WHISPERING P\|NES

BY KIMBERLY DIEDE

CELIA'S GIFTS SERIES
WHISPERING PINES (BOOK 1)
TANGLED BEGINNINGS (BOOK 2)
REBUILDING HOME (BOOK 3)

WHISPERING PINES CHRISTMAS NOVEL
CAPTURING WISHES

FIRST SUMMERS NOVELLA
FIRST SUMMERS AT WHISPERING PINES 1980

WHISPERING P NES

A NOVEL

Kimberly Diede

Celia's Gifts Book 1

To Mom and Dad, my first and my forever cheerleaders

*Sometimes the roadblocks, setbacks, and heartbreaks of life
turn out to be the greatest gifts of all . . .*

CHAPTER 1

Gift of a Wake-Up Call

*R*enee Clements couldn't have anticipated the tidal wave of changes one surprise phone call would unleash on her work life, family life and love life.

Looking back, the day started like any other. Fresh cup of coffee in hand, Renee sat down at her desk and fired up her laptop. She sipped the scalding brew, waiting for the heat and caffeine to give her system a needed jolt on the frigid Monday morning. She was ten days away from a week of vacation, but with Christmas and the company's year-end approaching, her "to do" list was long. She needed to wrap up two large projects. Once those were done, the pressure should—key-word: *should*—be off.

She opened her Outlook calendar. Four scheduled meetings wouldn't leave much time to work on her projects; she would end up taking a pile of work home again. One project stalled because costs came in too high and her boss challenged her to find cuts, the other was slow to progress because of some internal politics. It was hard to get things across the finish line. This wasn't anything new, but rather a symptom of corporate bureaucracy. She should be used to it by now.

"Key-word," she said aloud, "*should*."

She tolerated the frustrations because, well, she needed her paycheck. The steady stream of bills gave her little choice. Some days were more tolerable than others, and she had no desire to end up a bag lady. A week off with her kids would finally break up the monotony.

A new Outlook invite popped up for a call with her manager and peers.

"What now?"

They would probably get another time-sensitive project to work on—she'd *never* get it all done in time. At least the call didn't start for two hours.

She started pulling together a response to a request for a new report when her cell phone rang. Fighting irritation at the disturbance via a deep breath, she answered her daughter's ring tone.

"Hi honey, how are your finals going?"

"Hey Mom," Julie replied breathlessly. "I'm walking into my last test. I hope I studied enough. I was up until two this morning. Zoey kept her music on low the whole time, and it was so distracting."

Renee sighed. Zoey was Julie's best friend from high school. She was a good girl, but her study habits didn't match Julie's. Julie was used to having her own room and was still learning to adapt to a shared living space.

"What time will you get on the road?" Renee asked.

"We should get out of town by one, putting us home around five. It could take longer if traffic is bad."

"You know it'll be tough that time of day. Take your time and give me a quick call if you don't think you will be in by six. I threw a roast in the crock-pot this morning, so we can eat whenever."

This should give Renee time to swing by the high school, pick up Robbie, and get home so her daughter didn't arrive to a dark house. Renee wasn't used to going two months without seeing Julie. It had been too long since she popped home for that short weekend in October.

They said a quick goodbye, Renee wishing Julie good luck on her "final" final. Renee was glad her daughter would be done with classes. It would be fun to have her home without the stress of homework hanging over her head.

As Renee tried to get her mind back to the task at hand, her desk phone rang. It was turning into another typical day at the office where her time was not her own. Piles of work would go home with her again tonight. She may or may not pull them out once she got through dinner and caught up with Julie.

"Hey, Renee, what do you suppose our call is about this morning?" blurted her friend and colleague on the other end of the line. "I have so much work to do, and now Blaine decides to pull us onto a call? So rude, especially right before Christmas."

"Oh, hi Kate. I don't know what he wants, but I'm sure he thinks it's important," Renee said with a hint of frustration.

"I don't know, Renee. I'm hearing rumors out here . . . about *layoffs*," Kate whispered.

Kate's office was in New York City. Renee stayed closer to home, not venturing farther than Minneapolis. She was asked to relocate three years ago to take on a bigger role, but she declined—she didn't want to move her children any farther away from family.

Renee's pulse quickened. "I can't imagine they would do another round of those this close to the holidays . . ." But Kate's words snagged her attention. Being the sole provider for a fifteen-year-old son and eighteen-year-old daughter was scary enough without acknowledging the lack of job security in their industry. Days of feeling like you could work somewhere your whole adult life and retire with a secure pension were long gone. But the sheer busy state of her life prevented her from dwelling on it. It was so much easier to think it could never happen to her because layoffs only happen to "other people."

Renee didn't want to speculate about the upcoming call. She tried to assure Kate it would be another "task" to complete before the holidays.

"I sure hope you're right," Kate sighed. "I don't want to have to start over with another company. The thought of that makes my blood run cold. Guess we'll know in an hour." And she hung up.

Renee listened to the dial tone for a second, her mind wandering. She hung up and sat back, sipped her now-tepid coffee, and gazed out the office window she landed four years earlier when she moved up to a manager role. She recently "celebrated" her twenty-year anniversary with the company by ignoring her disappointment when she opened a small wooden plaque she received in the mail from HR on her anniversary date. It wasn't even personalized. She remembered when they used to give out small gifts of money on milestone dates. Twenty years of her life, and they couldn't bother to recognize her in person, or even give her a damn cake.

Renee shook her head to clear it again. The upcoming holidays must be making it hard to concentrate. She buckled down and was able to shoot off an email in response to a request for month-end sales results before a reminder ping sounded: time to jump on the call.

Taking a deep breath and ignoring a slight hitch of foreboding—blaming Kate for putting nasty thoughts in her head—she dialed in. If everyone was working today, there would be six on the call, plus her boss. A beep sounded as each person joined the teleconference. Renee was surprised to hear at least ten beeps.

After the beeping slowed, then stopped, Blaine's voice came across the line. "Thank you, everyone, for joining our call this morning. I am sorry for the short notice. I need to take a quick roll call, then we can get started."

Renee announced when Blaine called her name, then hit her mute button.

"Also on the phone with us today, we have Tom Jones and Rebecca Anderson from HR, along with Samantha Jensen. I'll turn it over to Samantha now."

Renee was surprised by the names on the call and puzzled to hear . . . was that a catch in Blaine's voice?

"Thank you, Blaine. We have some important news to share with all of you. We would have liked to have been able to share this with each of you in person, but the time-sensitive nature of our news would not allow us to do that."

Samantha was a seasoned executive, and Renee was always impressed with her ability to connect with her audience, regardless of whether it was over the phone or in person. But today she sounded stilted, as if she might be reading from a prepared script.

"As all of you are aware," Samantha read, "our industry has been hit by a number of different headwinds. We are making progress in growing our revenue streams in an effort to offset increased costs. We are all committed to our shareholders to continue to improve our bottom line.

Cost containment is an important aspect of this commitment. Staffing is one of our most significant areas of expense and much work has been done to determine where we can streamline some of our staff support areas. The decision has been made to centralize a number of functions previously handled by various departments across our footprint. The duties you and your teams have been handling will be transferred to our headquarters in Texas, effective immediately."

Renee gasped in shock.

"Please understand, we recognize one of our most valuable assets is our people, and we will do what we can to help each of you find another position within our company if you are interested in continuing to build your career with us."

"Does she believe this shit?" Renee wondered out loud, automatically glancing at her phone to make sure it was still on mute.

Realizing she was tensed up over her speaker phone, almost hugging it as her body naturally bent toward a fetal position to protect itself from the words coming out of the small black box on her desk, she took a deep breath—albeit shaky—and sank back into her chair. Samantha continued to drone on in an uncharacteristically flat voice. Renee pulled her attention back to the call.

"In addition to scheduling this meeting, we set up a second call that will start in a few minutes. We wanted you to hear the message first; however, we recognize you may be in a bit of shock and did not want to burden you with having to personally share this message with your staff. They will be joining us so we can share this same message with them as well."

Renee could hear Samantha take a deep, rattling breath before continuing.

"You will each receive a personalized information packet via courier within the hour. This will delineate the individualized severance packages you are each being offered. Please take time to review the information carefully.

"You will be allowed to take the rest of this week off. Your severance period will officially start next Monday. HR will set up a call with each of you to review the severance offer and make sure you understand its implications. If you agree to accept the package there will be requirements you need to comply with to receive your payout. Today is not the day to go into those details. We understand you will need the opportunity to process this news. We do ask that you clear out your desks while you wait for the courier to arrive. Arrangements have been made in each geographic area for someone to come to your desks shortly. You will be asked to turn over all keys, electronic equipment, and company property and vacate the premise. Please stay on the line and wait for the rest of your teams to join the call."

"Holy shit," she said aloud again. "So this is what it feels like?" The proverbial rug had just been ripped right out from under her feet. How could she have been so stupid? She never gave this possibility serious consideration. Where was the loyalty? After twenty years, how could they kick her out the door two weeks before Christmas?

But Renee already knew the answer. "They" weren't individuals, but "it" was a huge company doing what it needed to do to survive in this economy. When she allowed herself time to process what happened, she would need to face the fact it wasn't personal. All her years she gave to the company meant nothing to anyone but herself.

She pushed away from her desk and stood, arms crossed, slowly turning as she surveyed what had been her home away from home. Her eyes came to rest on her anniversary plaque, too new yet to sport any dust.

She picked up the memento and dropped it in the trash.

CHAPTER 2

Gift of Closing Doors

*F*irst, the courier arrived on time with a thick white envelope stamped CONFIDENTIAL in scarlet letters and addressed to Renee Clements. Her hand shook as she scribbled the stylus across the electronic signature pad.

Next, Joe arrived. Joe joined the local HR team in her office building right out of college. He rapped lightly on her door jam and poked his head in. His ears burned red, and he couldn't make eye contact with Renee.

"I have a few boxes you can use for your personal stuff and a cart to wheel them out to your car," Joe mumbled, not bothering to move the cart out of the corridor. "Let me know if you need any help when you have your things boxed up. I'll be back in forty minutes to collect anything you need to turn in."

Joe started to back out of the doorway but hesitated, shoulders drooped. He didn't know what to say. They exchanged small talk in the elevator on the way up this morning. Joe seemed as shaken by the news as Renee, and his unpleasant task was making him squirm.

"I'm sorry, Renee. You've worked here a long time and . . . it's bullshit. Please know how bad I feel." And with that, he was gone.

Renee grabbed the cart and pulled it into her office, closing the door quickly but not letting it slam. Did others on the floor know? Would they stop by to offer condolences while secretly thanking God they hadn't received the same news? Would some wish the packet sitting on her desk right now was addressed to them instead? She wondered if others in the building had also been given notice. All Renee knew for sure was she needed to get out and get out fast, with her back straight and her eyes dry. There would be time to crumble later, when she was alone.

She scooped pictures of her kids off her desk and placed them in one of the boxes on the cart. She looked around—there was little else she even wanted to take from this small, dull room.

Two scrawled drawings, ripped out of coloring books years earlier, hung on her credenza. Smears of dark pink and turquoise marker ran haphazardly across heavy black lines that formed a Santa on one page and a Christmas tree on the other. She easily pulled them down, tape brittle with age. One page bore a carefully penned "Julie" on the bottom, the other a quick "R" dashed off by her then-toddler son.

More than anything else, these pieces of precious art gave her pause. So many years, dedicated to this company. Her eyes welled. She shook her hands and blew out air, fighting tears.

"Not now, not now!" she scolded herself. She refused to let on how broken she was feeling. "What do I need to take now while I have the chance?"

In a moment of clarity, she realized she needed to print out her most recent performance evaluations. She had meant to keep a file of them at home but never took the time to do it. She would want to have them to show prospective employers. Quickly she pulled up the electronic files and sent them all to the printer in the corner of her office. Thank God they hadn't taken away her computer access yet. It was a little surprising, in fact. She certainly could have fired off a nasty email to a broad audience, expressing her anger and frustrations—but she only gave that tempting thought five seconds of serious consideration. No way was she going to burn bridges. She grabbed the evaluations and added them to a box. Finally, she tossed in a few additional personal items.

She looked at the results: two partially filled cardboard boxes; pathetically little after twenty years.

Looking at her watch, she realized Joe would be back in a few minutes. Should she call her staff? As their manager, shouldn't she at least check on them? Deciding they were probably in as much shock as she was, she grabbed her emergency contact list out of her drawer instead. It contained the home phone numbers for her team of five women and three men. She hesitated for a moment, considering how this would impact each of them.

"Stop!" she insisted. The thought of them right now was a surefire way to end up with a salty puddle on the carpet squares at her feet. She would figure out how to reach them and be sure they were all right later, once everyone came to terms with this.

Joe again rapped lightly on her now closed door.

Shit, Renee thought, *might as well get this over with.*

She strode over to open the door. "Come on in, Joe, I'm finished here."

Joe appeared even less composed than earlier.

"Is everything all right?" Renee asked him.

"Actually, no," Joe said. "It's so hard to see all of you being let go like this. I feel terrible, collecting keys and kicking you out of the building by a certain time."

Maybe you should follow me out the door, Renee thought, *before you give up the next twenty years of your life to this place, too.*

"Wait," Renee said, "did you say 'all of you'? Are there others here in this building? I was thinking I might be the only one, locally."

"No, you aren't the only one. You're one of several in this building. I'm glad I don't work over at the main complex. There are a couple hundred over there receiving notice today."

"Oh my God," Renee gasped, "I had no idea. Those numbers are big enough to hit the press. I haven't called anyone to let them know yet . . . I don't want them to hear it on the six o'clock news."

"Don't worry, I think they've kept this under the radar, at least for now. I haven't heard talk of any media inquiries yet. But you are right, it probably will get out pretty quickly." Then, somewhat sheepishly, "Could I . . . could I have your keys and . . . other effects?"

It was time to go. She pulled out her ring of work keys and her access card and dropped them on her desk. Next she removed the remote-access fob from an inside pocket of her purse.

No more signing in from home in the evening, she thought. This was the first positive thought to cross her mind since Samantha's statement.

"Anything else you can think of, Joe?" she asked.

"Nah," he said quietly. "If you forgot anything, you can send it to us. Do you need any help with these boxes?"

"You know, Joe, I appreciate the offer, but I can handle these without any trouble." Renee smiled at him. She was able to leave, but poor Joe would stick around and escort others out when he was done with her. She could tell his heart wasn't in it. While this was an obvious eye-opener for her, she hoped it served a similar purpose for Joe and all the other younger employees.

"Just hold the door for me, and I will call it a day," she said.

Pulling on her winter jacket, she threw her purse over her shoulder and grabbed her two boxes. She spared a glance at a small planter filled with near-dead violets on the corner of her desk. It wasn't looking like the little plant would survive until Christmas; a quick trip out to her Toyota, through the frigid December air, would probably finish it off. And seeing the pretty little pink vase later would bring this ugly day back. She knew this would be a day she would want to block from her memory.

"Help yourself to my plant if you like, Joe," she offered as she juggled her armload of mementoes out the door.

Eyes straight ahead, she shot toward the elevator. Off to her right she could just hear muffled crying. She absolutely did not want to encounter one soul on her way out. Since it was shortly after 1:00, she hoped everyone would be back at their desks by now, returned from lunch. There was a good chance people had heard what happened and would be as anxious as she was to avoid having to exchange words with anyone.

Renee managed to make it down the elevator and out the front door alone. As she stepped through the heavy rotating door, wind stole her breath and her eyes stung, watering from the cold. Her tears froze almost immediately. Nothing like a brisk winter gale to clear the senses.

Renee shifted the bundle in her arms and started the two-block trek to the parking garage. Normally she would have taken the skyway to avoid the elements, but she feared her new, unemployed status would be too obvious if she walked through the halls with her boxes. Might as well sob with abandon in that case.

Damn, why did I have to wear heels today? At least the sidewalks were clear of ice. The air felt too cold for snow.

Renee made it to her SUV, feet sore and arms tired. She beeped open the back hatch and dumped her boxes with relief. Slamming it shut, she climbed behind the wheel. She let her forehead fall to the steering wheel and let out a heavy sigh as she turned the key. Cold air blasted from the defroster, still set on high from her bitter morning commute. Music blared. She snapped the dial off, welcoming a moment of peace and quiet.

"What am I going to do now?" Renee asked out loud, glancing at the glowing digits on the dashboard as she slowly exited the ramp. Robbie wouldn't be done with practice until 4:30. She hadn't started her holiday shopping, but the thought of a loud, crowded mall was just too much. A quiet place to gather her thoughts before facing the kids, *that* would be better. Hopefully news of company layoffs wouldn't reach them before she could tell them herself. She merged onto the interstate and headed toward Maple Grove so she would be closer to Robbie's school when the afternoon wound down.

Driving aimlessly now, her mind churned over the day's happenings; she was still trying to process the news, so she decided it would be best to get off the road and grab a cup of coffee. She needed to think through her options. A blank journal was in one of the boxes behind her—an early Christmas gift from a co-worker.

Renee always felt better if she could brainstorm in writing.

***

Warm air surrounded her, filled with the rich aroma of ground coffee beans and a hint of peppermint, as she entered a small coffee shop. She ordered a hot dark espresso and settled into an armchair strategically placed by a cozy fire.

As she was digging through her purse for a pen, her cell phone vibrated once. The screen read "Mom" and a text came through: *Call me when you have time.*

She cringed a bit. How did her mother always know when she needed her? Renee dropped the phone back into the depths of her purse. She would call her later, when she felt she "had time."

She opened her new journal and held her pen poised above the creamy white page. She sat there. Where to start? All she could think was "Now what?" Taking a shaky breath, she decided to let the pen flow. She started jotting down anything that came to mind.

She scribbled. Confusion and fear topped the list. What was she without her J.O.B. to give her definition? Sure, she was a mother, but her kids were getting older; they seemed to need her more for a financial contribution than anything else these days. She hadn't been a wife to anyone in a long time and wasn't even currently anyone's "significant other." She was a daughter, friend, sister, aunt . . . but so were most of the other women in this city. What was she now? Unemployed. She grimaced at the thought. She sighed—this wasn't a productive vein to follow.

Renee titled the top of a new page "Things I Love to Do" and underlined it. A quote came back to her as she contemplated where to start with her list. Someone once told her if you love what you do, you will never work another day in your life. A phenomenon she had not yet been lucky enough to experience. Her work could have been described as *busy* and *hectic*, certainly, but seldom *peaceful* or *uplifting*.

She pulled her mind back to her writing. *Focus, focus.* Items she noted that brought her joy included spending time with her family, coffee or lunch with girlfriends, reading, time outdoors, and the occasional auction. Her list grew and she flipped the page. This was kind of fun, focusing on things she loved to do.

Next she decided to get a little more practical. On the top of the next page, she wrote "Items Needing Immediate Attention." She needed to review her severance package, make sure they would have insurance coverage, update financial records, and determine how much was in her savings account. A few holiday "to do" items made the list, too.

She thought her severance package would give her almost one year of pay—a relatively generous policy. Her years of service would earn her significantly more on the way out the door than the generic plaque she'd originally received for her anniversary. How ironic.

She hadn't allowed herself to think too much about the financial implications of her layoff up to this point. Despite all her fears and uncertainties, she was smart enough to recognize how lucky she was to have any type of severance package. Unfortunately, these days most people were left with no safety net when jobs were cut.

One of her first orders of business would be to figure out how she could stretch her severance dollars as far as possible, if need be. She needed an updated resume, but few companies would even talk to her before the first of the year. No one was interested in bringing on new employees before the holidays. She gave herself permission to not think about looking for a new job until January.

Her hand was starting to cramp, and Renee realized another hour had slipped by. Snowflakes drifted by the window. She'd need to pick up Robbie soon. Should she tell him what happened right away, or should she wait? She'd tell the kids together, during dinner tonight. It would be easier to go through the story once.

She gathered her purse and pushed out of the comfortable chair in front of the fire more than a bit reluctantly. She noticed a $20 bill fall to the floor when she pulled her gloves out of her coat pocket. She scooped it up. *I'm going to have to be much more careful with my money now,* she realized. There would no longer be a steady stream coming in, at least for a while—a *short* while, hopefully.

As she exited the coffee shop, bells rang in the crisp air. To her right was a common sight of Christmas: a volunteer huddled near the red Salvation Army kettle, giving his bell a hearty shake, waving to her with the other hand.

Probably trying to keep his hands warm, Renee thought as she shivered in the growing dusk.

The $20 bill was still clasped in her hand. She suddenly felt compelled to drop the money in the kettle. Normally she would throw in a few loose coins, but today was not a "normal" day. She crunched through new snow on the sidewalk and quickly stuffed the bill into the kettle before she could talk herself out of it. The volunteer paused to smile brightly at Renee. Renee could now see it wasn't a man but a woman, probably in her eighties, braving the cold to gather funds for the needy.

"Bless you, my dear," the woman crooned. "May you have a wonderful Christmas and may the New Year be filled with abundance and opportunities for you." Then, with a quick wink, the woman turned away to thank another customer who dropped a few noisy coins into the bucket.

Walking back to her vehicle, Renee felt warmed by the woman's smile and sentiment. She made a promise to herself to follow the woman's example and focus more on others. Besides, she needed a distraction from her own troubles.

CHAPTER 3

Gift of Wine and Reflection

*R*enee picked Robbie up from practice. She was never sure which Robbie would show up when picking him up. Would he be the bright, animated boy who loved to visit and share the day's events, or would he be the surly young man, willing to share nothing more than grunts when asked about his day? Renee knew this was normal for a teenager.

She was relieved when a happy Robbie plopped into her front seat. Hot and sweaty from his workout, Robbie talked all the way home about the "butt-kicking" he gave to Brent and Joel at practice. Renee didn't have to do anything more than offer a few words of encouragement to keep him talking. It never crossed Robbie's mind to ask about her day, thankfully, so there was no need to sidestep any issues. She could keep her secret a while longer.

She pulled into their snowy drive and cringed at the *crunch* sound beneath the tires; she knew she shouldn't drive over the newly fallen snow and pack it down before they could clear it, but she wasn't in the mood to shovel or to cut off Robbie's stream of conversation. She would ask him to do it later, and she wouldn't criticize him when he couldn't get the tracks cleared.

Years of habit allowed them to navigate the dark garage, Robbie still sharing tales of his exploits. Two things hit them at once when Renee opened the kitchen door: the warm, homey smell of a roast, and a barking bundle of energy which immediately jumped up on both of them.

"I'll take Molly out," Robbie offered, "I have to call Brent and see if he wants to go to a movie Friday," and with that, boy and cocker spaniel both went back out through the garage, kitchen door slamming behind them.

Renee could already hear Robbie on his cell, talking to Brent. At least he was actually *talking* to a friend, not texting. Texting was the main form of communication for her kids these days. *Maybe Mom thinks the same thing about me,* Renee thought, suddenly remembering the text she got from her mother earlier.

Relieved to be home, Renee kicked off her shoes. She tossed her briefcase and purse on the counter and headed straight to her room to change. Her kids didn't care what she wore at home, and tonight she needed comfort. She would deal with the boxes from her office later—and she still needed to tell the kids what happened.

Times like this I wish I weren't a single parent.

It was too soon to know what impact, if any, her layoff would have on Julie and Robbie. Hopefully she would be able to insulate them from hurt as much as possible. She dreaded the upcoming conversation. They were in an expensive period of their lives with college, cars, and insurance for teen drivers. Renee had some savings but planned to take out loans for the bigger ticket items and pay them off out of her salary. Not a good plan. Now what? Shaking her head, she headed back to the kitchen.

Robbie was still outside with the dog. She could hear him telling Molly to hurry up. No sign of Julie yet. In an uncharacteristic move, Renee grabbed a wine glass from a high cupboard and blew dust off the crystal. The goblets were a wedding gift; price stickers still stubbornly attached to a few gave testament to how little she used them. She pulled an equally dusty wine bottle down from above the cupboard. No better time to put the decoration to better use than today—she needed something to soothe her nerves, and alcohol was as good as anything. She found a corkscrew in the jumbled utensil drawer and freed the cork.

Renee took a deep pull of the warm red wine. She grimaced; she'd always preferred a cool white over the heavier red. Placing the bottle on the counter, she turned on a small television and she started peeling potatoes. Mashed potatoes were the required side dish to a roast, especially on Julie's first night home from college.

She turned the set off when she finished peeling—the nightly news had made no mention of job cuts.

She turned on the outside Christmas lights and then flipped a switch on the living room wall to set the room aglow. A large tree in the corner was covered in white lights. Her small village in the front window looked like something out of a Thomas Kinkade painting. Renee loved to decorate for Christmas. This was the first year Julie wasn't home to help, so it took her twice as long, the weekend after Thanksgiving, to get all the decorations down from storage and up in a way she knew Julie would love. Robbie didn't say much about the decorations, but Renee knew he would miss them if they weren't up.

With nothing more to be done before dinner, Renee settled onto the couch with her glass of wine and let the twinkling lights mesmerize her. Her mind wandered back to earlier Christmases in this house. Years ago, the four of them would pile into a pickup and drive an hour and a half north to a tree farm. They drove up and down the rows in search of the perfect tree, sipping hot chocolate out of a thermos. They would stop and walk out to a tree spotted by the kids, only to realize it was not one but two stories tall and wouldn't possibly fit in the living room. Back they would pile and continue their search. It would make for a long but memorable day by the time a tree was actually up in the corner of their living room.

As years passed and family dynamics changed, tree-cutting trips faded away. Now their tree could be assembled in half an hour and never needed water. While Renee appreciated the practical aspects of it, she missed the adventure.

Each of the tiny, New England-style cottages and businesses displayed in their bay window were given to her as a gift throughout the years. All brought back memories. Each box designed to store the tiny buildings eleven months of the year bore a note listing the giver's name and the occasion behind each gift. One special box, containing a quaint little bookstore, was marked with an outline of Julie's and Robbie's small hands. Her husband had given this to her as an early Christmas present during the last holiday season they all shared.

Staring at the miniature community she'd created, her mind wandered further back, to when she was a child. Christmas Eve always brought the same routine. After lunch, Renee, her brother, two sisters and parents would pile into the car with gifts and their dog. They would make a sometimes-white-knuckle drive across icy highways to her aunt's home. Renee's grandmother and her aunt Celia would step out onto Celia's front porch to greet family arrivals. If they were lucky enough to be the first to arrive, they would have first pick of the cookies, before Renee's cousins got there and devoured her favorites, the ones with the chocolate stars on top.

Supper always consisted of ham and scalloped potatoes, followed by steamed chocolate pudding for dessert. An extra card table or two had to be set up because they wouldn't all fit around the formal dining table. Cousins didn't graduate to the "big table" until they were at least in college and a space opened; if they were lucky, an aunt or uncle had a conflict and couldn't make it. On sadder occasions, a spot opened because a loved one was no longer with them.

Impatient kids didn't linger over dessert, encouraging adults to gulp down coffee and clear tables because *gift opening* was next. They always started out opening one at a time, but with so many people, order would dissolve into chaos. Keeping everyone's pile separate proved challenging and, inevitably, someone's instructions for toys with assembly required would be lost. Each family was assigned a bedroom at Aunt Celia's house. Opened gifts were stored back in the rooms for safekeeping; favorite new toys stayed out and were played with until it was time to get ready for Midnight Mass.

Once kids entered the third grade, they were expected to attend Mass. Younger cousins stayed home with two uncles who volunteered to stay with them. Everyone else piled into cars and headed to the old church. The women made sure everyone got there a half hour early so they could all sit together (and the men always grumbled about leaving home too early). They would grab two long pews, one in front of the other, and settle in, enjoying hymns and watching for old friends before the ceremony began. The air would be thick with incense, and a child or two would inevitably fall asleep. Afterward, the drive back to Celia's house was always subdued. Younger cousins would pretend to fall asleep and older cousins would carry them into the house.

Christmas morning started early, despite the late night. Santa always left presents for the kids, plus stockings for everyone, but no one could come out alone on Christmas morning. Cousins waited impatiently until everyone assembled in the upstairs hallway, and a stampede of slippered feet pounded down the stairs. The air filled with exclamations of excited kids, the robust smell of coffee, and, one year, even the yips of a terrified little puppy Santa left under the tree for Renee's brother. Breakfast consisted of caramel rolls and a huge pile of scrambled eggs. Everyone knew to fill up—there wouldn't be another meal until late afternoon, when turkey and all the fixings topped off the celebration.

Renee's reminiscing was cut off by a slamming car door. Molly heard it too and set off barking and pawing at the front door.

Julie was home.

"Robbie," Renee hollered up the stairs, "your sister is home! Come down!"

"Be right there, Mom," he hollered back.

Renee set her wine glass down and hurried out onto the front porch. Arms extended, she caught Julie in a huge hug at the top of the stairs, fighting back tears. Julie hugged her back, hard, laughing the whole time.

"Mom, you're squishing me," Julie yelped, and she giggled, pulling back at last.

Her friend Zoey was struggling to pull suitcases out of the trunk. Robbie jumped down the stairs to give her a hand. He thought of Zoey as a second big sister, and so he immediately started teasing her about weak arms. Zoey gave him a hip bump and told him to shut up, laughing the whole time. Between the two of them, they lugged a huge suitcase, a smaller one, and what looked like either a body bag or an enormous hamper of dirty clothes up the wooden front steps and plopped them at Renee's and Julie's feet. Renee extricated herself from Julie's arms so she could hug Zoey.

Herding them all through the front door, Renee felt the weight of worry lift off her shoulders. The girls were home safely and wouldn't have to go back to college for a month. Molly was crazy with excitement, jumping all over them both. Julie threw her coat over the back of a recliner.

"Would you like to join us for dinner, Zoey?" Renee invited. "We have plenty."

"Thanks, but Mom and Dad are waiting for me to get home. We're meeting friends for dinner. Besides, you guys have lots of catching up to do. Merry Christmas!" Zoey waved as she headed back out the front door.

Renee thought she noticed a look pass between Julie and Zoey—but maybe it was her imagination. Or the wine.

"Julie, why don't you take your stuff up to your room? Robbie, I need you to get the table set. Dinner will be ready in ten minutes."

"Thanks, Mom, you have no idea how good a home-cooked meal sounds," Julie said as she started hauling all her stuff upstairs. "I'll be back down in a minute to help."

Renee smiled. A home-cooked meal with both her kids was exactly what she needed, too.

Chapter 4

Gift of Space

*J*ulie bumped open her bedroom door with her suitcase and wheeled her larger one behind her.

"Thank God," she whispered and sunk onto her bed.

These past two weeks were awful. She was teetering between an A and a B in two of her core classes, thus spending what felt like hundreds of hours preparing for finals. Had it been enough? She wouldn't know until grades posted online a couple days from now. She had worked hard to lose herself in her studies ever since Thanksgiving, too . . . but it wasn't only because she wanted to pull up her grades.

Julie was worried about Lincoln. She met him at the homecoming football game. He was super cute and seemed nice, but now he made her feel . . . claustrophobic. He called and texted too many times every day, always wanting to study or hang out with her or know what she was doing. He wanted to take her home for Thanksgiving, but she'd already agreed to spend her first holiday away from home with her roommate and two other girls. Lincoln was upset when she turned him down. First he said he wouldn't take no for an answer, but she ignored his tirade and went with her friends anyway. He seemed to move past it, but he still wanted to be by her side any chance he got. Julie had been glad to climb into Zoey's car and head back to Minneapolis. She needed a break; she hoped he wouldn't contact her continuously during vacation. She and Zoey talked about it for most of the ride home. Zoey wanted her to end it, didn't feel Lincoln was a good fit for her. Julie was starting to agree.

She only wished she hadn't gone so far with him. During those first couple of weeks they were getting to know each other, she thought he was amazing. She didn't sleep with him, thank God, but she went further with him than anyone else before and was already regretting it. How could she have been so stupid?

"Well, I'm going to have to tell Lincoln we are done and cut myself some slack on this one," Julie muttered to herself.

She hadn't mentioned Lincoln to her mom. She wasn't sure yet if she would, if she could. Mom might get a little freaked if she thought Julie already paired off with someone, might even launch into the whole "safe sex" talk again.

"No," she muttered, "definitely not saying anything yet."

CHAPTER 5

Gift of Time

*R*enee wrestled with her own thoughts as she and the kids gathered around the dining room table, all the while keeping a grin plastered to her face. She hated knowing she would ruin their festivities tonight; this was supposed to be a time for celebration. If only her one struggle this Christmas were finding that elusive balance between treating her kids like the young adults they were becoming and still creating some Christmas magic.

The voice of their local news anchor cut through her thoughts, coming from the kitchen: "Stay tuned for recent employment developments at a large business in town, after these messages."

Renee popped out of her chair and hurried into the adjoining room to snap off the TV. She would only be kidding herself if she thought she could hold off telling them. If they didn't hear it from her, they would hear it somewhere else, or see it on social media, and be hurt. Tonight was a time to treat them like adults.

Renee let the kids catch up but wasn't able to concentrate on their conversation herself as they filled their plates and dug in. With no good way to start, she cleared her throat and told them she had news. Her tone shut off the easy flow of conversation. Both kids stopped eating and turned wary eyes her way. Neither liked her opening comment and knew her well enough to be worried about what she was going to say.

"Don't worry, no one died, and no one is sick. But I did get some tough news today, and it affects all of us," Renee said, looking from daughter to son and back. She took a deep breath.

"I got laid off today."

She said the words quickly, feeling an ache settle in her stomach and behind her eyes.

No one said anything at first. Then Robbie—her precious boy who despised conflict—quickly tried to reassure her.

"Oh, Mom, it's OK. You'll find another job, no problem. You'll probably find something before New Year's. Don't sweat it." He offered his mom a hopeful smile.

Julie said nothing right away. She eyed her mom carefully, her face flushing. When she finally spoke, it came out in a rush. "Are you frigging kidding me, Mom? Are they insane? Who does that two weeks before Christmas? You've worked there for what, like twenty years, and this is how they treat you?" Julie spluttered. "How did they tell you? Please say they told you in person."

Renee welcomed Julie's frustration. It helped to share the burden; despite Renee's not wanting to dump this on the kids, it was a relief to find that Julie's initial thoughts matched her own.

"Actually, no. They pulled us all on to a teleconference this morning and gave us the news. But I was glad I wasn't told in person. My boss has always been a prick, and it was a relief not to have to face him. This way I never have to see him again," Renee said, and she meant it. It felt good to know she wouldn't have to interact with that man ever again.

"Do you have to go back at all, or are you done?" Julie asked. She was processing what this might mean to the family quicker than Robbie appeared to be.

"I don't have to go back," Renee explained. "I still need to read through the severance package to get all the details, but as long as I follow the requirements, I'll get paid for a while yet. I could try to find another position within the company, but my package would stop paying. If I either don't want to try for a new position or fail to get one, my package should pay me for almost a year."

Julie digested this, then started throwing out more questions. "So, you mean, if you get a new job with them, they stop paying you your severance, but if you don't, you'll get paid for a year for not working? That is crazy!"

"Yes, it doesn't make much sense," Renee agreed, laughing a little. She hadn't thought about it from that angle. She could get paid for a year for not going to work, or she could find another job with them and be back on the regular payroll. Kind of made a person think they didn't want you back. At this point, she had zero interest in ever going back anyhow, but she knew that might change if she didn't find something else. Right now her wounded pride felt too raw to be more realistic about it. She couldn't make any rash decisions.

Renee struggled to share her feelings with Julie and Robbie. They always worked to be open with each other; they were a team of three—a strong family unit—and Renee knew she would draw on their strength in the days and months to come.

"I lost my job today, but we are not going to be destitute, OK? We have some equity in this house, I have money in my 401K, I have decent college funds set up for both of you, and I have some money in savings."

Robbie's eyes were glazing over, and she knew he wasn't following most of this. Today served as a wake-up call for her, and she wanted the kids to learn from this, too. She needed to stop operating on auto-pilot. This morning, she woke up as a long-term employee at one of America's largest companies; she thought she was valued. But she arrived back home unemployed, feeling like a knife was stuck in her back. She didn't know how, but she was going to figure out a way to protect her back from now on. And her kids'.

"All right, enough doom-and-gloom talk," she said. "I suddenly find myself with at least the rest of December off. Julie, you are home and have no homework since you are between semesters. Robbie, normally you would still have class for the next week, but that water main break in the school cafeteria last month means you get an extra week this year while they make some major repairs. You are free now until early January, too. Brainstorm with me. Help me come up with some crazy, fun things we can do. I was stressing about only having a few days off with you two, but now everything has changed. What do you guys want to do?"

Suddenly she saw the next few weeks as an unexpected gift, to be spent with her children. She had never taken more than one week off at a time before today. She vowed to make the most of this time.

Julie started throwing out suggestions, each one crazier than the next. "What if we went to Grandma and Grandpa's for a week at Christmas to see everybody? Or what if we call all of them to see if we could all go on a ski trip together? Maybe we could even fly to Colorado!"

Robbie darted nervous glances between his mom and sister. It was starting to dawn on him his holiday break wasn't going to consist of sleeping late, lounging around all day, and hanging with his buddies. He wasn't feeling too excited at this prospect of a whole lot of togetherness in the coming weeks.

Renee did point out they would have to be a little sensible with their plans, as far as costs went. "We can spend some money, and if we decide to take a trip, that would have to be part of your Christmas gifts. Be careful so we don't eat into your college funds for a few whirlwind weeks!"

Robbie finally got caught up in the excitement, too, and both kids wheeled off more ideas. Renee let them dream and finished her cold dinner. She got up and cleared the table, watching their animated exchanges with a small smile. She may be unemployed, but she wasn't going to let that stop her from giving her family a Christmas to remember.

She rummaged around in the junk drawer, pulled out two legal pads and pens, and tossed them onto the table in front of the kids, raising her hands to quiet them down.

"Today is December fifteenth. There are ten days until Christmas, another week until New Year's, and one final week before you both go back to school. Why don't we all take some time tonight to think about what we want to do for the holidays? Make a list of your top five ideas. Do some research. If you think a trip would be fun, check out travel websites and maybe get some cost estimates. If we are going to travel far, we will need to make arrangements right away, including for Molly. Tomorrow we'll go to lunch. Bring your ideas. We'll talk through all of them and make our plans. I promise we will do at least one activity from each of your lists." She beamed at them, and they sat breathlessly watching her. "Now go! I will finish cleaning up the kitchen. You guys have work to do."

Never having to be told twice to let someone else clean the kitchen, both grabbed their legal pads and ran up to their rooms. Doors slammed, and Renee was left with Molly to keep her company. She finished clearing the dishes and wiping down counters. Music drifted down from above, but she was in the mood for holiday carols, so she masked their music with "Have a Holly Jolly Christmas."

She refilled her wine glass. Back to the living room and her decorations she went, determined to come up with an amazing plan for her family for the next few weeks.

CHAPTER 6

Gift of Focus

*B*efore turning in, she spent a few hours thinking through and researching different possible activities for the holidays. She liked some of her ideas, but she was more interested in what the kids dreamed up. The task kept her mind busy, kept her from dwelling on more serious matters, but those matters were harder to ignore in the quiet of her own bedroom. Despite wine and exhaustion, Renee struggled to fall asleep. It would have been nice to have a man to share her bed, to keep her mind off her worries and tell her it was all going to be all right.

This surprised Renee. She rarely gave her love life much thought. Or maybe the sheer lack of a love life didn't give her much to think about. But she could have used both a distraction and comfort.

Her mind jumped between feeling sorry for herself because she didn't have a "significant other" to feeling sorry for herself because now she didn't have a job. By 1:00 a.m. she was thoroughly sick of her own personal pity-party and got up and took a Tylenol PM. She finally dozed off, but still felt drugged when her alarm went off at 6:00 a.m.

"What . . . the hell?" Renee moaned.

She'd set her alarm out of sheer habit—there was no reason to get up early when the kids would sleep for a few hours yet. She punched her pillow and tried to go back to sleep but gave up after half an hour. Molly would be ready to go out now, anyway, so she stepped into her slippers and headed downstairs. Her nighttime attire always consisted of sweatpants and an old T-shirt, so she threw on a hoodie too, to combat the chill.

Robbie didn't drink coffee—"yet," Renee always amended jokingly—so she seldom brewed a pot at home during the week, and instead filled her cup at the office. Today was different—of course it was, her whole *life* was different now—so she put the pot on. Maybe Julie picked up the habit during her first semester at college; she might help her drink it. Otherwise, Renee would drink the whole pot by late morning and be jittery for lunch.

Renee let Molly out, who was waiting patiently by the door, and followed behind her to grab the newspaper from the top step. A headline snagged her attention, spread in bold print above the fold.

Hundreds get pink slips from Santa

"Lovely," Renee sighed. *Let's bring the big guy into this whole fiasco.*

Slapping the paper down on the kitchen island, she poured herself her first cup of coffee. Only half the water was through the grounds so far, promising a powerful first cup.

Just what the doctor ordered, Renee thought ruefully.

She wisely decided against turning on the television. Quiet seemed appropriate this morning. What should she do until the kids got up? She considered making them a big breakfast but scratched the idea, knowing it would take the edge off their lunch plans. They could scrounge up cereal for themselves.

Instead, Renee fired up her laptop and checked out a few more ideas, rounding out her "Adventure" list, as she dubbed it. This gave her plenty to talk about with the kids at lunch, so she could switch gears until then.

During sleepless hours the night before, her mind had ping-ponged between different areas of her life where she now realized she wanted to make some improvements. Yesterday morning she felt relatively content with her life—even if she knew she was often going through the motions. She no longer felt that satisfaction, small though it was. Yesterday's wake-up call made her realize it had been ages since she'd challenged herself with anything tougher than getting through a busy day.

And so, this quiet morning was the perfect time to continue the soul searching she'd begun at the coffee shop the day before.

Yesterday, she'd filled a dozen pages with her jumbled feelings and lists. Starting a fresh page, Renee headed it up with "Things I am Thankful for in My Life Today." Another revelation from last night's tossing and turning was that she'd decided she was done focusing on just "getting by," and on all the negative feelings brought about by her layoff. She refused to let this turn her bitter.

Like many, she was familiar with the concept of the "Law of Attraction." She'd read *The Secret*, a popular book on the subject, a few years earlier. She'd even listened to the audiobook in her car during daily commutes. At the time, she thought there was merit to the ideas, but she didn't do anything with the information. Now was a good time to dust off her copy and place it beside her bed. Re-reading a few pages before turning off the light might put her mind on a more productive path and help prevent the insomnia she suffered last night. Or it could have the opposite effect, and make her mind race even faster. Regardless, it would be worth a try.

She often heard about the importance of feeling and expressing gratitude. Unless she was grateful for what she already had, would she be open to receive more to be grateful for in the future? The experts said no, and not having anything more reliable than their teachings, she decided to trust them and make an effort to show more gratitude.

She started writing again. First came the usual—her kids, her parents, her home, a vehicle that seldom broke down, her friends. But she wanted to dig deeper, beyond the obvious: she truly was grateful to have a financial buffer with her severance package; she didn't have an updated resume yet, but was thankful she would be able to display the loyalty she had showed her company when she did pull one together; most people jumped jobs every few years, but she worked hard, climbed the proverbial "corporate ladder" within the same company, and earned higher levels of responsibility.

Despite being scared to death now, she might have ridden it out at her old company until retirement, if not for the layoff. She might never have tried anything new. Had she done anything in recent years to benefit anyone other than the company's shareholders?

Looking at it now, it all seemed so . . . *shallow.*

The multitasker in Renee got up and filled her cup with fresh coffee. She felt like she should be cleaning house or doing laundry instead of sitting at the table, writing. Taking the time to think about her life felt foreign and unproductive. So, she would compromise. It wasn't even 8:00 a.m. yet! She would stick with this for one more hour and then start in on domestic chores.

Slowly, Renee realized feeling gratitude did give her spirit a boost. She committed to start each day with a fresh list of things she was thankful for and to limit her exposure to the news as much as possible. If something truly significant happened in the world, she would hear about it. Her daily newspaper subscription was due, but by God, she wouldn't renew. She would also fight the habit of turning morning and evening news shows on. She would limit her Internet surfing, too. The sensationalistic spin placed on so much of the news was too depressing.

She needed to lay out some goals. The categories were probably going to be pretty obvious. One would be "Career Goals," given she was sitting at her kitchen table this morning instead of an office. She also recognized she took her health for granted and didn't actively do much to keep herself healthy, so "Health and Fitness" was going to have to make the list. What else should she work on?

Maybe, since the only other individuals in the house were less than half her age—and her offspring—"Relationship Goals" needed to be on the list. She didn't want her goal to be "to get a man," of course. At times she thought it would be nice to share her life with a guy, and she wouldn't rule it out, but why hadn't she felt compelled to call any of her friends yet about what she was going through? Probably because most of them were actually co-workers or people she met through work. If they didn't have work as common ground, what basis for friendship was left? Relationship goals were going to need to encompass relationships with men, friends, and family. *That reminds me,* she sighed, *I haven't called Mom back yet.*

She sat back and chewed on the end of her pen. She needed to face it— she was boring. Where was the spontaneity? Where was the excitement? The fun?

That was it. Another area of focus would be "Fun."

Nothing else came to her and she was starting to feel anxious again. She left it at that for the day, set her journal aside, and rinsed out her cup.

She took the next half hour to review her severance package. As she'd hoped, based on her years of service, she would receive full pay and benefits for thirteen months.

The clock would start running next Monday. She needed to figure out her next steps.

But first, laundry.

CHAPTER 7

Gift of Adventure

$\mathcal{J}$ulie voted for her favorite pasta restaurant for lunch, and they all agreed. Once they finished eating and the mess was cleared away, they each pulled out their list. Renee was delighted to see both kids had made an effort.

"OK, how should we do this?" Renee asked. She wanted to let them take the lead.

"Maybe we can divide our time between now and when school starts again into three parts," Julie suggested. "We could say Leg One of our time is between now and the day before Christmas Eve. Leg Two could be from Christmas Eve to the day before New Year's Eve. The last part, Leg Three, could be New Year's Eve until January eighth, when classes start again for Robbie."

"Not bad," Robbie conceded. "I kind of like that—we need to use at least one idea from each of us. Plus, each of those parts has a different feel. Leg One feels like prep time, Leg Two feels like family time, and Leg Three feels like party time!"

"That works," Renee said, laughing.

So the sharing began. Some ideas were quickly laughed off. Some caused Renee to catch her breath in surprise. The kids loved her suggestion to catch a flight to a beach somewhere. They hadn't dared be that extravagant themselves.

Their adventure started to take shape.

An idea from each of them made the cut for Holiday Prep. Most of it could be done close to home. Originally, without taking the time to plan their days leading up to Christmas, each of them would probably have gone their separate ways with friends or working, taking a little time to buy each other gifts, but otherwise focusing on themselves.

Family Time would involve some travel, not only in miles but also back in time. One of the accepted ideas caused Renee lots of heartburn—but in the spirit of making this a true adventure, she agreed.

Party Time felt the craziest to Renee. It would eat into her savings and would require some scrambling on the front end to pull off, but it would likely result in memories they could all hold dear for years to come.

During a three-way phone conversation with Julie over Thanksgiving, when they couldn't be together, they'd promised to spend a few days together at home over the holidays. Circumstances were converging now that promised a much more exciting time together. Little did any of them appreciate how much this time would change all of them.

CHAPTER 8

Gift of Preparation

*S*pontaneous adventure sounds wonderful, but reality requires work on the front end.

Renee needed to make arrangements so their second two legs could happen. She didn't waste any time. As soon as she got home from lunch, she got out her legal pad and her laptop to plan her attack. Her goal was to have preliminary arrangements made by the end of the day.

Together they decided to make the extra effort to spend Christmas with extended family, as long as their family didn't already have other plans. Her first call was to her parents. It had been five years since she took enough time off at Christmas to drive to her parents' home. The first few years were hard and Renee dealt with the guilt—either real or imagined—of disappointing her parents by not going. Would there even be room for them now?

Her mother answered the phone when she called. "Hey honey, did you get my message yesterday? Did Julie make it home?"

"Hi Mom, sorry I didn't get a chance to call you back until now. Things were crazy with Julie coming home, and yes, she made it back fine. Say, Mom, I have a favor to ask . . . the kids and I were wondering if it would be all right for us to come home for Christmas this year? We weren't sure what your plans were, or even if you were going to be around, but we have a little more time off and thought it would be fun to come back and see everyone."

Renee always felt welcome, but she recognized time moves on. Her absence in recent years left her in the dark as to what holiday celebrations looked like for her parents these days.

After a beat of silence, her mother's voice came over the line again.

"Really? You're considering coming home this year? To be honest, we haven't made many plans yet. You know you are always welcome. We would *love* to have you! When will you get in?"

The planning continued from there. Renee avoided going into any detail when her mom asked why they would have more time this year, promising to explain later. Her mom didn't push, thankfully. With a sigh of relief, Renee checked off the first item on her list. It would be so much fun to get together with everyone.

The next item made her hands sweat and heart thump. This was the sticky point. Julie wanted to visit their other grandparents over Christmas. It had been ten years since Renee stepped foot in her in-laws' home, and almost as many years since she last talked to them. But at Julie's suggestion, Robbie's eyes lit up and Renee didn't have the heart to deny them. She agreed to at least find out if they would be home. She dug out her old address book—she had no idea if the phone number for Jim's parents would still work; she wasn't even entirely sure they were still alive, although she thought someone would have gotten word to her in the event of their deaths.

Hands shaking, she dialed the number. She wasn't sure if she hoped they would answer or hoped they wouldn't.

On the third ring, someone picked up.

"Hello?" said a familiar voice.

"Hello," Renee replied, trying to sound braver than she felt. "Marilyn, this is Renee . . . I know, it's been a long time. I'm glad this is still your number . . . I'm sorry we've let so much time pass and not kept in touch. I have no idea what your plans might be, but the kids and I are going to be home over Christmas and they asked me to call you to see if we could stop by?" She was relieved when her voice didn't quiver nearly as much as her stomach.

Similar to the discussion with her mom, her request was met with silence, but the pause was longer this time. She only knew her mother-in-law was still on the line because she could hear shallow breathing. Renee jumped in to fill the uncomfortable silence. "Listen, I know it has been a long time and you might not want to see us. If you're busy, I completely understand. I could even tell the kids I wasn't able to reach you if you would feel more comfortable with that, instead of me telling them you don't want to see us."

"No, wait, I didn't say that," Marilyn finally replied. "It's a shock to hear from you, that's all. I wasn't even sure who you were at first. I need time to think about this. Can I get back to you? Why don't you give me your number and I will be in touch?"

Since Renee wasn't entirely sure she wanted to see her in-laws, she was fine with this response. She gave Marilyn her cell number, again apologized for contacting her from out of the blue, and hung up. It was a huge relief to cross *that* item off her list.

Renee gladly moved on to the third item: planning their tropical vacation. She loved the idea of ushering in the New Year and new possibilities with a frozen cocktail in her hand and sand between her toes.

They should be able to get a direct flight out of Minneapolis to somewhere tropical without the hassle of connecting flights. Renee normally would have booked a big vacation like this months ago. Now she didn't have that luxury, but maybe she would find some last-minute deals. The kids agreed to keep an open mind, and Renee would surprise them with their final destination on Christmas Eve.

She jumped online and started with standard travel sites. She was thankful her dad insisted on taking the kids to Canada fishing a couple years ago so their passports were current. Thanks to an overseas work trip, Renee's was current too.

She didn't know where to start. She had never been any place considered "tropical."

She started by poking around online, selecting "Top 10 Tropical Destinations" from the search results. Her screen filled with beautiful pictures of turquoise water and white sand beaches. All were wonderful, scenic pictures with no people. The list read like a fantasy honeymoon extravaganza. Names like Bora-Bora, Fiji, and Hawaii jumped out at her. Wasn't the bottled water she treated herself to once in a while from Fiji? Her interest was piqued.

She set a budget for the trip. It was significantly higher than she would normally spend on Christmas, but this wasn't a normal season. Careful review revealed they wouldn't get a five-star hotel at that price point—probably nothing more than a three-star—but some were offering specials to help the resorts fill up for New Year's. She jotted down contact information for a few resorts that looked promising. There was no way Renee was going to drop that kind of cash without talking to a live person before booking something.

She called the first resort on her short list of three. It was the most expensive, barely within her budget. Renee was disappointed when he told her, in a thick accent, they were full for that week. She heard the same from the next resort. She might have to pick a different destination. The last resort on her list was a bargain compared to the first two, but would still challenge her budget. The cheaper rate made her hesitant to call, not sure what they would get if she picked it. But she was tired of working on the logistics, so she would make this one last call and then take a break until tomorrow.

After six rings, a woman's voice came over the line. "Hello, thank ya for calling Sailor's Cove. My name is Lulu, how can I be of assistance?" The woman sounded like she was from Boston instead of an island in the South Pacific.

"Yes, hello, my name is Renee Clements and I am calling to see if you have any vacancies for the week of New Year's? It would be for myself and my two children." Renee doodled on her notepad as she waited while the woman checked.

"Well, honey, today is your lucky day. We had a cancellation earlier today so we have one two-bedroom cabin open," Lulu confirmed. "We would love to host you and your kids for a week in paradise. Why don't you take a little time to decide—I can hold the cabin for you for four hours."

Renee thanked Lulu and spent the next three hours surfing the web, finding out everything she could about the area of Fiji where the resort was located. She studied the resort's website and read through all the reviews. Something about it just felt . . . right. Taking a leap of faith, she called Lulu back with her credit card number and booked the week of December 29.

Their holiday adventure was starting to take shape.

CHAPTER 9

Gift of Joy

*R*enee kept thinking about the Salvation Army lady she had encountered outside the coffee shop earlier in the week, hours after receiving the news about her job. Something about the older woman calmed her. Maybe it was the knowing look and warm smile she offered on that cold, unfortunate afternoon. Renee admired the senior for braving the elements and giving her time to help others, so she suggested to the kids they should all give back in some way before leaving for Christmas. Despite what had transpired, Renee knew they were so much better situated than many. She always gave to the United Way through payroll deduction, and used to help at an occasional emergency drive. When Renee suggested they use the first few days of their break to volunteer, both Julie and Robbie agreed.

Julie had made a new friend named Anna at college. Anna lived on her own and struggled to pull together enough money for tuition, books, and food after paying for her apartment. She would sometimes go hungry when grocery money ran low. This was a first for Julie, something she'd never encountered in her own life, and she worried about her new friend. So she decided she wanted to pull together a care package for Anna. She would have to be a "Secret Santa" because her friend would never knowingly accept anything more than a token gift. Julie started brainstorming on what she wanted to include in the package. Robbie thought it would be fun to be the elf to deliver the goods, since Anna wouldn't know him. Renee offered to get in on the fun, too, by baking some Christmas goodies to include.

There was a large-ish bowl of loose change in the laundry room. With Renee's permission, Julie took it to the bank and was shocked to come out of there with $261 in cash. She used the money to buy Anna food, toiletries, new pajamas, socks, a warm new hoodie, and a pair of jeans. Julie guessed they were the same size but purchased the clothes at a chain store so Anna could exchange them if necessary.

Julie also talked to their next door neighbor Suzy, an avid knitter, in the hopes she would have something to donate. She'd just completed a cute hat-and-glove set she was planning to donate to the mitten tree at church. The tree would be covered with cold-weather accessories and made available to those in need. Suzie loved Julie's enthusiasm and was happy to add the set to the growing bundle of treasures for Anna. She would knit something else for the mitten tree.

Within two days, Julie gathered an impressive box of items for her friend. She could hardly wait to get it delivered. Renee carefully bubble wrapped cookies and a box of homemade peanut brittle to include, too. Robbie called his old scout leader and was able to borrow a Santa suit they used for holiday parties. He would wear it when he delivered the box to Anna.

Once Anna's package was ready, Julie carefully put it all in a large cardboard box, sealed it up, and stored it in a corner of the garage. They would drive up to Anna's small hometown on the 23rd to make their stealthy delivery. Julie knew Anna was working as a waitress to earn enough money to get her through the spring semester. Anna's old boss let her stay in an efficiency apartment above the restaurant. She didn't have family there anymore, but to her, it was still home.

Together, they also thought it would be fun to help at a local toy drive Robbie heard about through school. The junior and senior classes were looking for volunteers to pick up donated toys from local businesses, wrap and code the gifts, then deliver them to kids registered through Social Services. It could be a three-day process. Robbie paired up with buddies to help bring in donated toys.

On Friday, Renee, Julie, and Robbie piled into the SUV and headed to the Civic Center to work on the toy drive. They stepped into the gymnasium and a frazzled teenager met them at the door with a clipboard in hand, pointing them toward long tables containing rolls of wrapping paper, tape, and scissors. He gave them a three-minute overview of the process and then hustled off to educate the next group filing through the door behind them.

"How about if I pick out presents for some little boys first? I'll go grab a wish list from over there," Robbie suggested, motioning to the table the teenager had pointed out to them. "Once I get the toys picked out for each one, I'll bring them to you, Mom. Since you're the world's best wrapper, you can get the toys wrapped and labeled. Then Julie can take it all over to the clothes section over there and finish up for each little boy."

Since the toy drive was Robbie's idea, Renee and Julie let him take charge. When Robbie couldn't find any more toys he thought little boys would like, he switched places with Julie so she could work on lists for girls. They worked until the organizers called it a day. In a span of five hours, the three of them managed to put together gift bags for thirteen boys and seven girls. Because so many people and local businesses donated time and products, over a thousand kids would receive gifts from the toy drive.

Julie and Robbie seemed subdued on the drive home. Carols softly streamed from the radio.

"You two are awfully quiet. Did you have fun today?" Renee asked as she turned onto their street.

No one answered right away.

"Kind of sucks that a stranger has to pick out gifts for those little guys," Robbie grumbled from the back seat. "I tried to pick out toys they will like, but there weren't any video games or stuff like that to choose from on the tables. Just a bunch of board games, toy cars, and books. Not exactly super fun stuff for Christmas morning."

"I suppose it wouldn't make sense to give them anything that needs to be played on a system the kids might not have or that would need batteries their parents wouldn't be able to replace," Julie said. "Most of these toys are ones they can play with for a long time, using their imagination. Robbie, you used to love playing with all your little cars."

"True," Robbie agreed quietly. "Just a lot different than what other kids will be finding under the tree this year."

Quiet descended again as Renee pulled into their drive, each feeling a mixture of gratitude and guilt for having so much when others had so little. The day served as a not-so-subtle reminder that Christmas was about so much more than receiving everything on your own wish list.

CHAPTER 10

Gift of Generosity

December 23 dawned crisp and cold. Julie rose early, wanting to finish her Christmas shopping before leaving to deliver Anna's package. She was giving Mom and Robbie one gift each, so she wanted each of the presents to be extra meaningful. She was excited about Robbie's, but was still searching for an idea for her mom. Her mom put on a good front, but Julie caught her sitting at the kitchen table the night before, staring at a cold cup of tea, tears trickling down. She'd quickly brushed the tears away, probably hoping Julie hadn't noticed. But Julie did notice, and she worried. She knew her mom had a lot on her mind. But, in classic Mom style, Renee refused to let any of them dwell on her job loss, and she was keeping them all hopping with volunteer work and packing to go to Grandma and Grandpa's house.

Julie enjoyed working alongside her family at the toy drive, and she knew she was doing something worthwhile for Anna, too. Plus, all of it kept her busy enough so she didn't constantly worry about Lincoln. She avoided talking to him on the phone. When break first started, he called or sent texts a few times a day. Now he was calling every hour, leaving messages. His tone was getting harsher. He couldn't understand why Julie wasn't responding to him.

"Probably because you're starting to creep me out," Julie mumbled to herself, turning her cell off again so she wouldn't hear it vibrate. She knew she should talk to him, tell him she didn't want to be a couple anymore, but she kept putting it off.

Julie grabbed her purse off the back of her chair, tossed her phone in, and headed downstairs. She let Molly out the back. A pot of hot coffee sat on the counter—her mom must be up, but Renee wasn't in the kitchen. Robbie would sleep for a few hours yet, tired from late night hours on his Xbox most likely. Julie poured coffee and watched Molly bounce in the snow in the backyard. The dog stopped playing and started sniffing a line of footprints from the back alley up to the garage. Julie could see the small door leading from the backyard into the garage was open.

She remembered Anna's package, propped in the corner. Alarmed, she jammed on her mom's snow boots, yanked open the sliding patio door, and ran across the icy deck. She slipped going down the back stairs, catching herself before she fell on her butt. She scraped her palm on the wooden railing, but it was so cold she only felt a quick twinge. Molly ran over, barking at her heels, and followed her to the garage door.

Still in a panic, Julie reached her hand inside and groped along the wall for the switch. Snapping on the light, she shoved the door open the rest of the way. With a sigh of relief, Julie spied Anna's box, still in the corner, right where she left it. Sitting next to it was a second box—probably the Santa suit Robbie borrowed.

Snapping off the light and turning the little lock button in the door handle, she gave the door a hard pull and hurried back to the house. A blur of movement near the neighbor's shed caught her eye. She glimpsed a bright red parka. Someone rounded the corner, but he or she moved quickly out of sight before she could see a face. Julie didn't give it much thought and scurried into the house, Molly still tight on her heels.

She kicked the boots off and picked up her coffee cup, warming her icy fingers. The heat made the scrape on her palm sting. She noticed her coffee was now a pale caramel color. Her mother must have doctored it up for her while Julie was outside, with a shot of creamer—just like she liked it.

Good old Mom, Julie thought as she rummaged around in the junk drawer for paper and pen. She sat down to make her shopping list, enjoying her coffee.

An hour later, Julie headed to the mall. She had a few names on her list, but not many gift ideas. She still felt bad about all the needy kids. She wasn't in the mood to buy people the usual gifts this year. She didn't want to buy her friends a useless little trinket or her mom yet another sweater.

As Julie approached the mall doors, tinkling bells caught her attention. To the right of the entrance stood an elderly woman, bright white curly hair poking out from under a cheap Santa hat. She gave the little bell in her hand a hearty shake every few seconds. A red kettle stood in front of her. Julie felt around for change in her coat pocket. Pulling out a few quarters and what she thought was a dollar, she went to throw the money in the kettle. She noticed it wasn't a dollar but a slip of paper in her hand, so she only pushed the coins through the slot. The woman handed her a candy cane in return with a wink.

"May God bless you and keep you safe this Christmas, sweet girl," she said as she handed Julie the candy cane.

"Thank you," Julie automatically replied. She thrust the paper and candy into her pocket, continuing into the mall. She thought the woman's comment was weird, but she forgot about the encounter until she took a lunch break. She picked up a soda and piece of pizza and found an open seat in the food court. She arranged her packages around her feet so she wouldn't lose or forget any of them. When she finished her slice, she remembered the candy cane and figured it would be as good a dessert as any.

Reaching into her pocket, she pulled out the candy—along with the piece of paper. She unfolded it and, with a start, saw it was a note from Lincoln.

Dear Julie,

You are the best thing that has ever happened to me. I am so happy you are a part of my life. I already miss you and can't wait until we get back from holiday break. I wish we could spend the holidays together. Maybe in some small way, we can.

Love, Lincoln

Julie dropped the paper onto her tray, shuddering despite the crowds around her. When had Lincoln put that in her pocket? She glanced around as if expecting to see him at the table next to her, but all she saw were busy, frazzled holiday shoppers. No one noticed her jitters. She wasn't sure why the note bothered her so much. She considered calling Zoey to talk about it, but remembered her friend already left town to visit relatives in Nebraska. She would call her later.

Trying to put the disturbing note out of her mind, she decided she was tired of the crowded mall. She was glad it was still early when she walked out to her mom's SUV. She threw her packages in the back and drove over to Barnes & Noble. While walking through the bookstore, she finally came up with some good gift ideas. She finished her shopping and headed home.

Robbie was home when Julie got back, excited to play Santa. She laughed. "There's still plenty of time before we have to go," she told him. "I don't want to get there until we're sure Anna is at work."

Julie wrapped the presents she bought while they waited. Finally, they ate supper and got on the road. It was a bitter cold evening with a brilliant moon. Stars twinkled against the black sky. Renee opted to stay home and let the kids make the delivery together, telling them she had holiday tasks she needed to work on alone.

Julie and Robbie pulled into Anna's hometown around seven o'clock. They found the Golden Spoke restaurant on Main Street. All the parking spots in front were full and it looked crowded through the frosty plate-glass windows.

"What's our plan?" Robbie asked.

"I guess I didn't think that far ahead," Julie replied with a sigh. "I suppose you could put on the Santa suit, walk in, and hand the package to Anna. But that might embarrass her. Maybe we could see if there's a back door?"

They decided to call the restaurant and tell whomever answered there was a delivery at the back door for Anna. Robbie put on the Santa suit, grabbed the package, and walked toward the back. It was dark and quiet in the alley.

Julie drove to a gas station on the edge of town, hoping they would have a pay phone. She didn't want to take a chance on the restaurant having caller ID and Anna recognizing her cell number.

Julie hadn't used a pay phone in years and was surprised, but relieved, to find one. A phonebook hung from a stiff cord, pages yellow and curled. She found the number for the diner, again relieved when a man answered instead of her friend. He chuckled when Julie told him about the delivery and muttered something like "Good for you, Anna." He promised to send her back for the delivery and hung up with a "Merry Christmas!"

In the shadows behind the diner, Robbie stomped his feet to stay warm, anxious as he stood in the cold and waited for the back door to open. He felt the strangest sensation that someone was watching him.

Ridiculous! he thought. While it was busy out front, it was dark and deserted back in the alley. No one would hang out back here at night, not in this cold.

Finally, the back door opened and a light above the door snapped on, illuminating the surrounding area. Warm air rushed out at Robbie. Anna stopped dead in her tracks when she saw Santa standing on the back stoop.

Robbie knew it was Anna based on Julie's description. She wore short, spiky black hair and a tiny stud in her nose. Earrings lined both ears and makeup was a little on the heavy side, in Robbie's opinion, though he did think she was cute. She looked like a punked-out elf. Instead of being frightened by a strange man in a Santa suit, Anna burst out laughing.

"Well, Santa, I don't see any flowers," she said, eyeing the white wrapped box with the huge red bow at Robbie's feet. "If there is a bouquet in that box, it's freeze-dried by now!"

"No, Anna," Robbie said with a deep chuckle, doing his best Santa impression. "We heard you were an extra special girl this year and wanted you to have an extra special gift this Christmas. Please enjoy. May you have a blessed Christmas and continue to spread holiday joy."

With that, Robbie gave another deep, Santa-like chuckle—at least he *hoped* it was Santa-like—and turned on his heel. Anna stood there in shock for a minute, staring after him, unsure what was happening. She hadn't received an unexpected gift from anyone in years.

"Wait!" she yelled after Robbie. "Who are you? I can't accept this!"

But after standing there another minute or two in the cold and getting no response from the retreating Santa figure, she carried her box inside and shut the door.

Robbie hugged up against the building after he walked out of reach of the overhead light, to make sure she took the box with her. Once he saw her go back in and the outside light flicked off, he pushed away from the building. Suddenly, a heavy weight smacked him on the side of his face, shoving him hard into gravel and gritty snow.

Because it was so dark, he could hear and feel but not see a figure towering over him.

"Stay away from her if you know what's good for you," a voice rasped. "This is your only warning!"

There was a slight rustling noise, and then all was quiet. Robbie lay there, trying to get his bearings. His gut told him whoever pushed him down was gone. Then he remembered Julie. He didn't want the psycho that decked him to come across her sitting alone in the car.

He eased himself up, brushed off the snow and dirt as best he could, and jogged out to the street. He wasn't hurt, but he was pissed. Here he was, dressed up in a dorky Santa suit, doing a good deed for some girl he didn't even know, and some guy smacks him in the head!

Robbie knew Julie would go crazy if he told her what happened. He needed time to think. Was the guy warning him to stay away from Anna? Or was he some lunatic and Robbie was in the wrong place at the wrong time? Maybe he was a scrooge with a grudge against Santa. No matter what, Robbie didn't want Julie to know what happened. It'd ruin the whole thing for her.

Plus, if Julie knew, Mom would find out—and Robbie didn't want to give his mother anything else to worry about. So he pulled off the smudged suit and tossed it in the trunk before jumping up front with Julie. He forced a big smile and announced to her expectant expression, "Operation: Christmas Miracle, a success!"

CHAPTER 11

Gift of Family

*R*enee woke early on Christmas Eve. She allowed herself the luxury of hitting snooze. *Merry Christmas, me.*

She couldn't believe all of this was happening. If you would have asked her at Thanksgiving what they would be doing for Christmas, she wouldn't have had anything exciting to report. She expected "low key" would have been her answer. Now her surprise status as unemployed meant there was time for so much more. There was time for *excitement.*

Renee knew, without a doubt, she wouldn't have made the effort to go home for Christmas. She certainly wouldn't have reached out to Jim's family. The call she received back from Jim's mom two days ago, while somewhat stilted, did result in them making plans for Renee and the kids to go to her in-laws' home for dinner on the 26th. She hoped this time to reconnect with their families would turn out to be a blessing and not a curse.

The biggest excitement was taking the kids on their tropical getaway over New Year's. She was insane to spend the money, given their uncertain future, but she was living the motto "Carpe Diem!" She better "seize the day," because, if she was lucky, she would be working at a new job by this time next year and it would be a while before she could take time off to seize anything again, least of all a tropical getaway. "Lucky" wasn't quite the right term; it was more like she despised the thought of *less* vacation time.

Hating to let melancholy sneak in, Renee got moving. Suitcases for this leg of the trip were down by the door. Suitcases for the New Year's trip were supposed to be packed, too, and stashed in everybody's room. The plan was to drive back on the 27th, finish getting ready, and fly out early on the 29th. She highly doubted the kids were packed for the second trip, but she would deal with that later.

As planned, they were on the road by noon. Traffic was heavy, but Renee was happy to be part of the wave heading toward family and friends. She wasn't sure what their schedule was and she didn't care. She just wanted time to catch up with everyone and not think about her worries.

Other cars were already there when they finally pulled up. Similar to Christmases of her past, grandparents met them on the front step. The difference was now it was her children's grandparents instead of her own. Her own grandparents died years earlier. Aunt Celia was gone now too, having died just this October—but she lived a long, fulfilling life.

Renee never fully appreciated how remarkable Celia was until after her death. Celia was a woman before her time. She died in her sleep at ninety-two. Celia took care of many people throughout her lifetime, and no one ever had to take care of her—she stayed strong and independent until the end.

Her aunt's absence from the front porch was a poignant reminder to Renee to reevaluate her priorities—a reminder of that line in her notebook that said "Relationship Goals." She needed to spend more time with her aging parents and rebuild relationships with her brother and sisters.

No time like the present, she told herself.

Julie and Robbie bounded out of the vehicle before Renee even parked.

Who says teenagers can't appreciate family time?

Inside, they were greeted with hugs. Renee's brother, Ethan, grabbed her into a huge bear hug. He was as tall and handsome as ever. Unfortunately, his soon-to-be ex-wife was no longer enamored with his looks; she thought him a shallow flirt. As his sister, however, Renee knew better and still thought her big brother was the best around.

"Do you have the kids?" Renee asked him. "Julie and Robbie want to see all the cousins."

"Elizabeth is here and Stacey is supposed to drop the boys off in the morning," Ethan replied.

Looking closer, Renee frowned; she noticed more lines around Ethan's eyes and less sparkle than usual.

Next came a squeeze from Val, her loud and sometimes obnoxious baby sister, followed by a quick hug from her other sister, Jess—Jess's husband wasn't there; as a doctor, it wasn't unusual for Will to miss family gatherings. It was a whirlwind of *Hello!*s, and Renee was ecstatic to realize she would spend Christmas with all her siblings.

"Hey, kiddos, all the other kids are out back playing football. Why don't you go get dirty with the rest of them before dinner?" Val suggested.

Julie and Robbie didn't have to be told twice. Both shot out the front door and stampeded around back.

Everyone else headed in the direction of the kitchen. Warm smells of ham and cookies filled the air. Renee's dad, George, was overseeing a contentious game of Whist on a card table. That same table would become one of the kids' tables in a few hours, but for now, it was home to lots of ribbing and competition. George, along with Renee's mom Lavonne, was taking on Ethan and Luke, Val's husband. Val cooked, slapping at hands trying to sneak a taste. An aunt, uncle, and a couple of neighbors relaxed on the sofas.

Everyone was curious what prompted Renee to take extra time off work to make the trip this year. Her trips home over the holidays had started to dwindle after the problems with Jim years back. Renee didn't want to get into it with the whole group and kept her replies vague. There would be time later to share her sad tale. A few glasses of wine might help, too, so she took her uncle Gerry up on his offer of some "holiday cheer."

Conversation flowed easily around the room. George and Lavonne were excited to have all their kids under one roof. Jess was quiet, but that was nothing new. She was always the reserved one in the group. Val was up a few more pounds and becoming a little round. At only 5'1", extra pounds pushed her curvy figure toward plump faster than on someone taller. She was as loud and bossy as ever.

"So Renee, how have you *really* been?" Jess asked once the game ended and the two met in a somewhat quieter corner of the room. She was never one to mince words, and was always able to sense something amiss in her sister's world. "I know you wouldn't drop everything and come home over the holidays. You can never take that much time at year end. What's up?"

Taking a deep breath, Renee eyed Jess as she took another sip of wine. She knew better than to try to snow Jess over one to one. Her sister would see right through her.

"Actually, I have plenty of time to come home because I got laid off mid-December. I probably should have expected it was coming, but I can honestly say I didn't have a clue," Renee confided as frustration flushed her cheeks and her eyes started to well up. She hadn't been able to have a heart-to-heart with another adult since she received notice, and now the words threatened to tumble out. Jess recognized the signs of a pending flood and held up a finger to stem the flow.

"Hey Mom, Renee and I are going to run to the store," Jess called out, quickly improvising. "I forgot to bring whipping cream for the steamed pudding. Be right back!"

"OK, girls, don't be late for dinner," Lavonne warned them, sparing them a quick glance over her shoulder as she took on George and the other guys in a Wii bowling match.

"God, you would think we were teenagers," Jess quipped as she grabbed Renee by the wrist and dragged her out of the kitchen. They climbed into Jess's Land Rover and just like that, they were away.

Leaning back against the headrest, Renee took a deep breath, thankful for the reprieve. She soon realized Jess wasn't actually headed for the store. Probably driving out toward the lake, Renee guessed. Growing up, the lake was their place for solitude or talks.

Pulling into an empty lot overlooking the frozen lake, Jess let the car idle so they wouldn't freeze. She waited patiently—another one of her strong suits. She didn't have to wait long, though. Renee put up a brave front, not wanting to crumble in front of her kids—but Jess knew how badly Renee always wanted to be strong. She worked hard and provided a nice life for Robbie and Julie all by herself. Both kids were well-adjusted and gave her little trouble. To have her foundation rocked like this would be hard on Renee. Jess knew Renee was only pretending to be fine, and Renee knew Jess knew this.

Jess had read a news blurb earlier about layoffs at Renee's company, but hadn't mentioned it to anyone since she wasn't sure, until today, whether it impacted Renee. She knew her sister would share any news with her when the time was right.

Finally, in one continuous flow, Renee gave vent to her fears and frustrations. While she loved Val dearly, Jess kept a level head and always gave her good advice. But today Renee wasn't looking for answers. She needed a shoulder to cry on; she needed to be heard. Jess understood, and listened quietly, offering soft words of encouragement as Renee ranted and cried. She let out a deep sigh, allowing her chin to fall to her chest.

"Am I too old to find a new job? What if I want to do something entirely different? Starting over just feels so . . . *daunting!*"

When Renee had nothing left to spill, Jess gave her hand a squeeze and looked her in the eye.

"Honey, when one door closes, you know another one always opens," Jess counseled, "and often what is on the other side of the new door can be bright and exciting. I don't want to hear any more dumb-ass comments about your age. You have lived your life for those kids these last ten years. Maybe now it's time for you to think about yourself a little. Don't make any rash changes right now. Give yourself time to figure out what you want to be when you grow up."

Both chuckled at the reference to a game they played as kids. All four of them would play the guessing game, trying to figure out what their brother and sisters would want to be when they grew up. They didn't realize it at the time, but they were learning to dream big and encourage each other. Somewhere along the line, though, they stopped playing. Adulthood seemed to have that effect on most people.

As only a sister can, Jess sensed when Renee was ready to face the family again. It was getting dark and Mom would be furious if they were late. Jess drove back, stopping to pick up cream on the way. Turns out she truly *had* forgotten it.

CHAPTER 12

Gift of Suspense

*V*al was still cracking the whip back at the house. Her face was as red as her current hair color, but her eyes twinkled as she ordered the kids to set platters of ham, fresh rolls, scalloped potatoes, and other dishes on the table. Someone—probably Lavonne—set the tables beautifully while Renee and Jess were gone. The dining room table stretched as far as it would go, ringed tightly by twelve chairs. Two additional card tables stood in the adjoining living room. Gold linen covered all the tables and creamy white china crowded their tops. This would be their first Christmas dinner without Aunt Celia, but they would be eating from her prized dishes.

Every place setting included Lavonne's silver and a crystal goblet of ice water. Paper napkins festooned with a Christmas tree rested on each plate. Even though the card tables were perfectly set, as soon as the kids were called to dinner, they would scoop up their plates and crowd around the dining table to dish up before the adults sat down.

The final bowl was nestled into the last open spot. The eight youngest cousins headed to the card tables—no exceptions or the arguments would start. Everyone else settled at the big table. (Julie and her older cousin Nathan couldn't *believe* they still hadn't graduated to the big table even though they were in college.) Grandpa George sat at one end with Grandma Lavonne across from him. Renee and her three siblings took their usual spots with Luke sitting next to Val. Uncle Gerry and his wife Letty, along with the two neighbors, filled in the remaining open chairs. New to the adult table was Ethan's daughter, Elizabeth, at Lavonne's right, sitting in Aunt Celia's usual spot. It was one of those sad years when a grandchild moved up because a family member died.

Renee felt sad for Jess. No spot was saved for her husband. He wouldn't be joining them.

As tradition dictated, Lavonne dimmed the lights. The room filled with the soft glow of candle light. Everyone bowed their heads for Grandpa's prayer.

"Lord, thank you for bringing all of us together to celebrate Your birth. This past year has brought many changes to our family. Gone from the circle around our table tonight are loved ones, some to serve Your will by helping others, some who have passed through our lives but are choosing to move away from our circle, and some who have been called to rest by Your side. While they no longer sit among us, they will always be a part of us. We thank You for bringing all of us safely together. Thank You for helping us appreciate the importance of family and for our commitment to each other. May You help all of us be strong to face the trials yet to come and help us find ways to make this world a better place. Amen."

Renee caught her dad's eye as he uttered that final phrase of his blessing, and he gave her a quick wink. So much for him buying her story that nothing was wrong. Mom was probably watching her out of the corner of her eye, too. But when she glanced in her mother's direction, Lavonne was watching Jess. As if sensing their eyes, Jess gave a tiny shake of her head, looked up, and smiled to no one in particular.

The noise level ramped back up in the room and dishes were passed.

"I can't see the damn food on my plate," Gerry grumbled, so Lavonne turned the lights up.

"God, it is so good to be home," Renee whispered as she sat back and scanned the room. The most important people in her life were all in these two adjoining rooms right now. Why in the world had she waited for something like this to happen before she took the time to come home for the holidays? She vowed she would not miss this again. Even if her new job—whatever that might be—required her to work over the holidays, she would figure it out. Her niece sitting in Aunt Celia's chair served as an important reminder to get her priorities in order.

George tapped his fork against his water goblet. The vibrating crystal sent out a clear ringing sound, catching everyone's attention.

"Hey, you be careful there, mister—don't you break that crystal," Lavonne piped from the other end of the table. "This isn't a wedding reception. You don't expect me to come all the way down there and give you a big smacker, do you?"

That statement was met by groans coming from the next room.

"Oh, gross, Grandma, old people don't kiss!" Val's four-year-old yelled.

Laughter rang out again, and George raised his hands in an attempt to silence the ruckus.

"Hey there, little Jakester, I will have you know your Grandma is a great kisser, and if you don't believe me, I am going to send her in there to give you a big smooch on the lips!"

Grandpa's warning was met with more hoots, none of which came from "Jakester."

"All right, seriously now, I want to make a couple of toasts. First of all, thank you to Renee, Julie, and Robbie for coming to Christmas this year. Your presence makes this holiday extra special."

Cheers and glasses rose around the room.

"Second, I want to take a minute to say a few words about my dear sister Celia. For many, many years, she was gracious enough to have all of us in her home for our Christmas celebration. She always went out of her way to make us feel welcome.

"I am sure you will agree, Celia was a remarkable woman. She worked in what was considered a man's world back then. Few women worked in construction offices. She started out as an office clerk, but worked her way up the ranks by being twice as smart and working three times harder than the men. Celia was one of those women that helped change the working world. It isn't uncommon for women to do what she did now, but back then it was almost unheard of. Blasphemous, even. She was tough and demanding, but she was also respected. She truly cared about the people she worked with, and they knew it. She was held in the highest regard."

George paused for a drink of water, wiping at his eyes before he continued.

"Celia was successful. She was also smart with her money and, as all of us know, she was extremely generous. She was a major donor to the women's shelter and taught classes there to help battered women become self-sufficient. She paid to fix the stained glass windows in the church. She even helped pay for college for all four of you," George said, motioning to his adult children.

Renee, Ethan, Jess, and Val all glanced at each other and grinned, proud to know they each worked hard and earned degrees with Celia's help.

"Celia lived a long and happy life. She was able to stay in her home until the end. I hate the thought she died alone, but I suspect that is what she wanted. Celia never wanted to show weakness of any kind. She helped so many people throughout her life. Celia always kept her financial affairs private. She had a trusted lawyer who handled her affairs for her as she aged, and he did right by her. You hear so many stories of crooked lawyers. We tend to think all people end up victims of those characters as they age. Not true. Have faith—good people still exist. No better a person existed as Celia, though. During her life, Celia took great joy in helping people. In death, she has found a way to continue with this mission.

"I admire all of you for never once asking about Celia's will. All of you came to her funeral, showed your respect, and laughed and cried with us as we reminisced about her life. But no one had a hand held out, wanting anything material from your precious aunt. Not many families can say that, and I want you to know how much Gerry and I appreciate it. But we thought tonight would be an appropriate time to share news of Celia's continued generosity with all of you. Mom, do you have the envelopes?" he asked Lavonne.

"I do." Lavonne stepped over to the sideboard. Tucked behind a silver bowl piled high with holiday cards was a stack of cream-colored envelopes. She was all grins as she handed the envelopes out. Each adult and older child received one; envelopes for the younger kids went to their parents. Ethan received three envelopes: one for him and one for each of his two sons, set to arrive in the morning.

Clearing his throat to gain their attention again, George made one request. "Please don't open your envelopes right now. Celia's wish was for each of you to read her message in private. She put much thought and prayer into the bequests, personalizing each one. Now let us respect her wishes. Let's have dessert, clean up the kitchen, and get ready for Mass."

"But Grandpa, what about the presents?" a young voice quipped.

"Be quick and we will do that too, little one," Grandpa George teased.

Tucking their envelopes into safe places, everyone obeyed Grandpa George. Waiting heightened the air of mystery and excitement. Blessed Aunt Celia was still running the show, it seemed.

The rest of Christmas Eve passed quickly. Everyone enjoyed a slice of warm, chocolate-steamed pudding. Following their familiar routine brought comfort. Little had changed during Renee's recent absence, she was happy to find.

Gift exchange was next. Everyone gathered in the living room, crowding around the tree. Robbie and a younger cousin were assigned "elf duty" and handed out gifts. One change to the tradition was the exchanging of names. They no longer attempted to buy for everyone. This made for less chaos and more appreciation for the time spent selecting fewer but more meaningful gifts.

Renee loved to see the kids getting more excited about the gifts they were giving than the ones they were receiving. She, Robbie, and Julie had agreed earlier to exchange gifts with each other on Christmas morning, when they hoped to find a little private time, so they could enjoy giving the rest of the family gifts tonight.

As soon as they finished opening gifts, little ones put on their pajamas, and Uncle Ethan volunteered to stay home with them. Everyone else headed to Midnight Mass. Aunt Celia's presence was even felt at church. Moonbeams streamed through the stained glass windows she once helped refurbish. The church wasn't as crowded as Renee remembered from years ago. Back then, the pews were packed. This year, no one had to stand in the back. The church itself felt smaller, too, but the music, white lights, and candles made the experience feel magical.

Merry Christmas, Aunt Celia, Renee thought, and she smiled.

CHAPTER 13

Gift of Traditions

*E*ven at eighteen and fifteen, both kids were still excited to see what Santa brought. They were shaking Renee's shoulder by 7:00 the next morning, just like they had done when they were eight and five. They could hear the rest of the cousins gathering outside their door in the upstairs hallway. Throwing on robes and grabbing glasses and a camera, they all thundered down the wooden staircase together.

After Renee grabbed a cup of coffee for reinforcement and the kids peeked into their stockings, together they headed to the empty sunroom to exchange their gifts.

Robbie gave Julie a CD of her all-time favorite songs. Julie was touched he remembered so many of the songs and surprised he took the time to pull it together.

Next, Robbie gave Renee a beautiful, leather-bound journal and matching pen. Looking a bit uncomfortable, he said, "Mom, you have some changes coming up, and I heard girls like to write in journals when they are trying to figure things out."

Up until then, Robbie had said little to Renee about her job loss. His gift proved he thought about it more than he let on, and he wasn't only worried about how this might impact him. Renee gave Robbie a squeeze, quickly blinked tears out of her eyes, and handed each of her kids an oversized box wrapped in shiny turquoise paper and tied with a big red bow.

Technically, Renee's gifts to Julie and Robbie contained lots of goodies, but they didn't complain about her stretching their rule of one gift per person. Each box included things they needed for their upcoming trip like underwater cameras, swimsuits, flip flops, snorkeling gear, and bottles of sunscreen. At the bottom of each of their boxes, Renee had pasted a photo of the three of them onto a stunning beach shot from a Fiji website. The kids finally knew where they were going, and their squeals filled the room. Also in their boxes were travel guides and little notebooks with pockets so they had a place to put any little brochures or ticket stubs they collected during their trip. They immediately started paging through the travel guides, both talking at once.

"Wait, wait, guys!" Julie finally shouted over the noise. "You still need to open my gifts to you!" she said, scooping the last two packages off the coffee table.

Robbie grabbed his out of her hands and ripped the paper off unceremoniously, grinning hugely at his sister.

"Oh, *cool*," Robbie gasped. It was a big, 12"x12" scrapbook. As he started flipping through the pages, Renee could see Julie had made her brother a photo album of his school years, starting in kindergarten. His grinning, gap-toothed face filled the early pages. Grade school and middle school pages consisted mostly of sports shots, including baseball, basketball, and football. Sprinkled in were a few shots of first and last days of school and a teacher or two. Family shots of the three of them popped up, too. Julie sat back with a smile, watching her mom and brother enjoy their trips down memory lane.

Pictures filled half the book. The remaining pages were blank.

"You can put our vacation pictures in there after we get back and fill up the rest with your high school days," Julie said. "Mom, I raided your boxes of pictures before I left for school; I hope you don't mind."

"Mind? No way," Renee laughed. "I have always meant to get those pictures organized into books, but I never find the time. I am so glad you did that. This is something Robbie will always have. Who knows if I would have gotten around to making you books?"

"Well, good, I'm glad you feel that way, Mom . . . because I also made myself a book so I wouldn't get so lonesome when I was at school," Julie said. "It isn't as fancy as Robbie's, but I keep it in my dorm room. I have pictures in there from the time I was a baby through high school, and when I'm having a tough day, I pull it out and look through it."

Renee knew if the book contained pictures of Julie from babyhood, the pages up until third grade would likely include pictures of Julie's father as well. Renee's heart ached as she pictured her daughter lying on the twin bed in her dorm room, staring at laughing pictures of the four of them. She found it interesting Robbie's book started *after* their family numbered three rather than four.

Julie handed Renee a beautifully wrapped box and a card. Opening the card first, Renee read the words from her daughter.

Dear Mom,

Thank you for always standing so strong behind us, supporting us in all we do, and being there for us as we move forward. Please know how much I appreciate all you have done for both Robbie and me. You have worked hard and sacrificed to give us a great life. You also need to take time for yourself, though. Be sure you take the time right now to decide what is best for you going forward. I thought these books might help you think about your life and finding your own happiness.

All my love, Julie

Welling up again, Renee offered Julie a watery smile. Lifting the top off a fancy Christmas box, she pulled out three books. Renee was an avid reader but usually lost herself in romance or mystery novels. It was her way of escaping the demands of single motherhood and a busy career. She'd never spent too much time reading the kind of books in her hands now.

The books were all written by authors Renee knew of but had never read. The first was *Rich Dad Poor Dad* by Robert T. Kiyosaki. The second was *Goals!* by Brian Tracy. The third was *The Magic of Thinking Big* by David J. Schwartz.

Julie gave Robbie something he could cherish forever . . . and she gave Renee permission to explore doing something different with her life.

Jumping up, she gathered both of her children in a hug. The hug didn't last long, quickly dissolving into tickling and wrestling. Worried her two big teenagers might break something in the sunroom, Renee pulled them apart and sent them up to their shared room to put the gifts away.

She took a moment to reflect before joining the rest of the family. Her kids were growing up. She hadn't been a total screw-up raising them, after all. She reflected on the care they each took to pick the right gifts for each other. Throwing up a quick note of thanks to God, she grabbed her cup of cold coffee and the garbage bag stuffed with shredded wrapping.

Lavonne called everyone to the table for eggs and rolls. As Renee walked by the window over the side yard, a blur of movement caught her eye. Intrigued, she stopped and looked more carefully at the snow-covered bushes, but saw nothing out of place.

Must have been a dog, or maybe a deer, she mused, heading out the door to join the rest of her family.

CHAPTER 14

Gift of Encouragement

*A*fter a big breakfast, everyone kept busy and the rest of the day passed quickly. A turkey roasted in the oven; there were card games inside, football and sledding outside, and lots of visiting.

Everyone talked about it, and Renee's sisters and brother all agreed to hold on to their envelopes from Aunt Celia and keep them sealed for a little while yet before opening them on New Year's Day—this would give them the proper time to open them in private, as per Celia's request.

For their last night together, another enormous meal was laid out. Turkey dinner was a family tradition on Christmas Day. Even when Renee stayed home in Minneapolis with the kids, she always prepared one.

Two more cousins crammed around the kids' tables this night: Ethan's boys, who had joined them mid-day. Will still hadn't made it—Jess would only say that he was on call. Renee started to wonder if something more was going on, but wasn't about to bring it up in front of everyone. Jess seemed fine, and her two kids enjoyed hanging out with all the other cousins, most of all Robbie and Julie. Renee wondered if maybe something was bothering Julie, too. She seemed distracted. Maybe she was missing her college friends?

Determined to enjoy her dwindling time with everyone, Renee shook off her worries and joined the lively conversation around the table. At one point, it flowed back to the subject of Aunt Celia. Celia had lived twenty miles from George and Lavonne; her home was a point of pride for her—a full two stories, plus a basement and a walk-up attic.

When Celia died, Lavonne, Jess, and Val took care of things needing immediate attention, like the food in the kitchen. They gave the place a thorough scrubbing and debated about what to do with Celia's household goods, so George talked to Celia's lawyer. The lawyer informed them things were to remain "as is" for the first few months following Celia's death. That was when he gave all the sealed envelopes to George and asked him to hold them until the holidays, explaining only—and enigmatically—that more would become clear once the family read the correspondence.

George's sister had always been eccentric, so he accepted her last wishes in stride. He dutifully readied the old house for winter, drained pipes, and cleared away leaves and sticks from the yard and gutters. The house had been shut tight ever since. The lawyer agreed to check it once a week. George hated to have the stately old home sit empty even for one winter. He kept the furnace on low to help prevent damage from the extreme cold.

"Celia was such an amazing lady, and her house was always full of surprises," Val reminisced. "It wasn't Great Grandma's old recipe box or the antique icebox full of her china that seemed out of place in her kitchen—it was her laptop, where she saved all of her healthy new recipes. Now, *that* was unexpected."

"I know," Jess chimed in. "Remember the old bristly curlers, the blow dryer, and the flat iron we found in her bathroom vanity? She was always updating her hairstyle. There were three boxes of that auburn hair dye she loved so much, in the linen closet. Celia never believed in going gray. She fought the aging process tooth-and-nail the whole way. By eighty, the red hair began to accentuate the blue veins in Celia's temples—but no one would have dared point that out to her!"

Conversation continued to flow around the table, everyone reminiscing. After the tables were cleared one last time, Lavonne remembered the box of photo albums she brought from Celia's. They hadn't wanted to leave the books in the empty house, she explained; they were irreplaceable.

Everyone moved to the living room, thumbing through the albums, the memories. Most were full of pictures, but some also contained wedding announcements, graduation programs, funeral cards, and all other manner of documents journaling major life events. The photos were either black-and-white or sepia or grainy color snapshots, fading now with age. There were a few pictures from when Celia, George, Gerry, and Beverly were children, snapshots of vacations and trips to the lake. Beverly had been sickly and died young.

There were laughs and there were tears as they enjoyed the old pictures. Older grandchildren stuck around to hear family stories, sometimes for the first time. Slowly, people drifted off to bed or headed back to their own homes until only Renee and her father remained.

"You know, honey, you still haven't said why you decided to come home for Christmas this year," George said, settling deeper into his old armchair. "Don't get me wrong—it's been wonderful. You just haven't been able to make it home these past few years. Is everything all right?"

"Everything will be fine, Dad. I suddenly found myself with extra time on my hands this year. I was laid off from my job a couple weeks ago," Renee finally told her father. "I guess I am still in denial. It hasn't sunk in yet that I won't be going back after the holidays."

"I figured it was something like that," said George. "You put on a brave front, honey, but I could tell something has been eating at both you and Julie. Robbie seems fine, but you girls have seemed a little out of sorts. Have you thought about what you want to do?"

"Dad, I didn't want to brood about it during our visit. I need a little more time to process what happened before I start to think about what I want to do next. We'll be all right financially, at least for now—I got a decent severance package. But I would like to get back to work so I can save some of that money for emergencies."

"Those goddamn bastards," George muttered. "How can they do this to you after all the good years you gave them? No loyalty anymore, is there? Used to be if you worked hard for a company, they'd do their part up until and through retirement. Now days, seems like they would rather get rid of people with experience earning more salary and bring in kids that don't know much but come cheap. Maybe you want to explore other ways to make a living that don't involve working for a thankless corporation, huh?"

"You know, Dad, I would have guessed you'd encourage me to get back out there and find another job right away. Honestly, that was my first inclination. Write up a resume, start scouring the want ads, and dust off an interview suit. But the thought of starting over somewhere turns my stomach. How does a person do that at forty-five? Pretty much all I have ever known has been working for this one company and raising my kids. If I go somewhere else, won't I have to start again with barely any vacation? How am I going to get Robbie to all his games and go visit Julie at college? This could change my life."

"Now don't panic, Renee, you hear? You have shown you are a loyal, dependable employee. There will be other companies out there that would love to have you. Hell, maybe you don't even want to go back to a traditional job. Maybe you want to try your hand at something different."

"Jeez, Dad, what else could I do? I know I need to think harder about this. Remember when we used to play 'What Do You Want to Be When You Grow Up'? We all used to have such big dreams. Have we *settled*? Are we living up to our potential?"

"Renee, never doubt you have done what needed to be done for you and those wonderful kids of yours. But maybe this is a gift from God. Maybe he is giving you a wake-up call along with a safety net. It would have been too easy for you to drift along, doing what you've been doing, for years to come. Yes, you made a decent living. But there were also sacrifices. You seldom had time to come home. When was the last time you painted a picture or threw a pot? Remember how you loved your art classes in college? What about writing? You used to write in those journals of yours every day. Do you still do any of that?"

"You're right, Dad, I was in a rut and I didn't even know it. But hey, it's getting late." Renee hoisted herself off the couch, crossed over, and dropped a kiss on her dad's head. "You've given me plenty to think about. You always give me solid advice. I'm sorry it's been so long since I took the time to ask for it. You better turn in. I am going to head up too. I can't remember the last time Robbie and Julie beat me to bed—they went up an hour ago already."

"OK, honey, good night," George said, squeezing her hand as she straightened. "I will go up in a minute."

But George didn't go up right away. He was concerned about his kids. It didn't matter how old they were; he would always worry. Ethan was suffering through his divorce, trying to keep his kids on the straight and narrow and not lose everything to that selfish ex-wife of his. Renee finally opened up to him tonight, but he knew something was up as soon as she called to ask if they could come home for Christmas. Jess still hadn't shared too much about Will, but George suspected their marriage was on the rocks too. Will didn't bother to come for any part of the holiday and George wasn't sure if he even called to wish a quick "Merry Christmas" to his own family. What kind of husband and father did that? Not a good one, in George's book. Then there was his little Val . . . always the strong, loud one. They seemed to be doing fine, but George worried about her too. Four kids already and Luke didn't make much money, and Val stayed home with the boys. Maybe once they were all in school she could go back to work.

George had some inkling about what each of the letters from Celia contained. If his instincts were right, he hoped each of them could do good things with Celia's generosity.

But there were risks as well.

CHAPTER 15

Gift of Intuition

$\mathcal{T}$he only day Renee dreaded during their three-week adventure dawned with a biting cold wind and gray skies. She hoped it wasn't a sign of what was to come. Today she would take Julie and Robbie to her in-laws for dinner. *Do you still call them "in-laws" when you no longer have a husband?* Renee wondered. Her eyes felt gritty and her head throbbed. Her talk with her dad last night sent her mind racing again. It was well past 2:00 a.m. before she finally drifted off. Robbie must have taken Molly downstairs to go out, because his sleeping bag was empty on the floor. Julie was stirring next to her.

"Hey Mom," Julie said with a yawn, pushing her white-blond hair out of her eyes. "What time is it?"

"A little after seven. I am going down for coffee. Are you going to get up, or sleep a little longer?"

"Sleep sounds good," Julie said and rolled back on her side, pulling the warm quilt with her. Renee considered asking her daughter if anything was bothering her, but it didn't feel like the right time. As she belted on her robe, she heard Julie's phone vibrate on the dresser. *Who would be texting Julie so early on the day after Christmas?* She suspected most of Julie's friends were also sleeping. Curious, Renee picked up the phone.

Renee always made it abundantly clear as long as she was paying the kids' cell bills and they were living under her roof, it was her prerogative to check their phones. She hadn't touched Julie's phone since graduation, but Renee's dad was right: Julie was distracted these days. Initially Renee thought her daughter was worried about her, but maybe it was something else. Maybe she was struggling with classes or her roommate. Renee opened Julie's phone as she took it with her out of the room.

Thirteen new text messages? And all since late last night, it seemed. Snippets of the texts made little hairs stand up on the back of her neck. Someone was obviously trying to get Julie to respond. All the texts were from someone named Lincoln. Renee had no idea who this Lincoln was.

Feeling like she had trespassed enough into Julie's business, Renee dropped the phone into the pocket of her robe and vowed to talk to her about it.

An empty kitchen met Renee when she got downstairs. Light snow was falling and Renee was surprised to see the back door open a sliver. She walked over to close it, glanced through the window in the door—and was met with another surprise: Molly was out back, playing with a bone in the snow. She didn't see anyone out with Molly. Stepping onto the back step, she whistled. Molly ignored her at first, chewing intently on her bone. She turned toward Renee at the second whistle and came bounding to her, leaping up the steps.

Bracing herself for the inevitable puppy assault, Renee caught the dog's front paws at her waist as Molly greeted her with her usual exuberance. Molly's paws were crusty with ice but Renee couldn't tell if she was shivering from excitement, or cold, or both. Glancing around the yard again, Renee felt the hairs on the back of her neck stand up for the second time in less than five minutes, neither of which were from the cold. Why was Molly out alone? And why was the back door open? How long had she been out?

Intent on finding her folks or son to see if they knew why the door was open, Renee ushered Molly back in and closed the door, throwing the deadbolt. The house was quiet. George might already be out for coffee with his buddies, ready to get back to his usual weekday morning routine after the hustle and bustle of Christmas. Some days he dropped Lavonne at her gym for a senior yoga class.

Molly went straight for her water bowl in the far corner of the kitchen. After a few laps, her ears perked up, and she stared toward the living room, stiffened, and let out a low growl.

Renee stood still, listening carefully. A couple thumps from the floor above followed by Julie's shout at Robbie to open the bathroom door snapped Renee into action.

"What's the matter with you, Molly?" Renee bit out in exasperation, rushing around the dog to the living room. The front door was locked tight. Open drapes on the large picture window let in weak, watery sunlight. Now Renee—and Molly—heard a crunch on the front porch, setting the dog off in a full-blown barking frenzy.

Rushing over to the window, Renee saw someone scurrying down the front walk, away from the house. Not sure if she should be alarmed, she watched the person jog to the corner and turn out of sight. *The paper boy, maybe, getting a late start to his day?*

Renee pulled the front door open, cold air rushing in. Sure enough, a rolled-up newspaper lay on the top step. Crossing the porch, she grabbed the paper and hustled back toward the house. She was cold, clad only in her robe and socks, but she noticed a package sitting to the left of the door. It was a small white box with a green velvet bow. Renee could see a gift tag below the ribbon. *To: Julie* was all it said. The *From:* was left blank. Frustrated, Renee scooped up the little box and went back inside, again making sure to lock the door behind her.

"What the hell is going on?" Renee muttered. First a bunch of texts on Julie's phone, then the dog is out back by herself and the door is open, and now a package is sitting on the front porch addressed to Julie. Did her daughter have a secret admirer? That still wouldn't explain how Molly got out.

Renee almost hollered up the steps for Julie to come down, but something stopped her. If someone wanted to give her daughter a present, why didn't they knock and say hello? And come to think of it, who knew Julie was at her grandparents' house?

Renee took the small box back to the kitchen and laid it on the table to take a closer look. Maybe she should open it? The box was seven inches long, but less than an inch deep. Deciding to check it before giving it to Julie, Renee carefully slid the ribbon off and undid the tape, taking care not to tear anything. If the gift was a harmless present, she would wrap it back up and give it to Julie. Her motherly paranoia would be satisfied and nobody would be the wiser.

Lifting the lid off the box, Renee could only see white tissue paper. Folding the tissue back, she was surprised to see a photograph lying at the bottom. No wonder it weighed so little. Gasping in disbelief, Renee stared down at a slightly faded photo of her daughter's dad, playing happily in the snow with Julie. *I remember snapping this picture!* It was one of her favorites. How in the world had it ended up in a wrapped box on Renee's parents' porch, addressed to Julie?

Hearing someone coming down the stairs, Renee scooped everything up and shoved the picture, box, and wrappings into her robe pocket.

Robbie sauntered into the kitchen, pulling a sweatshirt over his Nike T-shirt and shower-dampened head.

"Hey Mom," he said. "Anything around here for breakfast?" He barely glanced at his mother as he scratched Molly's head on his way to the fridge.

Renee kept a tight grip on the kitchen table, trying to act normal. "Ah, yeah, honey, there's some orange juice in the fridge and rolls left over from yesterday." Casually, she added, "Did you let Molly out this morning?"

Catching something in her tone, Robbie stopped his ransacking of the fridge and looked her way. "Nope. Hey Mom, you look kind of pale. You OK? You look like you saw a ghost."

He has no idea how close he is to the truth.

"I'm fine, Robbie," Renee replied, keeping her voice even. "I'm just tired from the past few days and, honestly, a little nervous about going to visit your other grandparents. It has been a long time since we last saw them. I'm not sure what to expect."

Robbie took this answer easily enough. "Don't worry, Mom. It'll be fine. Julie wants to see them—and I kinda do, too. I barely remember them." Brushing her concerns aside as only a teenager intent on food can, Robbie succeeded in temporarily distracting Renee. Together they shared warmed-up sweet rolls, talking about the times Robbie could remember spending with his father's parents. He was getting more excited for their big trip, too. He was ready to head back to Minneapolis to pack and go.

Renee loved catching up with her family, and while she hated to see it end, she was getting excited for their trip to Fiji, too. The photo shoved in her pocket only served as a reminder of the mess her life was becoming.

She wanted to get far away from all the drama—which now included a mystery person leaving disturbing gifts for her daughter.

CHAPTER 16

Gift of the Unexpected

*R*enee forced her hand to quit shaking long enough to ring the doorbell. Julie and Robbie crowded behind her on the icy step, anxious for their first glimpse of their grandparents in a long time.

Marilyn opened the door slowly—probably nervous, too.

"Look at how you children have grown," she exclaimed, glancing over Renee's shoulder at the kids. "Come in, come in, it's cold out today."

She backed away from the door, allowing them in. A television played in the background. The room felt warm and stuffy. Marilyn's once-auburn hair had faded to a dull gray streaked with copper. She reached only to Renee's shoulder, slighter than she remembered. James wasn't in his favorite chair, but the chair was still there. Looking around, Renee felt transported back in time. The formal wedding photo of her and Jim still sat on the mantel. Everything was as she remembered it, from the drapes to the carpet to the wallpaper.

"Please, come with me to the kitchen. Dinner is almost ready," Marilyn said.

Renee hoped they would find something to say to each other after all this time. She felt an awkward void between them. Julie and Robbie hung back, not knowing how to act or what to say. They followed Marilyn into the kitchen. Renee recognized the heavy stoneware already set out on the table. Marilyn busied herself with something bubbling on the stove. The kids and Renee sat, leaving one empty chair.

"Marilyn, is James not joining us tonight?" Renee asked, confused by the four place settings.

"I'm afraid it's the four of us tonight," Marilyn said, her back still to them. Eventually she gave a loud sigh and turned back to the table.

"James is at Oak Tree Manor. Has been since last summer," she finally said, looking from Renee to her grandchildren. "He suffered a number of strokes, and I couldn't take care of him anymore. It's just me here now."

"Oh, Grandma," Julie said, bouncing up out of her chair. "I am so sorry. We didn't know."

She wrapped her arms around her estranged grandmother in a warm hug. Marilyn stood with her arms stiffly at her side, clearly surprised and uncomfortable with the human contact. But after a moment, she melted into Julie's embrace and rested her head on her granddaughter's shoulder, hugging her back.

Robbie was less of a hugger than his sister. He stayed where he was, looking uncomfortable. He was only five years old the last time he was in this house. He barely remembered any of it. But Julie was old enough to remember both Marilyn and her grandfather. Renee hoped her daughter didn't remember the last argument in this house.

Finally extricating herself from Julie's embrace, Marilyn again checked her pots on the stove. "It will be another half an hour, looks like. Would any of you like a cup of coffee while we wait?" She seemed more relaxed now that she had told them James was in a local nursing home.

After filling cups for Renee, Julie, and herself, she gave Robbie a can of Orange Crush and joined them at the table.

"I'm glad you called, Renee. We should have kept in touch. Time slips by. After what happened to Jim, I kept busy cooking at school, and James spent all of his time either at work or tinkering out in that shop of his. He struggled with his blood pressure and terrible arthritis in his back, but he was getting by until the strokes started. At first he bounced back, but then he had a big one. After that, he couldn't walk without help. I wasn't strong enough. His doctor was afraid James was going to get hurt, or I'd get hurt helping him move around the house. It's been an adjustment, living alone these last six months . . . but enough about me. You kids tell me what you've been up to. How is school going?"

"College is a *blast*," Julie chimed in. "My roommate Zoey is a friend from high school. It was an adjustment, being away from Mom and Robbie, but I made some new friends. Classes were ridiculously hard, but I finished finals right before break."

"Have ya found a fella yet?" Marilyn inquired with a wink.

Julie's clearly evasive "Aw, Grandma" reply caught Renee's attention. Had Julie met someone? *Someone named Lincoln, maybe?*

"I can't believe my granddaughter is already in college," Marilyn said with a sigh. "And how 'bout you, young man, what do you like to do these days?"

"School is OK, I guess," Robbie replied with a shrug, "but basketball . . . now *that* rocks! We're ranked, like, second in our district, and I even get to dress varsity sometimes. We scrimmaged right before break and I crushed my buddy Brent. And the ladies, they won't stop texting me." As if on cue, Robbie's phone vibrated. He pulled it out and glanced at the screen, stopping mid-sentence. Renee kicked her son's foot under the table and he clearly understood the look she shot him. His phone disappeared back into his jeans.

Finally it was Renee's turn, but she wasn't sure where to start. She didn't want to get into her whole job situation or admit she was still a single mother with no love life of her own. But she did feel the need to apologize for keeping the kids away so long.

"Marilyn, thank you so much for having us over tonight, and I truly am sorry to hear about James. If we'd known he was sick, we would have come sooner," Renee said—but even as she said it, she wondered if that was true. "Jim died a long time ago, and we all said things we shouldn't have. We were all just shocked by his death and running on emotions."

Renee could picture the ugly scene in her mind only too clearly. After Jim's funeral and graveside service, everyone came back here. It was packed with people, many Renee had never met. The children were only five and eight. Robbie didn't understand what was going on, confused by what he had witnessed at the cemetery, and Julie didn't know how to explain it to him. Why was the box his daddy was in lowered into the ground? Why did the strange man in purple robes talk and talk while they all had to stand quietly in the wind and cold? By the time they got back to their grandparents', they were tired and cranky. Renee was overwhelmed and not paying attention to them. They got a little wild near the table and one of them knocked the bowl of red punch all over the living room floor.

Marilyn lost control, screaming at the kids and sobbing. James was usually quiet and mild-mannered, but when Marilyn became hysterical, he snapped too.

"You take those two little brats and get the hell out of this house. Our son might still be with us today if he hadn't run off with you and worked himself to death so you could live the big city life and pay for those expensive private schools you insist on," James hissed at her.

He was being completely irrational, clearly out of his mind with grief. Maybe if Renee hadn't suddenly found herself both a single mother and widow at only thirty-five, she would have given him some leeway for his behavior. They lost Jim to an ugly disease. Renee knew his death had nothing to do with her or the kids, but dammit, she just lost her husband and the father of her children, a man she loved with her whole heart. James's words sliced through her when she was most vulnerable. Her own parents hadn't been at the house at the time, so there was no one there to come to her aid. A man she didn't know did step in and tried to quiet her in-laws while everyone else looked on in shock and dismay, but the damage was done.

Grabbing her stunned children, she ran out of the house and they never went back.

That was ten years ago.

Once the sharpest edges of grief dulled, they made half-hearted attempts to reconcile. For the first few years, Renee sent school pictures and Christmas cards. They sent the kids birthday and holiday cards. The limited communication dwindled even more through the years and eventually ceased altogether.

Renee knew Julie harbored some hope her father's parents would show up for her high school graduation. She'd insisted Renee send an invitation. Marilyn left a message on their answering machine offering Julie their congratulations, saying James wasn't feeling well and they couldn't make it. They mailed a card. At the time, Renee was relieved, too busy to give much thought to the void their absence must have left in her children's lives. It was hard enough to lose their dad, but to not have contact with grandparents had to have been confusing, too.

Renee felt relieved to be in this kitchen again. The woman sitting across from her raised Jim, and he had been a wonderful man. Without him, Renee wouldn't have been blessed with Julie and Robbie. It was time to let go of the past and move on.

She knew it was only right to be honest with Marilyn and share what finally brought them back here. She explained about her recent layoff and how they decided to spend this extra time with family. She was open about the fact it was Julie and Robbie that insisted they try to reconnect with Marilyn and James.

"But Marilyn, I'm glad we're here now," Renee said. "I'm sorry James can't be here and that he has gotten so sick. These past two weeks are helping remind me to get my priorities back in line. We should have learned this lesson ten years ago, when Jim died. We need to appreciate what we have every day, because everything can change in a heartbeat. Let's work harder to keep in touch." Renee reached across the table to squeeze Marilyn's hand. Marilyn said nothing, but offered a small smile back and nodded.

Sensing the need to lighten the mood, Renee stood and walked over to the counter, prompting Marilyn to get up as well. Together they got dinner on the table while Julie and Robbie filled Marilyn in on other aspects of their teenage lives. Renee cringed when Robbie started talking about wanting to get his driver's permit. She still got nervous when Julie drove; she wasn't ready for another driver in the house.

After they finished eating and dishes were cleared, Marilyn was drained.

Renee stood and the kids followed suit.

"Thanks again for having us over for dinner, Marilyn. It's a shame about James. We probably should get going now—it's getting late—but we'll keep in touch."

Marilyn stopped her. "Now, just a minute. You can't go yet. Sit back down."

Renee threw a glance at Robbie and Julie, suspecting they were getting anxious to go. They all took their seats again.

Marilyn struggled with what to say next. She cleared her throat and made eye contact with each of them before speaking. Renee felt a flutter of nerves . . . Marilyn was acting strange.

"I have something to share with you that I probably should have shared a long time ago. I used to think I would take this secret to my grave, but now I realize this was never my secret to keep. I should have shared it with Jim. Now it is too late for that. James never wanted me to tell you this. He is a private man, but something has happened and I changed my mind."

What the hell is Marilyn talking about? Renee glanced at her kids. Both looked apprehensive.

"Renee, you know how much we loved Jimmy. He was our pride and joy. The only child we ever had. When he died, we just . . . *shattered.* But what we never shared with any of you was that Jim . . . Jim was not our biological son. We adopted him when he was an infant."

Shock ran through Renee. Julie and Robbie stared at their grandmother.

Once she started talking, Marilyn didn't stop. "Back when we were first married, we thought we would have a houseful of children. But it never happened. Back then, they didn't have all the tests and medical procedures young couples can try today to start a family if it doesn't happen on its own. We came to realize that if we ever wanted to raise a child, we would have to adopt.

"There was a young family in town. They already had three kids and the wife was pregnant again. Her husband ran off before she gave birth, leaving her completely overwhelmed. Our pastor approached us one day because he knew we were exploring adoption. The young mother found out she was carrying twins and was terrified she wouldn't be able to raise two more in addition to the three she was already struggling to feed. We would have loved to adopt both babies, but she was only interested in putting one up for adoption. For some reason, she thought she could handle four kids on her own but not five."

Marilyn paused to draw in a shaky breath, gnarled fingers wringing a white tissue she'd pulled out of her sleeve. She had their undivided attention.

"We went home and talked about it. We prayed. We decided this might be our only chance to raise a child, so we agreed, and within three months, we had our baby . . . we had our little Jimmy. The young mother took her other four children and moved out of the area. We never met her, but we were told she was a good mother and that it almost killed her to give up one of her babies. I sent her little notes and pictures of Jim through the years as well, through our pastor, whom she'd asked to deliver cards and letters to Jimmy for her. To my knowledge, she never attempted to find our true identity or visit her son."

"But . . ." Renee said, trying to wrap her head around this. "Why didn't Jim ever mention any of this to me?"

Marilyn took a deep breath. "Because . . . I kept the correspondence she sent, but I never shared any of it with Jimmy. We never told him any of this, in fact. I don't know if she ever suspected we didn't tell him he was adopted. We decided we just . . . we *couldn't* tell Jim he wasn't our biological child. When we adopted him, we lived in Ohio. We moved to Minnesota when he was still a baby, so no one around here knew we adopted. We didn't have much family around, so it was an easy secret to keep."

"But why?" Renee asked.

"We thought it would be less confusing for Jimmy, growing up, if we kept the secret."

Renee just stared back, still in shock.

"The first time I questioned our decision," Marilyn continued, "was when they finally figured out what was wrong with Jim and the doctor mentioned aplastic anemia can sometimes run in families. Should we have told him he was adopted at that point? If he had known his biological family and someone else in the family had it . . . what if he could have been diagnosed sooner? But he got so sick so fast, we were afraid to tell him for fear the shock might hurt his weakened body. So we kept our secret—but the doubt drove us mad.

Renee swallowed. "So . . . so why now? Why are you telling us this now? Now, when Jim has been gone for years?"

"As I said, we decided long ago to keep our secret. But something has happened that made me rethink that decision. Recently, I received a letter. Our old pastor died twenty-five years ago, so we hadn't had any correspondence with Jimmy's biological mother in a long time. Suddenly, a letter shows up. I could hardly believe it. I took it to James and told him what it said. But the man is failing, and I don't know whether he understood. He wouldn't say anything to me about it. He shook his head 'no' time and time again and got upset. An aide came in and asked me to leave for the day. The next day, he didn't remember any of it.

"So this is my cross to bear. You reaching out to me after all this time seemed to be a sign. Maybe it was a sign from God. Maybe it was Jim giving guidance from heaven. But when you called me, I knew this was something I had to share with you."

Pushing up slowly from the table, Marilyn went over to an old desk in the corner of the living room. Flipping down the oak lid, she pulled out an envelope and brought it back to the table, handing it to Renee.

"Please read it out loud, Renee," instructed Marilyn, taking her seat again. "My eyes aren't as good as they used to be."

Renee unfolded the letter. It was handwritten in bold cursive. She cleared her throat and began to read.

"Dear Mr. and Mrs. Clements. My name is Grant Johnson. Please forgive me for reaching out to you with what may seem like a strange request if my research is wrong. I believe you were the adoptive parents of my twin brother. My mother passed away recently, but before she died, she confessed to me I had a twin whom she gave up for adoption when we were born. I had no idea I had another brother. My mother was a strong, caring person and I can hardly believe she gave up one of her children. Believe me when I say her circumstances had to have been extremely difficult. When we cleaned out her home, I saved boxes of correspondence, intending to go through them when I had time. Lately, most of my time has been spent taking care of my daughter Grace, who is critically ill.

"A few weeks after my mother's death, I gave more thought to what she had told me. You see, it is possible to effectively treat the disease ailing my daughter if a bone marrow match can be made. If a match can be found with a family member, the transplant is much more likely to be effective. Unfortunately, no matches have been found within our family to date. Acting on a whim, I decided maybe something in my mother's files might give me a clue as to my missing brother's identity. Imagine my surprise when I did find some limited information. I worked with someone with good investigative skills and we eventually uncovered enough information to determine, with reasonable certainty, that you were the adoptive parents of my brother."

Renee spared a glance at her kids to gauge their reactions as she shuffled to the second page of the letter. Robbie fidgeted in his seat, peering into the blackness beyond the kitchen window. Julie met her mother's gaze with the briefest of nods to encourage her to continue reading.

"If this is indeed true, I am also saddened by the knowledge your son died an early death. It is possible he died from the same disease my daughter Grace is suffering from now. Please know how sorry I was to learn of Jim's death, and I convey to you my deepest sympathies. If not for my daughter's illness, I likely would never have acted on the information I discovered in my mother's files. I would have respected your privacy. But if there is any chance of finding a match for my daughter, I hope you can understand my desperate need to explore all possible paths.

"I know Jim fathered two children prior to his death. I am writing to plead for your assistance in reaching out to them.

"My daughter is very ill, so it is critical we act quickly. I can be reached at 555-290-2828. If my research was flawed and you were not the adoptive parents of my brother, please call me immediately so I can continue to pursue other paths to find potential matches for Grace.

"God bless, Grant Johnson."

"So you see," Marilyn said once everyone had absorbed Renee's reading of the letter, "it was no longer my secret to keep. Now it is your turn. It is up to you whether or not you want to reach out to Mr. Johnson. I have not, nor do I plan to. I have done what I can with the information."

"Wow," said Robbie. "That is some heavy stuff. We might have an uncle and cousin, and maybe more family we never even knew about before today."

Overwhelmed, Renee sat quietly, again reading the letter from a possible brother of her dead husband. A thousand questions raced through her mind. He was a twin. Would they have been identical? Would they have similar mannerisms even though they weren't raised by the same parents? Would Grace look like Julie or Robbie?

She refolded the letter, placed it in the envelope, and rose. She put it in her purse and turned to Marilyn again, ready to leave before any more surprises could be shared. She didn't know if she could process any more.

"One last thing, Renee," Marilyn said as she rose again from the table. She went back over to the secretary and slid open the bottom drawer. From it she removed a covered box the size of the photo boxes available in craft stores, but this box was much older.

"Here is all of the correspondence we received from Jim's biological mother in those years before Pastor Mike died. I think you three should have it. And I promise, no more surprises tonight. I am tired—and I know you need to get back to your folks."

At the door, Renee gave Marilyn a quick hug and a small smile. What could she say? She hadn't yet begun to think through the ramifications of everything Marilyn shared with them. Promising to call her when they got back from their trip to Fiji, they left the overly warm house.

No one said much on the way back to Renee's parents. They agreed to take some time to think about everything, and they would decide how they wanted to handle it all after their New Year's trip. Since it was late and they planned to leave early the next morning, they also agreed to hold their newfound secret close for a while longer. It was a secret Marilyn had kept for almost fifty years; a few more weeks couldn't hurt, right?

CHAPTER 17

Gift of Conversation

Renee settled into her seat on the plane. An ice cold, crystal clear morning had greeted them when they left the house at 4:00 a.m. Despite the hour, both kids chattered with excitement during the drive. Now the three of them were scattered throughout the coach section. Booking flights so close to departure hadn't allowed them to get seats together. Renee suspected both Robbie and Julie would sleep once the plane leveled off.

Once in the air, the reality of this excursion hit. With nothing else to occupy her thoughts in the darkened cabin, Renee started second-guessing her decision. Their adventure was going to be expensive—obviously not the most prudent choice. Renee's mind skipped ahead to next Thanksgiving . . . what if her severance package ran out before she found a job? Would Julie have to withdraw from college? How would Renee keep their medical insurance? Would Robbie be able to stay on his basketball team if she couldn't afford the costs of participating at the high school level? Her anxiety rose with the elevation, and she started fidgeting in her seat.

The seatbelt light above flicked off. To calm her nerves, Renee walked back to the lavatory. Once in the confined space—not the best solution for her anxiety, she realized—she splashed cold water on her face. She looked up, staring at herself in the mirror.

"Get a grip," she muttered at her reflection. She was not going to ruin any of their fun with a sudden case of regret, she told herself.

After a few deep breaths, she folded the door open and walked back to her seat. A cart bearing heavenly smelling coffee approached her row. She felt better as she drank the dark brew. Reaching under the seat in front of her, she hoisted up her carry-on bag, careful not to spill her coffee. She pulled out one of the books Julie gave her and the journal from Robbie.

It didn't take Renee long to become engrossed in one of her new books: *Rich Dad Poor Dad*. Julie's thoughtfulness was opening up a whole new world. She quickly devoured the first few chapters, capturing comments and favorite passages in her new journal.

Renee closed the book and laid her head back, shutting her eyes. The book was giving her lots to consider. Instead of sitting down and writing out a bunch of goals, as she started to do after she was laid off, she needed to think long and hard about how she wanted to live her life from now on. She needed to understand the "why" behind the key areas she would choose to focus on, before she tried to figure out the "how." She sat quietly, giving herself time to start assembling her jumbled thoughts. As she relaxed, she drifted off.

When she woke, strong sunshine streamed in and flight attendants were serving boxed lunches. Stowing her book and journal back under the seat, she noticed the woman sitting next to her put away her laptop. The woman offered Renee a friendly smile as they both opened their lunches. They'd exchanged hellos before the flight took off but hadn't talked beyond that in deference to the quiet of the dark cabin.

"Hi, I'm Renee."

"Hi Renee, I'm Susan," the woman replied with another warm smile.

Renee unwrapped her sandwich. "Are you going to Fiji for fun or for work?"

"I'm meeting friends in Fiji. We plan to usher in New Year's with fun, sun, and friendly natives. I was working in Minneapolis for the past month, but I live in Virginia. I noticed you were reading a book by Robert Kiyosaki. What do you think of it so far? He has written a few good books and I really love the one his wife Kim wrote. Have you read *Rich Woman*?"

"Oh, I haven't, I'll have to check that out next. I *love* this one! It's got me thinking, that's for sure. My daughter Julie gave it to me. My son Robbie gave me the journal for Christmas. We're heading to Fiji to celebrate New Year's, too. They're in seats up ahead. This trip was spur-of-the-moment, so we didn't get seats together."

"Wow, what a great thing to do with your kids," Susan exclaimed. "I booked this trip last February. Helped me tolerate Minnesota in December, knowing I had a tropical vacation to look forward to. What prompted you to take a last-minute trip all the way to Fiji?"

Renee pondered how best to respond. She was surprised at how comfortable she felt, talking with this stranger, and decided to be open about her current predicament. Why not?

"We originally planned a quiet holiday at home, like we always do. My daughter was coming home from college, and my son is still in high school. I always find it tough to unplug from work for long. We even stopped making the short trip to my parents' for Christmas the past few years. But in mid-December, I was laid off from my job, effective immediately—*such* a surprise."

Susan gasped sympathetically.

"It *shouldn't* have been a surprise, given the state of the economy and other recent layoffs, but I never thought it could happen to me, you know? Suddenly, we had free time on our hands. I had to decide whether I wanted to sit home and wallow in self pity or suck it up and celebrate the holidays. In hindsight, I feel like this trip was totally irrational . . . but as you can guess, we decided to celebrate and here we are, on a flight to Fiji! We also spent time with extended family over Christmas. It was great to reconnect with everyone. Made me realize what a mistake it's been to stop going home for the holidays."

Susan didn't act surprised by Renee's story. Renee was relieved when she didn't immediately reply with standard comments like "It'll be fine," or "You'll find another job right away." Instead, she listened and she nodded periodically, helping Renee feel comfortable enough to share her situation. Susan looked ten years younger than Renee, but she had an air of maturity about her.

"Renee, it sounds to me like you made the right decision to bring your family on this trip. It's scary to find yourself unemployed, but that's your situation as it stands today, and you're making the best of it. It can be maddening to have your life thrown upside down, but it happens all the time—just usually to other people, right?"

Renee laughed, nodding.

"Sometimes," Susan said, "these dilemmas, while painful, can be just what you need to force some much needed change in your life. Life can get pretty boring and stale if you don't shake it up once in a while."

Renee smiled. "You know, Susan, you sound a lot like the author of this book. Have you ever been laid off?"

Susan laughed. "I sound like the book's author because I've *read* that book, and many others like it. My work revolves around helping women who find themselves in much the same situation as you. It isn't always a job loss. It can be a sudden divorce, illness, even death—anything that's turned someone's life upside down."

"I can't believe this," Renee said. "What are the odds we end up sitting next to each other on a plane to Fiji?"

"It probably isn't a coincidence," Susan replied. "Keep reading those books, and I think you'll see what I mean."

"Please, tell me more about what you do," Renee prompted. "How do you help women?"

"I'd love to tell you about what we do. But first it would probably help if I told you a little more about myself. You were so generous in sharing your story—I owe you the same candidness."

Susan wrapped the remainder of her sandwich in her napkin and dropped it in her boxed lunch. She folded the box shut and took a quick sip of water before continuing.

"I graduated from college nine years ago and found a nursing job, working in an emergency room. I won't lie to you, it was tough. The hours were long, the work draining, and I struggled with the despair I witnessed every day. We were taught to keep a professional distance when working with patients, and I understand why they see the need to take that approach. If you allow yourself to think too deeply on the dire situations many of those people are facing, you go crazy. You want to help, but often there is little you can do."

"I can only imagine," Renee said.

Susan nodded. "You see families ripped apart when a spouse dies from an accident or a sudden heart attack. You see people, usually women, come in repeatedly because someone that supposedly loves them keeps beating them. You see kids coming in so messed up on drugs their brains will never heal. Sometimes you can serve their immediate needs, but often, you know some of them will make choices that will put them back in the same position again, or worse.

"I worked lots of hours, didn't socialize much, and was still single at thirty. My sister Maggie—she's two years younger. She met her husband in college. When they completed their undergrad, they decided to get married and he went on to law school. Maggie was pregnant a few months into the marriage so decided to stay home instead of starting her career."

Renee was so engrossed in Susan's story, she forgot to finish her sandwich. A flight attendant came by to collect trash, prompting Renee to continue eating as she listened. Susan handed her box to the attendant.

"They lived a few hours from me, so I didn't get to see them often. When I did, they seemed happy, excited to start a family. Tim, Maggie's husband, passed the bar and landed a job with a big firm. Life clicked right along, and Maggie kept busy raising their twins."

At Susan's mention of twins, Renee flashed back to her mother-in-law's kitchen, reading about her late husband's long-lost twin. A twin with a dying daughter. *Jim would have loved having a brother.*

But then there was the accident," Susan said, pulling Renee's attention back to her story. "Tim picked the twins up from a play date and was bringing them home. A drunk driver slammed into their car. Killed Tim instantly."

"Oh my God," Renee exclaimed, shifting in her seat to more fully face Susan. "That is terrible! What about the kids?"

Susan closed her eyes and shook her head. "I thank God every day that Maggie's son and daughter survived with barely a scratch. But Maggie struggled. Tim never actually bought the life insurance policy he told her he took care of. They bought a beautiful home when the twins were three. There wasn't much equity yet when Tim died.

"Maggie was forced to sell and move home to our parents with her twins. I helped when I could, but I was working full time, and so were Mom and Dad. Maggie couldn't find a job that paid enough to cover daycare. She got through each day in a state of limbo."

I remember those days all too well, Renee thought, shivering as she recalled life immediately following Jim's death.

"She tried her best with the kids, but Tim's death and her lack of financial security crushed her. She started going out at night, once someone was home to stay with the kids. She met a guy who liked to party—hard—and she started a downward spiral." Susan gazed down into her glass of water, lost in her own life's story. "We should have worked harder to get her help, but we were busy with our own lives and helping her to raise her kids. We thought she would eventually snap out of it.

"We realized she was in big trouble when she ended up in my ER one night as I was coming off shift. A girlfriend brought her in. She was badly beaten. Barely conscious. There was a point where her brain started to swell, and we didn't know if she would make it. Mom and Dad arranged for a priest to give her last rites." Susan looked back up and smiled at Renee. "But heaven intervened and she pulled through.

"Maggie had two choices. She could continue down the path she was on. The man who put her in the hospital was dangerous. He was good-looking with a great smile, and he could be a charmer. He tried hard to convince her it would never happen again. He'd made a terrible mistake because of the booze, but he swore he would never lay a hand on her again. Or, Maggie could start making different choices. She could reevaluate her life and recognize all her blessings. She had two beautiful, healthy children. She also had a supportive family, one willing to help her get back on her feet.

"Maggie made the right choice. She cut all ties with her new group of friends. She became close friends with Jane, a counselor she met while recovering in the hospital. Jane worked at the YWCA, and she encouraged Maggie to volunteer at the shelter. Our parents agreed to watch the twins every other Saturday so Maggie could go. When I had a Saturday off, I would go with her.

"Maggie and I both came to realize there were many women in the shelter that needed more help than they were getting. Maggie decided to start a support group. She saw that by the time women found themselves at the shelter—often in the middle of the night with their kids in tow—they had suffered in silence for a long time. Sometimes for years. Maggie wanted to find a way to help women before they hit rock bottom. Her enthusiasm for her new mission was contagious. She didn't know how she could earn a living helping other women, but she knew she needed to find a way. After living through hell with Maggie, my parents wanted to be part of the solution. I finally felt like this would be a way I could make more of a difference in people's lives, too. I was no longer satisfied patching up the wounded only to send them out to do battle again.

"It took a year of trial-and-error—by then the twins were in first grade—but Maggie finally figured out a format of women's retreats that felt like it could work. Dad decided to retire from the local university so he could help Maggie figure out the logistics. The retreats are often held on weekends. Mom prepares meals for the attendants and Maggie facilitates the sessions. Her friend Jane was instrumental in helping Maggie bring in experts, often for no charge in the early days of the retreats, before they were making any money with which to pay contributors.

"I kept my day job up until a year ago. Then I made the leap, too. Joined the family business! Now I work full time with our retreat program."

"That's amazing!" Renee exclaimed.

Susan beamed.

A thought suddenly occurred to Renee, for which she immediately felt ashamed, but she voiced it anyway: "And you make enough money doing this?"

Susan nodded, understanding. "We knew we could only help a limited number of women through our own retreats, so we came up with a way to duplicate ourselves. Now much of what I do is travel around the country and train other people that want to establish similar retreat businesses of their own. This expansion still fits our main mission to help as many women as possible. We charge enough for our services so we can support our family, but we aren't getting rich off the business. We're trying to take our own advice and also find other revenue streams so we can gain some financial independence while still continuing to provide a service we're all so passionate about."

Renee was engrossed in Susan's story. She had feared Susan would say her sister died at the hands of her abuser. Instead, she shared how her sister took her own painful life lessons and turned them into something positive.

Beeps rang through the cabin, signaling their descent to the islands. Renee was sorry their discussion had to end. She thanked Susan for sharing her story and jotted down her new friend's contact information. Both agreed they wanted to stay in touch. They weren't staying at the same place in Fiji, nor were they returning on the same flight, but maybe they would run into each other during their stay. If not, both promised to get in touch with the other when they returned to their lives state-side.

The end of Susan's story resonated through Renee's mind throughout the landing procedure, and she kept returning to a single question.

What am I passionate about?

Chapter 18

Gift of the Tropics

*R*obbie, Julie, and Renee met in the gate area after their long flight. Just as Renee had predicted, Robbie slept most of the trip, his hair tousled and clothes now a wrinkled mess. He woke up in time to see the ocean and beach as they started their descent. Julie, on the other hand, had only slept for the first part of the flight, then watched a movie and started reading her beach romance from her gift box. After a bathroom break, they stretched their legs and found the baggage claim. All three suitcases slowly rotated around the conveyor belt—a benefit of their direct flight. Robbie was starving—he'd slept through lunch, after all—but they needed to pick up their rental car, so he settled for a bag of chips and a soda.

A warm breeze, perfumed by flowers and rain, met them as they stepped out of the terminal. Renee paused to enjoy it, nearly getting run over by the kids.

We made it!

Their crazy plan actually worked. They were in Fiji, and there was no snow on the ground, even though it was December 29. The wind would be biting and the ground white back home.

"I could get used to this," she said out loud.

They all laughed.

"Yeah," Robbie said, "you might have to find a huge job when we get back so we can do this more often."

They found a shuttle bus full of holiday travelers, to take them to the rental cars. The bus driver wore a flowered shirt, shorts, and sandals. No stuffy uniforms here. He was deep in conversation with the couple sitting immediately behind him. Julie snagged the last three seats across the back of the shuttle.

A small rental car waited for them; the desk attendant jotted down directions to their resort. It would be a forty-five-minute drive, which made Renee apprehensive. She had no idea where she was going or what the traffic would be like. *I wish someone else could drive.* But since her only options were a college student or a high schooler, she knew she was still the safest bet. Renee put on a brave front as they piled into the little compact, their suitcases barely fitting in the trunk. *Should have opted for an upgrade.*

The directions were good. In no time, they left the congestion of the airport and followed the coast, ocean on their left, green mountains on their right. Fresh air rushed through open windows, Robbie throwing his head out the window and screaming out in excitement.

"For God's sake, Robbie, get your head back in here before you lose it!" Renee scolded her son, but her words lacked bite as she laughed.

An occasional flock of chickens roamed the side of the highway. Most cars were small, older models. There was some traffic, but nothing like Renee often endured in her daily commutes—commutes she might never have to endure again, she realized.

After twenty minutes in the car, Robbie reminded his mother of his state of near starvation. She pulled off the road to grab something quick at a small hamburger stand on the beach. After downing their burgers, they waded into the water for their first dip in the ocean. The beach wasn't crowded: a group of kids was building a huge castle of caramel-colored sand; down the beach, a group of older adults lounged, watching another group of teens play sand volleyball; a few others strolled up and down the beach by themselves.

Feeling like outsiders in their heavy travel clothes, they headed back to the car so they could get to their resort. Renee dug in her purse. Julie, accustomed to her mother losing things in the huge purse she lugged around, sighed in exasperation.

"What's the holdup, Mom?" she asked.

Robbie pressed his face to the glass window. "Crap," he said.

Dismay filled Renee. She'd left the keys on the car seat. They had no way into their rental.

She exhaled heavily. "Shit . . . *now* what we are going to do?" The long travel hours caught up with her as she sagged against the locked car. Julie and Robbie knew to keep quiet. They didn't have any good ideas, but they could sense Renee was getting close to losing her temper. What were the chances there was an On Star service tied to the car? "Guess I'll call the agency," she muttered. Renee plopped her purse on the car hood and dug for the rental agreement. Thank goodness she hadn't thrown it in the glove compartment. Number in hand, she went to place the call . . . only to discover her cell was dead. "Shit," she said again. "Phone's dead."

Robbie held his hands up in defense. "You made us leave our phones at home for this trip."

Exasperated, she plunked down on the curb next to the car, staring out at the water. Not knowing what else to do, the kids joined her. All three sat, looking dejected. Life continued moving around them; no one seemed to notice their dilemma.

Gravel crunched behind them and Renee heard a car stop. She turned around: a beat-up old police car had parked directly behind her rental. Hoisting herself off the curb and dusting sand from her butt, she walked back to the cruiser. A man was getting out of the driver's side. Though it was clearly a law enforcement vehicle, he didn't *look* like a cop. His "uniform" was similar to the shuttle driver's, although he was wearing long pants. His bright shirt was loose and untucked, probably in deference to the heat. His eyes were shielded by sunglasses and his dark hair, lined with a few silver streaks, fluttered in the wind.

Smiling a slow smile, he rounded the front of the cruiser as Renee came around the back of her car. "You three look like you could use a little help. Locked your keys in the car, huh?" the man said to Renee in a gravelly voice.

"Um, well, yes, I did lock the keys in the car . . . but how could you possibly know that? Didn't you just drive into the lot?" Renee asked, confused. She was tired, hot, and frustrated.

Chuckling, the man gave a small nod and walked over to her driver's side door, gesturing casually back at the beach. "Pete over there at the food stand noticed your little predicament and gave us a call. I was in the area so I thought I would stop to see if I could be of assistance. Name's Matt Blatso, and I have the dubious distinction of having the title of 'Sheriff' around here. Sorry—forgot to introduce myself. This kind of stuff happens all the time. People juggle so much gear when they head for the beach, keys get left behind. This'll only take a minute." He sauntered back to his car.

Returning, he worked his magic, and Renee's door popped open. The kids, hanging in the background, let out loud whoops of joy.

"Hey, thanks!" Robbie exclaimed, stepping forward and extending his hand to the man. "It's been a long day. We were afraid Mom was going to lose it when she realized the keys were locked in the car."

Matt returned the handshake and quietly sized up Robbie. Renee was surprised by her son's adult gesture.

"Not a problem, just doing my job," Matt replied. "By the way, where you folks from? Your accent sounds northern."

At that silly comment—because obviously *he* was the one with the drawl—Renee gave a little grunt, but quickly remembered her manners.

"Thank you so much for helping us out. We just got in from Minneapolis, Minnesota. My name is Renee Clements, and these are my kids, Robbie and Julie. Since you went out of your way to help, I hate to disagree with you, but I don't think we have much of an accent. You, on the other hand, sound like you have to come from the South."

"Ha, all you folks that come from snowier climates think you talk normal and the rest of us have accents. Enjoy your stay, relax a little, and your clipped tone might loosen up a little, too." And with that, he gave her a little salute and was off.

Left standing alone next to her car, she wasn't sure if she should take that as an insult or not. Julie reached across from the passenger's side and tooted the horn, anxious to get to their resort. Renee quickly crawled back in the car.

Shadows stretched across the road as they pulled into their resort's parking lot. They couldn't see a single building one could easily call a hotel. There was a cluster of small cottages, roughly ten in total, as well as a long rambling building next to the parking lot, bearing a sign that said LOBBY.

Each cottage was painted a different bright color with the same turquoise trim. The turquoise continued in a kidney-shaped pool and again in small glimpses of ocean behind the quaint resort. Lush green plants and brilliant tropical blooms ringed every structure and walkway. Lofty palm trees swayed gently above. It was easily the prettiest sight Renee had seen in a long time. She inhaled deeply again, the scented air a perfect balance of fragrant flowers and salty ocean.

"Think it's too good to be true?" Robbie asked.

Glancing at one another, all three piled out of the car and headed to the lobby.

"Welcome to Fiji!" rang a voice from behind the counter. "You must be the Clements, from Minnesota!" Looking around for the source of the voice, Renee took in a bright white room decorated with nautical knickknacks and boasting a wide expanse of glass looking over the ocean. A huge bouquet of tropical blooms sat squarely in the center of the long counter.

A short, round woman appeared, arms extended. She carried delicate flower leis and ceremoniously placed one around each of their necks. Surprised by the warm welcome, they all stood smiling from ear to ear.

"My name is Lulu! I'm the proprietor here at our little slice of paradise. You'll also meet my husband Bill. Together, we'll make your stay here everything you hoped it would be. You are getting in a little late, so you missed the picnic we held an hour ago—but don't worry," she added, perhaps catching Robbie's crestfallen expression, "we wrapped up goodies and stashed them in your fridge. As part of your vacation package, we like to keep you well fed, but it's just the two of us, so we don't have an open kitchen all day long. The place would fall to shambles if we spent our whole day cooking," she explained with a chuckle.

Lulu continued about the business of getting them checked in. She talked non-stop as she took care of the financial end of the transaction. She offered up fun activities they could do on the island and gave the kids glossy brochures.

"Or you can lounge on the beach all day and enjoy our sunshine. You can be as busy or as lazy as you want to be. Even a little of both if that's your desire. Come, now—let's get you settled in your cottage. You're in number seven, this little pink number on the end facing the ocean."

Lulu led them down a path of crushed shells rimmed with bright flowers to a wide, ornate door. She slipped a key into the hammered black lock and clicked it open, handing the key to Renee. She walked through a living area, straight to large glass doors overlooking the ocean, and slid them open to let in the ocean breeze. All business, she pointed out features of the small, two-bedroom cottage. It was airy and bright but not fancy. Slightly worn furnishings gave a sense of having been collected over time. The place was spotless. Dark wooden cabinets in the kitchen broke up the expanse of white; bright tiles on the backsplash added color.

A plate of cookies sat on a small kitchen table, which Robbie got to first. Lulu opened the fridge, motioning to the promised leftovers. "Please join us for brunch 'round the pool in the morning. We'll have plenty of fresh fruit and local flavor for you. If you need anything, track us down—enjoy!" Lulu let herself out the door with a wave.

Julie was enthralled with the cottage; she wandered from room to room, admiring all the homey touches. Robbie grabbed up a second cookie, remarking through a mouthful, "Not a TV in sight," then adding, at the look from his mother, "but I'm sure I'll manage." Before he could lament any further over what this might mean for his vacation, screaming seagulls caught his attention, and he was out the sliding door, heading to the beach.

Renee was as tickled about the cottage as Julie. It was nicer than she dared hope, since she booked it with so little notice. Renee got to work unpacking. She claimed the room with the queen-size bed and window opening to the ocean. The kids would share the other bedroom with two twin-size beds. A small closet off the kitchen revealed a stackable washer and dryer. *We won't have to drag sandy, salt-glazed clothes home,* she thought with a smile. It was getting better and better. To top off their welcome, Renee found a cold bottle of white wine in the fridge. *Well . . . we're settled enough,* Renee thought, and popped the cork, filled a wine glass, and, after changing out of her grungy clothes into a loose fitting sundress, followed her son's lead to the beach. Jess had insisted she borrow the dress when learning of their trip; the light cotton fabric was perfect for enjoying the sunset.

It was still hot outside but would cool quickly, according to Lulu, once the sun went down. Julie was already lounging on a white plastic recliner on the beach. A half-empty bottle of water sat on a little table next to her. Renee sank into a neighboring chair. They relaxed while Robbie explored the beach. The ocean turned purple as the reddish-orange sun dipped low. Renee could not imagine a place she would rather be as she sipped her wine and watched her teenagers unwind. The only sound was of the waves and birds. No cars honked; no phones buzzed. A couple walked past them, hand in hand, looking like honeymooners.

"Mom, this is amazing. Thank you so much for bringing us here," Julie said quietly.

Renee reached across and captured Julie's hand. Together they sat and enjoyed the glorious sunset.

CHAPTER 19

Gift of a Sunrise

*R*enee shivered as he ran his hands up and down her arms, lightly brushing her breasts in their journey to encircle her waist. He pulled her close and she tipped her head up, tasting his breath as his lips came down to capture hers. Soft chirping sounds floated in the air, muffled at first but growing louder until the man in her arms dissolved and the squawking brought Renee straight up in bed, disconcerted from both the dream and the sudden racket.

"Dammit," she muttered, trying to get her bearings. She hadn't enjoyed a dream like that in a long time. *Where am I . . . and what's all that damn noise?* It was dim, but her eyes started to adjust. She could see the outline of her bedroom in their Fiji cottage.

She had left her window open when she went to bed, to enjoy the lull of the ocean. The sun was starting to reach pale fingers across the sky. A flock of birds must be perched in the tree right outside her bedroom window, all fighting over the same worm. Renee got up and slid her window shut. She lay back down, trying desperately to pick the dream back up—*his lips . . . his skin*—but it was hopeless. Although the clock on her bedside table read 6:00 a.m., she was wide awake. Her internal clock was all screwed up after the long flight and time zone difference between Fiji and Minneapolis. Sighing in resignation, she plugged in the coffee pot. Might as well go for a walk on the beach while it perked so she wouldn't wake the kids.

Her hair was a wild mess after going to bed with a wet head, so she threw it up in a high pony. As she quietly squeezed out the sliding glass door, a cool breeze made her glad she grabbed a jacket. The sun was high enough so she could see her way to the beach. No one else seemed to be out yet. Wisps of fog lay low on the water. She walked down to the water's edge. The tide was low and the beach littered with mysterious relics from the sea. Renee spied a small shell next to her bare foot. Stooping, she picked it up and brushed off the sand. No chips marred the concentric ridges ringing the outside, and it was as smooth as silk inside. She dropped the perfect little shell in her pocket.

She meandered her way down the beach, head down. She found a few more shells and slivers of tumbled sea glass, adding them to her pocket from time to time. She ambled on, not paying attention to her surroundings in her quest for treasures. She spied a bigger shell a few feet up the beach and switched course quickly, stooping to scoop it up.

A soft crunching of sand and a grunt brought her up sharply and something banged into her shoulder, knocking her down. More stunned than hurt, she lay on her back, gazing at the sky instead of the sand.

"Jesus, are you trying to kill me, lady?" a vaguely familiar voice muttered next to her.

Turning her head, she was shocked to see the sheriff from the day before kneeling in the sand next to her, a hand on his heart. His light gray sweatshirt was stained with sweat, and he wore long shorts, his feet bare. Gone were the sunglasses, and vivid green eyes glared at her. Recognition dawned in those eyes as he realized who he mowed down on the beach. He plopped down on his butt in the sand, stared at her for a second, then burst out laughing. He laughed so hard, he couldn't talk. He was trying to say something and motioning to her with his hands, but she couldn't understand him.

Renee's first thought, the split second before she recognized him, was that the man from her dream was back. But in a huff she realized who it was and she jumped to her feet, brushing sand off as best she could.

"What the hell is so funny?" she yelled at him; the whole incident had knocked her equilibrium off. "First you almost kill me and then you sit there and laugh like an idiot!"

In her rage, she stepped toward him, jabbing her finger to emphasize her points. When she got close enough, he grabbed her hand and pulled her down next to him. Instinctively, she recoiled and tried to scoot away, but he was stronger. With his free hand, he reached toward her hair and she felt a tugging. Suddenly he was holding a grotesque, multi-legged creature in front of her face. His eyes streamed from laughter, but he took note of the look of horror on her face. Afraid she was going to start screaming again, he quickly tossed the harmless sand crab far up into the sea-grass rimming the beach. He rose to his feet and offered her a hand.

Ignoring his offer, she rolled away and got to her feet. Embarrassed—and still angry at him for laughing at her—she gave him one last glare and headed back up the beach toward her cottage.

Watching her retreat, the man seemed to realize an apology was a good idea and jogged to catch up with her, this time keeping a safe distance between them.

"Look, I'm sorry I ran into you back there," he said. "I saw you combing the beach, although I didn't recognize you, and had no intention of disturbing you. The sheriff, remember? Matt. I jog out here most every morning and always see people combing the beach. You veered right in front of me at the last minute, and I didn't have time to turn and miss you. I'm sorry—I hope I didn't hurt you . . .?"

Renee ignored him for a minute then stopped, turning to face him.

"Oh all right, I admit I should have been watching where I was walking. I didn't hear you and thought I was alone on the beach. Not real smart on my part. I think it was your laughing that ticked me off. By the way, what the hell was that creature you pulled out of my hair?"

"Oh, he was harmless," Matt replied, waving off her question. "Those little guys are always scurrying around on the sand early in the morning, before the birds try to pick them off as lunch."

"Gross." Renee shivered, not appeased by his response, feeling guilty for being rude. "Sorry I overreacted. It was as much my fault as yours. Can I offer you a cup of coffee to make up for my rudeness, and to properly thank you for helping us yesterday? I put the pot on before I left for my walk."

"As tempting as a good cup of coffee sounds, I'm gonna have to pass. I need to shower and get to work. Early shift today. Thanks, though. Maybe if I run into you again during your stay you can make it up to me then." He turned on his heel, jogging off in the direction he'd been running before they collided.

Still shaken, Renee rushed the rest of the way back to her cottage. What was the matter with her? Here she was, in a strange country where she didn't know a soul, walking alone on the beach in the early morning, paying no attention to her surroundings. Matt could have easily been someone else, and she could have found herself in a much different situation. *Gotta keep my wits,* she vowed, and headed back to the cottage, thinking as she went that the sheriff was kinda cute, even if he was irritating as hell.

The kids were still sound asleep, so Renee filled her coffee cup, grabbed her carry-on bag, and went back to relax in one of the chairs by the shore.

Today was Sunday, December 30, and tomorrow was already New Year's Eve. *Time flies in paradise,* she thought. She was so glad they didn't have to leave until the following Saturday. Lulu had invited them to an annual New Year's Eve party. There would be dancing, good food, and people of all ages, so the kids were looking forward to it, but they still had today and most of tomorrow before the party. She would leave the schedule for the next couple of days to the kids.

Renee dug around in her bag. In addition to her books and journal, there were also four envelopes. Three bore her dear aunt's scrawling handwriting. She would open hers on New Year's Day, probably sitting right in this same spot as the sun rose to greet a brand new year. The fourth envelope was addressed by a different hand and was made out to her in-laws. While she was excited to open the missive from Celia, opening this envelope and reading this letter again filled her with trepidation.

Renee knew she needed to give Grant Johnson's request serious consideration. She shouldn't put it off any longer—certainly not till New Year's Day. She pulled the yellow legal pages out and unfolded them on her lap, again reading the words. Words written by a man claiming to be the brother of her dead husband.

As her eyes scanned the letter, undoubtedly worded carefully by Johnson, her mind spoke in her husband's voice. It was as if he were asking her to help the brother and niece he never knew.

Renee set the letter aside and reclined farther in the lounging chair, eyes closed, considering her different options. Unbidden, the volunteer working the Salvation Army kettle the day she lost her job popped into her mind. Hadn't she promised herself she would focus more on other people in the future? But she was scared. Her husband had been gone for ten years. She was afraid to meet his other family. She considered the possibility of this being a hoax, but she didn't think that was the case. Marilyn admitted they'd adopted Jim as an infant, and knew he had a twin through her correspondence with the birth mother—had proof of it, even.

What worried Renee most was the possibility of opening her children up to more heartache. What if they did reach out to their cousin, tried to help her, and she still didn't survive? Close on the heels of that thought was the realization her children could also be at risk. If either Julie or Robbie were facing a deadly—but possibly curable—disease, wouldn't she do everything in her power to get them the help they needed? And her kids already knew about the situation because Marilyn shared the story in front of them. What message would she be sending to them if they didn't try to help?

She needed to call Johnson when they got home, maybe even before that if she could. She couldn't ignore his request for help. She had no way of knowing if either Robbie or Julie would be a match, or if the girl was healthy enough for a transplant, but she knew they needed to try. Decision made, Renee felt better. She would discuss it with the kids, of course, but she felt confident they would agree.

The sliding door interrupted her thoughts. Julie carefully made her way through the door with full hands, using her foot to push it shut behind her. She carried a steaming mug in one hand, a plate of donuts in the other, and a thermos tucked in by her elbow. Renee folded up the letter and stashed it back in her bag.

Setting her goodies on the small plastic table between the same seats they used the night before, Julie plopped down next to her mom. She looked relaxed, sipping from her cup. The contents were so pale, Renee wasn't sure if she was drinking coffee or hot milk.

"Is that coffee?" she asked Julie.

"Of course," Julie replied. "I figured out it was easier to stay awake for study sessions if I had a cup or two. But I can't stand it black. By the way, thanks for doctoring my cup for me last week when I was outside with Molly. That was a nice surprise. Forgot to thank you."

Renee peered at her daughter. "What are you talking about? I didn't doctor anything up."

Julie's brow furrowed. "Hmm, maybe I did it myself and forgot. I poured a cup and then Molly was having a fit so I went outside with her. When I got back inside, it was how I like it—lots of milk and sugar. I thought you did it . . . but I must have. Robbie wouldn't think to touch my coffee." Julie took another sip, shrugging it off.

Déjà vu . . . Renee was reminded of the package left on the porch at her parents', addressed to Julie, and feelings of unease returned. She hadn't told Julie anything about the gift. But she didn't want to scare her; it was time for some discreet digging.

"So how is school going, honey?" Renee inquired, keeping her tone light, refilling her coffee cup from the thermos. "We haven't talked much about your first semester except for your classes. Are you and Zoey getting along? Have you made lots of new friends? Any boys catch your eye?"

"Let's see . . ." Julie sipped from her cup, thinking. "Zoey and I are fine. Sometimes we get on each other's nerves but that's probably normal. I met some fun girls. You remember Anna, the girl we took the Christmas presents to? She's great, lots of fun. She dresses a little crazy and you might think she was a partier, but she isn't. When she isn't working, she spends most of her time studying. She doesn't have a safety net, like I told you, so she has to make this work. Then there's Emma. She's the girl on our floor with family twenty minutes from school. Remember she invited me, Anna, and Zoey over for Thanksgiving? I think you would like her folks. Her mom even had us help her pull out all her Christmas decorations after Thanksgiving dinner was cleaned up so she could decorate the next day. Made me homesick, wishing I was home setting up the tree with you like we always do."

Renee nodded. "It was strange for us too, Julie, not having you home for Thanksgiving. Robbie helped me get everything out but disappeared when I started doing the actual decorating."

"Typical Robbie," Julie muttered, and they both laughed.

"It took me twice as long without you, honey, and it wasn't nearly as fun," Renee finished.

Both sat quietly for a bit, knowing there would be more holidays in the future when they might not be together.

"And how about boys?" Renee prompted. "Did you go out with anyone? You haven't said much about the guys at school."

"Well . . . as a matter of fact, I *did* meet a guy. His name is Lincoln."

Now we are getting somewhere, Renee thought as she sat a bit taller in her plastic chair.

"We met at the homecoming football game. He's cute, and seemed nice—"

" 'Seemed'?" Renee cut in.

"He was getting too clingy," Julie admitted, "so I've been trying to let our relationship slow way down. We went out some, when we had time, and studied together, but it isn't anything serious. Dating started out fun, but he wanted to be together all the time and it got old. I was glad we would get a break during the holidays. I probably need to tell him officially that it's off when we get back to school. I thought he'd get the hint when I stopped wanting to do everything together, but . . . he doesn't take hints."

"Sometimes people only see what they want to see. You probably do need to sit down with him and tell him you don't want to see him anymore," Renee counseled. "Have you talked to him since break started?" As she said this, those thirteen unread texts popped into her mind.

"I have, but he called and texted so much, I tried to ignore him for the last few days. Mom, honestly, I was so happy to get on that plane and leave my cell at home for a week. He was smothering me. I slept great last night, not having to wonder how many times my phone would go off."

Renee wasn't thrilled about what she was hearing.

"Did he ever scare you, Julie? Did he threaten you or anything?"

"No, nothing like that. He never yelled at me or pushed me around or anything, Mom, really—don't worry. I'll take care of it when we get home, maybe even before I go back to school." Julie looked at her mom. "I don't want to talk about Lincoln anymore, if that's all right with you. I just want to enjoy the beach, sun, and fun for the next week."

"Fair enough," Renee replied. "No more talk about boys, or school, or anything even remotely depressing. From here on out, let's just enjoy ourselves."

And with that, the subject was closed for the rest of the trip.

CHAPTER 20

Gift of Night Waves

*B*oth Robbie and Julie voted to hang out at the beach Sunday and Monday—which was perfectly fine in Renee's opinion. Neither wanted to do any formal excursions, and Renee was glad not to have the added expense. The beach behind their cottage got busier late morning through early evening, filling with families, teenagers, and retirees, all out to enjoy the beautiful weather. Renee couldn't believe she was sitting in eighty-degree temperatures in late December.

Julie sunbathed, read, and snorkeled. She floated around in the bay for an hour at a time. Renee constantly reminded her to keep putting on more sunscreen so she wouldn't fry.

Robbie quickly made friends with two boys visiting from Georgia. They spent their time playing volleyball and watching pretty girls. At one point they even talked the girls into a match. Renee laughed when the girls beat them without any trouble. The guys weren't as cocky after that.

Renee loved watching the kids. She felt more relaxed than she had in years. Lulu and her husband handled all the cooking and cleaning. All Renee did was soak up the sun (she wore a hat so the rays wouldn't bleach out her new hair color she'd splurged on before Christmas). Her kids didn't yet appreciate how lucky they were to have a mother who kept them slathered in sunscreen since they were babies. If they kept up the habit, they might avoid sunspots like the ones dotting her arms, legs, and back. Renee grimaced when she thought back to her teen years at the lake with friends. They'd all doused themselves in iodine-infused baby oil to dye their skin even darker. The only reason she ever wore sunscreen when she was younger was because it smelled like "yummy coconuts," as she used to say.

By Monday afternoon, they were water-logged and drained from so much time in the sun. Robbie fell asleep in a hammock strung in the shade next to their cottage. Julie decided to nap in a covered cabana next to the pool to get a break from the sand. Renee laid down in the cool cottage. A band began warming up for the night's festivities down the block, waking Julie up first. Eventually all three were up and showered, dressed in the only festive clothes they packed.

Julie looked stunning in a yellow halter dress, her hair lighter from two days in the sun and her skin a shade darker despite all the sunscreen. Robbie put on the bright coral shirt he'd bought earlier from a shack down at the market, and donned his best pair of shorts. Renee slipped on the other dress Jess sent with her: a pretty aqua with a pale shimmery shade on top bleeding into nearly black at the gauze hem. Robbie surprised her with a dainty sea-glass necklace from the market. It looked perfect with her dress. She wore simple white flip flops to avoid sore feet by the end of the evening.

Together they walked down to the party, now in full swing.

"Don't feel like you have to babysit me all night, kids. I'm just going to mingle a bit. I won't be offended if you want to hang out with any of your new friends. Be home by one, and stay with the other kids." *God, it's hard to give them space, but they're good kids and they'll be careful,* Renee tried to reassure herself as her mind conjured up past news stories of kids traveling to the tropics and going missing.

It didn't take long for Robbie to spot his new buds and take off. Julie also saw girls she met on the beach earlier and wandered off with them, giving her mom a brief wave and encouraging smile. Renee found herself alone. She was surprised to realize this didn't even bother her. Everyone was friendly and she meandered from group to group, making small talk and introducing herself as "Renee from Minneapolis." The crowd included both visitors and islanders. At one point, Renee saw Matt, but he was in uniform and keeping an eye on the party. She watched him greet people as they passed, but didn't approach him. He caught her eye on one occasion and nodded a hello, but that was the extent of it.

Picnic tables had been set up around the parking lot to give party-goers a place to relax and visit. A group of six noisy women congregated at one such table, their laughter snagging Renee's attention. She was delighted to see Susan, the woman she sat next to on the plane, among them. She strolled over to their table.

"Hey Susan!" Renee greeted her new acquaintance. "I'm so glad to see you again! What brings you to this part of the island?"

"Oh my God, hi Renee! Everyone, this is Renee. We met on the flight over here," Susan introduced her, and the other women greeted Renee warmly. "The Chamber of Commerce provides a shuttle service around the island and we heard about this party, so we thought it would be fun to come hear the live music."

Renee sat down with them and joined in their conversation. All were there without their significant others, now enjoying girl time. Twenty minutes before midnight, they decided to catch a shuttle back so they could enjoy their resort's champagne and fruit bar.

"I am so glad I got to meet all of you," Renee said. She gave each of her new friends a quick hug as they left. "Happy New Year!"

Renee again found herself alone. Shirtless male waiters in flower leis and cutoffs walked through the crowd with plastic flutes of champagne, offering them to the adults as midnight drew near. Helping herself to a glass, Renee felt a sudden need for solitude.

The beach was off to the left. A bright moon illuminated the sand. Slipping off her sandals, she made her way down to the water's edge. It was so peaceful, the waves masking most other sounds. She could still hear a bit of the noise from the party behind her and see a group of kids with a fire burning farther down the beach, but she couldn't hear their voices. She was in her own little bubble, sipping the fruity, dry drink, pondering both the year now ending and the new one ahead.

She jumped at a slight touch on her arm. Standing next to her, eyes focused on the water, was Matt. He also held a flute.

"Trying to surprise me again?" she asked.

He smiled but said nothing, still staring at the water.

They stood quietly for a few minutes, and then heard the band's countdown to midnight begin. Matt silently put his hand on Renee's elbow, gently turning her to face him. *Oh man, am I really going to do this?* Renee pondered, poised to retreat. As the clock struck midnight, he dipped his head toward her, his intent clear. *What the hell,* she conceded, and she tilted hers up, meeting him for an innocent brush of lips to welcome in the New Year. It felt natural and unhurried, neither backed away to end the contact. They kissed again as the crowd behind them whooped it up. They stepped closer, their kisses becoming more urgent as Renee leaned into Matt, her bare toes bumping against his boots.

Something landed with a thud in the sand at their feet and both jumped back. A teenager jogged up, noticing them as he reached for his Frisbee. He was part of the group down the beach.

"Oh, sorry about that, didn't see you there," the boy apologized. "Hope we didn't hit you with our disc, Sheriff."

Off he ran with his bright yellow disc. The spell broken, Renee and Matt stepped even farther apart. Feeling embarrassed, Renee turned back to the water, draining her glass.

"Jeez, Renee, I'm sorry about that," Matt said, filling the silence with his deep voice. "I got off duty but didn't want to head home before midnight. I saw you wander this way, and I guess I followed you out. I was tired of the noise from the party and liked your idea of some peace and quiet. I wasn't thrilled with the idea of you out here alone, either. I certainly didn't follow you out here to kiss you."

"Well, I certainly didn't *want* to be followed," Renee replied, again put off by his comment—she didn't need to be looked after.

"No, no, that didn't come out right," Matt replied, exasperated, running his hands through his hair. "We just seem to keep rubbing each other the wrong way. Kissing is what people do at midnight on New Year's Eve, right? And I enjoyed kissing you. I just don't want you to think I'm following you. Hell, we barely know each other. I guess I wouldn't have been surprised if your first New Year's resolution was to slap me."

Giggling, Renee felt foolish for squabbling with this man yet again. They were both adults and didn't have to apologize to anyone. Unless he wasn't as "unattached" as she was.

"Are you married?" Renee blurted, touching her own lips in dismay.

At that, Matt laughed, his deep chuckles filling the tropical air. "Oh God, no. I'm single. There's no Mrs. Blatso to worry about," he said, turning toward Renee and putting his hands on her upper arms, pulling her against his chest. "I can kiss anyone I want to at midnight, and I enjoyed kissing you."

"You said that already," Renee said slyly.

Suddenly Renee was caught up in another long kiss with Matt.

The party of kids down the beach started breaking up and small groups of them walked in their direction. Renee snapped back to her senses when she heard Robbie's voice among them. She smiled up at Matt in the moonlight as she pulled out of his arms. She didn't know what to say, so she didn't say anything. She walked back toward the thinning party crowd. She didn't want Robbie to find her in the arms of the sheriff. He would have been mortified.

Robbie didn't see her, thankfully. Julie was at a picnic table with a few girls when Renee stepped back onto the blacktop. She saw Renee hustle out of the darkness, and rushed over to meet her halfway across the confetti-strewn parking lot.

"Mom, are you OK? You're flushed and . . . barefoot. Is everything all right?"

"Of course I'm fine! I just went for a little walk on the beach. I heard Robbie coming toward me with a bunch of kids and I was afraid if he saw me, he'd think I was checking up on him, so I wanted to get back here before he could see me on the beach," Renee improvised, pleased with herself for coming up with that little story. *Not a lie, right? Just an omission of the part about kissing a near stranger on the beach at midnight.* But she had no intention of sharing how she kicked off the year.

Julie accepted Renee's explanation at face value and, linking arms with her mom, turned toward their cottage. As she turned, she noticed the sheriff coming off the beach in the exact same spot her mom had a couple minutes earlier. For a split second she wondered if maybe her mom had been out there with the sheriff, but then decided that was ridiculous. What would her mother be doing on the beach with someone she barely knew at midnight on New Year's Eve?

CHAPTER 21

Gift of Guidance

*R*enee welcomed the new day from her plastic recliner on their beach, steaming mug of coffee in hand. Today was special. It was the first day of a new year—and the morning she'd waited for to read her letter from Aunt Celia. Even though she was up late the night before, the birds wouldn't let her sleep in. She didn't mind. She reveled in the early morning quiet.

Setting her cup aside, she pulled out Celia's envelope. She ran her finger across her name, carefully scrawled across the front in her aunt's looping hand. Renee missed Celia terribly. Aunt Celia's presence was always a given in her life. Growing up, all her holidays and special times included Celia. Unfortunately, as an adult, she hadn't spent as much time with her aunt, but Celia was always there if Renee needed her. News of Celia's death had been an utter shock. Despite her age, Celia had seemed timeless.

Unable to wait any longer, Renee broke the seal and pulled out three sheets of monogrammed stationery. The scent of roses lingered on the morning air as she unfolded the crisp pages. The letter was dated September 1, 2015, a few weeks before her aunt's death.

My dearest Renee,

I feel the time is near to say my goodbyes to you. I do not know exactly when the Good Lord will call me home, but I suspect it won't be long now. My body weakens and my vision fades. Leaves will soon turn golden outside my window. It may be their last glorious show I will see, these trees which have sheltered my home most of my life. The wind will again turn sharp and cold, whisking the leaves away for another winter from which I may be absent.

I believe the time has also come for me to do something special with my resources, before I no longer have a say in matters.

Renee ignored a teardrop as it meandered down her cheek.

As you read my final words to you, my dear niece, do not sit with a heavy heart and feel guilt over our time spent apart. You and I are similar creatures. We take the responsibility of providing for others seriously. You were a young woman when you lost your husband; I was a young woman when my father was struck down. I had to quickly learn how to help provide food and care for my younger siblings; you had to focus on building a career to provide for your Julie and Robbie. I have watched you work hard. Please know how proud I am of your strength and dedication.

As my days on this earth slowly wind down to the inevitable close, I have only a few regrets. I share these with you now because you are still young. You have time to consider some slight adjustments to your own path. You have helped guide your children to the brink of young adulthood. When they were younger, they needed you beside them to keep them safe and happy. They are now entering a time in their lives when they no longer need your constant presence, but they will always need you near. Close enough to watch out for them and step back up to their side in times of struggle.

The time also came in my life when I could have stepped back from some of my hard work. My brothers were grown. My savings would have kept my mother comfortable for the remainder of her days. I could have made the effort to share my own life with someone. Instead, it was easy to stay with the routine I knew best. People at work respected me and felt like family. It was easier to stay there. But each evening, my co-workers would go home to a spouse and children of their own. I often worked late because no one was waiting at home for *me. Never being a mother to a child of my own is one of my few regrets. Another is not having a husband at home to greet me at the end of a long day.*

Renee thought back, ashamed, to the times she felt irritated by the need to rush out of work at 5:00 to get dinner on the table or to attend a school function. Celia's words conjured up a picture of her dear aunt sitting alone in an office, surrounded by quiet and dark, losing herself in bookwork to delay going home to an empty house. *I never guessed Celia was lonely,* she thought, turning back to her aunt's letter. She read on, chuckling at her aunt's not-so-subtle hints to build quality relationships with other adults and not rely on her own kids too much. *She's right,* Renee conceded, *I am guilty of that!* She sobered as she read Celia's next passage—encouraging her niece to strive to find meaningful work, something her aunt felt she herself had never accomplished. Renee lifted her eyes from the page to gaze at the undulating ocean waves. *Does everyone struggle to find fulfillment in their work?* Since work was such a large part of Celia's life, Renee always assumed she'd thrived there. It couldn't have been easy for her, battling the discrimination she faced.

Renee read on:

Please do not misunderstand me. I know I have lived a blessed life. I have always felt the strong bonds of family with all of you. I loved being a part of all the important and mundane moments of your lives. My work provided me with the means to help many people throughout my life as well. Material possessions are meaningless if they cannot be used to lighten the burdens other people carry and to make the world a little brighter place.

Do you remember traveling to the lake and vacationing at Whispering Pines? We used to stay in the cabins for two weeks each summer, before all of you kids got too busy as teenagers.

Celia's abrupt change of subject gave Renee pause. Some of her favorite childhood memories included Whispering Pines.

Years ago, when I was in my forties, a business acquaintance was unable to pay a debt he owed me. Eventually, he signed over the deed for Whispering Pines to me to settle his debt. It wasn't worth much back then. There were a handful of cabins and one home, but our family spent many glorious vacations there.

Up until early last spring, an elderly couple, Ed and Mary, maintained the property for me and rented the cabins out to vacationers. It was a beneficial relationship for both of us. Ed and Mary were wonderful people, but unfortunately Ed died last May, and Mary couldn't work the Pines alone. She moved out East to live with her daughter. I had a service go in and close up the buildings. They performed some ground maintenance and minimal upkeep over this past summer, but it sits vacant now.

I have put much thought into whether or not I should keep Whispering Pines in the family or sell it. The property has always held a special place in my heart, even though I have spent little time there during the last few decades. I always hoped to do something more with it. My days spent there were some of my most peaceful.

After much deliberation, I have decided to pass the deed for Whispering Pines to you.

Renee stared at the page. She reread those words maybe a dozen times, shocked. "Um . . . *what?*" she said aloud.

There is no mortgage on the property; however, upkeep is still expensive. So to avoid placing a financial burden on you, I have established an escrow fund to cover taxes and insurance on the property for at least the next twenty years. If you sell the property before the fund is depleted, any remaining funds are to be donated to various charitable organizations. I also established a smaller fund to cover ongoing property maintenance for your first few years of ownership. My hope is you will use the property to generate income that more than covers future ongoing expenses.

If you choose to accept my gift to you—or even if you choose not to—I have but one request. Please do not sell the property for at least five years. Give yourself time to come to love it as I did and find a way to make it work for you. I have left further instructions with my lawyer; he will work with you on the transition.

Always remember to work hardest not on someone else's dreams, but on your own.

If this single statement doesn't yet resonate in your heart when you read it, you aren't yet ready to appreciate the meaning behind the words. I pray in time you will come to understand their wisdom.

Stay strong, my dearest Renee. Use your God-given talents to make this world a brighter place and enjoy each and every day.

All my love,
Celia

Renee let her hands, still clutching the pages of her aunt's final message to her, fall to her lap as she again stared across the pale gray ocean before her. Her mind's eye was seeing a different body of water: an old wooden dock jutted into crystal clear lake water as her ten-year-old self splashed around with Jess and Val, trying to catch minnows with a bug net. Her mom and Aunt Celia sat in green-and-white webbed lawn chairs on a brown sliver of sand, sipping cans of Tab. *I spent hours in that lake, floating around on air mattresses and jumping on huge tractor-tire inner tubes,* Renee reflected as she unconsciously touched the scar on her upper thigh; she'd gashed it on a metal valve stem sticking out of one of those tubes.

She hadn't thought about their summer weeks at the lake in a long time. She had no idea Celia still owned the property. *Why did we get too busy and stop going? Summer jobs? Ball games?*

It was all too overwhelming. Renee couldn't imagine being the owner of a lake resort in Minnesota. As a single mother, it was a struggle to keep up her own house in Minneapolis. *I can hammer a nail and mow a lawn, but I'm not handy enough to keep a lake property going!* The resort was hours from her home. It was an extremely generous gift, but Renee wasn't sure why Celia gave it to her and not someone else in their family.

God . . . this may be the first winter I'm actually glad *for the long months between now and spring. It gives me time to try to figure out what the hell I'm going to do now!*

CHAPTER 22

Gift of a Stroll

*J*ulie, Robbie, and Renee joined a tour group with twenty-five others on New Year's Day. Their guide was a native, and transportation consisted of an open-air bus and various boats. They took tons of pictures—"A whole 'nother photo album's worth," joked Robbie—using up all the film in their underwater cameras. Robbie would have plenty of photos to fill more pages in his new album. Lunch on a large sailboat consisted of fresh fish and exotic fruit.

By the time the shuttle dropped them back at their resort, they were in desperate need of cool showers to wash away the salt, sweat, and sand. After cleaning up, all three dozed in the cool cabin—until their grumbling stomachs woke them. Refreshed, they walked to a small diner down the road, since they'd slept through dinner served poolside.

They all ordered the lobster roll special, served in red-and-white checkered containers, along with glasses of pulpy lemonade. Not wanting to spend the glorious evening indoors, they carried their meals out to an empty picnic table at the end of the parking lot, overlooking the beach.

Robbie quickly devoured his food and finished off Renee's, then jumped up to join a volleyball game on the sand. Julie squeezed her mom's hand. "Thanks for the wonderful day, Mom," she said, and sauntered down to the water's edge.

Renee sat quietly, her mind wandering back to Celia's letter and the lake of her childhood. She could almost taste a crunchy, gooey s'more and feel the hot campfire on her face, mosquitoes buzzing in the dark outside the ring of light cast by flames. Big logs stripped of their bark, worn smooth by years of use, provided crowded seating for her family.

Grownups sat in webbed chairs and told stories. Younger kids fell asleep in laps. Bigger kids usually got tired of talking and started a game of "ditch." Fun but dangerous, the game often led to scratches and bumps. One bad spill resulted in a trip to the small emergency room ten miles up the road.

A brief touch on the small of her back brought Renee's attention back to the beach. The bench she sat on tipped up on the concrete as Matt settled next to her. Gone was his uniform, in its place a blue tank top, shorts, and boat shoes. Renee couldn't help but notice how the tank stretched taut over his chest. Based on the size of his arms, he did more than run on the beach to work out. If he was a beer drinker, he didn't have the belly to prove it. He smiled his slow smile and relaxed next to her, staring out at the water too. She liked that he didn't seem to feel the need to make idle conversation. She turned her attention back to the beach, making a conscious effort to stop glancing at him.

Renee was happy to see Julie was again chatting with the two girls she spent time with the night before. Robbie was still playing volleyball. Neither of them paid any attention to Renee. She shifted slightly closer to Matt.

"Off duty tonight?" Renee asked, grinning at the handsome man seated next to her.

"Yeah, just got off at seven. We all have to put in long days and nights around the holidays. Lots of tourists around. Short staffed, too. I have three deputies plus myself, so none of us get much time off. I hated to go back to my house and open a can of soup for dinner, so I decided to come down here for lobster rolls. Can't beat 'em," Matt declared, motioning to his tray of food. He winked at her. "Imagine my surprise when I saw a lovely lady sitting at a picnic table all alone, looking like she needed some company."

Renee laughed. "As a matter of fact, I *do* welcome the company of someone over twenty-one and not related to me. Don't get me wrong, I love spending time with the kids, but none of us are used to this much togetherness. I suspect they're ready for some space, too."

As Matt ate his lobster rolls, Renee asked him about life in Fiji, and what had brought him to live in such a place.

"I've been on the islands for three years, but I was born and raised in North Carolina. I studied criminal justice in college, considered becoming a lawyer, but hated the idea of being stuck inside all the time. My fiancée, on the other hand, wanted the financial security of being a partner in a big law firm. She wasn't too happy with me when I joined the police force. She eventually become a lawyer herself. We started dating in high school, and it seemed like the logical next step to get married when we graduated from college. I was a rookie on the force, worked lots of nights and weekends, and she was studying for the bar. We didn't see each other much. Drifted apart. Then she met someone at the office and decided she hated the uncertainty that came with being the wife of a cop. Turns out she preferred a quiet, boring life married to a tax attorney."

Matt took another bite and chewed a bit before continuing, "After that, I put all my focus and energy into work. By thirty, I was a detective in Charlotte. Those were tough years. I still have some sleepless nights, remembering the shit I saw working that job. It finally got to be too much and I quit."

"And you ended up in Fiji," Renee concluded.

"Well, not directly. I tried my hand at carpentry work with a buddy from college. He owned a small construction firm. We worked hard all day and drank beer and played pool at night. The guy's name was Jack. It was a fun year, but just a waste. Then Jack met Gayle, and the fun times were over for him. Three months dating her and she had him heading to the altar."

Renee cut in. "Jeez, Matt, when is this story going to get to Fiji?"

Matt laughed. "An old-fashioned church wedding wasn't their style. They decided to do a beach wedding . . . in *Fiji*. A group of fifteen of us came down here. I was supposed to be Jack's best man."

" 'Supposed to'?"

He nodded. "The bride and her sister were set to arrive the day after we got in. Guess she got cold feet because she never showed. At first, Jack was royally pissed off, then he was distraught, then he decided to drown his sorrows in alcohol throughout the whole week. He acted like a total ass. Couldn't stand to be around the guy. By the morning we were scheduled to fly home, I couldn't stomach the thought of going back to the construction gig with Jack. So I turned off my alarm, rolled over, and missed my plane ride home. That was three years ago, and I've only been back to the States a couple of times since to visit family."

He suddenly flashed his quick little grin at her, eyes crinkling in the corners. "How did you do that?"

"Do what?"

"I don't normally share my life story—even with ladies as pretty as you."

He tried to sound casual, but Renee suspected it bothered him some, having told her so much without much prodding on her part. She reached across the table, squeezed his hand lightly, then wrapped her fingers back around her sweating glass of lemonade.

"Your turn, Renee," he said. "Now that I spilled my sad tale to you, tell me: what brings you all the way to Fiji for New Year's with two great kids but no man?"

After glancing around and seeing her kids were still busy with their new friends, Renee took a sip of her lemonade and told Matt much of her own story. She shared how she wound up working for a large firm after college and married Jim. She told him briefly of Jim's illness and early death, how she'd found herself a widow at thirty-five. Feeling uncomfortable, exposed somehow, she skipped ahead to more recent events. But she still felt so comfortable with Matt, she told him about her job loss—and the bitterness it brought. She also shared how grateful she was to have this time with the kids and time to figure out what she wanted to do next. She even shared the contents of the letter from Aunt Celia, despite not having shared the news with her own kids yet.

Matt whistled. "That's a lot to deal with, Renee. Do you . . . want to go for a walk?" He seemed to want to lighten the mood after such heavy conversation.

"Sure," Renee replied. "Just let me tell Julie and Robbie." She gathered their garbage and tossed it in the trash on the way over to the kids. Robbie gave her a quick wave and grin when she approached him discreetly. He was listening to another boy tell stories around a bonfire someone had built when their game wound down. He promised Renee to be back at the cabin by eleven o'clock. Julie also committed to being home by the same time. She had a later curfew at home, but Renee wasn't comfortable letting her stay out any later in a foreign country.

Looks like I just gained myself a couple hours, she thought while she meandered back to the table, feeling shy yet oddly thrilled about the prospect of time alone with Matt.

But his calm smile and unhurried attitude put her at ease. They walked back out to the small parking lot in front of the diner and headed in the opposite direction from their resort. There was little traffic on the blacktop road that skirted along the beach. A sand-strewn path ran alongside the road, allowing them to stay out of the way of the occasional vehicle that drove by.

"That's old man Driso's bait shop on the corner," Matt pointed out as they strolled. "Ornery ole cuss, but ya need anything for fishing, he's the man. One of our dispatchers, Isabel, lives in that pink little number with her grandmother. The girl's sleeping with our newest deputy . . . they think no one knows but the whole precinct is on to 'em. Oh, and if you want to go home with some amazing shells, best place to find them is on the little beach down at the end of this path—one of our best-kept secrets." He continued to add local flavor to their walk with his commentary, constantly making her laugh. Renee was thoroughly enjoying herself and the company.

Eventually Matt turned toward a small cottage covered with bleached cedar shakes, sporting bright blue trim. A patch of scruffy sea-grass was neatly trimmed in front. Empty window boxes flanked each side of the white door. The place looked neat, but lonely.

Matt reached out and took Renee's hand, gently pulling her down the white shell path toward the cottage. "This is my place," he explained, "and Hank isn't going to be able to wait much longer to be let out."

"Hank?" Renee asked.

A sudden flurry of high-pitched yipping came through the open windows. Matt released her hand, reached in his pocket, and pulled out a key, unlocking the front door. "Please—come on in. This will just take a minute and we can keep walking."

A small gray terrier—the same color as the house, Renee observed with a smile—jumped all over their feet and shins, his little butt wagging his tail so hard he could barely stay upright. Hustling the dog to another door at the back of the kitchen, Matt got him outside quickly to avoid an accident. Renee took the opportunity to glance around the small kitchen and sitting room. Everything was neat and tidy, though bland. The only color in the kitchen came from kid's art posted on the white fridge.

I wonder if he has children he neglected to mention . . . ?

Before she could investigate further, Matt shouted for Renee to come out back. She exited the rear of the kitchen to a backyard. A small brick patio held wooden lawn chairs and a small table. The far edge of the patio was rimmed with sand and tufts of sea-grass stretching back a hundred feet, followed by a ten-foot drop to a wide expanse of yet more sand, and, finally, the ocean. A narrow path cut through large black stones lining the drop off, allowing access to the beach.

Hank ran in circles through the grass and sand. After he completed his business, he sniffed toward the path, but Matt called him back. Back he came, carrying a stick as long as he was, wanting Matt to play. "Not now, Hank, we can play later," Matt told the pup. Hank promptly rolled over at his feet, so Matt, laughing, scratched his exposed belly. Matt clipped a long leash to his collar. "Don't trust Hank to stay close," he said to Renee, chuckling.

Renee stood on the patio, enjoying the expansive ocean view. Matt wandered back to her side.

"There's a small pub down the road, another ten minutes or so. Would you like to walk down there for a glass of wine before we head back to your cottage? Or I might have a bottle of white in the fridge—Christmas gift from the local Chamber of Commerce."

It was an easy decision for Renee. She had no interest in sitting in a dark, noisy bar when instead they could sit out in the fresh air and enjoy this view. "Definitely stay here for a bit, if you don't mind."

"Sounds good," Matt said. "Why don't you sit and keep an eye on Hank while I go get us a couple glasses of wine?"

He headed back into the house. The wooden screen door, most of its white paint peeled off, knocked shut behind him. Renee was left alone with the dog, now sitting on his small haunches, staring at her with the stick at his feet. He lay down in the sand, his nose pushing the stick in her direction, eyes begging her to play.

Matt was only gone a few minutes. He came back with two unmatched wine glasses and an open bottle in the crook of his arm. He claimed the chair next to Renee. Filling her glass, he passed it to her, then filled his own. Everything about the evening felt right. It had been a long time since Renee spent a quiet evening with a man, undistracted by kids or household duties. Their conversation picked back up on lighter topics. Matt told her about his first months on the island, landing his job as sheriff, finding this property. While there was little major crime he had to deal with, there was the usual stuff.

"We're also starting to see more drug trafficking, unfortunately," he said.

As they talked, the sun slowly sank into the water, first turning the ocean a dark violet color and then an inky black. A bright white moon rose. Wine gone and stiff from sitting, Matt put the dog back in the house and together they took the sand path down to the water's edge. For the second time in two days, Renee found herself on a dark beach with Matt. He no longer felt like a stranger.

This time when he put his hands on her shoulders and turned her into his embrace, she stepped into him, her arms stretching up to circle his neck. He lowered his face to hers. Tonight's kiss was more urgent. While last night was a chance encounter, tonight was not. Renee now realized she had been attracted to this man ever since she first saw him in the dusty parking lot on their first day. Sure, she had been annoyed and slightly offended, but she couldn't deny her natural attraction to him.

Matt deepened their kiss and pulled her in tighter. Renee groaned softly. Her hands found his thick hair; his skimmed up under her loose white blouse and cupped her breasts, the filmy lace of her bra offering little protection from his warm palms. A cool breeze touched her now-bare back and she went up on the tip of her toes to better fit into him. When this still wasn't enough, together they sank into the soft sand at their feet. Matt pulled Renee on top of him with a laugh in an effort to keep her off the damp sand.

Lightheartedness was quickly replaced by a sense of urgency. Matt yanked his shirt off and Renee's blouse and bra followed, leaving them skin-to-skin from the waist up.

It felt like they were the only two on earth.

Maybe it was the secluded beach on a moonlit night; maybe it was the fact she would only have a short time with this man before she had to go back to her real life. Whatever it was, all of Renee's inhibitions fell away. Caught up in the moment, instead of stopping his hand, she helped Matt when he fumbled with the snap on her shorts. She welcomed the cool sand on her back when he finally had to roll her off him to rid them of the rest of their clothing. Renee could feel Matt's desire, could sense it in his movements.

A shrill ringing stopped them both. Disoriented, Renee had no idea what she was hearing. Swearing in frustration, Matt rose to his knees and then to his feet, pulling Renee with him. He located her blouse and handed it to her before grabbing his shorts up out of the sand and yanking the cell phone out of his pocket.

"Blatso here," Matt grumbled into the phone. "This better be good." As he listened, he still held Renee close, not seeming to want to let her go. Renee couldn't make out what the caller was saying, but she felt Matt stiffen against her and he cussed softly. "Give me thirty minutes," he said to the person on the other end of the phone and hung up. His hand went behind Renee's neck and he pulled her in for a quick, deep kiss, then stepped back and pulled on his shorts.

"I am so sorry, Renee, but we have a report of a missing teenage girl. She's a local, and her folks haven't seen her since she left for work this morning. Apparently she didn't show up at work. They're out of their minds with worry. I need to go in right away. I'm so sorry," Matt repeated, tracing his hand lightly down her cheek.

Matt's words immediately wiped the fog of desire from her brain. Buttoning her blouse and brushing the sand from her clothes, she waved off his apology. "You have to go in right away. I'll find my way back to our resort."

"Absolutely not," Matt said. "I'll throw on my uniform and give you a ride back in my cruiser. I'm not leaving you to walk back alone."

He led her back up the moonlit path to his house. She waited in his small kitchen while he quickly showered off and dressed in his uniform. He gave her a quick kiss before he led her by the hand out to the small garage beside the house. Still reluctant to end their evening but knowing he didn't have a choice, he stole one last quick kiss as he sat her in the front seat of his police car.

He had her back to her resort in record time. It was only 10:30, so she didn't know if the kids would be back yet, nor did she know if she wanted them to see her with Matt. But Matt insisted on walking her up to her door and seeing her safely inside. She wondered if maybe there was something more going on with the missing girl that he wasn't sharing.

He's acting like it isn't safe to be out alone.

Renee worried for her own kids' safety. She hurried to their cabin to see if they were back yet. Inside she found both Julie and Robbie, along with Julie's two new friends and one of the boys Robbie had been playing volleyball with earlier. They were playing cards at the kitchen table.

Sagging with relief, Renee returned to the front door and thanked Matt for the nice evening. After he left, she visited with the kids, then headed to bed, giving them the chance to entertain their new friends without her hanging around.

In the dark of night, her thoughts returned to that moment on the sand, naked beside a strange man who was no longer a stranger, and she wondered if she'd have the chance with him again. And if she wanted to if she did.

CHAPTER 23

Gift of Incentives

*R*enee didn't get that chance.

The remaining days of their vacation were a flurry of activity. They tried to squeeze in as much fun as possible. Matt phoned the cabin and apologized to Renee for being tied up with the case of the missing teenage girl, but he just couldn't get away. Renee understood, but she was disappointed she wouldn't see him again.

For their last evening, Renee and the kids decided to go out for dinner to a nice restaurant. Tonight was the night Robbie and Julie had decided to open their letters from Aunt Celia. Renee also planned to tell them about her inheritance. The evening would be a celebration. Before they went out, they packed their bags; they would leave early in the morning.

When they arrived at the restaurant, they were ushered to a table on the open patio overlooking a small inlet below. The sun was low on the horizon; soft lighting and candles illuminated the tables. Renee was glad the kids had heeded her request to dress up. They were two of the youngest in the dining area and would have looked out of place in shorts and flip flops. Robbie flirted too much with the cute waitress, but Renee was still proud of her kids.

Glancing around at the tables, Renee wished for a moment she and Matt could have come here during her stay. But she wouldn't have missed this evening with Julie and Robbie for anything and turned her full attention back to them. They all laughed when Julie gagged down her squid appetizer and Robbie made an awful face, eyes watering, when he sampled the ginger pickled fish. Each tried a different kind of seafood for their main entree. They shared a decadent chocolate dessert.

"I see you liked the cake I recommended," their tall, raven-haired waitress teased Robbie as she refilled his water glass.

"Since you recommended it, I knew it would be tasty before I even took a bite," Robbie quipped back, causing Julie to gag again.

When they were too full to eat anything more and wait staff had cleared the table, Renee pulled their envelopes out of her purse and handed one to each of her children. Both opened them simultaneously and silently read their letters. After each finished and set their letters down on the blue table cloth, they looked first at each other, then at Renee, then back at each other again as grins slowly spread across their faces.

"Well," Renee finally burst out, "don't keep me in suspense any longer—what did your letters say?"

"*Jeez*, Mom, you are not gonna believe this," Robbie exclaimed, waving his letter at her. "Aunt C left me a boatload of cash! It says here that just as soon as I graduate with at least a four-year college degree, I'll receive *fifty–thousand–freaking–dollars!* I had no idea Aunt C was so flippin' rich!"

Robbie's voice got a bit loud for the other customers and Renee had to shush him. She was too shocked to say anything. Robbie was right . . . that was a boatload of money.

"Mine basically says the same," Julie said, still grinning from ear to ear but managing to stay a bit calmer. "Aunt C left me fifty thousand dollars, too, and I get it after graduating. She went on to encourage me to put lots of thought into what I want to do with the money. When we get back to the cottage, I want to take more time to read everything she wrote to me. She obviously put a lot of thought into the letter, and I need a quiet place to spend more time going through it."

"Yeah, I do too," Robbie spoke up, still flustered by his gift.

"Mom, did you read your letter yet?" Julie asked. "You haven't said a word about it."

"As a matter of fact, I did. I read it early on New Year's Day."

"What?" exclaimed Robbie. "Before us?"

"When we were all together at Christmas," Renee explained, "Ethan, Jess, Val, and I all agreed to open our letters at the same time. Your Great

Aunt C was a special lady. You've heard the stories. She earned a good living, and she did an even better job investing what she made. Celia was generous throughout her lifetime. She used to tell us she was blessed and felt it was her duty to pass those blessings on to others."

"So what'd she give you?" Robbie asked.

"I haven't mentioned what was in my letter yet to the two of you because I'm still trying to figure out how I feel about it. Just like yours, it was a . . . *generous* gift. I'm just not sure what to do with it."

"Mom, quit with the suspense already! How much did you get?" Robbie blurted, getting another *"Shhhh!"* out of both his mom and sister this time.

"OK, OK, give me a second," Renee admonished Robbie, settling him down with a look he knew well. "Many years ago, Aunt Celia acquired a small resort on a lake in central Minnesota. We used to go there as kids, but I haven't been back since high school. I honestly didn't even know Celia still owned it. My gift from Aunt Celia is that same resort."

Both kids were stunned into silence for the first time that evening. They had expected her to say she received money, too—maybe more, since she was a generation closer to Celia. To find out their mother had inherited lake property back in Minnesota was a complete surprise.

Renee reached inside her purse and drew out a half-dozen photographs Celia had included with her letter. Four were starting to fade; two were more recent. Julie recognized a much younger Renee in one of the shots, wearing a bikini and standing next to her sisters on a wooden dock. The other faded pictures included more of their relatives in their younger years. The newer photographs must have been recent shots of the resort. One shot was of three small cabins scattered around a central area. All were sided in dark wood with bright red trim around doors and windows. A larger building in another shot looked like a lodge. There were cars parked in front. It reminded Renee a little bit of the building in the front of their resort here in Fiji.

Julie passed the pictures over to Robbie and sat back. Robbie groaned his disapproval at the sight of his mother in a bikini. He spent more time studying the two newer pictures before passing them back to Renee.

"Now do you understand why I hadn't said anything to you yet?" Renee asked. "I'm not sure what I'm going to do with a resort two hundred miles from home. How could I even think about keeping a place like that up? Why in heaven's name would Celia leave something like that to me and not to Ethan? At least he might be able to handle the maintenance of the old place." It was a relief verbalizing some of the thoughts that had been keeping her up at night since she read the letter. Her brother was a carpenter by trade, and a talented one. What was she? *Unemployed,* she thought bitterly.

"Do you know what she left to Ethan or your sisters?" Julie asked.

"No, I didn't want to call them from here. Too expensive. I'll call all of them when we get home."

"Well . . ." Julie thought aloud. "As we all know, Aunt C was a smart woman. I suspect she had good reason for doing what she did. We just need to give it some time to figure out what those reasons might be."

At those wise words, they decided to call it a night and head back to their cottage. It would be an early morning.

CHAPTER 24

Gift of Home

Their exit from paradise went smoothly yet regretfully so, and they soon found themselves on a large jet headed home. The three of them were again scattered around the plane. This time, instead of the charitable Susan, Renee was seated next to an elderly man with little to say. Renee was fine with that. She needed time to think.

The past three weeks had been crazy. She had become unemployed, reconnected with family, had learned her daughter was being harassed by a boy from college, discovered her dead husband had family she hadn't known about, took her two kids on a spur-of-the-moment dream vacation . . . even found herself almost making love with a sexy sheriff on a beach. Now she was going home to reality and had to figure out how she was going to make a living, what in heaven's name she was going to do with a resort she now owned in Minnesota lake country, and make sure her daughter was safe as she headed back to college.

More tired than she realized, she dozed off after lunch. She was back on the moonlit beach in Matt's arms, and this time they weren't interrupted. Her mind played out the fantasies her body had not gotten to experience because of an ill-fated phone call. She gradually felt the dream slip away as the plane started its descent. Once fully awake, she realized they were almost back to Minneapolis. It was hot in the cabin. She fanned herself using a pamphlet from the seat pocket in front of her. She could have sworn the old man smirked at her, and Renee wondered, mortified, if she had unconsciously made any sounds or talked in her sleep.

Renee busied herself gathering her belongings and then watched out the window across the aisle. A week in the tropics left her unprepared for the completely white landscape below, crisscrossed by black ribbons of roads, rivers, and lakes. She pulled her watch out of her purse to check the time. (When they got to Fiji, she had tossed it in her bag, refusing to clock-watch on vacation.) Now it was turning to dusk in Minneapolis.

They landed, gathered their luggage from baggage claim, and hauled everything out to her Toyota. The frigid air felt brittle when they stepped out of the terminal. Renee crossed her fingers, hoping the engine would start after sitting so long in such weather. After a slight hesitation, the SUV turned over. Renee maneuvered out of the ramp. Thankfully roads were dry, despite high snow drifts lining the highway. They opted for a quick stop at a drive-thru on the way home to give them time to unpack versus figuring out what to cook.

"The fridge is empty, anyhow," Robbie reminded them, somewhat glumly.

As they turned onto their street, they were met with one last blessing for the day: one of their neighbors had blown the snow off their driveway, only a fine coating of snow remaining. Together they wrestled everything inside and kicked up the furnace to take the chill off. It was too quiet in the house. Normally Molly met them at the door, but their cocker spaniel had stayed at Renee's parents' house while they were gone.

After depositing suitcases in bedrooms, each of them collapsed onto a couch or recliner in front of the television, too exhausted from jet lag and time changes to do anything more. All the fun had finally caught up with them. Thankfully it was Saturday night, and they were free of any obligations.

It took until later Sunday afternoon for Renee to feel like she could function again. She made a trip to the grocery store, threw dinner together, and started laundry. Robbie had to head back to school in the morning, and Julie would leave Monday afternoon to get back to college for a Wednesday start.

Julia is heading back to college, Renee thought, *and back to Lincoln.*

CHAPTER 25

Gift of the Senses

Where do I start? Renee despaired.

Julie was back at college, Robbie in his regular routine of school, basketball, and buddies. Both kids had thanked Renee again and again for the fun of the past three weeks, but now they were back to their own lives, and it was time to figure out what her life was going to look like. No more procrastinating. But the thought of it all was daunting.

Once Robbie left for the day, Renee put on the coffee and again pulled out her journals and new books from her carry-on bag. First she read through her entries from the day she was laid off and the next few days that followed, before their three-week holiday adventure had taken over. Her frustrations and fear from those days jumped off the pages at her. As she worked to figure out her next steps, she knew it would be important to keep those strong feelings in mind. Many had been bubbling under the surface of her conscience for some time, but it had been easy to ignore them.

After thumbing through her entries, Renee read a few more chapters from the books. The authors offered up ideas she had not even considered. Here she was, forty-five years old, and she was so reliant on her regular paycheck from her corporate job it terrified her. She had fallen deep into the trap of the eight-to-five gig, taking only a few weeks of vacation each year. Weeks, months, and years had clicked by on autopilot.

She set her book aside when the doorbell rang. *Who in the world could that be?* Renee wondered as she pushed out of her comfy recliner and glanced through the front window. Out at the curb stood a delivery van boasting a picture of large, vibrant flowers painted across its side. A young woman stood at her door, holding a large bouquet carefully wrapped against the cold.

Renee quickly opened the door. "Please, please, come in," she said.

The woman gladly stepped into the warmth of the foyer after stomping her boots on the mat outside so she wouldn't track in snow. "Oh, thank you, it's freezing out there," she said. "I have a delivery for . . ." Balancing the bouquet in one hand, she read a name from the clipboard she held in the other. "Renee Clements."

Who could this be from? Renee thought, surprised. She'd expected them to maybe be a gift from Lincoln, arrived too late for Julie's departure back to college.

"Thank you," Renee said, and pushed a five-dollar bill she happened to have stashed in her pocket into the woman's hand, taking the flowers.

The woman smiled appreciatively. "Happy New Year's!" she said, and returned swiftly to her delivery van.

Renee stared at the flowers as she set them on the dining room table. It had been years since anyone had sent her flowers. As she pulled layers of first plastic and then tissue from the bundle, the warm scent of tropical blooms rushed out and perfumed the air around her. She tossed the wrapping to the side and pulled out a card tucked into the bright petals.

Dear Renee,

Thank you for locking your keys in your car and stepping in front of me on the beach. I am sorry we didn't get much time together. Sending a bit of the tropics to you in snowy MN, hoping to add some color to your winter day. Hope you don't mind—I sweet-talked Lulu into giving me your home address, me being the sheriff and all. If you would like to keep in touch, my email address is on the back.

Thinking of you,
Matt

Delighted by the flowers and note, Renee beamed at the fragrant bouquet before her. The idea of reaching out to Matt via email more than intrigued her, so she fired up her laptop. Phone calls with him would be challenging, given the time difference and cost. But emailing could be a fun way to keep in touch.

Renee refilled her coffee and sat down to compose her message back to Matt. She took her time. She thanked him for the flowers and attached a photo to the email so he could see them, too. Because she had told him all about her current situation, she shared a bit of her frustrations about not knowing where to start. But she was careful not to whine. No one likes to listen to that for long. Once she had a couple paragraphs written, she decided that was enough and sent off the note, along with a suggestion that maybe they try to touch base about once a week. She knew how busy he was and didn't want him to think she expected an immediate response when she emailed.

Closing the lid to her laptop, Renee sat back with a smile, inhaling the much fresher air of her kitchen. She decided to make a few phone calls and start the ball rolling. She had lots to do.

Suddenly I'm motivated, she realized. She looked at the flowers again, smiling.

"Thanks, Matt," she said aloud.

CHAPTER 26

Gift of a New Lens

"*I*'m done," Renee told herself, "letting life just happen to me." She'd made some loose plans before heading to her parents for the holidays, hadn't she? Well, she decided, now was the time to start putting more structure to those plans.

Molly was home now—George brought her home on Saturday—and was currently curled at Renee's feet while a soft snow fell outside. Julie had called the night before and was back in the swing of classes and social life at the university. Renee was relieved to hear that Lincoln didn't come back for second semester. In fact, Julie hadn't heard a word from him since she turned her phone off and went to Fiji. She sounded happy and busy. *I can cross that off my worry list,* Renee decided. Robbie was playing junior varsity basketball, and it was taking up all his after-school time. Renee was taking him to a tournament on Friday.

So now it was time for Renee to start making her own plans. She was still intrigued by the structure written goals could provide. She'd never tried writing them down in the past, but all the self-help gurus insisted it was the way to go. Before Christmas, she had sketched out a brief framework of areas she knew needed more attention in her life.

What did she want her life to look like years into the future? Should she try to sketch out a rough plan for ten or twenty years out? Her husband had been gone a little over ten years; it felt like a lifetime. She was five years away from turning fifty—*God, what a scary thought*—and that seemed like a more reasonable timeframe to use to set her long-term goals, still keeping in mind her hopes and desires for an even longer view. She used to think fifty was ancient. Now it wasn't too far off. *Celia lived well into her nineties,* she reminded herself. She needed to stop thinking she was getting old. She was just entering another phase in her life. What did she want to accomplish between now and then to make the second half of her life as rewarding as possible?

Focusing on the four major areas she had already identified, Renee designated one page for each area in the front of her journal. She labeled the pages *Financial/Career, Relationships, Health,* and *Fun.* Up until last month, she thought if she was careful about her finances, the rest would fall into place. Now she knew better. She spent the next two hours rounding out her goals on paper.

She knew she wanted to establish more than one stream of income going forward-no more reliance on one job. She would also find ways to reduce her debt and build up her safety net.

She would pay more attention to both her relationships and her health. Spending time with Matt reminded her how much fun it was to have a man in her life—even if it had only been for a few days. Her short time with Susan also made her realize she missed the company of girlfriends. It was sad she hadn't felt compelled to call anyone in those days immediately after her layoff. She needed to stop taking her own health for granted. She'd joined a gym when she turned forty, but rarely went. There had been a six-month period when she joined a Zumba class. She loved the dancing and made new friends at sessions, but she let life interfere and slowly stopped going. And that had been . . .

"Two years ago?" she said. "Holy shit, Renee!"

She had only been to the gym a handful of times in the past year, even though she paid for it every month. *What a waste!* She needed to stop being so complacent.

A primary goal would need to be creating a lifestyle with lower stress levels. Less stress would probably mean fewer migraines, too. *Now, that's a plus.*

She contemplated her goal of more fun. Their trip to Fiji had been a great event to kick off this commitment, so obviously more travel would be near the top of the list. She also wanted to get more comfortable with her personal appearance. She didn't think she was being shallow to acknowledge this fact. She was tired of feeling haggard when looking in a mirror. Exercising and eating better would help, but how about cute hair, polished nails, less wrinkles? *And more massages,* she added wryly. How about flattering clothes? Sexy lingerie? A thought occurred to her: *What lingerie would Matt like?*

Molly stirred at her feet, stood, and stretched. *Time to take a break.* Letting Molly out, she popped a chicken breast and sweet potato into the microwave for a quick dinner. Robbie wouldn't be home until late from practice. She popped a cork on a bottle of white wine and poured herself a glass to celebrate taking the time to clarify her goals. She filled Molly's dish with kibble and let the dog back in. Taking her food and wine out to the dining room table, she grinned at her bouquet of flowers. They were already beginning to wilt, but still offered color and a faint scent of the tropics. *I can't toss them yet.*

As she ate her dinner, she again pulled up the reply email Matt sent the night before. She hadn't been sure he would reply, even though it had been his idea to keep in touch.

Dear Renee,

It was great to hear back from you. Work is busy. We still don't know what happened to the girl that went missing when you were here. We don't have much for clues. It's as if she disappeared into thin air.

Hank is tired of me working so much. Yesterday I came home to a mess. He chewed and scratched his way through the cupboard under the sink, then flung garbage all over the kitchen floor. Guess that adds one more item to my fix-it list.

Talked to my little sister Laura, my niece Olivia, and my nephew Aiden earlier today. God I miss them. Laura has an ass of a husband and is going through a nasty divorce. We talk about once a week, but I wish there was more I could do. She spends lots of time helping Dad, too. Our mom died ten years ago and Dad has some dementia, plus he doesn't take care of his diabetes. Growing up, we always had cows and chickens on the farm. Now Dad is down to just his dog Henry and

Bessie, his cow. She wandered off on Sunday. Dad must have left the gate open again. Laura and the kids drove around for an hour before they found Bessie.

Sure wish it was easier to travel back home.

Hey, how is the job search going? Any good prospects? Hope you land something soon. I know you were worried about getting back to work. Send me updates.

Matt

Renee remembered the bright, childish artwork on Matt's fridge and suspected the kids he mentioned were the little Picassos. She would hate to be so far from her own family.

She planned to reply to Matt soon, but wanted to finish laying out her goals. Setting her dirty dishes in the sink and refilling her wine glass, she got comfortable in her favorite chair and focused.

Chapter 27

Gift of a Mess

*R*enee put on her walking shoes, jumped in the car, and headed for the mall.

Time to get my butt moving. I'll just walk for an hour and then head home. Way too cold to walk outside . . . I really miss Fiji.

She kept only her keys and her driver's license in her pocket—no real shopping today. *Nothing wrong with window shopping . . . and people watching,* she thought as she walked around the mall.

The hour passed quickly and she headed out to her vehicle, reinvigorated and ready to start working on her resume. But the phone rang.

"Mom, can you come pick me up? I feel like crap. Got a killer headache, puked after gym."

Renee couldn't remember the last time Robbie called because he was so sick that he needed to be picked up at school. On the way, she made a quick stop to pick up a digital thermometer and over-the-counter medicine.

Once home, she got Robbie settled on the couch in front of the TV. "Here, try to relax, sweetie. Use this if you get sick again." She thrust their popcorn bowl into his hands. "I'm gonna go clean up that room of yours so you get some sleep tonight. Call if you need anything. I'll bring you some 7 Up and crackers in a bit if you don't throw up anymore."

She stripped his bed, picked up all the dirty clothes strewn on the floor, and took the pile to the laundry room.

"Ugh," she exclaimed aloud. "Teenagers can be real pigs."

She usually cut him some slack and didn't get on his case unless a nasty smell started drifting out of his room. She picked her battles, and his room wasn't usually one of them.

As she went through his jean pockets before throwing his pants in the washer, she was surprised to find a small baggie containing two small white pills.

"What are these?" Renee stared at the pills, confused. Little warning bells went off—had she just stumbled on a big problem?

Now what the hell am I supposed to do? Maybe it's aspirin . . . should I just go ask him? She looked closer at the pills, looking for an innocent explanation . . . but there weren't any marks on the pills. If Robbie was getting into something he shouldn't be, she didn't want to talk to him about it when he was downstairs suffering from the stomach flu.

I'll approach Robbie about it later.

"I hope to hell it isn't anything illegal," she muttered to herself.

She stashed the pills in her room for now. She didn't know if she could deal with any more drama at the moment.

She had always been so sure her own kids would never get involved with drugs.

CHAPTER 28

Gift of Connections

$\mathcal{B}$y morning, Robbie said he felt better and wanted to go to school so he could still play in the weekend basketball tournament. "Thanks for picking up my room, Mom." If he remembered leaving a small bag with two pills in his pocket, he gave no indication. He caught a ride to school with his buddy Paul, leaving Renee in an empty house and a sick feeling in her gut.

I can ask Robbie about it when he gets home tonight. Maybe it's nothing. But do I just believe whatever he tells me? I need some facts.

She didn't know how she could figure out what the pills were, and she wanted to be careful. If the pills were illegal, she wanted to know what she was dealing with before involving anyone else. *I have to call Matt. He'll know what I should do, and I can trust him.*

She grabbed her cell, found his number, and dialed, her hands already clammy from nerves. The call took longer to go through, but it eventually started to ring. It rang so many times, she was prepared to leave him a message when his gruff voice came over the line.

Oh, shit, I forgot the time difference! Renee realized in horror.

"Oh, Matt, I am so sorry if I woke you. This is Renee. I feel terrible. Were you sleeping?"

There was rustling on the other end. Renee could picture Matt trying to get his bearings, probably snapping on a bedside light and rubbing his eyes to wake up.

"No, that's OK, Renee. What's up?"

Renee could tell he was trying to act as if he wasn't still half asleep. But this probably wasn't an unusual occurrence for a sheriff. Hopefully.

"I didn't know who else I could talk to," Renee began, trying to explain the unexpected call. "Feeling a little desperate here. I think Robbie might be in big . . . trouble." Her voice caught on the last word.

"Now, Renee, slow down a little bit. Robbie seemed like a good kid when I met him. Has something happened? Did he get hurt?"

"Oh, Matt, I don't know, maybe I'm just overreacting. I found pills in his jeans when I was doing his laundry last night. They were in a little baggie and there weren't any marks on them. He doesn't take any medication, only ibuprofen once in a while, that kind of thing. I'm going crazy here, thinking maybe he's on drugs. Could I have missed the signs?"

"Did you ask him what they are?"

"No," Renee said, feeling a bit silly. "He came home sick from school yesterday, so I didn't want to confront him. This morning he said he was better and rushed out before I had a chance to mention the pills. Besides, if he told me they were something harmless . . . I don't know if I could believe him. There's just so much shit in schools these days, you know? I'm scared. I thought you might know what I could do to find out what they are . . ." Her voice trailed off as she fought to stay in control of her emotions. "Am I overreacting?"

"Maybe. But you're right. Kids are exposed to a lot of shit these days. You're right to be careful here. Tell you what. I have a buddy on the force back in Minneapolis, name of Ross. Owes me a favor. I can give him a call, see if he can run the pills through the lab, find out what we're dealing with before you talk to Robbie. He'll do it on the QT."

"Oh Matt, you have no idea how much I would appreciate that."

"Tell you what. I'm gonna take a quick shower and head into the office. I'll give my buddy a call and let you know what I find out."

"Thank you so much. I'm sorry to drag you into this . . . I just didn't know where to turn."

"No problem, Renee. Glad to help. Maybe we'll get lucky and they won't turn out to be anything to be worried about. Sit tight, I'll give you a call back as soon as I can."

Unable to concentrate, Renee distracted herself by cleaning out drawers while she waited to hear back. Her cell phone rang forty-five minutes later, and she was relieved to see it was Matt. This time he sounded more himself and had some information. His old friend was willing to help. Matt gave her his name and phone number and told her the man was expecting her call. Matt promised his buddy would run the pills through the lab and get back to her, no questions asked.

"I trust him, Renee. He will get to the bottom of this for you."

"Thank you so much, Matt. You have no idea how much I appreciate this," Renee thanked him profusely for the second time that day. "I'll let you know what I find out."

***

Hands shaking, she dialed the number and held her cell to her ear.

A man answered. "Brown here."

"Mr. Brown, my name is Renee Clements. Matt Blatso gave me your name."

"Oh, hey, Renee," Matt's friend replied. "Yep, Matt told me you'd be calling. Call me Ross. I'm tired of owing that son of a bitch a favor. Glad to finally get the chance to pay up, get him off my back." Renee hoped he was joking. "Matt told me you found some pills in your kid's pocket and you just need to find out what they are. That the skinny of it?"

"Yes," Renee breathed, somewhat relieved.

"No problem. Can you meet me downtown somewhere? If I can get them to the lab by noon, we should be able to get an answer tomorrow morning."

They agreed to meet in an hour at a coffee shop downtown. Knowing it would take her time to find a place to park, she wasted no time heading into the heart of the city. *Traffic isn't nearly as bad at 10:30 as it always was before 8:00 a.m.,* Renee reflected as she drove around the block, looking for a parking spot. She hadn't been back downtown since the day she lost her job. Renee arrived fifteen minutes early, so she ordered a latte and found a small table in the corner. Feeling apprehensive, she watched for the police officer named Ross. Five minutes before they were to meet, a tall man in a black leather jacket entered the shop and looked around. Spying her in the corner, he approached.

"Renee?"

She gave him a quick nod. She was expecting someone in uniform but was relieved he was in street clothes.

He took a minute to order coffee at the counter and then came back and sat across from her.

"God, I think I'm gonna have to take a little vacation, take a trip to Fiji just to thaw out. Matt's been bugging me to fly out. Might have to take him up on it one of these days. Too friggin' cold here. So why don't you show me what ya got?"

Just as Matt had promised, Ross didn't ask any questions—not even how she and Matt knew each other. He made sure he had Renee's number and told her he would be in touch. With that, he was gone, and Renee was alone again.

She sighed. *I feel like I'm in a damn detective novel.*

CHAPTER 29

Gift of a Scare

*R*enee received a call from a number she didn't recognize at eleven the next morning. It was Friday and they were scheduled to leave town mid-afternoon for the basketball tournament. It had been incredibly hard not to say anything to Robbie the night before. *I hope I get good news today.*

It was Ross calling back with results . . . but the news wasn't great.

"Renee, it's Ross. Hey, I got some answers on those pills. They're a designer drug kids are getting off the Internet. They aren't exactly illegal, but they're dangerous as hell and you need to have a heart-to-heart with your son right away."

"Oh my God. Why would Robbie have those? How could he order them off the Internet? He doesn't have a credit card. Wait . . . how dangerous are they?"

"Because they aren't technically illegal, kids assume they're safe and take them in high doses. The pills are supposed to boost energy and precision, the drug of choice among athletes. Some kids are getting dangerously sick. A sixteen-year-old died last month from an overdose in St. Paul. As to how he got the pills . . . the unfortunate truth is that they're easy to get. Another kid probably got a bunch, probably going around school, selling 'em to others under the pretense they'll help the kids improve their grades or do better in sports."

"Oh man . . ." Renee replied. "You hear about this stuff happening, but you always think your kid is going to be smart enough to stay away from that shit."

"Yeah. Unfortunately, I see it all the time. Maybe you got lucky. Maybe you caught it early. But I'm serious when I say you need to talk to your son first chance you get. He can't take that shit. It's like playing Russian roulette."

"I will, I promise. Thank you so much for getting me answers so quickly."

"It's a good day when I can do something to keep a kid safe. Take care, Renee, and good luck."

Renee slumped onto a stool in the kitchen. *Now* what should she do? She decided to look the drug up on the Internet. She was surprised at all the sites that popped up. Many were splashy, making big promises to improve sports and academic performance. Other sites warned about the use of these same drugs. After only a few doses, some kids became lethargic and experienced severe headaches. Renee remembered Robbie's flu bug earlier in the week. *Maybe it wasn't the stomach flu. Holy shit, has Robbie already gotten sick from the pills?*

Disturbed by what she had learned, now she had a choice to make. Should she refuse to let Robbie go to the tournament? Or should she talk to him about what she found during their drive over? Or should she wait and bring it up afterward so he wouldn't be distracted during the games? He had worked so hard to make the team and might even get to dress for varsity. She was trying to be careful not to jump to any conclusions before giving Robbie a chance to explain. But she was having a hard time coming up with any explanation she would be OK with, given what she learned from Ross.

***

She still hadn't decided the best course when she went to pick him up from school.

"Hey Mom, Coach said I could ride the bus with the varsity guys instead of driving up separately. Sorry I didn't get a chance to call you. You OK with that?"

Robbie stood at the open door to the car expectantly. Paul stood next to him, all grins, apparently having received the same invite. Normally, kids on the junior varsity team had to find their own rides to out-of-town games and stay with their parents. The school only had enough money to put up the highest-level team. Renee was surprised they invited Robbie on the bus.

"That sounds fun," she said hesitantly. She didn't want to ask about the pills in front of Paul. "Go ahead. I'll get checked into our room, and I'll see you at the game."

***

Renee called Matt from the car on her way up to the tournament to report what she had learned.

"Ross was able to have the lab run the pills right away. Turns out they're called 'pearls.' Ever heard of them?"

"No," Matt replied. "What are they?"

Once she explained what Ross had told her, Matt asked, "So what did Robbie say when you talked to him, then?"

Renee had been dreading that question. "Well . . . I haven't had a chance to get him alone yet. Ross called me back just this morning. I'm heading up to that basketball tournament I told you about. Robbie's on the bus with the team, but I'm driving up separate."

"You *are* going to talk to him, right?"

"Oh yeah, for sure. I'm scared to death about those damn pills—what if he has more? I *have* to talk to him about this."

"All right, just do it as soon as you can, OK? Stick as close as you can to him until then and watch to make sure he isn't acting any different than normal. Now get off the phone—you shouldn't be talking to me when you're driving," Matt scolded.

"Yes sir, Officer, sir," Renee laughed. "Hanging up now." It felt good to have a moment of fun, even if she still had the heavy cloud hanging overhead.

***

Renee didn't have a chance to talk to Robbie about the pills until late Sunday afternoon when they got home from the tournament. Anytime Robbie was with Renee, others were around. Paul stayed in their room, since his parents couldn't make the tournament. It was a fun weekend, but she watched Robbie like a hawk, looking for any signs of trouble, all the while dodging guilt for not yet fulfilling her promise to Ross—and now Matt—to talk to Robbie right away. The games were exciting, at least. Robbie's team won their first two, but lost the last. He played most of the JV games, and dressed for one varsity game.

By the time they got home, Robbie was beat.

"Heading up to shower, be back down. How 'bout we throw in a pizza?"

By the time he got back to the kitchen, a pepperoni pizza and two sodas sat ready on the island. It was time to talk.

"Robbie, I have to talk to you about something important."

Her tone caught his attention and he looked at her warily. He didn't even pick up a pizza slice. It didn't sound good.

"OK, what's up?"

"Well, the other day when I was doing your laundry, I found something in your pocket. Do you know what it was?"

"Umm . . . no, I don't think so," he said, but he wouldn't meet her eyes.

"It was a small plastic baggie with two white pills inside. What were they?"

Silence. He continued to avoid looking at her. He finally picked up a slice of pizza, but instead of taking a bite he plucked a piece of pepperoni off it and tossed it to Molly.

Renee waited.

Losing his nerve, he looked up. His face was expressionless, but his eyes were wide.

"Mom, I swear, I only took them once—and I got so sick I was going to flush them. Nate gave them to me and told me if I wanted to play varsity, I had to step up my game. He said those would help. Stupid, I know."

His head hung low following his admission.

"Do you even know what they were, Robbie?"

"Something he got off the Internet. He told me lots of guys were taking them, and they weren't illegal. But I felt so terrible after I took them. I swear I won't ever take them again."

"Robbie, do you have any idea how dangerous that was? And how *stupid*? Kids have *died* taking that stuff!" Renee's voice rose with each word, and her teeth clenched. She was on her feet now, furious. She would have sworn he knew better. "When I thought you had the flu, were you sick from those pills?"

He nodded, eyes downcast now.

"Look, Mom, I swear, I won't ever do something that stupid again. I already told the guy to forget it, I wasn't going to buy any from him. He gave me a few to try. I honestly thought it was no big deal, until I got sick. I know you have a lot going on right now, and the last thing you need is me pulling a dumbass stunt like this."

"I can't just let this go, Robbie. That was a stupid, dangerous thing you did and you need to understand how serious it was. I'm tempted to go to your coach about this—"

Robbie's head shot up and he started to protest, but Renee put up her hands and continued.

"I need to think about that. For now, you will do nothing other than go to school and practice. No computer other than for homework, and you'll do that right here on the island in front of me." She held out her hand over the kitchen island. "Give me your cell phone. You can have it back in two weeks."

Robbie stood and took the phone out of his pocket. Renee knew this would be the toughest part of his punishment, but he at least knew better than to say a word about the inconvenience. He handed her the phone, red faced.

"Sorry, Mom. It won't happen again."

He headed upstairs, pizza forgotten.

Renee dumped it all in the garbage. She couldn't eat a bite. The confrontation with Robbie had her shook up. Where had she gone wrong? Why hadn't she taught Robbie not to do something so stupid?

No, this isn't about me. It's about Robbie and a terrible decision he made. The kids are going to have to start to experience the consequences of their decisions, good or bad, and I can't always protect them.

CHAPTER 30

Gift of Hope

*J*anuary sped by. Even though Renee was no longer going into an office every day, she tried to stay busy. She was having trouble getting traction. The episode with Robbie reminded her that life would go on and still be messy, and if she wanted to start making some life changes, she was going to have to fight to stay focused.

Renee spent Monday compiling her current year goals and Tuesday morning working on her monthly plan. By early Tuesday afternoon, she had her goals for that week committed to paper and got to work. Days flew as she started addressing the many areas in her life she wanted to change. She set appointments for doctor visits, for hair and nails; she promised herself a massage following her first job interview for a little additional incentive.

The one item she decided she couldn't put off any longer was the call to Grant Johnson. His daughter's medical needs had sounded urgent, so even if connecting with him scared the hell out of her, it was time.

Renee pulled out the letter Marilyn had given her at Christmas. Taking a deep breath, she punched the number for her dead husband's long-lost twin brother into her phone.

An authoritative voice came over the line. "Hello, Johnson here." Renee sensed the man was distracted and not happy to be interrupted from whatever he had been doing.

"Hello, Mr. Johnson, my name is Renee Clements. My mother-in-law, Marilyn Clements, recently gave me a letter you wrote her regarding a possible family connection."

Following a long pause, the voice replied more hesitantly now.

"Forgive me, Mrs. Clements. I was working on something when you called, and then I was shocked to hear your name. I wasn't sure if I would ever hear any kind of reply to my inquiry. You said Marilyn Clements is your mother-in-law? So did you know a man by the name of Jim Clements?"

"Yes, Mr. Johnson, I knew Jim. Jim was my husband. He's been gone a long time, so you can imagine my utter shock when Marilyn passed your letter on to me. I didn't know Jim had been adopted. His parents never told me until now. Jim never knew, either."

There was another pause on the other end of the line. Grant Johnson seemed to be choosing his words carefully.

"First of all," he finally said, "please know how sorry I was to learn that Jim died at such a young age. I can't imagine how difficult that must have been for you. I feel a huge sense of loss, and I didn't even know I had another brother—a twin, no less—until my mother made a death-bed confession to me. Part of me wishes she would have taken that secret to her grave, given I never even got to meet him. But if I am being completely honest, another part of me wants to hear all about him and the life he lived."

"Growing up as an only child was sometimes lonely for Jim," Renee shared. "He would have loved to have had brothers and sisters, but it was always just Jim and his parents. I met Jim in college, and we were married for ten years before he died. His illness was sudden and brutal. There wasn't even enough time to explore possible treatments."

"Mrs. Clements, what exactly was the illness that took your husband?"

Renee suspected this was the question that had plagued him since the day he learned he had a biological brother and that brother had died young.

"Jim died from complications associated with aplastic anemia. He went from being a healthy man to gaunt and weak in a matter of six months. He wouldn't go to the doctor for the first couple of months because he thought it was just a bug of some sort. Once he *did* go, it took the doctors another couple of months to figure out what was wrong. By then, there was nothing they could do, and . . . he just faded away."

Renee took a moment to compose herself, to swallow down the lump rising in her throat, and then asked the question she had been afraid to ask.

"Mr. Johnson, your letter mentioned your daughter was ill. Is she suffering from the same disease?"

"Please, call me Grant," he replied. "Yes, unfortunately, Grace also has aplastic anemia. I'm a single parent. Grace is my only child. She was in her second year of college when she started feeling rundown and lost her appetite. At first we just thought it was the stress from her tough class schedule. But when she didn't start to feel better after being home for a holiday break, I took her in to get checked. Luckily, the doctors were quicker to diagnose her than it sounds like Jim encountered. They were able to put her on a regimen to slow the progression of the disease, but she had to pull out of her classes and has been home with me for the past year. She was doing all right . . . until she contracted pneumonia this last fall. Now the medicine isn't as effective at holding back the disease. Her only long-term option is a bone marrow transplant. Up to this point, we haven't found a match. Everyone in our family has been tested, but . . ." His voice trailed off.

Renee's internal debate fired up again. *Can I do this again? Go back into a hospital . . . possibly relive what this awful disease can do to a person?*

"I am so sorry to hear your Grace has the same terrible disease Jim suffered from, and that you haven't found a match yet. Back when Jim was sick, a transplant wasn't an option for him. How do you test for a match?"

"A simple blood draw, initially. If a potential match is indicated, further testing is necessary."

We have to at least try to help. I already decided.

"Jim and I had two children together. Could it be possible for Julie or Robbie to be a match for Grace, if you have your facts straight and Jim was your brother?"

"It's possible. Would you be willing to have your children tested to see if they might be a match for Grace? I'm afraid we're running out of time . . . they might be her only option."

Torn between her natural inclination to protect her kids from further heartbreak and the anguish she knew she would feel if one of them were sick, Renee took a deep breath. "Yes . . . they want to help if they can."

"Oh my God . . . you have no idea what a relief it is to hear you say that. I'll contact Grace's medical team right away. Someone will be in touch with the necessary arrangements—process, time, place. It can all be done in Minneapolis." Since Grant and Grace lived a few hours away, they would have to plan when and where to meet in person.

"Thank you," Grant said, his voice finally breaking. "Thank you so much."

This is the right thing to do, we have to help, this is the right thing to do, Renee just kept telling herself as she ended the call and sank into a nearby chair.

CHAPTER 31

Gift of Distractions

*R*enee filled Robbie and Julie in on her conversation with Grant. She still worried a little it might be a mistake—Jim hadn't truly been Grant's brother, perhaps wasn't even his blood relative, yet she was letting strangers into her children's lives—but she knew there was no way Marilyn would have shared any of this with her if she wasn't sure. This whole time Renee had thought reaching out to Marilyn over Christmas had been random . . . but maybe it wasn't.

"Mom, we *have* to help. Even if it's scary to get involved," Julie reminded Renee. "I remember how sick Dad got—that was awful and . . . and *scary.*"

Robbie nodded his agreement. "Yeah, I don't remember much except you crying, Mom, and that creepy cemetery. This is serious. I know if Elizabeth or Nathan were sick, we'd help in a heartbeat if we could," he said, referencing cousins they'd known all their lives.

Julie's class schedule was light on Mondays, so appointments were made accordingly. Grant called a few times, so appreciative of their willingness to get tested. He let them know he'd decided not to tell Grace about their newly discovered family yet; since none of their other family members had been a match, he didn't want to get her hopes up until they were sure. He didn't say it out loud, but Renee could sense he was concerned about Grace's ability to continue to fight the disease if she didn't receive a transplant soon. Regardless of how the tests came out, Grant and Renee agreed they would get the kids together.

They quickly learned from the initial blood draw that Julie couldn't be a match—but Robbie's results looked promising. More extensive tests were performed, but results wouldn't be back for a week.

The week dragged on. Robbie kept himself busy with school and basketball, so Renee had more time on her hands. She continued to email Matt every few days, and they talked on the phone too. She welcomed his call when it came mid-week. She needed a distraction.

Matt seemed to need a distraction as well. Work was frustrating. There was an increase in drug-related cases on the island, but funds were limited and his team couldn't keep up. He was worried about his dad, too. His widowed father was stubbornly trying to maintain his small farm. Neither Matt nor his sister were able to convince him to sell or even rent it out and move to something smaller. Matt also shared with Renee that he missed his sister and her kids. Fiji was a wonderful place to visit, but it was harder to live there, so far from home.

Wanting to enjoy the call, they moved their conversation on to more pleasant topics. Their usual fifteen-minute call lasted an hour. Both felt better by the end of the call and made a "date" to talk again. She might have felt guilty about the cost of these international calls if Matt hadn't told her he switched his plan so the cost wasn't astronomical.

Energized, Renee knew she couldn't put off starting her job search any longer. She penciled out an updated resume and hired someone to critique and polish it. Originally, she thought she would be ready to start her job search once the holidays were over and kids back in school. Now it was late February, and she still hadn't started. Her pride was still banged up from her abrupt layoff. In spite of her reservations, she committed to getting her resume out within the week—even though she couldn't muster much excitement about the process.

CHAPTER 32

Gift of Courage

*R*obbie was a match for Grace.

The call came on Monday. The hospital called Renee first before letting Grant know, to give her and Robbie the opportunity to make a final decision as to whether or not to go through with the transplant. Bone marrow would have to be drawn, and it could be painful. Robbie and Renee had already talked about what they would do if he was a match, so Renee was comfortable telling the doctor they would go through with it. In turn, the doctor promised to call Grant, and his office would set up the necessary appointments. Easter was a few weeks away—they would schedule procedures so Robbie could recuperate when he had time off from school.

Not an hour had passed when the phone rang again. Renee snatched it up, still wired from hearing Robbie's test results.

"Hello?"

"Renee!" a voice said. "It's Grant! Just got off the line with the doctor." She could tell he was trying not to shout in relief. Her mind conjured up a man looking very much like her dead husband, grinning from ear to ear, pacing as he clutched his phone. "I plan to explain this whole convoluted story to Grace tonight—that is . . . if you're sure Robbie is still willing to go through with the transplant."

"Robbie's in school, so I haven't had a chance to tell him the news yet, but he was *adamant* he wants to help if all the tests came back OK," Renee confirmed. *God,* she squirmed, *I hope he doesn't chicken out.* "I wish we could have told Grace together." But even as she said it, she realized that was a bad idea, even if it would have been an option. Grace had been sick for a long time. Finding out she had cousins she never knew existed, and one of them was going to potentially be key to her recovery . . . that was going to come as quite the shock.

Grant interrupted her thoughts, graciously not mentioning the awkwardness of Renee's wish. "I know she'll be anxious to meet you, once she has time to absorb all of this. Renee, I know you probably feel like you're going out on a limb here, helping complete strangers. My gut tells me this might just be the answer we've been searching for, and I can't thank you enough."

I pray you're right, Renee thought, as they agreed to talk again the next day to start firming up logistics.

***

Renee picked Robbie up after practice, having stopped for his favorite takeout on the way to the gym. He would be a sweaty mess and not in any shape to go out for dinner after she shared the news. Instant burger and fries and a hot shower at home was the better course.

Seeing the food, Robbie immediately looked up at his mom, the question in his eyes.

A quick nod gave him his answer.

Robbie blew out a loud sigh, running a hand through his hair. Sweat made it stand on end. He stared out his window as Renee pulled away from the curb.

He finally said, "I figured as much. Man, gotta admit, I'm freakin' out a little here. Jeez, Mom, what if it hurts? What if I can't finish out my season?" After a brief pause, he continued, giving voice to the loudest question on his mind.

"What if we try to help . . . but she still dies?"

A heavy dose of reality for a teenage boy.

"We'll do what we can, honey. After that, we leave it in God's hands."

Renee proceeded to update him with what she knew during the rest of the drive home. He didn't say much more. He ate his burger, but the fries went untouched, along with most of his chocolate malt. Renee understood his hesitancy. She was just as scared about what the next few weeks would bring. Once they got home, Robbie let Molly out and then took her up to his room, saying he had homework. Renee jumped online to research the transplant information the doctor had mentioned earlier.

She printed some of it out, grabbed a bag of Oreos and a big glass of milk, and took it all up to Robbie—knowing her son, that burger hadn't filled him up. He was lying on his bed, freshly showered and staring at his ceiling. Glancing her way, he sighed and pushed up to sit against his headboard. Molly was curled next to him, tail wagging at the site of cookies.

"Hey, Mom. Sorry . . . I'm just a little freaked out by all of this," Robbie said. "Lots going on. I was so sure if either of us was a match, it would be Julie. Not sure why, I just didn't think it would be me."

"I know . . ." Renee began, but Robbie kept going.

"Now we know and I kind of wish none of this happened. A few months ago, we didn't know Dad had more family or that we had a sick cousin. Now they're gonna do God knows what to me."

"Robbie, I know—it's a lot. But we all agreed we at least had to try to help this girl. Now we know you may be able to do just that. I am so proud of you, Robbie, and I understand if it scares you some. Scares me, too. Scares me shitless!"

Robbie chuckled.

"But I know how *I* would feel, as a parent, if either you or Julie were sick. We haven't talked about the fact both your dad and now a cousin had the same disease. That means you might be at risk to develop it. We need to find out more from the doctors. I'm sure they already checked your results for any signs—they would never let you donate if you had the same disease in your system—but the more we can find out about symptoms and treatments, the better. We need to know what we're dealing with here."

Renee offered Robbie the papers. "I did print out some info for you," she said. "Take a look at it sometime soon. Maybe it'll make you feel better if you know what to expect going in."

Robbie took the papers. "Thanks, Mom. I already did some searches on it too, but I'll look at this later."

With that, Robbie pulled out headphones, turned on his music, and tuned her out. She took the cue and left him to his thoughts.

Molly followed her downstairs. Renee looked down at the dog and scratched behind her ear.

"You sensed the teenage angst up there, too, huh?"

CHAPTER 33

Gift of Science

*R*enee, Robbie, and Julie met Grant and Grace for dinner near the hospital the evening before the procedure. Julie was home for Easter break and insisted on coming along. A hostess showed them to their already occupied table. A man and woman lifted from their chairs as they approached.

He doesn't look a thing like Jim, Renee thought—unsure if this was a relief or a disappointment—but she sensed something . . . *familiar* about him as they made introductions.

"Renee," the man said, shaking her hand with both of his own before giving off a small laugh and embracing her in a warm hug. "I am so happy to finally meet you. And you must be Julie . . . and Robbie."

Despite having just met them, Grant hugged each of them individually, conveying his gratitude. Maybe that was the familiarity Renee felt . . . the kindness.

"And this is my daughter, Grace." He motioned to the tall wisp of a young woman to his left. Grace offered a brief wave, not nearly as demonstrative as her dad. Her hair was nearly white and fell straight to her waist. Her skin had a translucent quality.

"Please, have a seat," Grant instructed, sitting back down. "Did you guys get settled in the hotel? We'll have to be at the hospital early tomorrow . . . you were smart to get a room close by."

They all settled around the table. Small talk continued until they placed their orders.

"I can hardly believe we're sitting here tonight," Grant said with a hint of wonder in his voice. "It felt like such a long shot last fall, reaching out to the people I thought were my brother's adoptive parents. And now, here we are."

"We still find all this hard to believe, too," Renee agreed, glancing around their table. "Jim would have loved to have had the chance to get to know you. He hated being an only child. I think that's why he loved spending time with my brother and sisters. He fit right in with my family."

"What was Jim like?" Grant asked, clearly anxious to learn more about his twin. "Did he like sports? What did he do for fun? How did you meet? Do you . . . do you have a picture of him?"

Renee had to laugh—Grant was like a little kid, asking question after question. She dug her phone out of her purse and pulled up her photos.

"I thought you might want to see a picture of Jim, so I found an old album and snapped a few copies so I could show you," she explained, handing her phone to Grant. As he scrolled through the images, Renee continued.

"Well, let's see . . . Jim wasn't a huge sports fan, except for football. He played in high school and was a diehard Vikings fan. When he had time, he loved to fish. I remember shortly after we got married, his car had almost two hundred thousand miles on it, but instead of replacing it, he bought a *fishing* boat. I thought he was crazy. In the winter, it was ice fishing."

"Oh, I loved it when we went ice fishing!" Julie jumped in. "We had that little pop-up fish house and Dad would fire up his heater-thingamajig so the holes wouldn't freeze over. We would go with Uncle Ethan and our cousins. I loved how it would be kinda dark in the house but the holes glowed . . . *so* cool."

"That's right, I forgot about that, honey," Renee said, smiling. "You two would take off on Saturdays. I stayed home with Robbie. He was too little to go along. I worried he would step into one of the holes!"

This line of reminiscing was met with a groan and eye roll from Robbie but laughs from the others.

"Jim was a good man, Grant," Renee said. "You would have been proud to call him your brother. He was a good father."

"It sounds that way," Grant replied, still scrolling through the photos. When he finished, he looked up and turned to Robbie. "How 'bout you, Robbie? What do *you* remember about your dad?"

Robbie shrugged, slow to respond. "Guess I don't remember much. I was only five when he died." He glanced at Grace, catching her eye. She hadn't contributed much to the conversation, either, but a small smile hovered on her lips. She seemed at peace with the new hope. She wasn't upset by Robbie's mention of death.

Robbie's comment did dampen the enthusiasm around the table, but right at that moment dinner arrived, saving him from more awkward talk about the father he barely knew.

As they ate, Grant filled in any holes in the conversation, clearly excited but also a bit uncomfortable. Robbie fidgeted and pushed his pizza around on his plate. Grace's eyes were pained and she barely ate, but she never complained.

Eventually their waitress brought the check, and the two single parents remembered the main reason they were there.

"We better call it a night," Renee suggested. "Robbie and Grace both need a good night's sleep."

"Of course," Grant agreed, taking care of the check. "You're right, we better head over to the hotel and turn in. We'll see you three tomorrow morning?" he acquiesced with a hesitant smile, helping Grace to her feet.

***

Despite getting to bed by 10:30, Robbie didn't get much rest. Renee heard him flopping around on his bed. He finally settled down, but soon was muttering in his sleep and whining in some imagined pain. By 6:00 a.m., they all gave up attempts at sleep and headed across the street to the hospital. The nurses had already taken Robbie to the back by the time Grace arrived. She was ushered away, and the remaining three settled into hard plastic chairs, sipping bitter coffee while they waited. An hour later, a hospital volunteer came by with a large box of donuts on a metal cart—but they were all too nervous to eat.

Finally, one of the doctors came out to update them. Robbie had done well and was resting in recovery. Grace was receiving the transplant; once she was done, she would have to be in isolation to minimize any chance of infection. Relieved at the progress, they all relaxed a bit. Robbie would be able to go home either tonight or in the morning, depending on how he felt.

Grant, a writer by trade, said he planned on posting an update on Grace's condition to the online site they'd created to let family and friends know how she was doing. He moved off to work alone at a small round table in the back corner of the room. Julie and Renee played a card game to pass the time.

After losing three games of Rummy (and blaming it on her inability to concentrate), Renee stood and stretched. "Hey Grant, Julie and I are going to walk down to the cafeteria and grab some lunch. Want to join us?"

"No, you two go ahead, I'm gonna sit tight."

Gone was the talkative man from the night before. This man sat stoically, alone, unwilling to do anything more after he finished his post. Renee saw him discreetly brush a tear from his eye before it could make its way down his cheek. If this operation didn't work, there were no good options left—and all Grant could do was wait, pray, and hold vigil. Renee offered him a reassuring pat on the shoulder as they left the waiting room, conveying a silent offer of support.

Fresh coffee and bowls of soup with oyster crackers were enough to revive Renee and Julie. Nothing more substantial sounded appetizing, and they didn't want to be gone when Robbie came out of recovery. Grant was just finishing up with the doctor when they got back to the waiting room. Some of the tension had dissipated from around his eyes when he shared the update.

"Grace tolerated the procedure well, but she's weak. They expect her to sleep for hours yet. I won't be able to see her for a while, but I want to stay close. I think I'll grab a quick sandwich. Would you . . . would you mind staying here?" he asked tentatively. "Just in case there's any more news while I'm gone."

"Absolutely. Go, grab something to eat and stretch your legs," Renee encouraged.

When he left, Julie turned to Renee and said, "No news is good news. Right?"

***

Later, Renee and Julie were allowed back to see Robbie.

He was groggy and not making much sense when they walked in. Julie bit back a giggle when he asked if she brought Tigger. Tigger had been Robbie's favorite stuffed animal until well into his grade-school years.

Renee nudged Julie, giving her a look. "No, honey, sorry," she said to Robbie.

He shrugged. "Ah, well. He'd probably be scared anyway." And with that, he drifted back to sleep.

***

Mid-afternoon, Renee's parents stopped in. They had been shocked when Renee shared all the developments around Jim's family. Two more chairs were brought in and quiet conversation floated around as they waited for Robbie to wake up again. Renee worried he might sleep for hours—she knew all too well how much he enjoyed sleeping. But prodding by the day nurse woke him in the late afternoon and he was soon sweet-talking staff, trying to convince them to send him home. He felt fine, or so he said, despite the twinge he gave when he gingerly got himself out of bed to use the restroom, groping around to hold his hospital gown closed so he didn't flash his grandparents. Renee went to check on Grant and Grace, promising to be right back. The nurse agreed to send the doctor in so they could decide whether or not Robbie had to stay the night.

Grant was alone in the waiting room, sound asleep in what had to be an uncomfortable position in one of the plastic chairs. He jumped when Renee touched his shoulder. Rubbing his eyes, he took a minute to wake up.

"Oh, hey Renee, how's Robbie doing?"

"He's awake and trying to figure out a way to break out of here so he can go home. Any news on Grace?"

Grant took a deep breath and sat up straighter in the unforgiving chair, flexing his shoulders. "Doc Larson stopped in about an hour ago. She has a bit of a fever, so they're keeping a close eye on her. Said it wasn't a huge cause for concern, but, at this point . . . any hiccup scares the shit out of me."

"Do you think maybe you should go get a little rest back at the hotel? You've been here for hours, Grant."

"Hell, no," he said immediately. "I'm not going anywhere."

I get it, Renee thought. If Robbie experienced any setbacks, she wouldn't go anywhere either.

"Tell you what," she said, "I'll keep you posted on whether or not they let Robbie go home tonight. If he can leave, I'll take him home so he can sleep in his own bed. If he can't leave, we'll stay at the hotel again. Either way, I promise to come up tomorrow to look in on Grace."

Grant captured Renee's hand as she stood to leave. "Renee, thank you for giving us this chance."

She gave him a small smile of acknowledgment, then left to check on her boy.

CHAPTER 34

Gift of Spring

*R*obbie got his way—that boy could schmooze his way out of anything—and was sent home to sleep in his own bed. After Renee got him settled with the remote control, his tablet and his dog next to him, she left him to rest. He was asleep within minutes; the drive home had tired him out more than he would admit. She continued to check on him every couple of hours, even during the middle of the night, just as she had done when he was a baby. She stood quietly in the doorway, watching for his chest to rise and fall as he lay there so still. Despite the discomfort from the incision in his back, he slept better than he had the night before.

Good, she thought, smiling. *The big guy deserves it.*

Renee was up early the next morning. Keeping her promise to herself, she spent the morning sending out cover letters and resumes and searching online job-boards. She needed to get serious about finding a job. She wasn't excited about any of the prospects posted; nevertheless, she knew it was important to network and get her name out.

Julie spent the day on homework. Robbie was content to lounge in front of the television. Renee stopped up at the hospital but was not yet allowed to see Grace. Grant appreciated the caramel latte she brought and assured her he was fine.

"Just waiting for Grace to show some meaningful improvement," he said, with what Renee thought looked like a forced smile.

***

After the hospital, she headed to the salon. She wanted to have a new look before she started interviewing. She was tired of the same old hairstyle.

Haven't changed it in a decade! she realized, grimacing.

Once she was sporting a short new style, brightened up with highlights, she headed to the mall. She couldn't remember the last time she'd shopped at noon on a Thursday. Shopping wasn't her favorite activity, but she wanted a couple of fresh outfits for her job search. She was pleasantly surprised when clothes in her usual size were loose.

More time spent on daily walks with Molly and less sitting at a desk helped shave a few pounds off without my even realizing it! she thought. *Wish Matt could see . . .*

Once she purchased a few corporate-appropriate pieces, Renee headed to a sporting goods store. She picked up a new pair of tennis shoes and some cute exercise clothes. This shopping was more fun than picking out dress clothes.

Renee made one last stop on her way home to pick up groceries and a few Easter goodies. Even if her kids were too old to believe in the Easter bunny, she had to have a basket for each of them and eggs to dye. They were going back to her parents' for Easter, heading over on Saturday night and staying until Monday.

Renee was apprehensive about their Saturday plans. The days were getting longer. It was time to visit her lake property. She needed to figure out what she wanted to do with it. When she was able to land a job, there was no way she would be able to spend much time out there. Was there any way she could actually get the resort up and running again, albeit with her as an absentee owner? She had promised herself not to remain solely dependent on income from an eight-to-five again . . . and Aunt Celia had placed an opportunity for a second stream of income right in her lap.

But I don't know the first thing about running a resort!

CHAPTER 35

Gift of Place

Saturday dawned gray and chilly; a brisk wind pushed bare tree branches in a slow dance. A late-season snow flurry the previous night cloaked springtime muck along the roads. George had made the drive to Celia's property enough times over the years to remember how to get there. He made one wrong turn, but quickly got his bearings. Renee didn't recognize any landmarks. She had been too young to pay attention the times she made this trip.

George turned off the paved road, onto a gravel path. Renee pointed to a familiar weathered sign:

Welcome to
WHISPERING PINES

The sign's letters were faded; it hung askew, either from growth of massive tree branches pushing it off kilter or because the sign was falling apart.

"I hope the whole place isn't in as tough of shape as that sign," Renee muttered.

They drove slowly down the lane, anxious to see what awaited them at the end of the road. Their progress was hampered by mounds of crystallized snow. Sunlight, filtered by the tall pines lining the path, was not yet strong enough to melt it all.

Finally, a clearing was evident ahead. All five strained for their first view of the resort. First came the view of the lake—a large gray expanse intersected with veins of jagged black where the ice was relinquishing its winter hold on the water. As they rounded a final bend, log-sided buildings dotted the open clearing. Sun had managed to melt the snow off the open paths intersecting the grounds. A graveled parking lot curved to their right, beside it a bigger structure with green trim. The smaller cabins off to the left had red trim, now faded a dull pink. Renee recognized the green-trimmed lodge—childhood memories flashed in her mind of playing *Pac-Man* in its upstairs.

The whole place had an air of desertion. Only tiny prints left behind by wildlife marred the snow and thawing ground. The vehicle doors creaked open and slammed shut, and then the only sound was of a low moaning wind.

"Not exactly how I remember it," George commented, surveying the dreary surroundings. "Only ever came out here in the summer. Used to take you kids down to the water with your fishing poles and a big bucket of night crawlers. Remember that? Ethan, I never saw a kid get as excited as you did when you caught your first northern. It was only a few pounds, but you fought that damn fish the whole way in, acted like the thing was a twenty-pounder!"

"I do remember, Dad," Ethan said, laughing. "You showed me how to clean the thing, too. When we cut it open, there was a smaller fish in its belly."

"Oh God, how *gross*," Julie cringed at the image as she walked around the side of the vehicle, taking it all in.

"I remember playing kick-the-can at night and eating s'mores around the campfire," Renee shared.

"Yep," Jess agreed, "and my favorite days were spent in the hammock, reading a good book."

They all laughed at Jess's comment; she was still a bookworm—little had changed.

Julie started down a muck-filled path toward the lake. A booming *CRACK!* split the air and she jumped backward with a little scream. Grandpa George, laughing, cut off her dash back to the SUV.

"What the hell was that?" Julie said, her eyes still wild.

Laughing even harder, he assured her, "That, my dear, is just the ice cracking. Don't you remember hearing that when you used to ice fish?"

The contemplative mood broken, George dug keys out of his pocket. He brought them from Celia's house. Everyone followed him up to the lodge door. It took finagling with the lock, but between George and Jess, they were able to slide the deadbolt out of the way. The heavy green door groaned on its hinges as it swung inward.

Air colder than outside pushed out at them as they stomped dirty snow off their boots and entered the lodge. It was dark; dusty furniture loomed in hulking shadows. A flip of the light switch on the wall yielded no additional light.

"Stay put, folks," Ethan said, and he ventured farther into the dark space ahead, aided by a small flashlight he pulled out of his jacket pocket.

What a relief to have everyone with me on my first trip, Renee thought.

In no time, weak light streamed in as Ethan raised window blinds to admit the mid-morning sun. Knowing they would freeze their feet if they took off their boots, they stomped off any remaining debris and ventured into the lodge. Frigid air was heavy with the smell of old wood and an undercurrent of . . . something else. As more blinds were opened, a large, open space came in to view. A massive fireplace dominated the west wall and ceilings were at least twelve feet high. An old bar stood in front of much of the north wall. Mirrors and shelves, empty of all but a thick layer of dust, lined the wall behind the scarred wooden bar top. Another wall was covered with old photographs. Renee walked over to it, tracking dusty footprints across the open space.

It was a hodge-podge of images, hung there over the decades. Most of the frames were the cheap, simple kind, made up of different shades of wood and plastic. Some images were black-and-white, featuring countless groups of campers, hunters, and fishermen; others were taken more recently, but colors were fading and the images blurring more than the older shots. The massive collection of photos reminded her of the history surrounding this old place. Renee hadn't thought much about the legacy of the resort. A bit of the magic of the old place started to slowly creep into her soul.

A shriek snapped Renee back to the present. Ethan rushed over to see what his sister was panicked over.

Probably just a dead mouse, knowing Jess, Renee thought, smiling to herself.

But even Ethan took a step back when he saw what she'd discovered. Jess had opened the door to an old bathroom—only to find a nest of squirrels living in the sink, chattering incessantly at her as if telling her to get lost. Ethan quickly closed the door to prevent the squirrels from running into the main room.

He looked around at everyone in the lodge and said in explanation, "Family of honest-to-God squirrels. Must've gotten through that broken window above the toilet."

George snorted. "We'll need to figure out how to relocate that little family of squatters and fix the broken glass." He nodded at Julie and added, "And soon, if I know anything about teenage girls."

Julie scoffed, but she didn't disagree.

Next they made their way upstairs. The air was thick with dust motes. Limp café-style curtains, displaying a brown-and-orange tulip pattern and probably dating back to the '60s, maybe early '70s, covered the bottom two-thirds of the few windows upstairs. Pulling back the curtains did little to dispel the gloom—the windows were filthy. Renee was sorry there wasn't a bank of windows along the wall facing the lake. If this area were to be at all useful, more light was needed. Huge braided rugs covered most of the wooden floors. There was nothing more to see, so they all made their way back downstairs and outside.

Farther back from the water, behind the lodge and graveled parking area, was a large shed. A rusted padlock prevented them from rolling up the fiberglass door, but a quick glance through the window confirmed the shed held lawn equipment and other tools.

Renee used her phone to snap lots of pictures and take videos as they explored. She asked Julie to do the same and saw Ethan making notes on a small pad he kept pulling out of his jacket. There was so much to see, she wouldn't remember a fraction of it all by tonight if she didn't record it.

Next they made their way over to the smaller cabins. Three were situated in a loose semi-circle, set around a large fire pit. The other two stood farther away, nestled along the edge of the woods rimming the clearing. George's key-ring held keys with little numbered stickers on them, but they didn't know which cabin was which, so it took time to get the doors open.

Thankfully no additional critters were found in any of the cabins. Unfortunately, one did have some significant water damage: the cabin tucked farthest back from the lodge had water stains running down the corner of the back bedroom wall. Ethan pointed out where a tree had rubbed the shingles and worn a small hole through the roof, letting water trickle inside.

The three cabins by the fire pit all had similar floorplans. You entered into a small kitchen area containing a wooden table surrounded by four chairs. Beyond was a living room with a modest rock fireplace in the corner. A couch with nubby green upholstery—*the kind that wears like steel,* Renee noted—plus a recliner and a wooden rocking chair provided seating. End tables with heavy lamps completed the furniture ensembles. Bedrooms filled the back two corners of the tidy little cabins, flanking a small bathroom. Two of the cabins had screened porches off the kitchen which would provide a welcome escape from mosquitoes on summer evenings. Ceiling fans throughout the cabins would help keep them cool; there were no air conditioning units. Electric heating units were mounted low on some walls to chase away the chill.

If they still work, Renee amended.

The cabin with the water damage was small, with only one bedroom. The kitchen was so tiny only a narrow table fit in the space. The other cabin on the edge of the woods was much larger. It boasted two bedrooms, similar to the first three cabins, but it also had a small third bedroom instead of a screened-in porch.

All the beds were made up, but the cabins smelled of mildew. Renee and Jess inspected the bedding further and agreed it would need to be replaced. The mattresses would probably have to go, too. Renee was starting to panic a bit. The cabins weren't in terrible shape, but everything looked dated and tired. No telling what would need to be fixed once electricity and water was turned on to the cabins. It was too cold to consider checking pumps yet, and they didn't want to flip the breaker to the cabins until they had more time to inspect the electrical systems.

Thinking they had checked out everything as best they could, Renee headed back toward the lodge. Everyone followed, but when she walked to her vehicle, George continued on to the other side of the lodge, looking back at her, confused.

"Don't you want to check out the duplex?" he asked.

"What duplex?" Renee replied. "I thought we looked at all the buildings. I don't remember a duplex."

"You probably never had any reason to venture back in that direction when you were a kid," George speculated. "The caretakers for the resort always lived in the east unit back here, and various staff lived in the west unit. I have no idea what shape they're in, but as long as we're here, I figured you'd wanna check."

Renee still didn't see her dad's mythical building as she turned the corner at the back of the lodge. She and the others followed George down a paved path, warning him to take it easy as patches of ice made the walkway slick. The path turned first right around a big tree and then left around another, before the house came into view. Unlike the other buildings, this one wasn't sided with logs. Pale yellow siding with blue shutters and two pink doors stood before them. A small porch stretched across the front. The doors, probably red before time had taken its toll, were the only indication it was a duplex.

Two rickety Adirondack chairs sat on the porch with a wooden box set between them. An old rusted bicycle stood in a far corner. George mounted the stairs and unlocked the door on the east side—this time the two duplex keys were easy to distinguish. Similar to their entrance into the lodge and cabins, they were met with cold, stale air. A semi-circle of faded linoleum gave way to gold shag carpet. Heavy drapes covered the front window.

Renee followed her father in, Julie, Ethan, and Jess at her heels, and George showed them around like a landlord with a potential tenant.

"Stairs"—he pointed to a staircase climbing up into the darkness—"lead to an upper level." He pointed to the back of the main floor. "Kitchen back there, though I'm not sure what kinda condition it's in."

The furniture matched the era throughout the rest of the resort. Striped gold-and-orange wallpaper lined the walls of the front room. The kitchen was dark. Cabinets, almost black in color, absorbed the pale light streaming in the window above the sink. Avocado-colored appliances completed the early '70s vibe.

"Yeah," Renee agreed with George's first tentative assessment. "I doubt these still work."

Ethan pointed at another doorway in the kitchen. "Where's that lead?"

George scratched his head, recalling old memories. "Down to the basement, I believe." Ethan, Renee, and George headed down—Jess and Julie had gone off exploring somewhere else.

Ethan used his flashlight to light the way. The floor and walls were unpainted concrete. A washer and dryer stood in the corner, elevated on a wooden platform, perhaps to keep them off a sometimes wet floor. "Those bad boys look a couple decades newer than the appliances upstairs," George remarked.

Renee nodded. "Thankfully the basement's bone-dry at the moment."

Satisfied with the condition of the lowest level, they headed back to the kitchen.

Footsteps from above meant Julie and Jess were exploring upstairs, so Renee and the others joined them. There were three small bedrooms along with an obnoxiously pink bathroom on the second floor. Pink subway tiles lined the lower half of the walls of the bath, broken up by a thinner row of black tiles and topped with walls painted a paler shade of pink. A black toilet and sink stood in stark contrast to the pink tub. A large, plate-glass mirror on the wall above the sink was flanked by black lanterns suspended by ebony chains. Bedrooms were carpeted in the same shag as downstairs.

Julie started sneezing from the dust they stirred. They headed back out to the porch and then did a quick review of the west unit while she waited outside in the crisp air. The unit was a mirror image of the first, except it showed more wear and tear. Renee remembered her father saying the resort caretakers lived in the east unit. They would have been more likely to take care of their home than the more transient population of staff that lived in the west unit through the years.

Their exploration of the resort lasted for a couple hours, but the chill started to set in. Spring didn't have much of a grip yet. Renee was conflicted about all she had found during this first visit. There was something familiar about the old lodge and the grounds. Of course, the muck and partial snow cover made it all look worse. Mother Nature would no doubt brighten up the place in the months to come. But some damage on the buildings was evident. Renee worried closer inspection would reveal more problems. Interiors were in sore need of updates. She still had no idea why Celia had picked her to become its proud new owner either. Why not Ethan, with his carpentry skills? Why did Celia even hold on to it all these years? As far as Renee knew, Celia hadn't been out here in a long time.

Sentimentality, probably, she thought bitterly.

Knowing everyone was cold and hungry, she herded her daughter and sister back to the vehicle while George and Ethan made sure everything was locked up. She saw her brother and dad pointing around at the various buildings as they made their way back to her Toyota.

The group was more subdued on their drive home. George shot Renee an encouraging smile and patted her leg, but made no comment. Renee snapped the radio on as she drove, her mind jumping from potential project to project.

As they passed that decrepit sign, Renee thought to herself: *What in God's name am I going to do with Whispering Pines?*

CHAPTER 36

Gift of Experience

"So, Ms. Clements, tell me a little about yourself," Katy Harper prompted. "Work experience, team management, any project work . . . that type of thing."

Renee eyed the young recruiter sitting across from her. The small room they were in felt . . . close. Stuffy. *If she'd bothered to give my damn resume more than a cursory glance, she'd already know some of this,* Renee thought bitterly. *She was probably still in diapers when I started working, and now I have to impress* her. She took a deep breath and mentally adjusted her own snarky attitude.

"I held a variety of positions with increasing levels of responsibility at my last company," she began. "I managed teams ranging from three to ten and oversaw numerous complex projects."

"Give me an example of one such project," the recruiter prodded.

Nodding, Renee recited a response she'd rehearsed the night before. "One of my more challenging projects involved updating the servers across our network in locations stretching from New York to Reno. My team of eight techs traveled between our locations and I coordinated their work with independent contractors." The woman nodded as Renee delved deeper into her explanation. "We completed our work within the prescribed timeline and only exceeded budget by two percent, due in part to increased hardware costs. I was able to find cost savings elsewhere to offset larger overages."

For the next thirty minutes, Ms. Harper continued to quiz Renee on her work history. Eventually, Renee felt she had given the recruiter plenty of thoughtful responses, and she subtly began to shift the conversation, asking questions of her own. The interviewer became the interviewee.

"Now that you have allowed me to share examples of my experience with you, Ms. Harper, would you please take a few minutes to tell me more about this particular position? You obviously do this type of thing—interviewing candidates—on a daily basis, so I would like to cut right to the point. I have two decades of experience in corporate America. I know some people are a better fit for certain roles than others. There's give-and-take in every job, of course, but I plan to be selective in my next career move. I don't want to waste your time if this position doesn't feel right to me."

Katy paused before responding, meeting Renee's steady gaze. "You know, Renee, I appreciate your candor. You've been forthright with me, sharing your history and not adding fluff or embellishment just to impress me. I have to say . . . talking with you is like a breath of fresh air. So . . . yes . . . let *me* tell *you* more about the role."

As the woman reviewed key aspects of the position, Renee added a few notes to her list of questions she'd prepared ahead of time.

"Will there be much overnight travel?" Renee asked.

When Katy confirmed this, Renee pressed for details around duration. She continued to ask questions from her list, asking more about the comp structure and how much vacation the company offered as part of their benefits package.

"Believe me," Renee said, "I realize most people don't ask this many questions early in the interview process. I apologize if I'm coming across too strong. I just don't want to play games here."

Katy laughed, waving off Renee's concerns. "Renee, you've earned the right to ask these questions. You wouldn't believe the kids I get in here, straight out of college . . . no experience, demanding a certain pay level, more vacation . . . the list goes on and on." Renee gave Katy a brief nod, commiserating with her. Katy continued. "You don't project a sense of entitlement, just a desire to understand what this job entails and whether or not you have any interest in it." She stood to signal the interview was over. "I enjoyed our visit, and I hate to cut this off, but I have another appointment waiting for me."

"Don't let me keep you any longer." Renee rose, offering her hand to the woman. "You haven't scared me off, so I hope to be invited back to interview with your panel."

Glad to escape the tight room, Renee crossed through the reception area, her high heels echoing on the gray marble. Just as she reached for the elevator button, the brass doors slid open and a well-dressed young man, not much older than Julie, rushed out. He barely spared a glance in Renee's direction as he skirted around her, his eyes instead finding the attractive blonde receptionist off to the left.

Nice, buddy, Renee thought, snickering to herself. *If you are Katy's next appointment, she's gonna see right through that fancy suit.*

As Renee exited the skyscraper, she raised her face to the sunlight. The office upstairs had felt confining. Down here at street level, exhaust fumes masked the freshness of the early spring air. Interviewing was stressful. She had no idea whether she would advance to the final interview, nor was she entirely sure this position was going to be a good fit for her if she *did* get an offer.

I can't wait to get home to take Molly for her walk, Renee thought.

***

The next day, Katy Harper called to invite her back for a panel interview that Friday. *I wanted to go see Aunt Celia's lawyer about Whispering Pines on Friday,* Renee lamented, feeling some of her newfound, albeit temporary freedom slipping away already. She had never personally interviewed with multiple people at once, but she'd been one of the interviewers on such a panel the preceding year. She remembered thinking then how she would hate being the one in the hot seat. Now it was her turn.

What's that phrase? she thought. *"My, but how the tables have turned"?*

Friday dawned clear with a tinge of warmth in the air. Heading back downtown—taking the same route she had trekked for so many of her working years—Renee avoided the worst of the traffic and arrived early. With time to spare, she visited her favorite coffee shop and sat at one of the empty tables outside. As people hustled by wearing designer shoes, schlepping sleek laptop bags on their shoulders, and talking animatedly into cell phones, no one paid her any attention. No one seemed to pay attention to anyone else either, each caught up in their own hectic little worlds. Everyone had somewhere to be and something to do. For some reason, this made her think of Fiji . . . and then Matt . . . and then Whispering Pines.

Renee thought the panel interview went smoothly. She was able to answer most of their questions without too much trouble. She learned the company was currently going through a restructuring phase, and this was a newly created position. The overnight travel could prove problematic for Renee with Robbie at home, but otherwise most of the details they shared were favorable. They promised to get back to all the candidates with their decision the following week.

Waiting was always tough. Renee continued to contact additional companies over the next week. She also kept exploring ideas for her lake property. She made lists of things that needed to be fixed, ways she might be able to reopen the resort—while not going broke in the process—and possible impacts if she were to not open the resort this coming season. If all she did was hire a company to do maintenance on the property, would the buildings continue to slowly deteriorate due to lack of use?

On Thursday, a FedEx delivery man knocked on her door. After signing for a package, Renee poured a fresh cup of coffee and took the manila envelope out back on the patio, hand shaking a bit as she opened it. The return address was MNC, the company she interviewed with the previous week. Inside was an offer letter, along with information about the company's benefits package. The salary was 15 percent higher than what she'd been earning at her old job. There was an array of insurance products to choose from, and the position came with three weeks of paid time off, which would accrue monthly.

Which means no time off for the first few months, she thought grimly. Fiji flashed in her mind, and she sighed.

As she wandered back into the house, a blinking light on the answering machine caught her eye. She hadn't noticed it earlier. She pushed play—and recognized the voice immediately.

"Renee, this is Katy Harper, calling you back from MNC. Sorry I missed you. We're impressed with your credentials and think you could bring a certain maturity level to the role that has been missing. You will be receiving our offer letter in the mail shortly. Please review the information and call if you have any questions. I look forward to hearing back from you Monday and hope you are as excited to come to work for us as we are to invite you to join our team."

Staring down at the sheaf of papers in her hand, Renee wondered when that spark of excitement might hit. She had the weekend to decide.

So why was that old song "Take This Job and Shove It" playing in her head?

CHAPTER 37

Gift of a Girls' Day

"Oh God, I'm sorry I'm late, Tabby!" Renee apologized as she rushed up to her waiting friend outside an auction house early Saturday morning. "Robbie needed a ride ... and *then* I couldn't find a damn parking spot. There are a *ton* of people here!"

"Hey, no worries—let's just get in there so we can look around before the auction starts," Tabby said, giving Renee a push toward the door. A good four inches shorter than Renee, Tabby had always compensated for her small stature with a slightly aggressive nature. Renee laughed at her friend's typical impatience. Nothing had changed.

They entered a vast, noisy room that smelled of coffee and exhaust fumes.

"No wonder parking was tough," Renee said. "This place is *packed*! When you asked if I wanted to go to an auction, I figured it was some kind of estate sale ... but look at all this furniture!" She motioned at row after row of desks, couches, and beds.

"Actually, it's a hotel liquidation. Remember me telling you my sister might try to go off on her own and open a deli?" Tabby asked, and Renee nodded as the earlier conversation came to mind. "I've been encouraging her to take a chance and she finally decided to go for it. But she doesn't have much capital, so she needs to be really smart with her money. She had to work this morning—hasn't quit yet—so I told her I'd check and see if there were any good deals."

Renee wasn't surprised Tabby was here to help Jill out. Ever since they lost their parents in a car crash, Tabby had been watching out for her baby sister.

"Since we're getting a late start, I better find the dishes they advertised and see if any might work for the restaurant," Tabby said, scanning the room.

Renee pointed. "Looks like kitchen stuff is back there," she said, heading toward a corner of the room. Together they wove through the crowd, skirting the auctioneer's pickup parked at the end of one row. Indeed, there were multiple tables of dishes, glassware, and pots in a back corner. Tabby started hunting through the stacks, sending pictures of possibilities off to her sister.

Renee wandered back over to check out the furniture. A long row of mattresses leaned against an outer wall. Some of the sets still had tags and were wrapped in plastic. There were full, queen, and king sizes. A long row of various bed frames stretched in front of the mattresses. Renee's interest piqued, remembering the musty beds back at the resort. What if these sets went cheap? Mattresses were so expensive. She always loved the thrill of picking up an auction treasure at a great price. *But be careful,* she reminded herself. It was way too easy to get caught up in the thrill of it all and pay too much.

Renee pulled out her phone and reviewed the pictures she'd taken of the bedrooms in the cabins. They contained a wide variety of beds, probably replaced as needed over the years and arranged to increase the sleeping capacity of the cabins.

Why am I even considering this? I don't know what the hell I'm going to do with the resort yet. I have no business buying mattresses for the place. Besides, there were so many people at the auction—there was no way the sets were going to go cheap.

She wandered between tables stacked with towels, sheets, blankets, duvet covers, and comforters. All the linens looked to be in good condition.

Renee jumped at the crack of a loud speaker coming to life. "Thanks, everyone, for comin' out this morning," the auctioneer's booming, sing-song voice rang over the crowd as he attempted to make himself heard over the cacophony of voices. "We have a great sale for you today. Got lots of quality items here. Be sure to get your bidding number from the gals over at the front table."

Renee saw three women wearing blue T-shirts emblazoned with the auction company's name across the front. *Probably his wife and daughters.*

"Gonna have to ask y'all to keep your voices down. Have those numbers ready if you plan to do any bidding—which I hope you all plan to do, and often," he teased, drawing a couple of laughs from the crowd. He went on to announce the order of the sale and housekeeping topics such as the need to remove smaller purchased items by the end of the day's sale. Furniture would have to be picked up within the week.

Bidding commenced at a flat of tools and cleaning supplies. Neither Tabby nor Renee were interested in anything on the first trailer.

"Come on," Tabby suggest, "let's grab a cup of coffee and a donut and catch up."

Together they bought the treats and found open spots at an aluminum picnic table.

"All right, girl," Tabby started, "I need updates—updates! Last time I talked to you, you were heading to your parents' for Christmas. Not something you usually have time to do. What's up?"

Renee smirked. "How much time ya got? This probably isn't the time or place to get into everything, so the abbreviated version: I got laid off."

Her friend, who seldom stopped talking, was momentarily speechless.

"But," Renee added, "that's not all. I also inherited that place my folks used to take us every summer as kids—"

"Wait, wait, wait," Tabby finally cut in. "Back up a minute. You got *fired?*"

Renee laughed. "Well, technically, our roles were 'eliminated' in mid-December and I received a severance package. I prefer the term 'laid off' to 'fired,' though."

"You have *got* to be kidding me! And you didn't think to tell me all this until now?"

"I'm sorry, Tabby, I know I should have called. But everything's been so crazy, and I guess it's still hard to talk about. I'm still trying to figure out what I'm gonna do. I wish I was gutsy like you, wish I had the balls to see if I could re-open Whispering Pines."

"Whispering Pines?" Tabby was having trouble following.

"Sorry, I'm blabbing. Whispering Pines—it's the resort I inherited from my aunt."

"And again," Tabby bristled, "you didn't see fit to tell me about this until now? What the hell, Renee?"

"I know, I know, I should have called sooner. Actually, that's why I called you yesterday to see if you wanted to do lunch today. I was going to tell you everything. When you already had plans and invited me along today, this sounded fun. So here we are, and here I am, dumping all my crap on you."

Tabby shrugged off Renee's concern, her interest still piqued by Renee's mention of a resort. "Got any pictures of the place?"

"Of course." Renee laughed, relieved to be so easily forgiven by her friend for not reaching out sooner. "We went out to tour it Easter weekend. Here, I took a ton of shots. Feel free to flip through them."

Tabby took Renee's phone and started checking out her friend's new property. "Hmm . . . interesting," was all she muttered at first. She took her time looking through the pictures and handed the phone back to Renee. "The lodge and those quaint little cabins have some real potential," she finally said, arms crossed in front of her chest, eying Renee carefully.

Renee laughed again. "Of *course* you would say that. You're the interior designer!"

Tabby held up a finger. "Hold that thought, they're moving back to the kitchenware." She bounced up and grabbed Renee's arm, pulling her back toward the corner. "We aren't done with this discussion about the resort," she warned.

But Tabby wanted moral support if she was going to spend her sister's hard-earned cash on a pile of dishes. They inched as close to the front of the crowd as they could. The auctioneer was working fast and bids flew. Most of the bidders acted as if they knew what they were doing. Unwilling to be intimidated, Tabby and Renee held their ground as others tried to jostle their way in front of them to see better. They enjoyed the competition between bidders and the camaraderie of the auction team.

Finally, the dishes came up for bid. The first few sets went too high and Tabby held back. But as bidding progressed, she jumped into the mix. Her hands were shaking after, but her eyes sparkled as she rechecked her math and, with great relief, confirmed she was able to stay below Jill's $1,000 budget. Renee stayed with Tabby's dishes while her friend found a cart and a teenager willing to help get the sets out to Tabby's truck. The dishes were safely stowed and the helpful kid sauntered off with a $20 tip in his pocket.

By the time they were done dealing with the dishes, the auctioneer was halfway down a row of desks and armoires. Next, a row of couches were sold.

Finally, they reached the mattresses.

"I'm just gonna watch," Renee reminded Tabby.

The auctioneer tried to get an opening bid of $500 a set, but no one was interested at that level. He had to go all the way down to $100, still searching for that opening bid.

Oh, what the hell.

Renee couldn't help herself—she felt her right arm wave at the auctioneer, and he took her bid. After that, a few others jumped in the fray. Renee thought she had the bid at $240, but at the last minute, an ornery old woman gave another bid at $245.

Not today, granny.

Renee threw one last bid out there at $250.

Stop, she told herself.

But despite the efforts of the persistent auctioneer, the granny was apparently tapped.

Renee won the bid.

"Oh, *shit*," Renee half-whispered to Tabby. Was she stark-raving mad?

The auctioneer was waiting for her to declare which sets she wanted at $250 apiece. Waving her hand at two stacks of plastic-wrapped sets, she held up all the fingers of her left hand, but couldn't bring herself to say a word. She hoped others thought this was something she did all the time, no big deal. Her head was spinning.

"The lady is taking these five new mattress sets, two kings and three queens. And you, ma'am," the auctioneer said to the other bidder, "would you like any at that price?" Just like that, he'd moved on and the clerk labeled the sets with the same number as the bidding number Renee still clutched in her right hand.

"I need to sit down," she said to Tabby, and walked off, Tabby close on her heels.

"Now Renee, don't freak out," Tabby said. "You know those sets would be closer to one thousand dollars *each* retail, and all five of them are new. Even if you ultimately decide not to do anything with the resort, you could resell these individually at a profit. There are so many sets here . . . you got a great deal!"

Renee knew Tabby was right but wasn't over her mini panic attack yet. She had just spent $1,250 . . . and she didn't even have a job. The resort needed a ton of work and mattresses might not have been the wisest place to start. Sitting down wasn't helping with her lightheadedness. She started to hyperventilate. Tabby pushed Renee's head forward, down between her knees, and rubbed her back until Renee gave her a thumbs-up. Tabby stepped back.

Renee sat up, a sheepish grin on her face.

"Oh, God, Tabby, I'm so sorry I lost it there for a minute," Renee apologized. "This doesn't feel like a smart move at all right now . . . but I guess there isn't anything I can do about it at this point. I hope the bed frames at the resort will work with these mattresses. Otherwise, I'll either be switching all the mattresses out in our house, with one to spare, or I'll learn how to use Craigslist."

Tabby laughed. "If you start selling on Craigslist, let me know. I have crap I want to get rid of, too."

They meandered back to the auction. The rest of the furniture was sold off, leaving only the linens. After the furniture was gone, the crowd thinned measurably. The remaining tables were full of piles of towels, sheets, and blankets. When the auctioneer struggled to get a bid higher than $17.50 per pile, Renee raised her number to his request for $20. It was already four o'clock in the afternoon and the auctioneer was ready to be done. He hollered "Sold!" and Renee found herself again having to decide how many lots to purchase. Since she'd bought five beds, she selected ten sheet sets in king and queen sizes so she would have two sets per mattress. She also took ten sets of towels, five blankets, and five duvet covers.

And just like that, it had taken her a total of five minutes to drop another $600.

Tabby was ready for another panic attack, but surprisingly, this time Renee wasn't upset.

"I made up my mind. This was a wise investment in my property," Renee stated when Tabby looked at her questioningly.

Again, they used a cart and the same teenager to transport all of Renee's linen purchases out to her Toyota. The mattresses would have to wait. Renee was almost positive Ethan would help her out with his enclosed trailer.

The auction was quickly winding down. Tabby and Renee were starving and decided to go out for an early dinner before heading their separate ways. Renee called Ethan on her way to meet Tabby at the restaurant but got his voicemail. Figuring she better explain to him in a real conversation, she left him a short message, asking him to give her a call on Sunday.

He would probably think she was nuts. She *knew* she was nuts.

Renee turned in to the restaurant's lot and parked next to Tabby's tall white pickup. Tabby walked in with her, having used the running boards to jump down from the driver's seat. People always assumed the pickup belonged to Gary, Tabby's husband. Renee found her friend's choice of vehicle comical but also knew Tabby needed the truck for her interior design business.

The hostess showed them to a table by a crackling fire and they requested their favorite bottle of wine. Knowing they couldn't drink too much on empty stomachs, they ordered an appetizer to share and dinners of steak and potatoes.

"What a crazy day," Renee said.

Tabby nodded, laughing. "Girl, it sounds like you've had a crazy few *months*."

Renee nodded soberly, then took another sip of wine to change that. "Sharing a glass of wine and conversation with an old friend is exactly what I needed."

"So, spill it," Tabby insisted.

"Well, let's see . . . I've spent lots of time with my family . . . I experienced a once-in-a-lifetime trip to Fiji with my two favorite people in the world . . . we met extended family we never knew existed, I inherited valuable property, and I've started making changes in other areas of my life."

"Is that all?" Tabby joked before bluntly pointing out most of it wouldn't have happened if she hadn't been laid off. "So you should stop feeling sorry for yourself and recognize your many blessings, girl." Tabby took a sip of wine. "I've had my share of struggles, too, you know. Gary and I are in a good place now, but you know how bad we wanted to have kids. It just wasn't meant to be, and that was hard on us. When I couldn't get pregnant, I threw myself into my work. I was scared to death when I opened my own business, what? Five years ago?"

Renee nodded, smiling.

"There have been some lean times," Tabby continued, "but I'm finally getting some traction, and just hired my second assistant last month. It isn't always easy, but I love having my own business." She looked into Renee's eyes, holding her gaze. "What I'm trying to say is . . . don't be afraid to try something different."

"I know, I know . . . I'm scared, but I'm ready for change too."

As they sat around the fire and continued to catch up on each other's lives, Tabby shared funny stories about rich, hard-to-satisfy clients. Finally Renee had to insist Tabby stop; tears were running down her face and she was afraid she would wet her pants.

Shifting the conversation, Tabby broached the subject of the resort. Renee showed her the pictures again, taking time to tell her more about the property.

"You know," Tabby mentioned, looking closer at the photos, "I might have a few tricks up my sleeves as to how we could give the cabins and lodge an inexpensive facelift. This old furniture and the tired surfaces don't scare me." Renee shot her a skeptical look, but Tabby continued. "Paint some of the wooden pieces, maybe use a light-cream chalk paint to lighten up the interiors. The old dark-green, nubby-textured fabric on the sofas isn't that bad. If you throw on some funky pillows, it could work. Maybe you'll get lucky and find wood floors under the grungy carpet. Did you check?"

"No," Renee admitted, "I didn't think to look under the carpets. Next time."

Tabby continued with her suggestions. "Taking down the heavy drapes would let more light in. You could add simple shades for privacy. We could make the little bathrooms cute, too."

"But how can I possibly get all that accomplished on my limited budget? Not to mention my even-more-limited time?" Renee sighed. It was all so overwhelming.

"I could go out to the resort with you when it warms up, maybe in May," her friend offered. "We could spend a couple of days taking a look at all the cabins, deciding where we could have the most impact with the least amount of time and money, and put a plan in place. Obviously, this place will need to be a work-in-progress for the foreseeable future, but I think you'd be pleasantly surprised how quickly it could come together."

"You would do that for me?" Renee asked, truly touched by Tabby's offer.

"Of course! It would be fun. Kind of like a weekend at camp, but without anyone telling us what to do," said Tabby. "You know I love these types of projects. Heck, maybe I could even help you with some of the actual work, take before-and-after pictures, use them to advertise my services. I love what I do, and I'm always looking for ways to expand. I've never thought about working on lake properties."

"But I couldn't afford to pay you your normal fee," Renee said. She didn't want to dampen the conversation, but she felt it was important to be realistic.

"I would never allow you to pay me," Tabby replied, feigning a dramatically offended expression. "I wouldn't be able to devote a ton of time to the project, anyway, but let me at least contribute what I can. I think it's so cool your aunt left you that place. Why do you suppose she did?"

"I've thought a lot about that, but I'm still not sure. I certainly wouldn't be the most obvious choice. Maybe she could sense my growing dissatisfaction with my career. I don't know why she gave it to me."

They both took a sip of their wine, and Renee's mention of "career" reminded her about the job offer. "Oh, I forgot to tell you! I also have to decide whether or not to accept a job offer from MNC by Monday . . . a pretty solid company, and I'd make more than I did at my old job. But I'd have less time off and have to accrue it over time, meaning I wouldn't have anything more than weekends to spend at the lake this summer."

"It sounds an *awful* lot like what you did before . . . sure you want to go back to that type of gig again?" Tabby challenged, an eyebrow arched as she looked at Renee skeptically.

Renee shrugged in reply.

Pushing back from the table, Tabby scooped up their ticket and reached for her purse. "Well, my friend, you do have plenty of thinking to do, don't you?" She stood and gave Renee a hug. "Don't be afraid to take some chances. If something doesn't feel right, you should trust your gut. There are a million different ways to make a living. I don't want to get all sappy on you, but if something feels like it's sucking the soul right out of you, you probably don't want to commit another decade or two of your precious life to it. Don't be rash, but don't settle either." Tabby smiled warmly. "I have to say, this has been one of my more interesting Saturdays in a long time. Thanks for making it so much more than a quick buying expedition for my sister!"

CHAPTER 38

Gift of Trust

"*Hey*, sis, what's up?" It was Ethan, returning Renee's call the next morning. "What do you need with my trailer?"

"Believe it or not . . ." Renee replied, anxious about Ethan's response, "I need to pick up five mattress sets from an auction house."

"What the hell do you need with five sets of mattresses?"

"It's all Tabby's fault," Renee blurted. She was suddenly afraid to voice the fact she bought them for the resort.

Ethan laughed, making Renee sigh with relief. "That's not the first time I've heard you say that," he said. "You two still finding ways to get into trouble after all these years?"

Renee grunted. *We didn't get in* that *much trouble.*

"I went to an auction with Tabby yesterday. Turns out it was a liquidation sale for a hotel chain. They had stacks of new and next-to-new mattresses and all I could think about were the gross, musty beds at the resort, so . . . I bought some. Well, five. I bought five."

"Really? So does this mean you decided to fix up the resort?"

"I'm still trying to decide, but if yesterday was any indication, it certainly seems I'm leaning that way."

"Well, hey, I'm happy to help," said Ethan. Renee was grateful he didn't push for a more definitive answer. "My trailer is half full of tools and lumber, but I'll have the boys help me clean it out this afternoon. I can help you tomorrow, if that works for you."

"God, thanks, Ethan, you're a life-saver. Tomorrow would be great." A *beep* sounded as another call came in on her cell. "Hey, I gotta run, but

I'll call you in the morning after I find out what time they open for pick-ups. Thanks, bro!"

She looked down at the number. *Matt!* She quickly clicked over.

"Hi, Matt! How are you?"

"Tired. Just got off a long shift. Thought I'd give you a call, see how your weekend is going. Hope you're having some fun." Matt *did* sound tired.

"It has been a fun weekend. I have a friend, her name's Tabby, and she invited me to go to an auction yesterday."

"I love going to auctions," Matt said. "We used to go to farm auctions when I was a kid, and when I was doing construction, we'd go to auctions held by the county where they sold architectural salvage pulled out of old buildings. Damn, I miss renovating those old homes. You can get a hell of a deal at auctions. Just depends on the other bidders. Buy anything?"

"Actually, yes. I bought mattresses."

"You're kidding ... *used* mattresses?"

"No, not used," Renee laughed. "It was the liquidation of a bunch of hotels, so these were new. There were new and used sets for sale. I bought 'em for the resort. Then, after I bought them, I kind of lost it . . . thought it was a really stupid—*expensive*—purchase. But I've come around. Lots of beds at the resort are going to have to be replaced."

"Sounds like you might open the old place up," he said. It sounded like a question, but, like Ethan, Renee appreciated how Matt was careful not to pressure her.

"Giving it some serious consideration, but I'm still exploring my options. Oh, I almost forgot! I *did* get a decent job offer. Still trying to decide what to do about it. I'm having trouble getting excited about heading back to an office."

"Really?" Matt replied, his voice slow and measured. "I'm not surprised, to be honest. You have lots to offer a company. What kind of vacation do they have? If it isn't much, it could be years before I have the pleasure of another visit from you."

And I'm not too happy about that, Renee thought. They'd gotten closer through their regular phone chats and emails, but it wasn't the same as being able to go for a walk with him, reach out and touch him, or see his smile. She wasn't sure if he was dating, either. They hadn't talked about it, but Renee had the strong sense Matt wasn't seeing anyone else.

"Don't remind me," she groaned. "I need to make up my mind and let them know. I'll keep you posted."

"Sounds good. Anything else new?"

"Well, let's see. Talked to Julie this morning. She doesn't have too much school left. Finals the first full week of May and then she'll be home. She's stressed about not having a summer job lined up yet. I told her not to worry, she can look when she gets home."

"She should be able to find something," Matt agreed. "Hey, have you heard how that girl is doing? What was her name? Hope?"

"Close!" Renee gave a little laugh, but sobered. "Her name's Grace. Her father gives me periodic updates, but it sounds like recovery is slow. I do worry about her."

"That's tough. Robbie all healed up?"

"Oh yeah, good as new. Didn't take him long. Sometimes it's a relief to have a healthy growing boy."

Their conversation continued until Renee heard Matt yawn.

"You better get some rest."

"You're probably right. Hey, let me know what you decide about the job offer."

"Absolutely," Renee assured him, signing off so he could go to bed.

It would be so fun to see Matt again, but she didn't know how she would be able to pull that off. He was so busy with work, and her world was in an upheaval right now. She couldn't go traipsing off to Fiji anytime soon.

Robbie was at a friend's house for the evening, so Renee grabbed Molly's leash and took the dog for a walk around the neighborhood. The air was cool but the days were getting longer. Early tulips bloomed on the south side of her house. Spring was almost here. She wondered what kind of flowers might be popping up at the resort. The snow was probably gone out there by now. The weather had been warmer this week. She had only made the one trip to the resort, but, she was pleasantly surprised to admit, she was already anxious to go back.

Her night was spent tossing and turning. Renee just couldn't fall asleep. She missed Matt. She missed Jim. She missed Aunt Celia. She didn't know what to do about the job offer, and she'd dropped a huge wad of cash for the resort.

When Renee finally drifted off, her sleep was fitful.

***

She again stood on the warm sands of a beach in Matt's arms; she was so happy to be there with him. She reached up to wrap her arms around his neck, to run her hands through his dark hair—she loved the thickness, the sleek feel of it. But, as dreams often do, a shift occurred. The texture of the hair changed. She recoiled in surprise, her body stiffening. *What the hell?* She peered into the dusk, now finding herself eye to eye with Jim. *How is this possible?* She recognized that look—it hadn't changed, and her immediate response to it hadn't diminished, despite all the time that had passed—desire flaring in his piercing blue eyes. Her body registered what was happening before her mind. She relaxed against his familiar form . . . reacquainting herself with it . . . running her hands over the body she'd once known better than her own. As they collapsed on the sand in a tangle of limbs, desperate to satisfy a long-buried need, the beach of her dreamland suddenly filled with crowds of tourists and Jim vanished, again leaving her alone. Always alone, even in a crowd. Renee stood up quickly, mortified, brushing sand from her sundress, but no one paid her any attention. She walked up the beach toward a cluster of cabins. The beach changed, ground underfoot taking on the crunch of shale, her footsteps sinking slightly into the shifting, heavier dark sand . . . every step an effort. Now she was at her resort, alone on a hot summer day. She recognized the small cabins, but they looked different, fresher. Dark wood gleamed in the sunlight, trim painted an apple-red with new rust-colored shingles capping roof lines. Boats on the water filled the air with the sound of summer. But where were all the people? Why was she all alone?

The grounds were immaculately tended, green grass perfectly mowed with beds of flowers sprinkled throughout and stately trees crowned in green providing shade here and there. An empty hammock swayed softly in a summer breeze, but once the boats moved out of earshot, all was eerily quiet. The smallest cabin, tucked into the edge of the woods, appeared in stark contrast to the others; its shutters hung askew and everything had faded to a dull gray. Grass around this cabin, unlike the rest, was brown and crunchy. It was as if something inside the house had leached the life away around it. Unable to resist, Renee was slowly pulled toward the bleak structure. She stepped up on the small covered porch. Wood creaked ominously under her feet. A decrepit wicker rocker slowly creaked of its own accord in a far corner. A gentle push of the door sent it swinging silently back on its hinges. Renee was unable to make out much through the gloom inside. Not wanting to enter, but unable to stop, Renee stepped into the tiny kitchen, and the door swung closed behind her. A scratching noise, coming from the bedroom, pulled Renee deeper into the gloom. Sunlight barely penetrated filthy windows and did nothing to dispel cold, dank air. Renee stopped at the doorway to the bedroom, hit by a strong smell of rot and decay. The water-damaged wall now seemed to run with a shiny dark substance; flies buzzed in the air. The scratching, scuffling sound was coming from the bed. A quilt covered the mattress, its faded patchwork streaked with weak sunlight. *Something's under the quilt.* Stepping ever so slowly, quietly, toward the bed, Renee reached out and pinched the threadbare edge of the heavy coverlet. She tossed it back with a quick flick of her wrist and gasped in terror as a mass of chattering squirrels thrust up onto their hindquarters, interrupted from their feasting upon something lying in the middle of the bed. The enraged creatures terrified her. She spun on her heels, intent on escaping the cabin. It took so much longer to reach the small kitchen than it had to reach the bedroom. Renee was sure she heard the vermin jumping off the bed, pursuing her. She threw open the cabin door and burst back out into the sunshine, not bothering with the stairs, leaping off the porch and onto the dead grass. She ran all the way to the lodge, never looking back. Thankfully the lodge door was unlocked. Renee pushed her way in and quickly slammed the heavy wooden door behind her, collapsing against it. She could hear voices in conversation and the low strum of music from the back of the lodge. The inside of the lodge was bright and smelled of cigarette smoke with the underlying aroma of pine. Everything looked different. The collection of photos was still on the wall, but there were fewer of them and no colored shots, only the older black-and-white ones. As she approached the bar, she noticed well-stocked shelves sporting bottles of clear and amber liquid, sparkling in light reflected off the mirrored backdrop. A bearded man was wiping the counter with a dirty towel, talking to a woman with her back to Renee. The man glanced in Renee's direction, greeted her with a silent nod, and walked around the end of the bar out of sight. The woman turned slightly and patted the barstool next to her—an invitation to join her. Exhausted from her scare in the gray cabin, Renee gladly took a seat and swiveled to thank the woman. To her utter shock, she found herself looking into a familiar set of bright blue eyes. They seemed to smile at Renee, although the smile didn't reach Aunt Celia's lips. Gone were the laugh lines and wrinkles Renee had so loved, reminding her of wisdom and kind-heartedness. Celia appeared to be about Renee's age now. In front of Celia, on the counter, was an ashtray holding a smoldering cigarette with red lipstick smudged on the butt along with a neat glass of whiskey.

"I think you need this more than I do right now, honey," Celia said in that smoky voice Renee remembered so well, pushing the glass Renee's way. "Something must have given you a scare to send you rushing in here like that, white as a ghost."

Finding her dead aunt's comment ironic, Renee scooped up the glass and tossed back half its contents. She sputtered as the liquid scorched her throat, setting the glass down, and she worked to catch her breath. She waited for Celia to clue her in on whatever the hell was happening.

"This was always my favorite place to spend time," Celia finally said after sitting quietly next to Renee for a minute. "I first came here years ago, as a teenager, with a friend and her family. We spent a month here, and I fell in love. I never told anyone. We were crazy about each other, but I was heading to college in the fall and he was going into the military. We promised to write, and we did for a while, but he went overseas and the letters eventually stopped. I never knew what happened to him. I also never forgot how magical this place felt that summer. I always dreamed of coming back here, bringing a family of my own someday. Fate intervened. Circumstances were different from my idyllic dream, but I came back none the less. By then, buildings had fallen into disrepair. Many thought I was crazy—a single woman with no family of my own, taking on a project of this size? They just didn't understand. But it was always where I came to recharge my soul and restore my sanity. And everyone was wrong about me not having a family of my own. I *did* have a family. I had you and your brother and sisters, along with my siblings and other nieces and nephews. Renee, I know you're confused as to why I was inclined to leave this place in your capable hands. Trust me. I did not make the decision lightly. Notice how I once brought this old place back to life. I know, if you grace Whispering Pines with your spirit and time, it will breathe life back into you as well. Find a way to use it to give back, and you will always get more in return. I left the gray cabin untouched to serve as a reminder to me, and now to you, of what can happen to your life if you don't keep striving for more. Over time, with no attention and rejuvenation, things first turn stale and then crumble away. Don't be afraid of the light. Be afraid of stagnation and be afraid of predators. Make this place shine again. I never had enough time here . . . and I so regret it."

As Celia spoke to Renee, she visibly aged. She took on a look more familiar to Renee, but then faded away completely, leaving Renee alone again.

CHAPTER 39

Gift of the Leap

*R*enee's vivid dream stayed with her into the next morning. She felt lonelier upon waking. Her encounter in the gray cabin bothered her the most. She clearly remembered feeling empty and bereft entering that cabin. She supposed the nasty squirrel episode was prompted by their real-life encounter with the family of squirrels in the lodge, but her visions of tended lawns and freshly painted cabins sparked her interest. Everything looked so . . . fresh. *Alive.*

It had been a delight to dream about Celia. Renee missed her so much. Maybe she was finally starting to understand why Celia gave Whispering Pines to her and not someone more obvious.

She wanted to give me what she never had . . . more time to enjoy a place we both loved.

Renee *had* loved the resort as a child. She would beg her parents to let them stay an extra week each summer and bawl when it was time to go home. She specifically remembered Celia calming her as they loaded up the cars to leave.

"Honey," she'd say, "you can come back here next summer. You can come back every summer. And you wanna know a secret? Just between you and me?"

Renee would paw the tears from her eyes and look up at her larger-than-life aunt, in awe. "Yes!"

Celia would lean down, wink, and whisper only for Renee's ears, "I always hate to leave, too."

Renee knew, deep down, she needed to turn down the job offer. The job wasn't right for her.

I can't go back to corporate!

"I can't go back to corporate!" she said aloud.

***

Before she could second guess herself any longer, she made the call.

"I truly appreciate your offer," she thanked her would-be manager. "I realize it would be a great opportunity for someone . . . just not for me. My heart wouldn't be in it."

After she hung up, Renee bolted to the bathroom, afraid she was going to lose her breakfast. *Oh God, what did I do?!* She may have just thumbed her nose up at financial stability for her and her kids.

After the initial shock at her own audacity passed, Renee felt a strange sense of peace settle over her.

***

She called her dad.

"Good for you, Renee. That was a gutsy move, but I think it was the right one." George gave his daughter the reaction she needed to hear.

"I'm glad you agree, Dad. I may regret this someday, but today, it feels like the answer. I need something different . . . and flipping from a corporate job to getting an old, decrepit resort up and running . . . that's about as drastic of a change as you can get!"

"Our visit out to Whispering Pines has really got me thinking, too," George confessed. "Haven't been sleeping much. My mind spins. Weird dreams, too, like you wouldn't believe. I got lots of ideas, if you want to hear 'em."

The old place even invaded Dad's *dreams!*

"I would love to," she said. "Can you come up this week? We could brainstorm."

***

George made the trip to Renee's on Thursday. He brought their binder of ideas. They spent eight hours discussing options. They came up with a list of questions for the lawyer and made an appointment with him the following week.

This was *happening*.

Renee wanted to get the cabins back into decent condition so she could rent some of them out this summer. "We don't have to renovate all of them right away," she told her dad. "Celia gave me a little cushion with the reserve fund."

"Have you ever considered living at the resort? At least in the summer?" George asked, closely watching Renee to gauge her response.

She initially snorted at the idea. *There is no way in hell the kids would go for that!* But was that true? Why couldn't she at least talk with Robbie and Julie about the possibility?

"I know it sounds crazy," George acknowledged, seeing it in his daughter's expression. "You don't have to decide on that right away. Talk to the kids. But in the meantime, I know I can convince your mother and brother and sisters to help get the resort in . . . at least . . . *passable* . . . shape. 'Many hands,' as the saying goes."

"Dad, you know I hate asking for help."

"Honey, this time you don't have a choice. This is too big to do all on your own."

Of course he's right. Renee accepted, begrudging but grateful. This wasn't something she could pull off alone.

As the sun set, George headed home. Together they agreed to enlist everyone's help for Mother's Day weekend. If logistics worked out, Renee had lots to do between now and then. First she had to convince Robbie and Julie this wasn't a mistake. This would impact them, too, so it was important to her to get their support. Renee was afraid she might lose her nerve if the kids balked at her ideas. She thought through the pros, cons, and implications of what she was about to suggest before broaching the subject with either of them. When she felt as prepared as possible, she called Julie.

"Hi, Mom! Did you take the job?"

"No, hon, I turned it down."

"Really?" Julie was quiet for a moment as that sank in. "I was sure you would take it. You are *full* of surprises, Mom."

"Well, now that you mention it, Julie . . . I did want to talk to you about something else that might come as a surprise. Your grandfather and I have been talking."

Julie's voice sounded hesitant. "Yeah . . . ?"

"After my shock over the layoff, I vowed I would never again put our family in the position where our sole source of income was from a job working for someone else. If I accepted MNC's offer, I would have been right back in that same, scary position. Julie, honey, I am *tired* of working for a huge company where I'm a tiny fish in a big pond, where I have no control over my income. They would dictate what I earn, when and where I work, if they still need me . . . the list goes on and on."

"I know, Mom," Julie said, and she sounded sincere. "I get it."

Renee soldiered on. "Aunt Celia gave us an amazing opportunity by leaving me Whispering Pines. I want to build the resort back up into a viable business. I know Dad will help me, and so will Ethan. I want you and your brother to help, and I'm sure Mom and your aunts will help too. What do you think? You visited Whispering Pines with me over Easter, and you're an adult. I respect your opinion. Do you think I'm crazy, or do you think we could make it work?"

"Um, yes and *yes.*" Julie's voice came through the phone in emphatic bursts. "Yes, I think you're crazy! Yes, I think we could make it work, too. Seriously, Mom, I *loved* the resort. Yeah, it's pretty shabby right now, but there's *tons* of potential. To be honest, I keep thinking about our visit and how fun it could be to be out there on hot summer days. Are you thinking we could actually start renting cabins this summer, like a real resort?"

With that enthusiastic opening from her daughter, Renee launched into some of her ideas and rough timelines. Julie was excited at the prospect of living at the lake. She was wrapping up her freshman year and looking forward to time with her mother. She even missed her brother. Unlike the summer before, when she spent all her time with friends, she was ready for a change. She didn't have a summer job yet. The prospect of spending the upcoming summer working at a resort with family held plenty of appeal.

Promising to keep Julie updated on progress, Renee hung up . . . and braced herself for a similar discussion with her son.

Robbie is gonna be a harder sell than Julie. He hasn't even been out to the resort yet.

***

His initial reaction was shock.

"You've got to be kidding. Mom . . . are you *nuts?* I have my whole summer planned. I'm gonna get a job somewhere, hang with the guys, and sleep." Robbie was passing right through shock to outrage. And Renee didn't have the advantage of receiving it on the other end of a phone line, like Julie—she was sitting with Robbie at the dining room table, face to face, and Robbie's face was slowly turning redder as he let the anger out. "There is no frigging way I'm spending all summer at some resort where I don't know anybody. No . . . *way!*"

"Honey, I think the only way we're going to be able to keep the resort is if we actually live there this summer."

That was the final straw. Robbie shut down. He refused to talk about it and stormed out of the room. He wouldn't even look at her once she broke the news.

Well, that went well.

Renee quickly gave up hope they could have a civil conversation. She was more than a little frustrated at the silent treatment Robbie gave her, so she steered clear of him all afternoon. He said little at dinner and didn't come out of his room all night. His revolt gave Renee a few qualms.

Am I doing the right thing here?

Am I being fair to the kids?

***

In the morning, Robbie left for school without breakfast, muttering only that he was catching a ride.

Hoping kid number two would come around with time, and refusing to give up at the first bump in her plans, Renee spent her day putting things in motion. She had so much to learn. Initially, she was only concerned about the physical condition of Whispering Pines. She was quickly realizing there was so much more she would need to address beyond broken-down appliances and squirrels living in the lodge.

Plans were set to spend Mother's Day weekend at the resort with her extended family. Together, they would start the initial clean up and get a better idea as to what needed to be done before they could open for business.

And, surprisingly, Renee found herself . . . excited.

I can't wait to get back out there!

CHAPTER 40

Gift of Help

*R*enee was nervous about the weather forecast for Mother's Day weekend. Predictions: rain, wind, and cold.

Great.

Julie had finished finals, so Renee drove up to help her move out of her dorm. Friday afternoon, Renee and Julie picked Robbie up from school. He was still mad about the move.

"Hey there, kiddo," Renee greeted her son as he tossed his backpack in the backseat and plopped down behind Julie.

All she got in reply was a grunt.

Julie turned to partially face her brother. "Why don't you quit being such a dick?"

Robbie flipped his sister off.

"Julie . . . Robbie . . . knock it off *right* now." Renee didn't want the kids screaming at each other before they even got out of the school parking lot; experience had taught her diversion helped, so she plowed ahead: "We're going to meet everybody for an early supper. We can't do much out at the resort tonight. It still gets dark early and the power isn't on out there yet. We'll probably just get settled at the hotel after we eat and relax some."

Julie rolled her eyes at her brother but turned back around and ignored him for the rest of the trip. Renee glanced in the rear-view mirror; Robbie was sitting with a textbook in his lap, staring out at the passing scenery. Still not happy . . . but at least not fighting with his sister.

They were the last to arrive at the restaurant. Adults were at one table, kids at another.

"Hello, honey!" Lavonne rose to hug Renee. "This is going to be so fun."

"I don't know about *fun*, Mom, but I am excited," Renee said, hugging her mother back. "You haven't seen the mess out there yet."

"Nothing this family can't tackle," her mother noted reassuringly.

"Hi everybody," Renee greeted the rest of her family as she sat down next to Jess. Multiple conversations were happening at once.

Renee was just glad to be back in their midst.

***

The cousins got rowdy in the hotel pool, dunking and rough-housing. Likely annoying other guests, too. The adults relaxed in the small whirlpool.

"Here you go, guys." Val approached carrying two red solo cups. Luke followed close behind her, precariously balancing four more. "Thought we could start the weekend off with a few margaritas."

"Oh jeez, Val, you brought a friggin' blender?" Renee said with a laugh, reaching for one of the glasses Luke was juggling before he dumped the whole stack in the hot tub.

"I didn't think the whole weekend had to be all work and no play!"

"I like the way you think, sis," Ethan piped in, grimacing a little at his first sip of the tangy cocktail.

Once everyone was sufficiently waterlogged—and alcohol-logged—they headed off to their rooms.

Renee was too excited to sleep.

A low rumble of thunder echoed off in the distance and a steady wind slapped cold rain against their hotel window. The promised weather had arrived.

We are so screwed if this keeps up, Renee thought with a grimace, punching her pillow and trying to relax.

***

Old lawn chairs set out between two massive logs—fashioned into rustic benches decades earlier—provided enough seating around the fire pit for everyone. Kids were relegated to the logs so adults could rest their sore, aching bodies in the chairs. The cool night air had a definite bite.

What a day, Renee reflected, scanning the tired faces ringing the pit.

Luke worked to get the fire started to chase away the chill. "Nathan, want to help me pull some of this crap off the burn pile and keep this blaze going?" he asked of his older nephew, relatively confident the teenager wouldn't burn himself in the process.

"Lauren, your idea to stockpile all the musty old linens out here by the pit was genius," Jess complimented her daughter. "It would've been awful to lug all this crap to the dump."

"I know, right?" Lauren replied, happy to have contributed to the night's festivities. "Tonight we can have a ceremonial 'out with the old, in with the new' party!"

"Hopefully I managed to save what might still be salvageable," Lavonne added, grimacing at the massive pile. "I tucked a few old quilts and all the kitchen curtains in our trunk. Might be able to clean those up with a long, hot wash cycle and a thorough ironing. I hated to toss the drapes . . . those were so expensive back in the day. But the moths got to 'em first."

"Hey, can we have some s'mores?" one of the kids hollered.

The other cousins quickly chimed in on the request.

"You guys devoured six whole pizzas half an hour ago! How can you be hungry?" George asked, incredulous.

But the kids wouldn't be swayed. Val rummaged around in the picnic basket at her feet, found the marshmallows, and tossed two bags to Dave and Robbie to pass around.

"Come on, Gramps, you know it doesn't matter if they're full," Val reminded her father with a laugh. "It wouldn't be a proper campfire without s'mores." She balanced graham-cracker sections and chocolate bars on her lap, waiting for the kids to toast the marshmallows. More than a few of the marshmallows fell off their sticks into the flames; the make-shift skewers sagged a bit.

"*Mom*, tell Noah to stop touching my stick! He made my mellow fall off!" Jake yelled, trying to shove his brother away and stumbling when Noah didn't budge.

"Jesus, Jake, be careful!" Luke yelled, grabbing hold of his son's jacket to yank him back away from the fire.

"All right, everybody, let's settle down." Lavonne eyed the group, paying special attention to Jake and Noah. "We made it this far without anyone getting hurt."

"Speak for yourself, Mom." Ethan winced in his chair as he tried to stretch out the kink that settled into his lower back anytime he had to maneuver himself into tight spaces. "Didn't think we were ever gonna get that damn pump going. I think I tweaked my back trying to get it primed."

Luke and Ethan had battled the water pump earlier in the day; after much debate, banging on pipes, and swearing, they were eventually rewarded with belches of air, followed by a slow, rusty stream of well water trickling from the faucet in the lodge kitchen.

Renee leaned over to clap Ethan on the shoulder. "But I can't tell you how happy I was to hear that thing start to gurgle."

"Between getting the water running and the electricity working through most of the resort, I would say those were probably our biggest wins today," George pointed out. "Except for that blasted little cabin on the edge of the woods. I remember Celia used to have trouble with that cabin, too. Appliances always breaking down, roof leaking, and now we can't get the power to work back there. Renee, you're gonna have to get an electrician out here to look at it."

"Tell me about it," Robbie chimed in, rubbing his lower leg. "I smacked my shin wandering through that dark cabin, trying to find a light that'd work."

Flames licked high into the sky and sparks showered down. Since everything was still wet from the spring thaw and last night's rain, the sparks caused little concern. Nathan continued to feed the flames from the burn pile.

The weather had turned out to be perfect for an early spring day. The rain pushed through sometime during the night, leaving messy puddles but clear skies. With help from the kids, they had cut away most of the dead vegetation in the flowerbeds and picked up the trash that had been strewn around. Jess taught them to be careful of the young green shoots popping up in places. The hardy little perennials promised a decent start for the beds surrounding the lodge and cabins.

During a pause in the conversation, Renee heard George chuckle.

"What's so funny, Dad?" Renee asked.

"I was just remembering Jess's scream when she discovered that little family of squirrels in the lodge, back during our first visit out here," he replied, continuing to softly laugh at the memory.

"OK," Jess replied, defending herself, "you have to admit that was freaky."

"What squirrels, Grandpa?" Jake quickly inquired. "I didn't see any squirrels. I *like* squirrels."

"No, you didn't see any squirrels, little buddy," Ethan said. "They'd left by the time we got back this morning." He'd peeked into the corner bathroom first thing, to check on their little band of critters. Relieved to see the squirrels had moved on, he'd quickly nailed a piece of plywood over the small broken window, high in the corner, and shut the door tightly. There was a mess in the sink and on the floor—he didn't want any of the kids snooping around in there before it could be cleaned up. Given Jake's interest, he'd been right to keep his nephew away.

Jake's shoulders slumped upon learning he wasn't going to get to see any squirrels up close.

Renee cleared her throat to catch everyone's attention. "I just wanted to take a minute to thank *all* of you for your help today. We accomplished more than I could have hoped. I don't know how I will ever be able to repay you."

"Free lodging for a week or two . . . every summer . . . for life?" Val joked.

"You got it, sister!"

I wish I could help them, like they're helping me, Renee thought, looking from Ethan, to Jess, to Val.

Other than a brief conversation after New Year's to share what each of them received from Celia, no one else had said too much yet about their gifts. Renee knew all three were grappling with what to do with their inheritances. Similar to Renee's predicament, all of their gifts were complicated. Ethan received their aunt's beautiful old Victorian home but also a portfolio of other residential and commercial properties; already busy running his own construction firm, and going through a nasty divorce, he wasn't sure what to do with the properties, most of which came with a mortgage. Jess was deeded a large portion of Celia's stock portfolio; within this portfolio, they were surprised to find out Celia had been a not-so-silent partner in three different companies. Val's gift of a substantial sum of money came with strings attached: she could only use the funds for certain expenses, none of which included anything that would directly benefit her kids or husband.

But everyone was too tired tonight to discuss what they were planning to do with their bequests; Renee mentally filed the topic away for a conversation at a later date. She *would* help them, too.

Older cousins started to tell spooky stories and cast furtive glances into the woods; the trees now seemed to press closer against the ring of light cast by the fire. Noah and Logan, tired from the long day, subtly shifted positions to sit closer to Grandma Lavonne. Jake crawled up onto Val's lap, whimpering a little.

"Momma, are there ghosts out there?" the young boy asked, pointing a chubby little finger toward the towering black trees behind them, rubbing a sleepy eye with his other hand.

Val hugged her youngest closer. "No, baby, there are no such thing as ghosts."

Jake snuggled in, too tired to react to her calling him "baby."

The stories even had Renee glancing out into the woods. *I wonder what might be lurking out there,* she thought, not necessarily believing Val's declaration that ghosts didn't exist. The long day had her exhausted and jumping at shadows. She remembered feeling like this as a child too, never completely convinced that the woods held only trees and friendly little animals.

Once the burn pile was depleted and the shrinking flames failed to keep the cold at bay, it was time to call it a night. Ethan dumped water on the remaining embers, not wanting to take any chances. Once again, their caravan headed out, this time away from Whispering Pines.

I need to ask Ethan to check and see if he can fix that decrepit sign tomorrow, Renee reminded herself when her headlights glanced off the sign as she turned onto the paved highway.

As the last of their tail lights faded away, a flashlight blinked on in the woods behind the smallest cabin.

CHAPTER 41

Gift of Assistance

Sunday dawned cold and gray.

Everyone trekked back to the resort and work continued. Val brewed coffee (and heated a saucepan of apple cider for the non-coffee drinkers). A box of fresh muffins and doughnuts kept the workers fueled. Work picked up where they left off the day before.

The cabins had wall-to-wall green shag carpet in the living rooms. A good shampoo might have gotten rid of the grunge inevitably deposited into the carpet fibers over the years, but Renee was doubtful. Jess helped her pull up a corner of rug to peak underneath—no easy task, as it was tacked down. To their delight, they could see hardwood floors beneath. Renee decided to take a chance: the nasty carpet had to go. They quickly pushed furniture out of the way. Using muscle and an occasional crow bar, Renee and Jess pulled up the carpet in the first cabin. Julie and Lauren followed behind, prying up old tack strips so no one would impale a foot. Together the four of them managed to wrestle the heavy, unwieldy roll out onto the grass. After the carpet was out, Jess swept up debris left behind. Once the floor was laid bare, they took a closer look. Hardwood ran throughout. It was far from perfect, but at least there were no holes. There were stained areas here and there, probably caused by spills seeping through carpet, never properly cleaned up. The wood also ran under the edge of the linoleum in the kitchen. Renee was tempted to remove the linoleum too, but she worried she might have used up her luck. No telling if the hardwood covered the whole kitchen floor; it might, but the linoleum wasn't in bad shape and would be easier to maintain where spills were more likely. She'd have to pick up some strips of either metal or wood and tack down the edge of the linoleum to the wood floor; the previous strips had been ripped out with the carpet.

Sweaty and dirty from work in the first cabin, everyone shifted to the second and followed the same process. This time, they found a problem: In front of the fireplace, a section of the hardwood had been cut out and replaced with plywood. A log must have rolled out at some point and damaged the wood. The patch would be tough to conceal with the carpet out. Despite the issue in the second cabin, Renee was glad the old carpet was out. Now all the floors were either wood or linoleum throughout and would be easier to clean. She would have to research how best to deal with the patched floor in the second cabin.

Their last project of the day was to clean one of the duplexes. Because the east unit had been better maintained, Renee and the kids would use that one over the summer. The west unit was going to need repairs. Unfortunately, the stove wouldn't heat up in the east unit, but the stove next door worked fine. Luke and Ethan pulled out the broken stove and Renee cleaned up the grunge accumulated behind it. Nathan and Robbie muscled the stove out of the other unit and into Renee's side. Now she had a gold-colored stove paired with an avocado fridge and sink. But as long as all three worked, that was all she cared about right now. *I can deal with a psychedelic kitchen*, Renee assured herself. It would only be for the summer.

The kids were troopers throughout Saturday and part of Sunday, but eventually they'd had enough. "Julie, can you take the boys down to the lake and show them how to skip rocks?" Val suggested, tired of listening to her sons whine.

"You bet, Val. Come on, whoever wants to get in on a little rock skipping competition, follow me," Julie instructed, taking Jake by the hand and leading a line of her cousins down to the water's edge.

It was colder right next to the lake, but they didn't care. She gave the younger cousins a quick lesson. "Here guys, find the flattest, smoothest rocks you can. Now hold them in your hand like this." She modeled for them how to hold the rocks and flick their wrists to get the most skips. After some frustrating first attempts, they got the hang of it.

Then the contest was on.

***

Val and her troop were the first to head home. The boys were filthy and still had homework. Ethan finished securing all the junk—including the musty old mattresses—loaded onto his trailer. He offered to take it to the dump Monday and promised to hand the bill over to Renee to pay for the disposal. Jess had ridden over with Lavonne and George but jumped in with Lauren and Nathan for the drive home. Once everyone else was gone, Renee, George, and Lavonne gathered in the lodge kitchen. Julie was outside on the phone with someone and Robbie was studying algebra on the picnic table they had used to eat on throughout the weekend.

"It's *crazy* how much we accomplished," Renee said to her parents as she sagged into an old wooden chair. "I can almost believe we'll be ready to start renting cabins this summer. It won't take much more to get Cabin #1 and Cabin #2 ready for renting. I still need to make sure I have all the legal work done and the proper insurance. But it's starting to feel *real.*"

Renee hated to head back to the city—she wanted to keep getting ready.

We've barely touched the lodge yet, or the duplex, she thought, groaning to herself.

Sensing Renee's impatience, George offered to meet her back here next Friday, as soon as Robbie was out of class.

Lavonne had a better idea.

"Why don't Renee and Julie drive over and meet you here Friday morning? I can drive over to their house sometime on Friday and be there when Robbie gets home from school. We would probably wait and drive over Saturday morning."

"Mom, if you're sure you don't mind, that would be awesome. I'm afraid we won't have anything ready to rent in June if we only spend two days a week out here. We made lots of progress this weekend, and I so appreciate everyone's help, but there is still a lot of work to do," Renee said.

She grimaced as she raised her arms to hug her parents. She wasn't used to so much physical work, and her muscles screamed. George returned her hug, then stood back, shaking his head at her.

"What?" Renee asked, eyes narrowed at her father, head tilted.

"You remind me of Celia, with your determination to get this place up and running. I'm starting to see the wisdom in my sister's decision."

Renee smiled "You know, Dad, I'm starting to understand it all a bit better myself."

CHAPTER 42

Gift of Competition

*R*enee hit a snag. Because the old lodge used to have a bar, she figured she should get it up and running again. So it came as quite the surprise when she learned getting a liquor license was more time-consuming and expensive than she'd initially thought.

Jess called to check on their progress and Renee shared this news with her.

"Renee, I don't think this is bad news," Jess said. "First, scrap the notion of trying to get a bar up and running this first summer. You have plenty of other issues to work through. Second, I want you to think about what kind of atmosphere you want to promote at the resort. Do you want a family atmosphere? Or do you want to cater to sportsmen, more apt to want to kick back with buddies and drink at the end of the day? If you plan to live at the resort this summer with Julie and Robbie, without a grown man around all the time, maybe a bar is a bad idea. There are plenty of other bars in the area. People will sometimes want to drink in the cabins, or around the fire pit or beach, but there's nothing saying you have to sell the alcohol at the resort."

"You know, I hadn't thought about it like that, Jess. It probably isn't realistic to think I can turn this place into a destination offering a bar or a restaurant this first summer," Renee mused, appreciating her insight. "If customers show a desire for amenities like that, we can work it into our longer-term business plan."

Jess posed great questions and Renee realized she needed to figure out the answers. She promised to keep Jess in the loop and thanked her again for all her help.

Julie volunteered to work on a website for the resort.

"Mom, I found a company we can hire to help us set up a site and incorporate an online reservation system. They aren't cheap, but they have great reviews, and I really think we need to make an investment here."

"Oh man, Julie, I just don't know if I can *afford* that right now. I need to be really careful where I spend my money," Renee replied, concern evident in her eyes. "Can't you just work with one of those free templates to get us started?"

Julie threw up her arms in exasperation. "You've got to be kidding, Mother! Don't you understand how important our online presence is? Customers expect a fully functioning website. They don't want to have to talk to someone. They want to go online day or night, look at pictures, read reviews, and book a cabin immediately if they like what they see. If we don't capture them when they're interested, because our website is crap, we risk losing them to the next resort they find online." Julie stopped to catch her breath, hoping she was convincing Renee this was *not* optional. "We need to be able to capture renter information, too, so we can add them to our mailing list. We'll want to build up a clientele we can rely on to come back, summer after summer."

She has some valid points, Renee had to admit to herself, eyeing her daughter in a new light. There were definite benefits to incorporating Julie's ideas. They would need the website to share their story and attract the right type of clientele, too. *Maybe I really don't have a choice. Julie is probably right. I can't afford to take the cheap route.*

Julie and Renee spent a day surfing websites of other resorts in the area, taking notes on how their competition positioned themselves. Some sites were user-friendly, with enticing descriptions along with positive customer reviews. Other websites were not as well-constructed and had out-of-date information or boring pictures and narrative. They made notes of what they liked and didn't like on other sites.

Thursday morning, they sat down together again. Renee started the conversation with her description of what she thought their "perfect customer" would be like.

"Resorts around here talk up the wonderful fishing, but I don't have an interest in catering to fishermen. Same with hunters. It feels too . . . foreign. It would be fun to see kids fish for pan fish off the dock, but offering guide services or fish cleaning holds no appeal for me. When I think about the type of people I want to see enjoy a vacation at Whispering Pines, I picture parents with their kids, or maybe even extended families coming for reunions. Maybe we could offer packages for honeymooners or couples celebrating anniversaries. Maybe even girls' weekends. Have you heard about those tour companies that plan the whole trip for their guests without telling them exactly where they're going or what they'll be doing? How fun would it be to position ourselves as one of their stops?"

Julie laughed at her mother as she got more animated, eyes bright as she listed idea after idea. Both agreed families would be their focus. They would position Whispering Pines as a place for a peaceful vacation. They needed to get a couple of cabins photo-ready as soon as possible. Outside pictures could be updated as the summer progressed and flowers and shrubbery filled in. They talked price points. Costs would be figured in, but they would use estimates until they had some history.

"Mom, we have to be careful not to set the price too high, or we'll have some serious vacancies this first summer," cautioned Julie. "Summers are short here, so we want to be as full as possible. I collected rates for two-bedroom cabins at nearby resorts and noted significant points about each. I think we aim for rates in the top half of what we are seeing, but not *at* the top. If we go too low, we might not get the type of clientele we want."

Renee sighed with relief at her daughter's attention to detail. "Bless you, child," she said, and they both laughed.

After more discussion, they agreed on their starting rates. Adjustments would be made as they learned more, but they needed a place to start.

Julie helped her decide on many of the details Renee had been stewing about since making the decision to reopen the resort. It helped to have someone to bounce ideas off and Julie proved to be a useful sounding board. She was interested in how best to market their new enterprise and wanted to learn alongside Renee.

I can't believe how fast she is growing up, Renee thought as she sat watching her daughter articulate a point. *I couldn't have guessed how accepting Celia's gift would allow us to work together like this. This is going to be so much more fun than being holed up in an office all summer while Julie worked at some boring, part-time gig—which was exactly what would have happened if not for the resort.*

If not for Celia.

CHAPTER 43

Gift of Expertise

"*I* love these cute little cabins," Tabby exclaimed when they arrived at Whispering Pines the following week. "They have so much potential. How much time and how much money do we have to work with?" she asked, a Cheshire-cat grin on her face as she spun a slow circle in the kitchen of the first cabin, taking it all in.

"We have very little of either," Renee reminded Tabby with a more restrained grin. "That is exactly why I brought you out here, my miracle-worker friend. If anyone can help me spiff this place up fast and on the cheap, you can!"

They spent the remainder of their first day planning how to do exactly that.

Julie stayed home with Robbie. She would work on their website while Renee was gone. She had spent two solid weekends at the resort cleaning and scrubbing and was more than willing to sit this round out.

"Stripping, sanding, and staining these bad boys will take too long," Tabby explained. They hadn't yet come to an agreement as to what to do about the beat-up floors. "They aren't in great shape to begin with, especially in the second cabin. Trust me, we need to lighten up in here, and I know exactly how we should do it."

Renee sighed. "How?"

Tabby flashed that Cheshire-cat grin again. "I had a crazy-ass client a couple months back who actually had beautiful hardwood floors throughout her house, but she lived with floors like that as a kid, and hated the thought of keeping them dusted and polished. She hired me to distress and paint her floors to match a picture she ripped out of a high-end decorating magazine. I thought she was a lunatic. Who does that to perfectly good floors?"

After a pause for dramatic effect, Tabby continued.

"But I tell you, Renee, I was *shocked* at how good they looked, and it was relatively quick and easy. We took the woman's rooms from traditional to chic, despite my doubts. We could do the same here." Seeing Renee's still-dubious expression, Tabby added, "Look, if you hate it, we can try something else later when we have more time."

"Oh, all right, Tabby," Renee caved. "You're the expert, not me. So I'm going to trust you on this one."

"Great! You won't regret it, Renee, I promise. We'll do the treatment on the floors right before we leave. It will take time for them to dry since it's still chilly. We need to brighten these up, too," Tabby insisted, motioning to the walls, currently a dingy green. "Thank *God* they aren't covered in wallpaper or paneling. A fresh coat of paint is all these need. The floors will be a light gray . . . I think we should use a soft taupe with gray undertones on the walls and paint the trim white. We don't have time to do anything more with the kitchen cupboards other than give them a good scrubbing, unless you want to change out the hardware."

"I like that," Renee agreed, jotting notes quickly to keep up with Tabby's suggestions.

"Why don't we price out new faucets? Your sinks are fine, but the faucets are rusty and they drip. And the light over the kitchen sink is *atrocious.* An updated fixture would be an easy fix. Make a note of all the outlet covers and light switches—we need to update them. These are yellowed and have to go. Pro-tip: sketch the shapes, 'cause you won't remember exactly what you need if you don't."

She continued to make her way through the cabin, Renee following close behind with her clipboard. Tabby pulled out her flipbook of paint samples. Together they picked colors for all the rooms. It was important to coordinate paint throughout since all rooms were visible to each other. Old lamps would be spruced up with spray paint and they decided to tear the stained linen off the shades, leaving the metal exposed for what Tabby claimed was an "eclectic look."

The cabins needed accessories, too, Tabby explained. New pillows and throws on the old furniture would help give them the look they were after, but they would have to be savvy shoppers. There were no mattresses in either cabin yet. The old ones had been hauled off and her new auction purchases were still in Ethan's shop. Renee and Tabby positioned two cots in the living room of the first cabin, thinking a fire in the fireplace would help with the May chill. Neither of them knew how to work the fireplace, but how hard could it be? It wasn't difficult to get the fire started, but they forgot to open the flue, and the cabin quickly filled with smoke. Amidst coughing, sputtering, and giggling at their own stupidity, they figured out the problem and quickly flung open windows and doors to clear the air. This was before they opened a bottle of wine. The giggling continued as they gorged themselves on junk food and vino, having skipped dinner. They talked well into the night.

Matt called earlier that afternoon and Renee had excused herself to go outside and talk. She updated him on the changes they were contemplating to the cabins. Renee didn't say anything to Tabby after the call. Tabby didn't ask at the time, but later, when they were curled up in their sleeping bags and the wine was gone, she asked who called earlier.

Renee said nothing at first, considering how much to share. Julie and Robbie had met Matt, but she didn't think they knew she kept in contact with him since their trip.

"It isn't a big deal, Tabby. When we were in Fiji, I made a new friend, and we still talk once in a while. "

Renee was purposely vague, but Tabby was no dummy. She caught Renee's slight hesitation.

"Come on, spill it. Who is this 'friend'? And why am I just hearing about this now?"

Renee rolled her eyes. *Classic Tabby.* "Geez, Tabby, it truly isn't a big deal. We were tired and hungry after our long flight, we rented a car to drive to our resort but stopped at a hamburger stand on the beach, we were excited to take our first steps in the ocean and to finally get food, and I accidently locked my keys in the rental. I wasn't sure what to do and was on the verge of panic. Just so happened, though, that the local sheriff pulled in the lot and helped us out. After that, I ran into him a few more times on the island."

"The *sheriff*," Tabby teased.

Renee laughed. "His name is Matt. We had a nice visit, and I enjoyed the little bit of time I spent with him, but our trip was short. I didn't expect to ever talk to him again."

Tabby sensed Renee shrugging on her cot, even though she couldn't see her in the dim light from the embers.

"But . . . ? Come on, Renee. Why did he call you today if that's all there was to it?"

Knowing Tabby wasn't going to drop it, Renee sighed and continued.

"Shortly after we got home, a bouquet of flowers arrived, along with a nice card from Matt. He suggested we keep in touch and included his contact information. We emailed each other a few times, and I called him about something that came up with Robbie. He helped me out, we talked some more, and now I guess we're in the habit of talking once a week or so."

"Did you have sex?"

"Jesus, Tabby, I can't believe you asked me that!"

"Come *on*, Renee, you are a grown woman and you were on a beautiful island over New Year's. You hit it off with some guy. It's a logical question."

Renee laughed despite herself. "You never cease to amaze me, Tabby. All right, fine—to answer your *rude* question, no, we did not have sex."

Tabby was silent, but it was clear she didn't believe this.

Renee finally added, "We were interrupted."

"*What?*" Tabby yelped, flipping the light on and scrambling for her glasses. "Tell me more, I want details, details!"

Now Renee was laughing wholeheartedly. It had been years since she spilled about her sex life to a girlfriend, and it was somehow . . . a relief.

"The kids and I were eating crab rolls on the beach near the end of our vacation. They finished and wandered off. Matt happened by. He joined me, ate his dinner, and then invited me for a walk. I wanted to give the kids some space, so I agreed—"

"Yeah, I'm sure that's all you wanted," Tabby said, giggling.

Renee laughed. "Do you want to hear the story or not?"

Tabby put a hand over her mouth to stem the flow of giggles, then waved her hand in the "go on, go on" gesture.

"He showed me his place, we talked some more, then we took a walk down to a fabulous moonlit beach. But before we could do much more than some hot and heavy making out, like a couple of teenagers, duty called. Literally. A girl was missing and Matt had to go into work right away. The case kept him busy, so we didn't get a chance to see each other again before I left."

"Oh, man, that is so unfair! Do you think you'll see him again?"

"I don't see how," Renee lamented, her mood shifting. "It isn't like I can afford to go to Fiji anytime soon, and his work keeps him busy. Maybe, if he would come back here to the States to visit family, we could arrange it, but we haven't talked about it. We're enjoying our talks, and maybe it would amount to more if we lived near each other, but we don't. I don't know if he's dating anyone else at all. Like I said, he's a friend, and we talk. I would be interested in more if it was feasible, but I don't see how it could be. That's why I never mentioned him."

"Remember, my friend, 'where there's a will, there's a way,' " was Tabby's response.

I have plenty of will, but no conceivable way, Renee pondered as she lay there in the dark.

Quiet descended after Renee's confession and both eventually drifted off to sleep. It had been a full day.

***

Morning meant shopping—it simply wouldn't be a girls' weekend without it. And so, list in hand, Renee headed into town with Tabby. There was a decent-sized hardware store at the end of Main. After purchasing things off their list, coffee and breakfast were next.

"I saw a little diner in the middle of the street a block down," Tabby said. "I would kill for a gooey caramel roll and a cup of strong black coffee. It'll be ten by the time we're done eating, and a couple of those cute little shops should be open by then."

The diner had a glass-fronted cabinet under the cash register filled with baked goods, much to Tabby's delight. Sugar and coffee helped clear the little cobwebs left in their brains from their bottle of wine the night before. A couple ibuprofens each would take care of their sore backs. Sleeping on camp cots had been more comfortable when they were kids.

After breakfast, they got back to their shopping. A bell chimed as they entered the first little boutique through a pale pink door. The air smelled like fresh springtime; pretty knickknacks filled shelves and covered tabletops. As Renee had anticipated, prices were on the high side. In a back corner, a bin full of throw pillows was tucked under a clearance table. At 75 percent off, Renee had to have them. They would liven up the dark green couches in the living rooms.

The second boutique offered more beautiful things. There was a quaint picture of a lone seagull standing on a beach, framed in white, perfect for one of the small bathrooms. Renee couldn't pass it up, and Tabby wasn't about to let her either.

Walking back to the truck, Tabby noticed a thrift store down one of the side roads.

"Come on, Renee, you never know what we might find." Tabby was partway down the block before Renee could stop her.

Entering this shop was a completely different experience. The air smelled musty, and the place was jam-packed, floor to ceiling, with junk. A table of brightly colored plates and bowls caught Renee's eye. *These would look so much better than the chipped, mismatched junk in the cabins now.*

The dishes were also cheap. Renee couldn't pass them up.

"I'll go get my truck, Renee, while you finish up."

By the time everything was loaded in the truck and they got back to the resort, it was early afternoon. A pickup and trailer were parked in the lot in front of the lodge. Ethan was lounging against his bumper, smirking at them as they drove in. Their pickup was packed full, and he could tell how they had spent their morning.

"Come on, ladies, help me muscle these damn mattresses out of my trailer and into the cabins. I hope you have some food around here to feed the poor starving help."

The rest of the day passed quickly. Ethan's timing was perfect. He helped them unload all of their purchases after they placed the five mattress sets. Even though they hadn't been expecting him, the soup and fresh bread they picked up from the diner after breakfast fed all three of them. He stayed and helped paint the walls in the first cabin.

"I have the kids tonight, so I have to head out," Ethan shared as the shadows started to stretch across the grounds. "You've made lots of progress out here. I'm almost proud of you, little sis," he semi-complimented his sister with an easy punch to her shoulder. Catching him in a quick hug, she thanked him again for all of his help and sent him on his way.

Knowing they had to head back the following day, she and Tabby spent another few hours painting in the other cabin, wanting to get as much done as possible. Renee made up new beds in Cabin #1—another night on the cots might have left them both in traction. This time they called it an early night, exhausted from their second full day.

***

Sometime during the night, something woke Renee.

She sat up in bed, startled and disoriented. Had the door just creaked? Maybe Tabby got up to use the bathroom.

But the sound seemed to have come from outside.

Moonlight streamed through the window beside her bed. Old curtains had been ripped down, but new ones still needed to be hung. Slowly she leaned over the side of the bed to look out the bare window. The moon illuminated the area in front of her window, but it wasn't strong enough to chase all the shadows away.

She was too chicken to get out of bed. Trying to convince herself it was nothing more than her imagination, she lay back down. Everything was dead quiet now, except for the ticking of an old wall clock out in the kitchen and soft snoring coming from Tabby's room—so maybe she hadn't just gone to the bathroom.

Throwing the covers up over her head, Renee willed herself back to sleep.

CHAPTER 44
Gift of New Beginnings

"*I* think we're safe to open up our website to accept reservations," Renee declared when Julie meandered into the kitchen. "We don't have too much left to do in the first two cabins to get them ready. Tabby helped me take some interior shots we can post. Look at these."

Julie rubbed her eyes and pushed her hair back as she shuffled up to her mom at the kitchen island. Renee had already fed Robbie a big breakfast before he left for school. His final exams started today. In three days, he would be done with school and the three of them, along with Molly, would pack up and head to the resort for the summer.

"Mom, I had faith in you and Tabby. I already have two tentative reservations lined up for the first two weeks of June."

Renee jumped off her stool and caught Julie up in her arms, swinging her around the kitchen. Julie laughed.

"It's happening, honey—we're doing this! Thank you, thank you, *thank you*! I couldn't do this without you." She let go of her daughter. "Now if only your brother were more excited. He still seemed ticked at me this morning. I thought he would come around by now."

"Mom, don't worry about him. He's just pissed he can't spend his summer here, playing pickup basketball games and hanging out with his friends. Plus, I think he might like someone. He was texting more than usual, and a group of them went to a movie Saturday night when you were gone. He asked me if the shirt he had on looked all right before he left. *Dead* giveaway."

Renee raised her eyebrow at Julie. "How so?"

Julie stared at her mom expectantly. "Mom, he *never* cares about what he wears. I asked him straight out, but, of course, he didn't answer."

Renee groped behind her for her stool, sinking back down on it with a sigh. Robbie hadn't shown much interest in girls before.

"Wow . . . I hope I'm doing the right thing here. I want all of us to be happy about this."

Julie brought the coffee pot over to the island and refilled Renee's cup.

"Give it some time, Mom. Robbie will come around. It's only for a few months. Besides, we'll be so busy, the summer will fly by and we'll all be back here before he knows it."

"Oh, honey, I hope you're right. Robbie hasn't talked much since I made this decision about the resort."

Julie filled her own coffee cup and pulled leftover pancakes from the fridge, tossing them in the microwave. Her mom's cell rang and Renee excused herself to take the call. Julie could hear her laughing at whatever the caller said. She figured it must be Tabby. Those two had been talking constantly as they worked on the resort.

Julie plopped down at the island with her warmed-up breakfast. She'd worked hard these past few weeks, learning as much as she could about building websites. She lost herself for hours at a time online, going to other websites to see what seemed to work and what didn't. She wanted to help her mom make this work. She was no accountant, but she was worried getting their five cabins rented out as soon as possible—and keeping them rented out all summer—still wasn't going to bring in enough money for her mom to make a living from the place. She wasn't exactly sure how much money Renee had in savings, or what the arrangements were in Aunt Celia's will. Either way, she had already resigned herself to the fact there probably wouldn't be much in the way of income for herself this summer. Renee wouldn't be able to do this without her, and her mom probably wouldn't have extra money to pay her, either, which was fine by her. She was determined to trust it would work out and do what she could to help.

Renee came back into the kitchen, smiling about something. "Sorry about that, honey . . . what were we talking about?"

Julie looked at her. "Who was that, Mom?"

"Oh, just a friend, curious about how things are coming along at the resort. So do you think Robbie will be OK with all of this?"

Their conversation continued, but Julie hadn't missed how her mom sidestepped answering her question about the phone call. Renee was usually an open book with Julie, so this was new.

Maybe it was nothing.

***

Together they started packing for their summer move. Renee made arrangements with the young couple next door to check on the house and keep the lawn mowed. They were expecting their first child, and were excited at the prospect of earning extra money.

Renee hoped the living conditions in the duplex would be tolerable. All they did to this point was clean it. At least there were three small bedrooms—it would have been almost impossible for the kids to share a room at their ages. Renee would have loved nothing more than to start ripping all the old, outdated décor out of the duplex too, but there was neither time nor money for that yet.

By Thursday, Robbie was done with finals and they were almost ready to make their official move. Renee had made two trips over to the lake throughout the week, taking boxes and food over. There was no way they would have gotten it all in one trip. Renee's SUV was packed tight. Molly rode on Robbie's lap in the back seat. Her kennel took up too much room, so they'd disassembled it to make it fit. They would make further trips if needed later, but it would be a while.

Their first guests were scheduled to arrive on Monday afternoon. Renee's nerves were stretched taut. There was so much to do. Panic was starting to set in.

As the kids made one last check of the house, not wanting to forget anything, Renee took a cup of coffee onto the back patio. She needed to breathe. So much had changed over the past months . . . A year ago today, she would have been sitting in her office, probably on a conference call talking about what they could do to boost sales. She wouldn't have been able to be outside, enjoying the warm sunshine on her face. She wouldn't have been scared to death, like she was right now, but she also wouldn't have been excited or invigorated, either.

I'll make this work, she thought. *I have to. Remember your journal entries,* she reminded herself.

When she was packing her room the night before, she came across her journal. Since Christmas, she'd been faithful about journaling, up until she got so busy on the resort. She hadn't made an entry for a while, but her earlier entries served to remind her why she was doing all this. It would have been easier to go to work for someone else in an office somewhere. She would have earned a regular paycheck—barring another layoff—but she would have been right back to exchanging her time for money on the endless corporate treadmill. She was determined to do everything she could so she would never have to go back to a corporate job.

CHAPTER 45

Gift of Summer

*D*espite her previous resolve, when Monday morning arrived Renee would have given anything to be sitting at her old desk with nothing more than a monotonous day of meetings stretching before her. Now she was on the phone with her ornery plumber.

"Please, Burt, I know squeezing me into your already busy schedule is asking a lot, but I would *really* appreciate it if you could manage to drive out right away. I have a bit of an emergency." Renee tried to work her charms, desperate to get the old coot to come back out . . . again. He'd already been out and fixed a water heater for her. Guests were arriving mid-afternoon, and having no running water in Cabin #2 wasn't an option. "I made fresh rolls this morning," Renee threw in just as Burt was starting to give her his sob-story about already being behind schedule.

It worked.

"Oh for Christ's sake . . . all right . . . I'll be there in twenty minutes. Better have some coffee brewed up to go with that roll," he ordered, hanging up before she could reply.

Renee had to trust him to keep his word. Both cabins still needed to be stocked with the dishes she bought at the thrift store and the linens from the auction. Thankfully her dad had mowed, but the walkways were in tough shape from the weekend's rain and wind.

Renee rousted both kids out of bed and got them moving. Julie could do the stocking and Robbie the outside work; Robbie couldn't be trusted to get the right sets of dishes or towels set up, but he could run a hose and broom, even if he wasn't excited about it.

***

"Welcome!" Renee greeted their first customers when they pulled into the lodge parking lot five hours later. *Ready as we'll ever be,* Renee assured herself, making sure she had a welcoming smile on her lips. "Thank you for choosing Whispering Pines. We are so happy to be your hosts this week. My name is Renee Clements."

And she was officially in business.

The woman approached her, hand extended. "Hello, Renee. Nice to meet you. We're the Blacks from South Dakota. My name's Brenda, and that's my husband, Hank, back there with his head buried in the pickup box. We picked up bait on the way so the kids could fish, but Hank took your corner a little hot coming off the main road and we heard stuff shift in the back. He's worried the minnows might have spilled."

"Actually, we got lucky," the man said as he slammed the tailgate shut and wiped his hands on his pants before also shaking Renee's hand. "Little water sloshed out, but no big spill."

A girl climbed out of the extended cab just as Hank made his pronouncement. She looked a couple years younger than Robbie. "Oh, that's just *great,* Dad! There better not be any slimy fish water on my suitcase," she declared, stomping around behind the truck and again opening the back.

"Jeez, chill, Ashley, I'm sure your precious little suitcase is just fine," another kid said as he exited the truck from the other side, his voice laced with sarcasm.

"Excuse our children, Renee," Brenda apologized. "We've been stuck in the pickup for *far* too long today."

"Don't worry about a thing. Why don't you come on in? We can take care of some paperwork and then I can show you to your cabin. I'm sure you want to get settled and relax a bit."

I feel just like LuLu, Renee thought, remembering their spunky little host in Fiji. *Now I'm the host!*

As Brenda and Hank followed her into the lodge, she turned back to them and added quietly: "Don't worry about the kids. I have two of my own. I'm used to the drama."

Renee was pleased when she didn't fumble with the check-in process. Soon after she showed the Blacks to their cabin, a second vehicle pulled in.

Round two!

***

Her second group of renters was another family of four, a blended family named the Ortons. Sylvia and Barry were still newlyweds, married just six weeks earlier. Each had a ten-year-old son. This trip was meant to help them start feeling like a true family. Renee's first impression of the boys was that neither was thrilled to be there. She hoped a week at Whispering Pines might quickly change that.

It didn't take long for the two families to start interacting. By the second day, Renee spied all three boys out on the dock, fishing for sunfish. Ashley kept to herself, sitting in a lawn chair reading or playing with her phone. *Hope they have an unlimited data plan,* Renee thought with a grimace. That girl was constantly on her phone. Renee hadn't considered offering Wi-Fi throughout the resort . . . she might have to add that to the list.

There were no major issues throughout the week and everyone seemed to enjoy themselves. Renee and the kids hauled split wood closer to the pit so their guests could enjoy a campfire. The Blacks used the pit the first night and the Ortons the second. The third evening was drizzly, so all was quiet. By the fourth night, both families were out around the fire pit together, visiting long into the night.

At checkout, Hank complimented Renee. "You're doing a hell of a job bringing this old place back to life, Renee. Now Brenda wants to go home and mimic your floors at our house! We'll be in touch to book with you again next summer. We can't wait to see what you do with the old lodge."

The Ortons dawdled, reluctant to leave. Their boys seemed to be getting along better than when they first arrived, and Renee couldn't help but feel a small surge of victory. She flashed back to her childhood days at Whispering Pines, playing with Ethan, Val, and Jess down on the beach.

A kid would have to work hard not *to have fun around here!*

***

She had similar results in her second week of business. Renters showed up, had fun, did no damage, paid, and left happy.

Week three was supposed to consist of two full cabins, and Cabin #3 would be officially listed for rent. But things went haywire.

"Where the hell are they?" Renee asked Julie when the renters for Cabin #2 hadn't shown up by 5:00 p.m. "No calls, no cancelations, nothing!" She didn't expect Julie to answer; she was just venting her frustrations to relieve the stress. Renters for Cabin #1 had arrived two hours early, before the cabin was ready, and had complained to Renee about one thing after another since their arrival. On top of it all, Renee accidently knocked the faucet loose in the bathtub when she was cleaning the cabin they were getting ready to start renting, so Julie had to make it unavailable on their website until they could get Burt out for a *third* time.

Renee groaned. *Imagine how many fresh rolls and coffee he'll want this time.*

The one set of renters never did show up, and the week didn't get any better. By Tuesday, Renee was learning what it was like to deal with customers that would never be satisfied, no matter how hard she tried to make it an enjoyable experience or how much she catered to their every whim. The beds weren't comfortable, the husband and wife said; the water wasn't hot enough, the beach wasn't properly raked—it went on and on. By Saturday, it took all of Renee's strength to be civil with them.

"Ms. Clements, we suspect you realize how *deeply* disappointed we have been in our accommodations this week," Mr. Brimley said as he turned in the cabin keys the morning they were to leave, with a look on his face Renee usually reserved for scolding toddlers. "My wife suffers from terrible arthritis and couldn't *possibly* sleep in that bed. You may want to explore obtaining higher-quality mattresses for your facility."

The mattress is brand new, you jackass. You may want to explore obtaining a higher-quality wife, Renee ached to say to the ungrateful man, but she bit her tongue and instead offered him a cool smile.

The jackass went on: "I am afraid we must insist you give us a twenty-percent discount for this past week, given the poor quality of the service and amenities we have received."

Afraid her tongue would start to bleed if she had to keep biting it, Renee was more than happy to grant them a discount if it meant they would leave and she would never have to deal with them again.

"I am *so* sorry you have been less than pleased with your stay here at Whispering Pines," Renee said, speaking through gritted teeth and a forced smile. "We will take your suggestions under advisement."

When they finally drove out of sight, Renee called Julie up at the duplex on her cell.

"Is there a way we can block those idiots from ever being able to rent from us again?!" Renee asked her daughter.

She was only half kidding.

***

The last week in June looked more promising. Cabin #3 was officially open for business and rented out, as were #1 and #2. All renters arrived and were settled in by midday.

Renee walked back to the duplex for a quick break. Saturdays were always crazy, getting cabins cleaned and new renters checked-in. All she wanted to do was sit out in her backyard for ten minutes, enjoy a little sunshine, and sip a cold glass of lemonade before tackling the next thing on her "to do" list.

Julie was baking cookies in the kitchen when Renee went in to grab a lemonade. Julie liked to bake, and Renee liked to surprise their renters with a fresh baked treat on their first evening at the resort.

"Oh, hi honey. What time do your friends get in?"

"Hey, Mom. Anna had to work until five, and she's picking Emma up on the way, so I suppose about nine tonight. Thanks for letting us use the other duplex. I already warned them it's in kind of rough shape, but they're so excited to visit. They both took the week off. I hope it'll be hot and sunny and we can do some relaxing on the beach." Julie saw her mother's expression and quickly added, "Don't worry, I know you need help, too. Actually, Emma and Anna already offered to help. They know there's still a ton of work to do." She smiled. "It'll be a working vacation!"

Renee wondered how much work they would actually get to that week. Three cute college guys were renting #3, but Julie hadn't been there when they checked in so she had no idea. Renee suspected, unless all the young men were spoken for, that there could be some interesting developments. *At least* someone *might have a little romance in their lives,* Renee thought bitterly. Other than Matt's weekly calls, which Renee always looked forward to, there was time for nothing else in her life other than resort work.

Next week would bring the Fourth of July, which, of course, came with extra festivities. Renee's extended family was coming. The duplex would be crowded. Val and Luke were bringing their old camper. Jess and Ethan and their families would use the other duplex. George and Lavonne would have Julie's room, and Julie would bunk with Renee.

"Oh, Julie, did I tell you Grant called?" Renee asked.

"Recently?"

"Yeah, a couple days ago. I can't believe I forgot to mention it."

Julie turned to Renee, finally giving her mom her full attention. "Is something wrong with Grace?"

"No, nothing like that. It sounds like she's improving some all the time, but it's a long process. But that's not why Grant called. He was actually wondering if they could rent one of our cabins for the month of July."

Renee tried to sneak a cookie off the baking sheet but dropped it on the counter when it burned her fingers. Crumbs shot all over. "Shit!"

"Nice job, ace." Julie gave Renee a look very much like the one Renee often used on her. "Can Grant get a whole month off from work? Don't get me wrong, it would be great to have them here. A month is just a long time."

Renee cleaned up her mess, sweeping the crumbs into the sink, then replied, "He's a writer. Guess he can do that from pretty much anywhere. He mentioned a big project he's working on. He also wants Grace to have someplace quiet and peaceful to recuperate, away from hospitals and doctors. I told him we would be delighted to have them."

"That's awesome, Mom. It'll give us a chance to get to know them better." Julie turned off the oven. The last batch of cookies needed to cool before she could do anything with them. "OK, cookies are done. If you don't need me for anything else right now, I'm gonna run up and take a quick shower."

"Nope, go ahead and get cleaned up." Renee juggled her lemonade and a second cookie while she fumbled with the screen-door latch. "I'm just going to take five, then get back to work."

Taking a seat in the sunshine, she thought more about having Grant and Grace at the resort. It would be a win for everyone. Renee would have steady, reliable renters in at least one of her cabins for the full month of July; she wouldn't have to worry about getting some nutcase coming in. She was still getting used to the transient nature of this business. So far, other than those complainers, it had gone well, but you never knew what kind of people might show up. Grant and Grace would be arriving next week. Renee needed to finish Cabin #4 for them. Grant needed an office to work out of, in addition to two bedrooms. As soon as she finished Cabin #3, she started work on the larger cabin. Ethan helped her convert one of the bedrooms into an office. Because she only purchased enough mattresses for the first three cabins, she had to replace the ones in Grant's cabin with sets purchased at a furniture store, and it was twice as expensive as the auction had been. But if all went as planned this last week of June, Cabin #4 would be ready.

***

Julie's friends arrived on schedule. Tired from the drive, and having lots to catch up on, the three stayed in their side of the duplex. Renee could hear them laughing well into the night. Robbie had gone up to his room earlier to watch a movie on his iPad.

"Come on, Molly, hurry up," Renee tried to hustle the cocker spaniel to finish up her business and come back inside. It was after ten, and she was exhausted. She could see a group around the fire pit through the trees.

The resort had decent cell phone reception, despite its remoteness; a cell tower was nearby. Renee posted her cell number in the kitchens of all the cabins, so if there were any problems, she could be easily reached. She hoped her phone would be quiet for the night.

The little dog took her time, sniffing around and exploring before meandering back up the porch steps. It was a beautiful evening and the dog was reluctant to come in. As Molly reached the top step, she froze and let out a low growl. She turned and backed toward Renee, staring at something off in the trees, the low rumble continuing deep in her chest.

"Molly, it's all right. Probably an animal out there in the woods." Renee tried to calm her dog, reaching down to give her a reassuring pat. But now Renee felt uneasy too. She had the strange sensation of being watched. Hustling the dog inside, she shut and bolted her door.

"What's the matter with me?" Renee scolded herself out loud. *If I'm going to get scared over a little animal in the woods, or every time Molly barks, how am I going to run this resort?* "I need to find my backbone and get a hell of a lot tougher if I'm going to make this work."

Molly looked at her with liquid brown eyes, head tilted slightly, perhaps doubting the effectiveness of Renee's little pep talk. But the dog was quiet, having forgotten about whatever spooked her as soon as the door closed behind them.

***

It was a quiet night, and her phone didn't ring. The only sounds were the occasional shout or laugh from the girls through the adjoining wall.

By 7:00 a.m., Renee was at the kitchen table, enjoying her morning coffee. All three girls wandered in dressed in baggy sweats, two with hair up in messy buns. Renee loved Anna's short, spiky hairdo the color of black ink. A finger comb was all she needed to start her day—what a nice convenience that must be.

After gulping down large mugs of coffee laced with plenty of sugar and cream, they rummaged through the cupboards for cereal or toast.

"Mom, last night we stayed up late trying to devise a plan for the old lodge," Julie said, her speech thrown off by a mouthful of Froot Loops which dribbled out of her mouth.

Emma laughed. "Eww, *gross*, Julie!"

Swallowing her cereal before replying this time, Julie apologized, wiping her chin. "Sorry, got a little carried away there."

"So what ideas did you come up with?" Renee wanted to know.

Anna piped in. "Nothing concrete yet, of course, since we haven't even been in there yet, but we were brainstorming. Julie said you aren't putting in a bar or restaurant, at least not yet. Maybe you could fix it up so there're things for people to do if the weather isn't great outside or they want to get out of the heat."

Renee pondered this. "I hadn't considered folks might enjoy some indoor common areas. But you're right. Not every day is going to be as beautiful as today, and people might get sick of being in their cabins."

"Yeah, we were thinking maybe if you put in a big-screen TV and kept a bunch of movies on hand, or maybe an Internet connection for Netflix, something like that," Emma shared. "Maybe a cabinet for books people could borrow. We even thought a stash of board games and cards would be um, kind of *old-school*. But still good."

Renee started a second pot of coffee, enjoying the girls' ideas.

"I remember when I used to come here as a kid, there was a bookcase like that in the lodge," Renee reminisced. "People could take a book to read or leave one they finished and didn't want to drag home. In fact, I remember sneaking a pretty racy paperback off the bookshelf and hiding it under my mattress in our cabin. I read it under my covers with a flashlight late at night. I would have *died* of embarrassment if anybody caught me."

More Froot Loops sprayed from Julie's mouth in laughter. "That is *hilarious*, Mom!"

"I couldn't have been more than ten. I suspect the book was tame by today's standards, but I learned a few things!" Renee laughed. "Did you come up with any other ideas?"

Anna brushed the crumbs from her peanut butter toast off the table into her other hand and dropped them in the garbage. "We were throwing around a few other things you could maybe do, but why don't you let us spend some time in there, flesh out the ideas more? Then we can talk."

"Come on, ladies, time to get to work," Emma directed as they each rinsed their bowls and piled them in the sink.

***

It was a beautiful Sunday. Around noon, Renee stopped in to see how Julie and her friends were doing in the lodge. She was amazed at their progress. Old blinds were down from windows in the back of the first floor and the glass gleamed. Walls and ceilings were free from dust and cobwebs. The floor had been swept but still needed to be mopped. The half-dozen tables previously strewn about the main lodge floor had been folded up and propped against one wall, leaving a huge open area. Knowing the girls might lose interest if the week turned into more work than fun, Renee kicked them outside. They'd earned some fun.

Grimy from their morning work, all three stripped down to swimming suits under their clothes and jumped into chilly lake water. Yelps of shock and laughter rang out. It sounded like summer: kids swimming, boats out on the water, insects buzzing, and a lawnmower in the distance. The family renting Cabin #1 had already made their way down to the beach. Their kids were building sand castles. A screen door slammed and a shirtless guy trotted down the steps of Cabin #3, scratching his belly and rubbing his eyes. He was one of the three cuties Renee checked in the day before. She suspected he was drawn outside by the racket the girls were making. The other two followed not far behind, and all three wandered down to the water's edge.

After a perusal of the area, one of the three sauntered over to Renee, where she was weeding a bed of flowers near the lodge. "Say, Mrs. Clements, you wouldn't happen to have any canoes or kayaks we could borrow or rent, would you?"

"Please, call me Renee. Mrs. Clements is my mother-in-law," she insisted with a smile. "I did see an old canoe leaning against the back side of that cabin over there. Why don't you guys go take a look and see if it's sea worthy? If so, you're more than welcome to take it for a spin. But please make sure it seems sturdy enough first. There are life jackets hanging in the shed. I'll go grab some while you check the canoe."

"Awesome, thanks!"

Renee needed a stool to reach high enough to pull the life jackets down. She brought three out into the sunlight. The jackets would serve their purpose but should probably be replaced. *Like so much around here,* she thought. She also noticed a set of old wooden oars and grabbed those as well, piling it all where the grass met the sand.

The guys found the old canoe. It was made of heavy fiberglass. Renee laughed as they tried to make it look easy as they hauled the boat down to the beach; a few curt words whispered between them and stilted progress was evidence enough that it was no easy task. The girls lounged in old webbed lawn chairs along the water's edge, drying off and enjoying the show.

Renee had the boys rock the canoe up on its side and she grabbed a broom to sweep out all the debris. Nature had a way of taking over, especially back in the trees. The canoe's cavity was full of cobwebs and something resembling an old nest, but of what Renee wasn't sure. Thankfully, nothing crawled out to avoid her broom.

One of the little kids on the beach, a boy of about five, filled his sand bucket with water and brought it over.

"My name's Sam. Can I help you clean up your boat?"

"You bet, Sam, we could use some help," answered the blond in sunglasses, crouching down to be at eye level with the younger boy. "My name's Ben. These two guys are Craig and Denny. Dump your pail in here and then go grab more water. This canoe is filthy."

Sam smiled and agreed with a fervent *"Filthy!"*

Craig, a redhead with freckles, and Denny, tall and dark, held the canoe while Renee, Ben, and now Sam worked to get rid of the grime. Not wanting to miss out on the action, a little toddler waddled over to see if she could help, too.

Sam was not happy.

"Mom, get Olivia out of here! These guys need my help and she's gonna get in the way!"

Sensing her kids were about to disrupt the peaceful beach atmosphere, their mother came over and scooped up Olivia, tickling her as she took her down to the water to splash around.

After they had done their best to clean up the faded red canoe, and since Renee didn't see any cracks or holes in it, she allowed the three older boys to push it out into the water to see if it leaked. Sam hung close, watching their every move. He obviously wanted nothing more than to get in the boat and float off with the big kids.

Seeing Sam's expression, Ben came over and said, "We're gonna take this old boat out for a test drive, OK? If we don't have any problems, and if it's OK with your parents, we can take you out for a boat ride, too. But let us take it out first and make sure it floats. Deal, buddy?"

The look Sam gave the older boy when Ben promised to give him a ride left no doubt Sam would be Ben's number-one fan for the week.

Denny and Craig were busy trying to climb into the canoe in knee-deep water without tipping. Once they were seated, Ben shoved into deeper water and jumped in, all in one quick movement. The boat barely rocked; apparently this wasn't his first time in a canoe. They paddled around, staying close to shore, until they were certain they weren't taking on water. When they gave Renee a shout and thumbs-up, she waved them off. The boat was crowded, with three big bodies in it, but Renee had to trust they knew what they were doing.

True to his word, Ben steered the boat back toward shore a half hour later. Craig jumped out when they got into shallow water and motioned for Sam to come over, as long as it was all right with his mom. She waved her approval and Sam bounded over, grinning from ear to ear. He was already wearing a life jacket Renee had found in a smaller size. Craig helped him get in and Ben got him settled on the bench seat in the middle of the canoe. Off they went again.

"That was pretty cool of you to let that little boy go out in the canoe," Anna said to Craig as he walked back up out of the water. "You do know you made his week, right?"

"Yeah," Craig laughed, "leave it to Ben. He's great with kids, works at a camp for autistic kids. One of us had to get out so Sam would fit, so I volunteered. I hate to admit it, but I think I'm starting to burn."

"Julie," Renee hollered at her daughter when she heard Craig, "toss him your sunscreen! It'll be a miserable week for him if he starts out with a bad burn."

The redheaded boy smiled bashfully. "Thanks, Mrs. C, I totally forgot to bring some."

Julie tossed a tube to Craig, and he smeared the coconut-smelling lotion on his face, arms, and chest. He tried to reach his back, but it was useless.

"Here, give it to me," Anna ordered. She took the sunscreen and quickly applied it to Craig's back. He was turning beet red, to match his hair, and Renee suspected it wasn't all from the burn. Anna hadn't given him a chance to say a word. She was a take-charge kind of girl, leaving Craig flustered. Finishing up and tossing the tube back to Julie, she invited Craig to join them on the beach.

The family took Olivia up to their cabin for a nap. Julie promised to bring Sam up when they got back in. Wanting to give the kids some space, Renee went back to her weeding.

Robbie finished mowing, looking hot and tired. He grabbed a loaf of bread, a package of sandwich meat, a big bag of chips, and a six-pack of Cokes from their kitchen and took everything down to the beach. He knew the older kids would let him join them as long as there was something in it for them. Renee smiled to herself. *Smart kid.*

It stayed warm and sunny all afternoon. After Ben and Denny brought Sam back, others took turns going out in the canoe. Renee was going to have to look into getting a few other small boats for guests to use. The canoe was looking to be a huge hit.

Renee smiled, feeling that surge of excitement again.

"All aboard," she said to herself.

CHAPTER 46

Gift of New Friends

$\mathcal{T}$he week passed quickly. The girls managed to get the lodge cleaned up by spending their mornings working inside and the rest of each day playing. Even the young men in Cabin #3 pitched in—in the cleaning *and* the playing. They cleaned out gutters and scraped and repainted the outside trim, then happily joined the girls out on the lake.

"Let me pay you guys something for helping out around here," said Renee. "I feel guilty letting guests work on renovations."

"No way, Mrs. C," Ben said—apparently still not comfortable calling her Renee. "We don't want your money. How about if you feed us dinner tonight, and we call it even? I don't think I could eat another hotdog, and that's all we have in the fridge."

Renee smiled, shaking Ben's hand, who was brokering the deal on behalf of his buddies. "Deal. How about steaks and baked potatoes for dinner then?"

Renee's suggestion was met with enthusiasm, so she finished what she was doing and went to clean up a little so she could make a trip to the grocery store.

***

When she got back to the duplex, she was surprised to see the door of the west unit stood wide open. One of the girls or Robbie must have run back to grab something and didn't get the door shut all the way when they left.

"Hello . . . anyone in here?" she hollered, poking her head in the open doorway. The only answer was Molly barking in the adjoining unit, letting

Renee know she was there. But everything else was quiet, so she pulled the door shut and quickly forgot about it. No sense scolding the kids for carelessness; mistakes happen.

The teens spent most of the afternoon hiking in the nearby woods. By the time they returned, Renee had steaks grilling and a huge dispenser of lemonade ready. They were famished after their work on the lodge followed by an afternoon walking in the fresh air. Renee was glad she bought plenty of meat; the guys were big eaters. They tried to help clean up after the meal, but Renee wouldn't allow it.

Soon, they had a volleyball game going over an old net Robbie dug out of the shed and strung between two poles Denny helped drive deep into the ground. Sam was invited to play, too, so there were four on each side. Competition was fierce.

"That serve was out!"

"No way, it was right on the line!"

"Come on, you pansy, what's wrong with you?"

Renee was about to run over and tell them to cool it—little Sam might learn some new words if they weren't careful—but before she could, she heard Ben beat her to it and scold the rest of the group.

After that, the laughter and shouts continued, but the heat dwindled. At dusk, Sam's mother called him in for a bath, and the group decided to call it a draw, leaving the net up for the next day. Because it was such a beautiful night, they all congregated around the fire pit, laughing and having a good time.

Renee left them to their fun and headed home. *Home,* she thought. Funny how she had started to think of the duplex as home over the past month. Apparently its charm was growing on her. Molly followed Renee home. Together they wandered around back, and Renee checked to make sure she turned off the propane on the barbeque. They went in the back door and Renee flipped on a light.

Molly and Renee both saw it at the same time: lying in the middle of the kitchen floor was a squirrel.

A dead squirrel.

Renee's screams and Molly's barking brought the kids running. Julie bounded into the kitchen through the front with Ben, the others close on their heels.

"Mom, are you OK?"

"What's wrong, Mrs. C?"

Everyone talked at once. Renee felt behind her for one of the kitchen chairs and blindly dropped into it, not taking her eyes off the mess on her kitchen floor. Robbie grabbed Molly by the collar and pulled her back.

"Um, there's no *way* that crawled in here on its own," one of the boys said, stating the obvious. "Something must have dragged it in."

"Oh *God*," Renee groaned, dropping her head into her hands. Was some critter lurking in the shadows inside the house right now, frightened back when they came in?

Craig left the kitchen through the back door, but was back quickly, carrying the shovel Renee had propped next to the back stairs when she'd finished with it earlier. "I'll get rid of it. Ben, Denny, why don't you guys look around and see if you see anything else unusual?" he suggested. He didn't come right out and tell them to see if there was another animal in the house that might have carried the squirrel in, but they were all thinking it already.

Anna tagged along with them. They checked the basement, main, and upper levels but found nothing. Craig chucked the dead squirrel as far back into the woods as he could with the shovel.

"The back door was shut when we got here," Renee said. "When you kids came in the front, was the door open?"

"No . . . shut, but not locked."

"This is so strange. How did it get in here?" Renee wondered aloud, then remembered the open door from earlier. "Hey, the door to the unit next to this one was standing wide open this afternoon when you kids were all down at the lake. I figured somebody didn't pull it shut hard enough. Do any of you know anything about that?"

If anyone did, they didn't fess up. If the squirrel had somehow gotten in the other unit when the door was wide open, it would have made more sense. But it got in *her* unit. It hadn't been in the middle of her kitchen floor when she cleaned up after dinner, but it was there when she got back from the volleyball game barely an hour later.

Julie used a rag and pine-scented cleaner on the spot where the squirrel had been found. There was nothing more they could think to do. The dead squirrel ruined the festive mood. Ben, Craig, and Denny headed back to their cabin.

"Thanks, guys, you were a big help tonight," Renee yelled to them as they walked across her front lawn.

"See you tomorrow," they shouted back, and then they were swallowed up by the darkness.

The girls were on edge after they learned their front door had been wide open in their unit earlier. They gathered their duffle bags and decided to bunk in Julie's room, back on Renee's side, even though it was tight quarters. Renee felt more comfortable having them all together, too. Something had felt . . . *off* these past few days.

***

There was no more drama that night, other than Renee's dreams.

The dead squirrel stirred her previous dream back to her subconscious. She again found herself in the gray cabin, inexplicably drawn toward the back bedroom and the muffled scratching sounds. When she pushed the bedroom door open, furious squirrels bounded off the bed at her, faster this time. Her feet felt cemented, and she couldn't move. A squirrel was reaching her, ready to launch itself for her leg, when something cold pushed against her hand.

She bolted up in bed with a gasp.

Molly must have sensed her distress and was trying to comfort her. Normally the cocker spaniel slept in Robbie's room with the door shut, but Renee had asked him to let her roam tonight in case they had any more strange visitors.

Moonbeams streamed into her room, slanting through the side of the closed curtains. There was so much light it must be a full moon. Not that Renee was going to get up and check. She settled Molly up on the bed next to her and pulled the covers tight. It took a long time for her heart rate to level out and for sleep to come. The house was quiet. Molly fell back to sleep curled up next to her. Finally, she relaxed enough to drift off.

Moonlight was replaced by sunbeams when Renee next opened her eyes. It was stuffy in her room and Molly was gone. Renee swung her feet to the floor, meandering over to push open a window. Below, Emma and Julie relaxed on the patio with coffee. Molly was playing with her ball in the grass, grabbing it in her mouth, tossing it in the air, and chasing after it.

Throwing her old ratty robe on over baby-doll pj's, Renee headed downstairs, grabbed her own cup of coffee, and joined the girls out back.

When Julie saw her, she exclaimed, "Oh hey, Mom. Did you get some sleep? We didn't want to wake you. That was so scary last night. We figured you could use some rest."

"Yeah, I slept some. I keep having these strange dreams and waking up, but I feel good now. So, girls, what are your plans today, since it's your last full day together?"

"This morning we'll see what more we can get done in the lodge. Then we thought we could hang out here this afternoon. Hopefully it'll be hot. We can relax by the water, maybe play some more volleyball. The guys mentioned a street dance in town tonight. They heard it's a tradition to kick off the week of the Fourth. They invited Anna, Emma, and me to go with them. Would you mind?"

Renee stared at the three expectant teenage faces. "Mind? I think that sounds like a blast. But none of you are twenty-one yet. Does the dance have an age requirement?"

"Nah," Julie said. "It's open to the public. Sounds like there are beer gardens, but those are separate."

"I don't want any of you drinking. It's way too dangerous. Craig, Ben, and Denny seem like nice guys, but if any of them start drinking I want you to call me and I'll come pick you up." Renee stared at each of the girls in turn. "I am dead serious about this. Do you understand?"

"Of course, but don't worry," Julie said, and the others nodded emphatically. "They're pretty cool, Mom, and they already said they don't plan to drink. But if there's any trouble at all, I promise I'll call you."

Knowing they were used to being on their own after a year at college, Renee left it at that. They needed to take responsibility for themselves. She couldn't force them to do anything. She would have to hope and pray they behaved. She knew she wouldn't get any sleep until they were all home; no way around it.

Well, she thought, *at least I have Robbie.*

CHAPTER 47

Gift of Protectors

*R*enee relaxed in bed, still awake despite the hour, sitting against the old headboard. She tried to call Matt, but he didn't pick up. *Probably working.* Robbie was in his room on his iPad. Molly was somewhere wandering around.

Friday had been a long day of preparation, working until the light started to fade outside. It was hot, still in the low eighties. Renee's window was open, and she could hear people around the fire pit. Sound carried on the still night air. Little Olivia was singing a song from *The Wizard of Oz*, and Sam was hollering at her to stop. Renee hoped both families in the first two cabins enjoyed their week. The weather had been beautiful, and no one complained.

She finally started to drift off, tired from her day. It was a struggle to keep her eyes open so she set the alarm on her phone for 1:00 a.m. She had expected to be wide awake, worrying about the kids' safe return from the dance, but she was just too tired. Turns out *she* had gotten used to Julie being away at college, too.

A low growl from downstairs brought her out of a light slumber. Something had Molly uptight. Maybe the kids were back? But a glance at her watch showed it was only 11:30. She'd be surprised if they were done at the dance already. Through leafy foliage, she could see a bit of flame dancing in the fire pit but couldn't hear any voices. Everyone must have turned in. The little kids had to be exhausted. Robbie's room was quiet, too, but she supposed he could be using his headphones.

Renee walked down to the kitchen, nervous after the episode the night before but wanting to see what was up with Molly. The dog was standing in the kitchen, growling—but at what? The moon provided some light for Renee to see: her dog was fixated on the spot where they found the dead squirrel. Renee flipped the light on and the sudden glow from the overhead fixture abruptly cut off Molly's growl. She rushed over to Renee's side and rubbed against her leg as if nothing were wrong. Maybe it *was* nothing. Maybe the dog had heard an animal outside, or could still smell the squirrel even after all that pine-scented cleaner. Renee closed all the curtains on the main level before heading back up. She also made sure the front porch light glowed so the girls wouldn't come home to a dark house.

Now she couldn't sleep. Trying to keep her mind off things that go bump in the night, Renee took out her iPad and worked on her Pinterest boards. She had a growing collection of grandiose ideas for the resort. Molly stayed close, letting out a few sporadic growls. She couldn't, or *wouldn't*, settle down.

Renee heard a car drive up right at curfew. Gravel crunched in the parking lot. She held her breath, hoping they wouldn't make a racket and wake the other guests. If it had been a rowdy night, they might not be ready to settle down yet, might forget their surroundings as teenagers sometimes do. She hoped she wouldn't have to go all preachy on them.

There were some giggles and muffled conversations but nothing crazy. The boys walked the girls back to the duplex and they all loitered out on the front lawn. Renee wondered if any of them had paired off into couples. It was pretty convenient to have three girls and three boys in their group this whole last week. *Almost like Julie, our Whispering Pines booking agent, planned it,* she thought, grinning.

Since everyone was home, Renee relaxed enough to fall back asleep.

Sometime later, a shrilling sound filled her room, yanking her back awake. She fumbled around on her end table for her cell phone. A call at this hour was never good news. Ten different scenarios ran through her head before she was able to find her phone.

"Hello." Her voice cracked from disuse and she cleared her throat. "This is Renee."

"Mrs. C, this is Ben. Sorry to call so late, but there's something you need to see. I don't think you want to wait till morning."

Julie was standing in the bedroom doorway, having heard Renee's cell, her eyebrows raised in curiosity about the late call.

"What is it, Ben?" Renee asked, scooting to the edge of the bed.

"Craig is walking over now to get you. Can you come down and meet him on the front porch?"

Ben sounded stressed, worried about something. He was a level-headed kid, so his tone concerned her.

"Is everyone OK?" she asked, afraid someone might have gotten hurt.

"It isn't that, but you need to come over, OK? I have to go." Ben clicked off.

Renee pulled on sweatpants and a hoodie. She dropped her cell in her pocket, grabbed the flashlight next to her bed, and filled Julie in with what little she knew. Julie rushed back to her room to pull clothes on over her T-shirt and panties. She wanted to go with her mom, and Renee wasn't going to talk her out of it. Something was seriously wrong. She'd heard it in Ben's voice.

"Anna and Emma," Renee spoke softly as she stuck her head in Julie's room. "Are you girls awake? Ben needs me to come over to their cabin quick. I don't know why. Julie's coming with me. I need you two to stay here. I'll lock the door behind us. If Robbie wakes up, keep him here, too. I don't need everyone out wandering around in the dark. I'm going to go see what happened."

"Got it, Renee," one of them answered from the depths of a mess of pillows and blankets on the floor. "Be careful!"

An urgent knocking downstairs signaled Craig's arrival. Renee grabbed Molly's leash and snapped it on the dog. She'd bark like crazy if they left her behind.

"Mrs. C? It's me, Craig. Open up."

Renee flung the door open. She saw the same look of concern on Craig's face as she'd heard in Ben's voice. "What's going on, Craig? Is anyone hurt?" she asked again.

"No, but we have a big problem back at the cabin. Come on, follow me."

The three of them and the dog navigated the dark path, around the back side of the lodge, and made their way to the cabins. Cabin #3, where the boys were staying, was brightly lit, and the door was standing wide open. There were also lights on in one of the other cabins.

Ben stepped into the doorway as they ran across the lawn toward him. He jumped down the steps and blocked Renee's path. He put his hands on her shoulders and looked her straight in the eye, taking a deep breath.

"It looks like we had a visitor when we were at the dance. After we left your place, we walked back over here. The fire was still going a little so the three of us sat around it and bullshitted for a while. We were still jacked up, and, since we go home tomorrow, we weren't in a hurry to call it a night. But we got hungry, so Denny went in to grab chips."

Ben paused, reluctant to continue.

"It's a real mess in there, Renee. I want you to be prepared. When Denny saw it, he freaked a little. OK, a lot. He started yelling for us to get in there and was running from room to room, trying to figure out what the hell happened. I . . . think he woke up the neighbors, too. Sorry," Ben apologized, motioning over his right shoulder to the light in one of the other cabins. He took his hands off Renee's shoulders and moved to her side. "Whoever was in there is gone now. Come on, we'll go in with you."

Ben ushered Renee toward the cabin with a light hand on her shoulder. He discreetly clasped Julie's fingers with his other hand, pulling her in close as well. Craig took Molly's leash and stayed outside with her. She was growling again, sniffing around on the ground she could reach from the short length of her leash. Denny followed Ben and the women up the stairs.

"Oh . . . God," Renee exclaimed, her hand covering her mouth in horror.

Destruction was everywhere.

One of the kitchen chairs lay busted on its side. Drawers were pulled out and dumped in the kitchen. A deep slash ran down the length of the old sofa, stuffing yanked out and spilling onto the floor. Pillows were torn. Bedding was ripped off both beds and dressers were overturned. Big black slashes of paint marred walls they had recently worked so hard to paint.

Scribbled across the bathroom mirror in bright red were the words: *Go to HELL!*

"Oh my God, oh my God," was all Renee could manage as she picked her way through the ransacked cabin, hardly believing what she was seeing.

A thought occurred to her and she turned back to the boys. "Is any of your stuff missing?"

"I honestly don't know," Denny said. "We haven't even looked yet. We called you as soon as we were sure the asshole that did this wasn't still in here."

Julie stared around with wide eyes. "Mom, whoever did this must be sick in the head. I'm scared. I think you need to call the police."

"Right, honey, we need help here. We probably shouldn't wait until morning," Renee said, pulling out her phone and dialing 911.

She explained the situation to the dispatcher and asked him to send someone out as soon as possible, preferably without lights or a siren. It was late and she didn't want to bring negative attention to Whispering Pines.

Renee stepped outside to wait for the sheriff. Dan, Sam's dad from next door, was in hushed conversation with Craig. She stepped up to talk to him.

"I called the sheriff, he's on his way. Dan, I am *so* sorry. I can't imagine who would do something like this. I hope your family didn't all wake up, too. I would hate for something like this to ruin your vacation."

Dan gave her a sympathetic smile. "Renee, don't be silly. This isn't your fault. Angela woke up, too, but I convinced her to stay inside with the kids and not wake them. With any luck, they won't even know anything happened. I'd be happy to talk to the sheriff, but I'm afraid I won't be much help. The kids fell asleep on our laps when we were out talking around the pit, so we didn't go in till about midnight. I can't believe I didn't hear anything until these guys started hollering. Looks like

Tim and Jenny slept through it all." Ben motioned to the dark cabin of her other renters.

Renee's phone buzzed. It was a text from Robbie, wondering what was going on. Knowing it would be quicker, she called him instead of texting back. Now that she knew why Ben had called, she was a little nervous about Robbie, Emma, and Anna back at the duplex by themselves. She told Robbie she would come over and get them, but Craig heard her and insisted he would go instead. She needed to stay where she was until the sheriff arrived.

Dan offered to go with Craig. No one was likely to mess with those two big guys, even on the dark path between here and there. They headed off, with Molly trotting along between them.

Renee went back into the ravaged cabin. She felt uncomfortable standing outside alone, the yellow light over the cabin door highlighting her almost like a target for the criminal: *Her next.*

Ben, Julie, and Denny were standing in the living room, talking quietly. No one wanted to touch anything. Renee looked around again, tears starting to course down her cheeks. Who could be so cruel? Who would do this . . . why?

It must have been a busy night for law enforcement. By the time a squad car pulled into the lot, it was already 3:00 a.m. Robbie, Anna, and Emma were sitting around the glowing embers of the pit, silently staring into the orange. They had already looked inside the cabin and were sick about it.

Two officers exited the patrol car, illuminated by the solitary streetlight. Both were in uniform, one looking fit and not much older than Julie, the other more grandfatherly. Renee approached them across the dark lawn. Shock was starting to wear off, replaced with anger.

"Thank you for coming out, Officers. My name is Renee Clements. I'm the owner here at Whispering Pines. Unfortunately, one of our cabins was vandalized tonight."

"Aren't you Celia's niece?" asked the older of the two men. "Celia was one hell of a woman. Been a long time since she last came out here. We heard she left this place to her niece, and you were trying to get this old place going again."

Renee was a bit unnerved by how much this stranger knew about her. Her surprise must have shown on her face.

"Sorry, ma'am, I'm the sheriff around here, name's Thompson. This here is Deputy Winston." He gestured to his partner and then extended his hand to Renee. "Been a busy night, what with the big dance in town and all. Folks get all wound up and crazy this time of year. Must be a combination of heat, a full moon, and the holiday coming up. Why don't you show us what ya got?"

Renee escorted them over to the damaged cabin. Neither officer said anything initially. They gave slight nods to Dan and the teenagers, all of whom were standing outside, unsure what to do. As the officers entered the cabin, Sheriff Thompson gave a low whistle. Renee assured them whoever had done this was no longer in the cabin, but from their careful perusal through the rooms, it was obvious they wanted to make sure that was true.

Winston took pictures of the damage with his phone, and then the deputy had Denny, Craig, and Ben come back in and check through their personal items. Nothing seemed to be missing. The sheriff jotted notes in a little notebook he pulled from his shirt pocket. After surveying the cabin, he took everyone's name down and asked if there was somewhere they could go to talk, away from the chaos of the cabin.

"Yes, why don't we head over to the lodge," Renee suggested, pulling keys out of her sweatshirt pocket.

"We need all of you to come with us so we can take your statements," Winston informed the group, glancing around at everyone. "Any other renters out here? We should talk to everyone."

"We have three full cabins tonight," Renee said, ticking them off her fingers. "One is the messed-up one we were just in, Dan and his family are in the cabin next door—his wife is inside with their sleeping kids—and I don't think the renters in the cabin to the left of the fire pit are awake. I was hoping not to bother them with this."

"Better go knock on their door," Sheriff Thompson advised. "I know you don't want to inconvenience your customers, but I need to make sure everyone's OK, too."

"Oh lord, I didn't even think about that," Renee admitted. "I'll be right back."

Renee jogged over to the dark cabin. Winston followed her, just in case.

After a few moments of silence, there was some rustling from inside and the door opened. A confused man stepped out onto the front stoop in a tank top and boxers. "What's going on, Renee?" Tim asked, spying the uniformed man behind her.

"I hate to wake you, Tim," Renee apologized, "but one of our other cabins was vandalized tonight. The sheriff came out to check on things."

"No shit?" Tim said, running a hand through his longish auburn hair. Renee hoped his wife and little boy were still asleep. "I'm sorry to hear that. What can we do?"

Winston stepped up to Renee's side. "Would you mind coming over to the lodge with us, sir? We just want to check in with everybody, get an idea of anything you might have heard or saw that was out of the ordinary tonight, that type of thing."

"Oh, OK, sure," Tim agreed. "Let me throw some pants on quick. What about my family?"

Winston peered behind her renter, into the dark interior of his cabin. All seemed quiet. "If they're sleeping, leave 'em be. No sense getting everyone riled up. If your wife can think of anything she might have noticed, you can give us a call in the morning."

They all made their way over to the lodge. Renee was glad the girls had made so much progress cleaning it up. She asked Julie to make coffee; she feared this would take a while. Fortunately, Renee had already started stocking the kitchen for Val's return; there was a bag of ground coffee and large jugs of bottled water on the counter.

Renee provided the officers a brief overview of the evening, introducing Ben, Craig, and Denny as the cabin renters along with her own kids and Julie's friends. She explained Dan was renting the cabin right next to the one that had been vandalized.

Robbie pulled out two of the large, foldable tables, setting up one at one end of the large room and the other in a different corner. Taking a seat at the far end of the room, the officers started by taking statements from each of the college boys, one at a time. Then they talked to her other renters, Dan and Tim. Molly paced around the room, sniffing everything, all the people making her nervous. Finally, they talked to Robbie and the girls.

Once they had talked to everyone except Renee, Thompson suggested the rest could go get some sleep.

"Julie, why don't you take Craig, Denny, and Ben over and get them settled in the other duplex? They have to be exhausted, and no one is going to spend any more time in that cabin tonight. Robbie, Anna, and Emma, please go with them. I want you all to stick together. Take Molly too," Renee instructed, handing the dog's leash to her daughter. She turned to the two men standing beside the deputy and sheriff, who were still sitting at their make-shift interrogation table. "Thank you, Dan and Tim, for your support. Again, I am so sorry you had to deal with this."

"Don't worry, Renee. Like I said, it isn't your fault."

Deputy Winston stood, offering to escort everyone back. "I'll take a quick look around over at your duplex, too," he discreetly told Renee. "Make sure everything looks to be in order."

The lodge emptied except for Renee and Sheriff Thompson. She handed him a fresh cup of coffee and both sat back down at the table.

"I gotta tell you, Ms. Clements, this is unusual. Been a long time since I've run across something like this. I don't think your renters did it. They seem like a decent group of young men. This obviously has all three of them shook up. My gut tells me they weren't involved. If they've only been here this week, I'm not sure why anyone would specifically target them, either. All three of them, along with your daughter and her friends, gave me the same story as to how their night went tonight."

"I agree with you, Sheriff," said Renee. "I've gotten to know those boys a bit this week, and I like all three of them. They've even helped out around here, and they've been nice to the other renters and have always been respectful. I have no reason to think for a minute that they had anything to do with this."

The sheriff nodded, consulting his notes. "Does anyone hold a grudge against you, Renee? Have you had any bad experiences with any of your renters yet? I know you haven't been open long."

"No . . . I can't imagine why anyone would do something like this because they're *mad* at me. I have to tell you, we have been busting our tails over here, getting things back in shape so we could open for business. I had one husband and wife complain the whole time they were here, but I think they're probably difficult by nature. This attack gives me the creeps. It feels *violent . . .* intrusive."

"I tend to agree with you, Renee. The slashed furniture and message on the mirror concern me. This wasn't a simple B&E where they were looking to steal stuff. Doesn't appear anything is missing. How about your kids? Anything going on with them lately that could be related to what happened here tonight?"

Renee thought back to the pills she found in Robbie's pocket. She truly didn't think it had anything to do with what happened here, though, so she didn't mention it.

"I don't think so. We haven't been here long enough to meet people in the area. It's only been a month, and my kids have been working hard alongside me most of the time. This is a long way from the city for someone they know to come all the way out here and do something like this. Julie was away for her first year at college and is home for the summer."

Sheriff Thompson nodded, jotting down a few notes. "We'll do an investigation and let you know if anything turns up. You can go ahead and clean the place up, we have plenty of pictures to document the damage. I have to be honest with you, though—we might never know who did this. It could have been a drifter, passing through. Have you noticed anything else unusual since you've been here? Anyone hanging around you don't recognize? I know there's another resort around the bend, so it isn't like you're totally alone out here."

Renee flashed back to her horror the previous night when she found the dead squirrel in the middle of the kitchen floor.

"This is probably totally unrelated ... but we did have something weird happen last night, too." Renee told him about the dead squirrel and the open door in the other unit.

"Hm," the sheriff said, nodding. "You're probably right. Maybe your dog dragged the squirrel in when you weren't looking and a careless teenager didn't shut the door tight, but good to know. Be careful, OK? If you have anything else strange happen, here's my card. Call me direct right away. It's just you and your two kids out here, then, along with whoever is renting your cabins?"

Renee knew what he was asking without coming right out and asking it.

"I've been a widow for ten years. We don't usually have a man out here with us. But this coming week, my family is coming for the Fourth, so my dad and brother will be here. I also rented out one of the other cabins to my brother-in-law and his daughter for the month of July."

"Good, good to know. We should know in a month's time if the trouble has passed. Why don't you go home and get some rest now? I'll walk you back and we'll be in touch."

Hopefully, the next time we talk, it's so you can tell me you caught the bastard that did this, Renee thought. There would be no more sleep tonight.

CHAPTER 48

Gift of Expansion

Renee considered calling Matt after everyone was settled in for what was left of the night. But they had talked so often over the past few months, he would do a quick mental calculation of the time difference and know something was wrong. She didn't want to worry him, so she would wait. She would probably talk to him in a couple of days regardless, and she needed to get some rest. Her first order of business in the morning would be to figure out what to do about her renters for Cabin #3 for the upcoming week. After a couple hours of restless sleep, Renee gave up and headed downstairs. All was quiet. She made a quick list of all she needed to accomplish. She was expecting her family to start arriving midday.

Knowing her dad always got up early, she called him.

"Hey, Dad, hope I didn't wake you. We had a little problem here last night," Renee started to explain. She gave him a quick rundown on the vandalism.

"Well, shit—is everyone OK?"

"Yeah, I called the sheriff. He came and took a report. Everyone is fine, but the cabin is a mess. I have a full house this coming week, with it being the Fourth. To be honest, I need a little extra help. I know you and Mom were coming later today, but . . . any chance you could come earlier? I could use you."

"Of course, of course, Renee. You don't have to ask twice. I'll wake your mother right now. We will pack up and be there as soon as we can. Everything will be OK, kiddo." And with that, George hung up.

Ten minutes later, her cell rang. She expected it to be one of her parents, but it was a number she didn't recognize.

"Hello, this is Renee Clements at Whispering Pines. How can I help you?"

"Hello, Mrs. Clements. This is Joe Anderson. Sorry to call you so early. My wife Mary Beth and I are renting one of your cabins this week. Unfortunately, I had a bit of a fender-bender yesterday and our car is in the shop. It won't be fixed until Monday, so we aren't going to be able to get to the resort until later that evening. I was calling to let you know we won't be there today."

With a silent fist pump for this unexpected reprieve, Renee told Joe how sorry she was to hear about the accident and assured him she would hold his cabin.

The Andersons had been slated for Cabin #2. Since #2 and #3 were a similar layout, she was going to flip them around with the renters for #3. This gave her two extra days to get Cabin #3 back in shape. When the other renters arrived this afternoon, she would put them in Cabin #2 instead.

Problem temporarily solved.

***

George and Lavonne arrived at ten that morning. Ethan and his kids got in a half-hour later—George had called him immediately after talking with Renee. The plan had always been for the week to be a combination of work and relaxation; now they were going to have to work a little harder than expected at the front end.

Thank God for family, Renee thought.

Emma and Anna were scheduled to go home, as were Ben, Denny, and Craig, but given everything that happened the night before, they all wanted to pitch in to help clean up before leaving. Ethan brought his enclosed trailer back so some of the items they couldn't salvage were hauled out and stowed there. The sofa was ruined, but there was a similar one upstairs in the lodge. Celia or another previous owner must have gotten a discount and bought them in bulk. Craig and Denny wrestled it down the stairs and replaced the one taken out of the cabin.

Renee was thankful the floors hadn't been damaged. She had enough paint left for the walls to cover the black markings. George painted on a quick coat of primer first, and once that was dry, Ben re-painted the wall. It was a huge improvement. The nasty message on the mirror had been scrawled with red paint of some kind. It was tedious work, but Robbie managed to scrape it off with a razor blade.

Whoever had done this didn't leave either red or black paint cans behind.

It would take one last coat of paint to erase all traces of the black, then the room could be put back together. Luckily the new mattresses weren't damaged in the tirade.

Mid-afternoon, the teenage visitors loaded up their vehicles. Everyone gathered in the lot for a last goodbye. Renee enjoyed the college boys this past week and hoped they would be back. Emma and Anna already had another weekend planned later in the summer. There were hugs all around; Renee thought one shared by Ben and Julie might have lasted a bit longer than the others but she couldn't be sure.

I'll have to ask Julie about that later.

***

Renee suspected it had been a long time since the resort had hosted this many people at once, especially with family. Two cabins were full; two more would be filled by late Monday, leaving only one more cabin to get up and running. It was Cabin #5—the Gray Cabin, as Renee had come to call it, the one she visited in her dreams.

All bedrooms in both units of the duplex were also full, plus overflow in Val's camper.

It was all fun but overwhelming. Almost all of her family members were helping to get Cabins #3 and #4 ready for guests. Will, Jess's husband, was the only one not pitching in. He was on his cell phone most of Sunday morning and spent the afternoon out on the dock, fishing for pan fish. He didn't interact much with anyone. Renee noticed, was surprised that he had even come, but she was too busy to worry about him. He had always been aloof, as if he thought he was better than the rest of his wife's family.

Val kept everyone fed. They were all splitting the cost of food, but she was kind enough to plan the meals, cook the dishes, and get the food on the table, along with help from various "kiddos," as George called everyone.

Grant and Grace arrived Sunday afternoon. Cabin #4 was clean and ready for them. After they were settled, Renee gave them a tour of the resort and introduced them to her family. Grace's complexion had more color than before the transplant. Grant had warned Renee his daughter was fed up with the struggle to get her strength back. They were both hopeful time in the sunshine and fresh air, away from doctors and hospitals, would help.

The two of them joined the family for a barbeque in Renee's backyard their first night at the resort. Renee, Julie, and Robbie recounted the events of Friday night for everyone. Most had heard bits and pieces of the story but Renee thought it was important they all knew what had been happening. She wanted the kids to know, too, even if it scared them. She was hopeful they wouldn't have any more trouble, but she needed everyone to keep a watchful eye.

The three of them then shared other, admittedly less exciting stories from their first month of renting. George couldn't believe that old canoe could still float. When Val's boys heard there was a volleyball net in the shed, they jogged off to string it back up. Jess asked how Renee handled the no-show renters, pointing out they should clarify their policy on the website so they could still charge when a cancellation wasn't received on time.

As the discussion continued, the rest of the kids wandered off to join the volleyball game. Will disappeared, too. Grant and Grace turned in shortly after they finished eating; Grace still tired easily, and it had been a busy day.

This left Renee, her parents, her brother, sisters, and Luke relaxing in the backyard. With the smaller group, Renee felt comfortable sharing some concerns she'd been holding onto.

"I don't know, guys, I thought I was up for this. I was excited to start something new and thought Aunt Celia's gift was what I needed, when I needed it. Oh, I *knew* it would be a ton of work, but I don't think I fully appreciated what I was taking on. I don't know that I'm cut out for this."

Renee took a hefty gulp of her gin and tonic for some liquid courage and continued.

"I couldn't be more appreciative of the love and support you've all given us . . . but I'm starting to wonder if this is all worth it. Wouldn't it be easier to go back to a desk job? I had a call last week from someone at my old company. A job opened up in Minneapolis, and they think I might be a good fit for it. I can apply if I want to. I don't know what to do."

No one said anything at first. Renee had clearly caught them off guard. They knew she'd been working like a mad woman, and that she'd encountered some frustrations, but no one had any idea she was thinking about quitting already.

Her father finally broke into the silence. "Yes, honey, it might be easier if you went back to work. It certainly might be easier . . . but my fear is it would be much less rewarding in the long run. Think back to how you felt in December. You were furious at the company you had devoted so many years to, but you were disappointed in yourself for giving up the reins to your own life for so long. I think I speak for the whole family when I say this place has become a labor of love for all of us. While you might feel like you're in this alone some days, you always know we have your back. You need only to call and we will help however we can. Hell, this morning is *proof* of that! And that's just the thing—here we can do that. But if you go back to the corporate world, you're on your own there."

The others were all nodding their agreement with George's words.

Renee sighed. "Dad, you have been so awesome through everything—you *all* have. I felt so helpless Friday night, so violated. It scared me. I don't want to put anyone at risk out here."

"Stop right there, Renee," Luke scolded, his harsh words softened by the squeeze he gave her hand. "You've worked too hard to let one crazy idiot take this away from you. That could happen anywhere. It could happen back at your home in Minneapolis. It could happen at the resort down the way. Shit like this happens, like it or not, but you can't let the bad guys win."

"And I would hate to see you go back to your old company, Renee," Jess added. "If they cut you once, it could happen again. Why would you put your family's financial well-being back in their hands? I've been so proud of you these past few months. You dove right in, learning everything you could, as fast as you could, about running a business you knew nothing about. Most people don't have the guts to try something like that. You need to give this time. Dad said it, and I want to be sure you hear what he's saying: *We are all here for you.*"

More emphatic nods.

Jess went on, "You have had some tough blows through the years and you always rose to the challenge. Yes, it's hard right now, and it will probably continue to be hard. Most new businesses take a few years to find stability. This could be even tougher given the short summers around here. Maybe what we need to do is some brainstorming around how you can tweak your business model to make this place more financially lucrative."

"I know everything you guys are saying is true, and I love all of you." Renee laughed. "Nothing like family to tell you to stop whining and suck it up!"

"Got that right," Lavonne chimed in.

"Tough love, big sister!" Val joked.

Ethan piped up. "Renee, you mentioned Julie and her friends did lots of work in the lodge this last week. They must have had some ideas how you could use the space, something that excited them enough they took the initiative to work on it on their own. Did they share any ideas with you?"

"A few . . . but the cute college guys took up most of their spare time, so we didn't talk about it at length. They thought the upstairs could be fixed up and used for dances or exercise classes. Maybe some type of limited service restaurant or bar could go downstairs. They wanted to help get the place cleaned up as a starting point."

"OK, everyone, let's think," George ordered. "What could Renee do with the lodge to help generate more income?"

They started throwing out ideas. Renee ran into her kitchen, grabbed a notebook, and came back out. She captured some of the less ludicrous ideas on paper. They kept coming back to the limited number of summer months here in Minnesota. How could they turn her business model into something sustainable all year round? That became their first guiding principle. A theme that started to emerge was a desire on Renee's part to help other women. She had been widowed young, a single mother for years, and unceremoniously dumped from her long-term place of employment. She had weathered some storms and come away with lessons learned she could share with others.

Renee kept thinking about all of the other areas in her life where she still wanted to make improvements. This included her finances, her health, and her relationships, to name a few. If she was looking for ways to improve in all of these different areas, others were, too. How could she help them?

A thought occurred to Renee and she shot up as if struck by lightning. "Oh my God! Why didn't I think of this before?"

Everyone stared at her expectantly.

She stood up, too excited to sit. "Remember when the kids and I flew to Fiji for New Year's? I met this amazing woman on the plane. Her name is Susan Metzel. We had a great visit. I also ran into her at a party on New Year's Eve. She told me all about how her sister almost ruined her life through a series of poor decisions after her husband died. He left her with a young family and no life insurance. But instead of giving up, her sister eventually found a way to thrive. She started helping other women in similar situations, found ways she could help them before things were too far gone. Eventually, with the help of her family, Susan's sister created a retreat business for women where they could teach life skills to help them become strong and independent. What if we did something like that here? I *know* Susan would help us!"

"Hmm, you know, you might be on to something, Renee," Jess said, staring thoughtfully into her margarita glass, still containing an inch of melting pink slush.

"What if we reconfigured the lodge so you could hold retreats there?" Ethan asked. "Right now the main level is pretty much just a couple of large open spaces. Same upstairs. I would have to draw up some sketches and take measurements, but we could maybe add some dormitory-type bedrooms and expand the bathroom area on the main level. I think we could still fit a gathering area near the kitchen, but it would have to be smaller. The kitchen isn't too bad now. With some adjustments to the layout you could probably serve meals out of there to larger groups. Upstairs you could still have a big open space, plus maybe a library."

The idea was getting some legs. Renee could feel her spirits lifting. Discussions continued, with everyone adding thoughts and points of view.

Lavonne spoke up, playing the devil's advocate. "But we don't know anything about the retreat business."

"You're right, we don't," Renee said. She took another sip of her drink. "But Susan does. Once they had their retreats up and running, they realized there was more demand out there than they could handle. So in addition to running their own retreats, they travel around the country and help others set up similar businesses. I'm sure I would have to pay them a fee, but I bet it would be reasonable. I can find out. I got the sense from Susan they're passionate about reaching more women. I don't think they're in it for the money. Of course, they have to make a living, too. If they have knowledge and a system they can share to help others get up and running quicker, that's value added, and they should get paid for it."

"Very true," Val said. "You know, Renee, it's only a forty-five-minute drive for me to get here from home. Maybe I could help you run the kitchen. I've been thinking about using some of my inheritance from Aunt Celia to start a catering business. She encouraged me to explore ways to capitalize on my love for cooking and serving in some way."

George clapped his hands together. "*That's* the way to do it!"

Renee beamed. "We could feature healthy meals, healthy cooking. Heck, maybe you could even offer a course on it, Val. Not as many people know how to cook these days, especially healthy meals."

"I'd be happy to give you some pointers on the business end," Jess offered.

"And I could help out with the lodge," Ethan said, "if you decided you wanted to offer overnight retreats. The cabins alone don't offer enough space and would need some serious work to winterize them. I could get you materials at cost and do at least some of the labor for you."

"I appreciate that, Ethan. You really are the best. But I couldn't let you do it for free. You have your own business to run. You can't afford to spend all your time doing charity work for me out here."

"We can work out the details later," Ethan assured her. "Aunt Celia was generous with all of us. I have some financial cushion now with the income Celia's rental properties are throwing off each month. I know she would appreciate me helping out here. Celia always had a soft spot in her heart for helping other women. I think she would have loved this idea."

By the end of the evening, everyone seemed excited about exploring the retreat business further. Renee planned to call Susan after the Fourth and learn more.

Renee had to agree with Ethan. Celia would love this idea.

CHAPTER 49

Gift of a Grandfather's Wisdom

*T*he rest of the holiday week passed quickly. George, Renee, and Ethan spent hours sketching out possible layouts for the inside of the lodge. They considered dorm-style rooms of different sizes. Some women would likely want private rooms while others may travel in with girlfriends and be fine with sharing rooms. Renee needed to visit with Susan about the average number of attendees and logistics that worked for them in the past.

The three worked on plans for everything except the kitchen. Val and Luke put their focus there. If they wanted to serve larger groups on a regular basis, there would need to be some appliance upgrades. They would need an industrial-style dishwasher, upgraded refrigeration, and, of course, a newer cook top, ovens, and microwaves. The water would have to be tested. Not all meals would have to be cooked on site but it would be easier if some prep could be done here.

Julie studied Susan's family's retreat business on their website. She was as excited about possibly holding retreats here at Whispering Pines as Renee was, but Robbie said little about it. Renee was too busy to notice, but George sensed Robbie's lack of enthusiasm.

He saw his grandson down at the shore by himself, skipping rocks into the lake.

"Hey, kiddo, what's up? I know it's been a crazy week with all of us here, but you've been awfully quiet. Something bugging you?"

Robbie skipped another rock, looking out at the water. "Yeah, Grandpa, something *is* bugging me. At first, I didn't want to spend my whole summer out here, away from home. But it hasn't been so bad.

We've met some cool people and I don't mind working outside. If we stayed home, I probably would've been stuck working fast food or filling shelves in a grocery store somewhere inside all summer. So that part is cool. But I heard you guys talking about Mom maybe starting some type of retreat business here. What would that mean for me? Would we have to move here permanently? What about my school and my teams? Julie goes back to college in the fall, but . . . what about me?"

George didn't answer right away. He kicked around on the beach until he found a flat stone and skipped it into the water.

"I don't know, Robbie. It would be hard for your mom to run a business located here from home. It would be a tough commute, especially in the winter. Your grandma and I, and your aunts and uncles too, all live closer than you guys do. You know how much your mom loves you, right? She has worked hard to provide for you and Julie. If her work required you both to move here, do you think you could do that for her? I know it's a lot to ask, but sometimes family has to make sacrifices for each other."

Now it was Robbie's turn to take his time replying. He plopped down on his butt and rested his arms on bent knees, staring out over the water.

"It would suck, having to go to a new school and starting over. I never thought I would have to do that. Thought I'd get to play basketball with my team and graduate from my high school. But I guess Mom never thought she'd get fired, right? She wouldn't be here now either if Aunt Celia hadn't left this place to her. Part of me wishes she would go back to a regular job . . . but this place isn't so bad." Robbie looked up at George. "I don't know, Grandpa. I have to think about it, I guess."

George stepped over to him and patted his shoulder. "Fair enough. Change is always tough. But sometimes, good things happen when you take a chance."

George stood next to Robbie, his hand on his grandson's shoulder. He didn't want Robbie to feel like he had to be the "man of the house" for Renee. He was still a kid. But he was growing up, and Renee was going to need his buy-in. If Robbie fought her on this, she might give in and take the easier route, heading home and taking another office job. George didn't want that for either of them.

Ethan quietly approached them on the beach. "Hey, Dad, can you come here? I want to show you something."

George heard something strange in his son's tone. "Sure, Ethan, be right there." He turned back to his grandson on the sand. "So you gonna be OK, Robbie?"

"Yeah, Gramps, it'll all work out, right? Go help Ethan. I'm gonna stay here for a while, maybe think about what you said." Robbie turned his attention back to the water.

George followed Ethan back up the beach and across the grass, toward the back side of the resort. Ethan was striding toward the cabin tucked into the edge of the woods. This was the last cabin still needing repairs before it could be rented. George had heard Renee refer to it as the "Gray Cabin." He supposed the name aptly fit the little structure. For some reason, it looked forlorn, sitting off by itself. George had been in it the weekend of Mother's Day, and remembered some damage, but hadn't been in it since.

Ethan spoke softly as they approached it. "I wanted you to see this. Renee asked me to see what it would take to fix that water damage in the back bedroom, and I finally got around to it. Let me know how you think we should handle this."

The two crossed the small front porch and entered the cabin. Ethan flipped on a light. It was dim inside. Heavy curtains blocked out much of the noonday sun. Nothing had been done in here yet and a heavy film of dust coated everything. Ethan walked through the kitchen and living area, back to the room with the damaged wall. He pushed the door open and flipped on another overhead light. He stood back so his dad could enter the bedroom.

"What the hell is this?" George hissed, surveying the room.

There were stubby little candles on the dresser and nightstand. White wax had dripped down onto wood tops. It was obvious the candles had been used, but George knew for damn sure they hadn't been there in May. The bed was made, but poorly; the old quilt was slightly off kilter and a bit lumpy, as if bedding underneath the coverlet was mussed from use. The coating of dust had been disturbed.

It looked to George like someone had been in here, maybe sleeping here . . . but for how long? When the bedroom door was shut, it would be impossible to see light from this room out in front of the cabin. The only window faced back toward the woods, and it was covered with a heavy curtain regardless.

"I think someone's been staying in here," Ethan said, voicing George's thoughts. "Could have been the same person that trashed the other cabin. I wanted you to see this before I said anything to Renee."

"Shit . . . this could do her in. But we have to tell her. It wouldn't be right to keep this from her. When we show the others, it's going to get crazy. I think we should take a few minutes and look around a bit first."

Ethan nodded, still looking around. "Yeah, you're probably right. Maybe someone started staying in here after we left on Mother's Day but cleared out when Renee and the kids moved in. *Or . . .* maybe whoever vandalized the cabin was holed up in here."

"Maybe . . . hard to say. Is that window locked?"

Ethan checked the window. It slid open easily. There was no screen, which was unusual. No one would leave a window open in a cabin in Minnesota without a screen. The place would fill with mosquitoes. Ethan poked his head out the open portal and surveyed the nearby area.

"The screen's lying in the grass, propped up against this back wall. The grass is pretty high back here, but it's trampled under the window. My bet is whoever's been in this cabin is coming and going through this window so they won't be seen."

George was taking a closer look around the bedroom. The tiny closet was empty. He didn't see any personal items someone might have left behind. The top drawer on the old scarred dresser wasn't closed all the way. George slid it open, thinking it was empty at first, but there was something lying in the bottom of the drawer, a piece of paper maybe. He pulled it out and flipped it over.

"Oh, God . . . Ethan, you have to look at this."

Ethan took the item from his now-pale father.

"Holy shit . . . a picture of *Julie?*"

Now he was confused. Why was there a picture of his niece in the dresser drawer?

George nodded grimly. "Looks recent, too."

George quickly went through all the other drawers, but there was nothing else.

"I think we better call the sheriff. Maybe we don't tell Renee about the picture right away. The possibility that someone has been staying in here, without her knowing, is going to scare her enough. We'll show the picture to the sheriff first and see what he thinks."

"OK, Dad, but we have to tell Renee at some point. You do realize that, right?"

George sighed. "Right now I'm more concerned with catching whoever took that picture of my granddaughter."

CHAPTER 50

Gift of the Storm

George was right. As soon as they showed the others what they discovered, things got crazy again. Renee called Sheriff Thompson directly, using the number on the card he gave her last Saturday morning. She handled it better than her dad and brother expected—at least the intruder part. They kept the picture from her for the time being.

Adults checked out the back room, but they kept all of the kids outside. If there was any evidence as to who might have been in there, no one wanted it disturbed before the police arrived. Lavonne and Renee lectured everyone to be discreet. They didn't want their new guests to find out what was going on. There was a good chance the squatter in the forlorn little cabin was also the person that vandalized the other cabin, although they couldn't yet be sure.

Sheriff Thompson and another deputy arrived. It didn't take them as long to get out to the resort this time. Renee and George stayed in the cabin while Ethan offered to meet the officers in the parking area and bring them back. This gave him a chance to discreetly show the picture to the sheriff. Ethan explained it was a picture of Julie, Renee's daughter, but the sheriff recognized her from his previous visit.

The sheriff agreed to let Ethan tell Renee about the photograph.

After the officers surveyed Whispering Pines for the second time in a week, they talked with everyone on site—including Grant and Grace—to determine if anyone might have noticed anything.

So much for keeping it from the guests.

Thompson was relatively sure it had been someone passing through the area, back when it had been uninhabited. He promised to "look into it," similar to what he had said about the vandalism, but Renee started to get the impression it wasn't going to be a priority item for their department. After about an hour, they drove off, saying again that they would be in touch.

Renee's family was scheduled to leave on Sunday morning. The remainder of Saturday was subdued after the discovery in the Gray Cabin. Val cooked up a traditional camp meal of hamburgers, hotdogs, corn on the cob, and baked beans. After the mess was cleared away, Luke took the kids down to fish with old poles and a Styrofoam bucket full of worms.

Ethan grabbed three beers out of the cooler. "Renee . . . Dad . . . you guys got a minute?" He handed a can to Renee and walked back to her patio, gesturing for them to follow. Once behind the house, George settled into a lawn chair and Ethan handed him a beer before taking a seat himself.

"Sit down, Renee," Ethan directed as he cracked open his beer.

Renee caught something in Ethan's tone. "Let me guess . . . this isn't going to be a friendly Saturday night visit over beers?" she joked, hoping to fend off any more bad news.

It didn't work.

Ethan got straight to the point. He handed his sister the snapshot. "We found something else in the Gray Cabin earlier, and you aren't going to like it. Dad found a picture of Julie in one of the dresser drawers."

Renee looked blankly at her brother then glanced down at the photo in her hand, struggling to understand why there would be a picture of her daughter in one of those old dressers.

"We wanted to get the sheriff's take on it before we told you," George explained, seeing Renee's confusion morphing into anger.

"All right—for the record, I am *not* OK with that decision." Renee paused, working to keep her temper in check. "Tell me what Sheriff Thompson thought about the picture."

"I get it, Renee," Ethan acknowledged. "I'd be pissed if I were in your shoes, too. Thompson thought some kids might have used the room for a little privacy . . . might have been when those college boys were here the same week Julie had friends out. Maybe Julie paired off with one of the boys and they went there to be alone. Maybe she gave him a picture, but it was forgotten when everything got crazy with the vandalism."

"That is absurd!" Renee scoffed, furious an assumption like that would even be made.

"Now calm down, honey," George said, trying to soothe his daughter's temper. "Remember, we had every intention of telling you about the picture. We just didn't want to hit you with everything at once. You've had a few shocks lately. And for the record, we don't think the sheriff's theory about how the picture ended up in that drawer is accurate. Kids snap pictures constantly with their phones these days. They wouldn't need a printed photograph. Besides, if Julie knew who had been back in that room, she would have fessed up before the sheriff was called again. The sheriff agreed to let us tell you about the picture in private and to let you decide how you want to tell Julie." He took a drink from his beer, swallowed, and sighed. "This is probably going to scare the hell out of her."

Renee sunk back into her folding chair, at a loss.

George continued, "It's up to you if and when you think Julie should be told. But we don't want to leave you here alone with the kids—there's been too much going on—so your mother and I discussed it, and we're gonna stay an extra week in the other duplex unit. That will give all of us a little more time to see if all goes back to normal."

Renee looked up at George, Ethan standing just behind him. "Look, I appreciate it, but I'm a big girl, Dad. You don't have to stay."

"We know that, but we want to. We can even help if you decide it's time to clean up the Gray Cabin."

"Seriously, Dad, you guys don't need to stay. Whoever was camping out in the Gray Cabin is probably long gone. Even if they weren't gone before today, they will be now."

"I tell you what," Ethan said. "Why don't we all sleep on it? We can talk about it again in the morning."

George smiled. "Capital idea, kiddo."

***

Renee couldn't fall asleep. She didn't want to dream about the Gray Cabin again. She tossed and turned. A thunderstorm rolled through. The low rumble and flashes of light matched her mood. It began to rain but there was no wind. Finally the rain soothed her to sleep and, mercifully, there were no dreams.

Lavonne was already downstairs, the coffee brewed and sweet rolls baking, when Renee came down in the morning. She joined her mom at the kitchen table.

"Mom, it isn't necessary for you and Dad to stay. We will be fine, I promise. Besides, Grant and Grace are here, too. Seriously, you've already helped so much with this place."

Before Lavonne could respond, Jess came in the back screen door, letting it slam behind her. She looked terrible.

"Jesus, Jess, what's up with you? You look like shit this morning," Renee teased.

"Renee!" Lavonne scolded one daughter while she rose from her chair and crossed the room to take another in her arms. "Are you OK, honey?"

Lavonne pushed Jess's hair back from her eyes, lifting her head up with a light touch on her chin. Jess's eyes were red-rimmed and swollen. A single tear traced a path down her cheek, but she managed a weak smile for her mother.

"Got a cup of that for me?" she asked, gesturing to the steaming mugs on the table. She extricated herself from her mother's arms and took a seat, laying her head on her forearms.

Lavonne, looking at a loss for words, poured her a cup.

Jess took it gratefully, using it to warm her hands as she sat in silence. She took a sip, then eventually said, "Will left."

Renee's mouth dropped open.

Lavonne stepped up to her. "What do you mean, he *left*? Did he have to go in for a patient? Do you need to borrow my car to get home?"

"Will left because I told him to leave. He's been having an affair, and I got sick of pretending I didn't know about it. When I first confronted him about it, he told me he would end it, but I didn't believe him. Not this time." She looked up from her mug soberly. "This isn't the first time he's cheated on me . . . but it *will* be the last. I am not going to give him a chance to do it again. At least to me."

"Oh, Jess," Renee said, coming to her sister's other side. "When did you find out? Why didn't you say anything? That son of a bitch!"

"I had my suspicions at Christmas, but I wasn't sure. And you were going through your own crap, Renee. I didn't want to give you any more to worry about, like I'm doing now. God, I'm sorry. And besides, I wasn't sure then. Believe me, when something like this happens, you don't want to acknowledge it yourself, let alone have anyone else find out. I feel like such an idiot."

Jess took another sip of coffee to calm herself, then continued.

"Things have been rough for a while. Will was spending so much time at the hospital, we hardly ever saw him. And when he did come home, he was withdrawn. Never wanted to do anything with us. Now I know he wasn't at the hospital as much as he claimed. He's been seeing a nurse from the hospital." She laughed bitterly. "It all sounds like a goddamn cliché."

"Did he admit to an affair, honey?" Lavonne asked her daughter, gently rubbing her shoulder to comfort her.

"He not only admitted it, once he could tell I wasn't going to forgive him, he told me he's going to be a goddamn *father* again. He actually said to me that he sees this as his chance at a fresh start. That did it. I kicked his ass out right then and there. Told him if he didn't get out of my sight immediately, I was going to go tell his children what a fucking loser their father is right then and there." She looked up at her mother's and sister's shocked faces. "You guys didn't hear him leave?"

"No," Renee said, suddenly feeling guilty for being too wrapped up in her own problems.

Jess shrugged. "Probably because it was during the storm last night. The thunder was pretty loud." She laughed again, this time less bitter. "I actually prayed God would fry him with one of those lightning bolts as his sorry ass was running out to the car."

Not used to hearing her sister swear so much, Renee had to bite back a giggle. She personally thought Will had been acting like an ass for the past decade. While she was sad to see her sister so upset, she wasn't surprised by any of this. His professional success had gone to his head.

And after Jess had worked so hard to put him through medical school!

"Renee, I want to stay here and help you. I don't want to go home for a while. I can't stand the thought of being anywhere near Will right now. I think you are onto something with your idea to hold women's retreats here at the resort, but you're gonna need some help. I need something completely different to work on so I don't focus on the shamble my life has become. I don't know how long I can stay, but at least for the rest of the summer. Is that OK?"

"Oh, honey, are you sure? What about the kids?" Lavonne asked, concerned Jess was making an irrational decision in her current state.

"Well, Nathan will head back to college mid-August. Lauren would need to stay here with me, if that's OK. She did some nanny work in June, but the mother had a new baby last week and will be on maternity leave until September, so they don't need Lauren anymore, at least for now. If I can get Internet out here, I can do most of my work remotely. I'll have to go to the office once in a while, but I think I can make it work. They need me. They shouldn't have too much problem with it."

"You have been doing some thinking about this haven't you?" Renee asked.

"I can't lie. I knew things with Will were reaching the point of no return, even before he dropped this bombshell on me last night."

"Do the kids know yet?"

"I'm sure they know I haven't been happy. Will and I don't even fight anymore, not like we used to. It was like we didn't even care enough to bother to argue. They're smart kids and they aren't babies. But they don't know Will left last night . . . or that he's already started family number two. The ass." Another tear joined the first. "I'll have to tell them this morning."

Renee leaned in and hugged her. "Of *course* you're welcome to stay here as long as you like. In fact, we should see if we can't make a few improvements to the other unit. It's in pretty tough shape. You and

Lauren will need to have some privacy. But are you sure you would be OK with those living conditions?"

"Are you kidding? I can't imagine going back to our house right now. I never felt comfortable there, anyway. Will always wanted everything so fancy, and it's so big. Having somewhere to recover from this, somewhere Will has never been a part of, would be perfect. I don't care if it's a little worn around the edges. I'm feeling pretty worn right now, too."

Lavonne nodded. "I think your dad and I should head home today. You are going to want some space, some alone time. I think as long as you and Lauren are here with Renee and her kids, I won't worry like I would if it was just the three of them." She rubbed her daughter's shoulder again. "Are you feeling better, Jess? I can hear Val and her family starting to pull up camp and they will have to leave soon. We better update her and your brother and dad on the change in plans."

Jess nodded, steeling herself, and finished her coffee. "Yeah, let's get this over with. Putting it off isn't going to make it any easier. I don't want to get into the details with everyone yet. I'll tell them Will and I are going to take a break. I need to talk to Lauren and Nathan first."

"Why don't you go do that now, honey?" Lavonne said.

Jess nodded. "Before I lose my nerve? Good idea. Mom, will you please go tell the rest of them?"

Lavonne smiled reassuringly, and they all hugged.

Jess pulled away and voiced something that had been on Renee's mind for quite a while now.

"God bless family."

CHAPTER 51

Gift of Rest

*B*y noon, all of Renee's extended family—except Jess and Lauren—had left. Nathan rode with his grandparents; he had to get back to his summer job at the golf course. He didn't seem too upset about his folks. George and Lavonne took Molly, too. She needed a booster shot, so George offered to take her to a vet for Renee.

Renters in two of the cabins also headed home. New renters weren't due in until the following day. Renee was dead tired. She hadn't slept much the night before and she hadn't relaxed in a month. Two hours, just two short hours, should be enough to help her recharge.

Jess, on the other hand, wanted to keep busy. Sensing Renee could use some time to herself, she loaded up the three teenagers in Renee's car and headed to town for a round of miniature golf and ice cream.

Alone at last, Renee went upstairs. She needed a shower and sleep. She considered a nap in the hammock in the backyard, but a tiny voice in the back of her mind suggested that might not be the best idea. Given recent events, she knew she wouldn't be able to relax enough to fall asleep, alone in the open like that. The temperature was pushing eighty-five degrees, so she cranked up the AC unit in her bedroom and took a cool shower. She slipped on a light tank top and cotton pajama shorts, shutting her bedroom door in case the kids got home while she was still sleeping. She set the alarm on her cell for two hours. The room was comfortably cool, and it didn't take her long to drift off.

***

She slowly surfaced from a dreamless sleep. Something had disturbed her, but she wasn't sure what. All was quiet. She glanced at her cell: she'd only been asleep for half an hour. She started to fall back asleep when someone knocked at the front door.

"Oh, crap," she groaned. *Two hours is too much to ask around here. Now who needs something?*

Renee considered ignoring whoever was at the door; maybe they would go away. But the rapping sound came again.

Giving up on her nap, but still groggy, Renee grudgingly left the comfort of her bed and headed downstairs to see who was so persistent. She flung open the door, but paused in shock when she saw who was standing there. A second later her face split into a huge grin and she launched herself straight at the man on her porch.

Matt caught Renee up against him, strong arms wrapping around her and rocking her gently back and forth. Neither said anything for a minute or two. He breathed in deeply. Renee's damp hair smelled of fresh flowers, and her body was warm from sleep.

"God, I needed this," he finally said.

Pulling back only far enough to look up at him, Renee studied his face, delighted but confused by his presence.

"Oh my God, what are you *doing* here, Matt? I can't believe you're here!"

Matt gently brushed back a stray curl from Renee's forehead, letting it wrap around his finger. His eyes roamed over her face. "You're even prettier than I remember, you know that?"

She smacked his chest, laughing. "Don't dodge the question!"

"Well now, it's kind of a long story. Maybe you should invite me in. I personally love what you're wearing, but I don't know that you want your guests seeing you in this if they're out for a walk."

Looking down, Renee shrieked in horror. She'd forgotten how little she had on. She felt herself blush furiously, grabbed Matt's hand, and pulled him inside, laughing but appalled at herself for being so careless. She would have been mortified if it had been anyone other than Matt standing there. The fact that it *was* Matt thrilled her.

She didn't let go of his hand after she pulled him into the cool interior, shutting and locking the door behind them. He didn't move away. They had been talking on the phone and emailing each other for months, learning bits and pieces of each other's lives, but both had become achingly aware of their inability to experience true intimacy with the other. Suddenly, they were here, together, and the air around them felt electric.

Matt caught Renee up against the length of his body. He slowly stepped her back until she could feel the cool door against her shoulder blades and bottom, a stark contrast to the heat she felt all along the front of her body. Matt dipped his head, catching her lips in a hungry kiss. Renee matched his urgency, dropping his hand to wrap her arms around his neck, her hands burying in his hair. It was like she was right back on that beach with him, surrounded by inky black night, white sand at their feet. Desire washed through her like the tide. He pushed her more firmly against the door, and she could feel his need. She let her arms relax, exploring his broad shoulders and back until he was shivering against her.

"OK, Renee, either we need to slow down, or I am going to show you right here on your living room floor how much I missed you," Matt warned her, resting his forehead against hers and gulping for air.

"I missed you too, Matt. So much. I have to admit, I've wondered what would have happened that night on the beach if your cell phone hadn't gone off. I've wondered it almost every night."

"You know exactly what would have happened," Matt chuckled, pulling back to look at Renee. "You intrigued me from the minute I first laid eyes on you."

"Oh, I did *not*. Now you are lying. There was nothing intriguing about me that first day on the beach, rumpled from travel, hungry, and ticked off at myself for locking my keys in the car. And then we crashed on the beach the next morning when you were out for your run. We fell into the sand and I had that awful creature crawling in my hair . . ." Renee remembered with a shudder.

"That isn't the way I remember it at all. I remember how you kept your cool, after what I'm sure was an exhausting day of travel, when you locked your keys in your rental. The next morning, you were so engrossed in finding the perfect sea shell, you didn't see me coming. I should have been watching where I was going instead of running you down." Matt held her close again and brushed his lips against her forehead. "But what I remember most vividly is you standing at the edge of the ocean with moonlight shining in your hair and on your shimmery dress as the clock ran out on the old year and a new year was dawning. It was like I was drawn to you, time and time again."

"Matt, I want you. I want to be with you. I'm home alone right now, which never happens. Come upstairs with me. We've waited long enough."

Renee again took Matt's hand, this time leading him up the stairs. He followed silently, raising her hand in his, kissing each of her fingers as they climbed. She pulled him a little faster now, not wanting to think too much about what she was doing. They entered her bedroom and she shut this door, too, locking it behind her.

He met her eyes. "Are you sure about this, Renee?"

Renee pulled him farther into the room. "No, I'm not sure about anything. But this feels right. I missed you. Even though we haven't spent much time together in person, we've been getting to know each other for months." Renee beamed at him. "I *still* can't believe you're here."

A shadow briefly passed over his eyes, but he smiled back at her.

"I missed you too, Renee. I didn't know what to expect, showing up here unannounced."

"Let me show you."

Renee slowly reached out and took a hold of the bottom of Matt's shirt. She eased it up over his head and let it fall to the carpet. Her hands caressed his chest, broad and muscular. He groaned and followed her lead, pulling her tank top up over her head and dropping it on top of his. Shyness had her stepping closer to Matt to pull his eyes from her breasts back to her face. Despite her wanting this, it was still scary to allow Matt to see her in broad daylight, to touch her.

It had been a long time, and she was nervous.

Sensing her hesitation, Matt again asked her if she was sure. Not trusting her voice, she walked over to her rumpled bed and lay down on her side, looking up at him. Seeing the invitation in her eyes, Matt laid down next to her so they faced each other.

"God, you are so beautiful. Thank you for the warm welcome," he teased, breaking the growing tension. She gave him a playful shove and he rolled onto his back, pulling her along and settling her on top of him.

They kissed again, exploring each other with their mouths and their hands. Sensations rose, and Renee forgot to be nervous. She had dreamed of this moment, literally, over the past six months. Matt's hands played down her back, massaging and stroking, pressing her even more firmly to him. He raised his knee slowly, creating an exquisite pressure where an insistent throbbing had started at her core. When she couldn't take it anymore, she rolled off him, pulling him along until they reversed positions. He stayed on top of her, kissing her deeply, until both of them needed to be closer still. Matt rolled to his side and slowly eased Renee's shorts down her legs, following behind the shorts with butterfly kisses. He tossed the shorts aside and quickly wiggled out of his constricting jeans and briefs.

Now when he again settled on top of her, there were no barriers between them. She could feel the length of him. Unable to hold off any longer, he gently nudged Renee's legs apart and slipped into her, both of them shuddering and moaning as he buried himself deeper. Giving her time to accommodate him, he used his forearms to bear some of his own weight, searching her eyes but not moving until she started to rock against him, inviting him. At her signal, he matched her rhythm, starting slowly but gathering speed as they raced toward release together. Gone was the careful, exploratory pace. Renee wrapped her legs around him, pulling him in ever deeper. He moaned at the exquisite rush, and she gasped as she was racked with wave after wave of pure energy.

Neither moved as the intense sensations began to subside, both savoring their closeness and the magic they shared. But it was getting hard for Renee to breathe; Matt was heavy in his current state of utter relaxation. He rolled off her but gathered her close. Renee snuggled in, her head against his shoulder as they both caught their breath, gazing at the slowly circling fan above.

Eventually, Renee gave a little shiver as the sweat on their bodies evaporated into the cooled air. Matt pulled a light cotton blanket over them, wanting to hold Renee close a bit longer.

"You OK?" Matt inquired, absently stroking her hair. "You're awfully quiet."

"Oh yes, I'm . . . *wonderful.* Honestly, I was thinking how relieved I am we never had a chance to make love on the beach back in Fiji."

Matt's hand froze mid-stroke, more than a little surprised at her response.

"What does that mean?" he asked, not sure he wanted to hear the answer.

"If we had, there would have been no way I could have waited over six months to do that with you again!"

"Oh jeez, you had me worried for a minute there, woman!"

With a giggle, Renee started tickling Matt and the wrestling match was on. Matt was so ticklish, he could hardly stand it. Renee was quick, but eventually he again had her pinned on the bed below him, holding her hands above her head to stop the tickling. Slightly appalled at his lack of control—all her squirming was already getting him aroused again—he bent to give her a hard kiss and then pushed himself back up off the bed. He reached a hand down to her and helped her up.

"If you aren't careful," he said, "we're going to wind up right back where we were on that bed again. While I certainly wouldn't complain, aren't you expecting your kids to be getting back any time soon?"

Renee clutched her arms to her breasts as if she expected them to walk in right at that moment. "Oh my God, what time is it? They can't come home and find us like this!"

And aren't they going to be surprised to see you! Renee reminded herself—after all, the kids still had no idea she'd kept in touch with the sheriff from Fiji.

Matt laughed. "Hold on. Relax. It's about two o'clock. When were you expecting them?"

Still clutching her chest, Renee took a deep breath. "Oh, thank goodness . . . Jess thought they'd be back about three."

"OK then, why don't we get dressed, straighten your room, and head out back to talk? Unless," Matt said with a laugh, "you'd rather spend the time going for round two."

***

Five minutes later, Renee and Matt were sitting in the backyard. Each had a glass of lemonade on the table between them.

"Why, *Matthew*, it is so good to see you! Whatever brings you *here?*" Renee asked him with a twinkle in her eye.

But Matt wasn't so playful now. He leaned forward in his chair, resting his forehead on his fists. He didn't immediately answer Renee. But then he sat back, took a deep breath, and began to share.

"About a month ago, my sister called and said I needed to come home. Dad was going downhill fast. It took me a few days to make arrangements, and then I flew back to the States."

Matt paused for a minute, sipping his lemonade and collecting his thoughts. "She made the right call, insisting I come home. When I got to the hospital, Dad wasn't arguing with the doctors and nurses to go home anymore. Not a good sign. It was as if he'd resigned himself to the fact he'd never go home. He was glad to see me, but didn't say much. I stayed with him that first night, fell asleep in the chair." He glanced at Renee, then dropped his head back to gaze at the brilliant blue sky. Renee reached over and carefully took his free hand, offering him support. He squeezed her hand and continued, "In the morning he didn't wake up. He lingered for a few more days, but never regained consciousness."

"Oh, Matt, I had no idea. I am so, so sorry. Why didn't you tell me? I talked to you last week. And the week before that. You never let on anything was wrong."

He gave her hand another quick squeeze, then released it, sitting back farther in his chair. "There was nothing you could've done. I knew you would have wanted to help. Hell, you probably would have wanted to fly out yourself. With how hard you'd been working to get this place up and running, I knew there was no way you should be away from here. I didn't want you to be distracted." He looked at her. "I'm sorry I wasn't more open with you, Renee. Really, there was absolutely nothing you could have done," he repeated.

How could I not sense something was wrong? Renee chided herself.

After another pause to collect his thoughts, Matt continued. "We started to get his affairs in order and held a small graveside service. It was nice. Dad would have approved. It was a beautiful summer day and we didn't make a big fuss. Dad would have hated anything fancy on his behalf. Then my sister and I had to deal with the farm and Dad's house. Things were in pretty tough shape. Dad wasn't able to keep up. Laura kept Henry, Dad's basset hound. The poor little dude howled every night for a week, confused at Dad's absence. We aren't sure what we want to do yet with the property. So we cleaned things up, I hired a family friend to take care of the yard and check the house periodically, and we're gonna take some time to figure out what to do long-term."

Renee reached out and took his hand over the table. "How are you holding up? That's an awful lot to push through in a short amount of time."

He nodded. "It's been tough. Honestly, Renee, I feel bad I wasn't here for Dad these last few years. I knew his health was failing, but I got used to living on the island and never made the time to get back and see him often enough. Laura tried to tell me but I didn't listen. I thought she was exaggerating. Turns out he was even worse than she thought. My only consolation is I know Dad would have been miserable if we had moved him off his farm. He lived out there until the end. That's what he wanted." He took his hand from Renee's and cupped his head again. "I can't believe he's gone."

He was silent like this for a moment before sitting back up. "I guess I needed to see a friendly face. Thank you for being that bright light at the end of an awful month for me. Maybe I should have called first, but . . . . I wanted to surprise you." He grinned sheepishly.

Renee knew there weren't any words she could say that would be of much help. She held out her hand again and he took it, holding tight and staring off into the woods again.

"What is *that*?" Matt suddenly asked, squinting at something out beyond the outer edge of her backyard.

Renee couldn't see what he was looking at. Just a bunch of trees. "What?"

He pointed. "Why do you have a trail cam on that tree, aimed at the house?"

"*What*? What do you mean?" Renee didn't have a clue what he was talking about.

Matt pushed himself out of his chair, still staring hard at something. He walked purposefully toward the woods, stopping ten feet into the trees edging the backside of her lawn. Renee followed him.

"Right there," he said, pointing up into a nearby tree. "That's one of those trail cameras hunters use to take pictures of wildlife. They have a motion sensor, and when something walks by, it snaps a picture. They're so quiet, animals don't even know they are there."

"I had no idea it was up there," Renee replied, gazing up at the small box. It was hard to see, blended in with the tree bark. "Maybe the old caretakers had trouble with deer or something eating their garden?"

"Hmm ... maybe. But this doesn't look old. Doesn't look like it's been out in the elements through a Minnesota winter. Want me to take it down so we can take a closer look? I think I can reach it."

Matt was tall. He was able to unhook the strap holding the camera to the tree without too much trouble. Together they left the shade of the trees, walking back into the warm sunshine, and sat back down on the patio.

He turned the camera around in his hands, examining it. The small camera was encased in greenish-brown, hard plastic with a lens on the front and various dials on the side. It looked complicated. "Looks like this one is a high-end version. These can take pictures day or night. Hmm ... the SD card is missing."

"Wouldn't we see a flash if it went off at night?"

He shook his head. "It uses infrared. A flash would scare animals off."

Renee stared at the thing in his hands as if it were a live animal. "This isn't good. Matt, I probably should fill you in on what's been happening around here. I was going to tell you one of these days. Just like you didn't want to worry me about your dad because there was nothing I could do, I didn't want to worry you with this stuff."

Now it was Matt's turn to be confused. He set the camera down. "What's been happening that you didn't want to tell me about?"

Renee hugged her arms around her, even though it was warm outside. "At first, I thought it was my imagination. A feeling or niggling worry that something wasn't right. Like when my friend Tabby was out here with me, and we were getting the cabins in shape. Remember, I talked to you when she was here? Anyhow, I heard something outside in the middle of the night but figured it was probably an animal or the wind. I wasn't feeling brave enough to go check it out myself. And there were other times, too, when I felt like someone was watching. Something set Molly off a few times, times when I couldn't tell what spooked her."

Matt looked around, having forgotten about Renee's dog. "Speaking of Molly, where is she?"

"Dad took her home with him earlier today to get her in for shots. Saves me a trip. Anyhow, a little over a week ago, we started having some . . . incidents."

Not liking the sound of that, Matt prodded her a bit. "What kind of incidents?"

Renee took a sip of her lemonade, condensation dripping off the glass onto her shirt, as she tried to decide where to start.

"I had three college boys renting one of the cabins the same week Julie had two of her girlfriends come out. Good group of kids. They all helped out, put some extra effort in cleaning up the lodge. Two days before they were set to leave, I made them a steak dinner here, in the backyard, to thank them for all their help. After all, the guys were paying guests. It was a fun evening. They played volleyball in the yard by the fire pit, and I brought Molly back here to give them some space.

"Molly freaked when we came in. I freaked out, too, when I saw there was a dead squirrel lying in the middle of my kitchen floor. To this day, I have no idea how it got there. The doors were both closed tight. Earlier that same day, I came back here and the door of the other unit was standing wide open. No one was around, but I figured someone hadn't pulled the door shut all the way. But that wouldn't account for a dead animal on the floor in *my* unit. The kids helped me clean it up and checked the house, but we couldn't find anything else."

Renee shivered at the unpleasant memory.

Matt frowned. "Any other incidents?"

Renee nodded. "The next evening, Julie and the other college kids all headed to a street dance in town. When the boys got back to their cabin, someone had done major damage inside while they were out. Slashed and busted the furniture, painted the walls, wrote a nasty message on the mirror, the whole nine yards."

"Wait, what? Somebody vandalized one of your cabins?" Matt glanced down at the camera lying on the small end table. "What the hell is going on? Did you call the police?"

"I did. The sheriff and a deputy came out that night. Of course, whoever did it was nowhere to be found. The officers took pictures, talked to everyone, said they'd be in touch. I have some pictures, too. I can show you when I'm done telling you everything."

Matt raised an eyebrow. "You mean there's more?"

"Unfortunately, yes, and the last thing worries me the most. A couple of days ago, my brother Ethan went over to work on the Gray Cabin."

"Gray cabin? I thought in the pictures you sent me they all looked pretty similar."

"Yeah, kind of, but there's one last cabin we haven't fixed up yet, tucked a little ways back into the trees. All faded and gray. I even had a few nightmares about it, for whatever reason."

Unpleasant premonition, Renee thought now with the value of hindsight.

"Anyhow, we knew there was some water damage in a back bedroom. Ethan wanted to see what it would take to repair the wall. He'd already stopped the leak earlier in the spring. Maybe I would still be able to start renting it out yet this summer if repairs didn't take too long. When he unlocked the cabin door and went back to the bedroom . . . what he found was bizarre and scary as hell. It looked like someone had been staying in there. The bed was rumpled and there were stubby white candles sitting on the two dressers, wax dripped down onto the wood. The window was unlocked."

"Do you think maybe someone used the room for privacy?"

"It's possible, but I don't think so. We called the sheriff back to let him know, given the vandalism the week before, and he asked that same question. Thought maybe some kids had gone in there."

Matt nodded, trying to wrap his head around everything. "So the fact someone might have been staying here without your knowledge has you freaked."

"Of course, but there's more."

"Jesus," Matt said.

"Dad found a picture of Julie tucked in one of the dresser drawers. None of us had been in there much up to that point. Why in the hell would there be a picture of my daughter in a drawer?"

"Have you asked her about it?"

Renee shook her head. "She doesn't know it was there. I need to tell her, but I haven't yet."

"Renee, you shouldn't have kept this from me. I don't want to scare you, but . . . if my years in law enforcement have taught me anything . . . this could be serious. You know I care about you, and your kids are great. I hate the thought of you alone out here with all this happening. Do you have any idea who might be behind this?"

Renee shifted in her lawn chair, trying to get comfortable as a bead of sweat rolled down her back—whether from the heat or from fear, she couldn't say.

"I've thought long and hard about it. I'm at a total loss. We haven't met many people around here yet except our renters. Other than one couple complaining constantly, all my renters have been great. I don't have any enemies that I know of."

"Do you mind if I visit with the local sheriff about all this? Maybe I can help."

"Matt, with everything you shared about your dad, you don't have time to take any more on. Besides, when do you have to go back?"

Matt shrugged off her concerns. "I was hoping to spend a few days here, before flying back to Dad's for a day and then catching my flight back to Fiji. That is, if you're OK with me hanging around?"

"Absolutely! It's great to have you here. I still can't believe you actually *are* here. If you want to go talk to Sheriff Thompson, I don't mind. Anything to get some answers. And by the way, I'm not going to be out here with just the kids and an evolving stream of renters I don't know. My sister sprang it on me this morning that she told her husband she wants a divorce and she and her teenage daughter are staying in my extra unit for the next month or so. I also have one of our cabins rented out to Grant and Grace. Remember me telling you about the brother-in-law I never knew about and his sick daughter? Well, they needed to go someplace quiet so Grace could recuperate. They decided to rent a cabin from me for a month, too."

Matt grinned. "Sounds like you don't have room for me."

"Don't be silly, you can stay in Julie's room. She can bunk with me. Sorry I don't have a cabin open to put you in. Unless you want to stay in the grungy old Gray Cabin," Renee teased.

"If you're sure you don't mind, I'd love to stay here with you. It will be fun to meet more of your family. I don't suppose we can arrange to have them all gone for about an hour each afternoon like they were today? I don't think spending only one short hour in bed with you will be enough for me."

Feeling herself blush for the umpteenth time, Renee had no comeback for that comment. But she was saved from further embarrassment by the sound of a vehicle out front. Renee stood and Matt rose to stand beside her.

"Sounds like it's time to meet the family," Renee said, reaching for Matt's hand.

Matt took it and used it to pull Renee up tight against him to steal a quick kiss and then released her, scooping up the camera. "Maybe you want to go put this somewhere safe until we can figure out what to do with it. Probably don't need the others to see it until we know more."

"Good idea."

Renee ran the camera into the house and joined Matt back on the patio seconds later. Footsteps pounded up the trail toward them.

"Give me that back, you little shit," Julie screamed, hot on Robbie's heels. He had something clutched in his hand as he ran out ahead of his sister. Lauren wasn't far behind. None of them noticed Renee and Matt at first.

"Give me back my phone *right now*!"

All three teens slid to a stop in front of Renee.

"Whoa, what's up, guys?" hollered Renee.

"Robbie thinks he's being *cute*, taking my phone and texting Ben, pretending to be me. So now I'm going to kill him!" Julie lunged at Robbie, attempting to grab her phone out of his outstretched hand.

"Hey, settle down. Robbie, give your sister back her phone right now. You know better than that. If you two are done acting like you're three years old, I have a surprise for you. Remember Matt?"

Both Robbie and Julie finally noticed the man standing slightly behind their mother. Both looked equally confused.

Robbie was the first to speak. "Oh, hey there. Didn't expect to ever see *you* again."

Julie elbowed Robbie in the stomach as she stepped past him toward Matt. She gave Renee a sideways look, as if silently asking her *What the heck?* But she was gracious to Matt, extending her hand in welcome.

Matt gave Julie's hand a shake. Before he could explain his presence, Jess approached on the trail and came across the grass to join them all in the backyard, glancing between Renee, Matt, and the kids.

"Matt, I'd like to introduce you to my sister Jess and her daughter Lauren," Renee said, motioning to the two. "Matt is a good friend I met when we were in Fiji last winter."

Ever the calm, cool, collected sister, Jess eyed Matt skeptically, taking her time before replying. "Well, hello, nice to meet you, Matt. My sister didn't tell us she was expecting company."

Matt glanced between Renee and her sister. The family resemblance was noticeable, but Jess seemed more reserved. "Nice to meet both of you, too," he replied, nodding toward Jess, then Lauren. "Unfortunately, I had a death in the family so I had to fly home. I had some extra time before I'm due back, so I thought I would surprise Renee."

An awkward silence followed introductions. No one but Renee seemed to understand why Matt was there. The kids hadn't known she kept in touch with him after they got back. She had never talked about Matt to Jess. Other than telling Tabby about him, she had kept her friendship with Matt to herself. She was finding it entertaining that everyone was having such a hard time comprehending why a man would come to visit her.

"I bet everybody is getting hungry. I don't have anything fancy planned for supper. Why don't I throw in some frozen pizzas?" Renee suggested, not wanting Matt to feel too uncomfortable.

With that, everyone dispersed. Julie mumbled something about calling Ben to explain her imbecile brother. Robbie wandered over to the house. Jess and Lauren said they wanted to go freshen up before dinner.

"Well, *that* was a little awkward," Matt said, exhaling. "Apparently your sister has never heard my name?"

Renee grinned. "You noticed that, huh? Honestly, I didn't want to tell anyone about us. At least, I didn't want to when I didn't know if I would ever see you again. I so enjoy our talks. Normally I'm an open book and my family pretty much knows everything about me, so it's been . . . kind of *fun* having a little piece of my personal life stay personal, ya know?"

"But then all of a sudden I show up on your doorstep . . ."

"Yep, the cat is out of the bag now! And believe me, I am going to get grilled for this. If it was anyone other than Jess, she would be inside right now calling my mother and sister to tell them I have a man here. But Jess isn't like that. She will ask me about you, but she'll leave it up to me whether or not I want to tell anyone else. The kids, on the other hand . . . no promises there."

"So, how do you want to play this? Like platonic friends? Or hot lovers? Because I gotta tell you, hot lovers sounds like a whole bunch more fun," Matt teased, stepping close enough now to be in her personal space.

"Believe me, if Jess hadn't kicked her husband down the road last night and my kids weren't at such vulnerable ages, I would be all in for the 'hot lover' approach. But we are probably going to have to try for some discretion this time."

"I understand," Matt said, flashing his cute dimples. "But maybe we could sneak in a midnight swim or something when they're all asleep."

Renee frowned suddenly as images flashed through her head of hidden cameras, a trashed cabin, and a mystery person hidden away on the property.

"Normally I would be intrigued by your suggestion—I have to admit I've never had the opportunity to skinny dip. But now I'd be afraid someone was watching. There's been too much crap going on around here lately for me to be comfortable outside at night like that."

"Oh jeez, Renee, I'm sorry. I shouldn't even kid around about stuff like that until we figure out what has been going on. I promise you, I'll help you get to the bottom of this, OK?"

"I hope we can figure something out . . . this is driving me *crazy*."

CHAPTER 52

Gift of Loyalty

"So you gonna tell me what the deal is with Matt?" Jess asked when Renee went in to start the oven and Matt made a trip out to his rental to grab his luggage.

"I would if I knew what the deal was, but it's . . . complicated. We met in Fiji when I locked my keys in the car—he's a sheriff there—and I saw him a few more times while I was on the island. We exchanged contact information and have been talking on the phone about once a week or so. Sometimes we email, too. He's a nice guy. I didn't know if I would ever get a chance to see him again."

Jess nodded, but she was still suspicious of Matt. "What kind of family emergency brought him to the States?" she asked.

"His father died. Matt's sister asked him to come home because their dad was failing. Matt managed to see his dad shortly before he slipped into a coma. He took a month off from work for personal leave, but it didn't take him the whole time to settle his dad's affairs so he decided to surprise me."

"How much do you know about him?"

"Well, as I said, I know he's the sheriff in the area where we stayed back in Fiji . . . he has contacts in law enforcement back here . . . he even helped me out with a little situation I had with Robbie a while back. He was married, back when he was a cop on the East Coast, but he's been divorced for years. No kids."

"Don't you think it's odd, him showing up here like this?"

Jess cut off her interrogation when the front door slammed. "Where should I put my suitcase?" Matt asked good-naturedly.

"Julie's fine with you staying in her room. To the right at the top of the stairs. Why don't you put your stuff in there and come join us?" Renee suggested.

Matt joined them in the kitchen a few minutes later. Jess was leaning against the sink, leveling a less-than-welcoming look at Renee's visitor.

Renee shoved a frozen pizza in the oven, set the timer, and tossed her hot pad on the counter.

"As you can see, my sister here has suspicions as to your character and reason for showing up here unannounced," Renee said to Matt, nodding her head in Jess's direction. "It's hard for her to grasp why a man might be interested in paying me a visit."

"Oh, that is bullshit and you know it, Renee," Jess declared. "I never said that. I'm just trying to protect my sister. You have to admit, there's been some weird shit happening around here lately . . . and then this guy shows up out of the blue, who I've never heard a word about before today . . . Can you blame me?"

"You raise a good point, Jess," Matt agreed. "You should be skeptical, given what's happened. Renee updated me this afternoon. She agreed to let me go visit the local sheriff tomorrow to see if they're any closer to some answers. If you still have reservations about me, come along and have Sheriff Thompson check into my background." Matt nodded at her. "I like you. I like your attitude."

Jess continued to stare pointedly at Matt for another minute, then pushed off from the sink.

"All right, as long as you don't say or do anything that seems out of line, I am going to accept you at face value. Renee isn't stupid. I trust her to be a decent judge of character."

"Don't mind her," Renee said to Matt. "She's just mad at all men today."

Now Renee was on the receiving end of Jess's glare. But Renee knew her sister would come around, so she took Matt's hand and pulled him out the back door onto the patio, leaving Jess to sulk in the kitchen.

"Sorry about that . . . Jess isn't usually so cynical."

Matt chuckled. "Don't worry about it, she's going through some tough times right now. I show up unannounced . . . I get it. My plan is to enjoy some time with you before I have to go home. I promise not to do anything to upset your family."

"Does spending time with me include helping me get a couple cabins ready for new guests coming in tomorrow? Because that was how I was planning to spend my evening."

Matt beamed, spreading his hands in a welcoming gesture. "You bet!"

***

True to his word, after dinner Matt accompanied Renee to clean the cabins. He was impressed with how Renee, along with help from Tabby and her family, had cleaned up the resort. He remembered the "before" pictures she'd emailed him, so he could tell they had made lots of progress since early spring.

Matt vacuumed while Renee cleaned the bathroom in the first cabin. When she went to strip the bedding, he offered to help. Dirty linens were tossed in a large hamper, and before Renee could wrestle the clean sheets onto the mattress, Matt managed to pull her down onto the bed to steal a few kisses.

The sound of footsteps on the front steps and the slap of a wooden screen door had them both scrambling to their feet, giggling and adjusting their clothes like a couple of guilty teenagers. It was Julie, bringing in clean towels. If she noticed anything, she didn't let on.

It didn't take them long to get the two cabins ready. It was still light outside, so Renee took him over to the lodge next, chatting excitedly the whole way. She really *did* feel like an excited teenager all over again. A feeling she hadn't experienced in . . . God knew when.

"We've been doing some brainstorming the past week or so," she explained to him as they walked, "and have some ideas we want to pursue. If we only rent out the five cabins—and no one will rent out here in the dead of winter—there won't be much income left over after covering expenses. Celia ran the resort with just the cabins, and only in the summer, but she also had a day job. This was more like a hobby for her. And on top of everything, property taxes have really gone up, too. So I am seriously considering hosting retreats here. We would need to make some significant upgrades to the lodge, but I think we're on to something."

As Renee walked Matt through the lodge, she went into more detail around their preliminary plans. She told him about Susan and how her business helped people set up retreats to assist women in various aspects of their lives. She showed him where they were thinking about building in sleeping rooms and expanding the bathroom on the first floor, then took him upstairs.

"I'd love to build huge windows into this wall facing the lake and add a library down on that end, with a crackling fire and shelves full of wonderful books . . . just *imagine* it," she said, sweeping her arms in wide arcs to emphasize her big dreams.

"Wow, Renee, you've put some thought into this, haven't you?" Matt replied as he wandered through the upper level with her.

"We started brainstorming about this a few days ago. But I have to tell you, between wanting to find out whether or not we could make a go of some type of retreat business plus the strange crap that has happened lately, I'm not sleeping much."

"For the record, I'm happy to help keep your mind off your troubles tonight if you aren't able to sleep," Matt teased, reaching for her.

Renee laughed. Matt's hands glanced off her shoulders as Renee took a quick sidestep, pretending not to notice his attempted embrace. *Damn, it feels good to flirt like this. Much better than over the phone,* she thought, not wanting to come across as too eager—but not refuting his idea for a nighttime distraction, either. "It would be a welcome diversion," she assured Matt with a wink.

Now it was Matt's turn to laugh as he followed Renee back down the stairs. "Seriously though, you have me intrigued with your retreat concept," Matt said. "Tell me more. What kind of retreats?"

Renee halted, considering his question. "Well . . . we still have lots to figure out, but our initial thought was to offer retreats for women to assist them in different areas of their lives. We're thinking things like finances, relationships, healthy living . . . you know, that kind of thing. I really want to help people before they hit rock bottom."

This time when Matt reached for Renee, she didn't avoid him.

"I like it," he said, pulling her close. "Lots of women out there could benefit from a helping hand, before they find themselves in a really bad place."

A shadow passed over his eyes; Renee could tell he was remembering a few of the many tragedies he must have witnessed on the job.

Renee wrapped her arms around Matt's waist and held tight for a minute. It felt good to be in his arms. Eventually she stepped back, walking over to flip on a light. The sun was setting, casting the interior into shadows.

"Jess wants to help. My brother, Ethan, is a contractor and offered to help me make the physical changes to the building. My other sister, Val, is an awesome cook and she's been playing around with the idea of starting some type of catering business. She offered to help me provide meals to retreat guests." Renee led him into the kitchen. "And, of course, my parents want to help, too. There is so much to think about and figure out, but I'm excited."

Matt glanced around the large kitchen.

"I love how you think outside the box to find ways to make this resort work for you. I take it you've decided you're not going back to an office job anytime soon?"

"Believe me, I've given it serious consideration throughout these past few months. But I keep coming back to how awful I felt when I was laid off. I want to try to do something totally different. I figure, if it doesn't work out, that can be my Plan B. For now, I want this place to be my Plan A."

It was getting darker and Renee wanted to get home to the kids. They locked up and headed back to the duplex. Robbie was in his room listening to music, and Julie was over in the other unit hanging out with Jess and Lauren. Renee pulled two beers out of the fridge and sat down at the kitchen table with Matt.

"I still can't believe you're sitting here, having a beer with me in my kitchen," Renee said, reaching across the table to Matt.

He took her hand, tapped his bottle to hers, and took a pull of the icy cold beer.

"Yeah, it's been crazy. It seems surreal to me to be sitting here, too. All I've been doing since you left is working. When I first started working in Fiji most of the crime was low-level stuff. But it's ramped up—more drugs, some violence . . . more of the shit that pushed me out of the force years back. At first I loved the beautiful weather and beaches, but now . . . I don't make time to enjoy it. I go home after a shift but only my dog is there to greet me." He looked into Renee's eyes. "I look forward to our talks. Thank you for staying in touch."

"Are you *kidding*? I love our talks, too. *I* should be the one thanking *you*. Matt . . ." Renee stared down at her beer. "I have to ask. Do you date at all?" Before waiting for an answer, she went on. "Of course, it's OK if you do. We never talked about it. I know we live so far apart—it isn't realistic to think we can have a real relationship." She finally looked up at him. "But I do wonder about it sometimes."

Matt smiled, calming her racing heart. "Renee, you're wrong—I *do* think this is a real relationship. At least, it feels like the beginning of one to me. Yes, it's hard living so far apart. But you've kept my interest from the day I met you. I did go out a time or two, shortly after you left, but I was never interested in going out with anyone a second time. It's been . . . God, *months* since I even did that. You?"

Renee shook her heard. "Well, as you know, my life's been full since the beginning of the year. I don't know that I could have found time to go out with anyone even if I'd wanted to. My weekly calls with you have been the sum total of any romance in my life lately."

Matt stood and set his beer on the table. He pulled Renee up into an embrace, tilted her head back with a finger under her chin, and kissed her softly.

He pulled away after a moment. "Thank you for bringing this up. To be honest, it's been bugging the hell out of me. Some nights I would lie in bed and wonder if you were seeing anyone. I hated the thought but knew there wasn't a damn thing I could do about it if you were. Your life is here, and mine is there. But all of this with my dad is making me do some serious thinking. Maybe my life isn't meant to be in Fiji. It's definitely been a nice three-year hiatus, but it might be time for me to come home. My niece and nephew are growing up so fast. I want the chance to be part of their lives, not someone they see once a year, ya know?"

Renee looked up at him, surprise registering in her eyes. "You're considering moving back to the States?"

"Yeah, I'm considering it . . . haven't made up my mind yet. Maybe I could move back and live at my dad's farm. We don't want to sell it."

"If you lived somewhere within driving distance, even though it would be a long drive, we might actually get to see each other once in a while."

He pulled her in closer. "We just might at that. I could certainly get used to *this* . . ."

And they were kissing again. Standing in the middle of her kitchen, no less, with her kids not far off—but Renee didn't care. He deepened the kiss and she welcomed it, desire again coursing through her. A thud from above broke them apart. Matt had a way of both exciting her and grounding her at the same time. She had pretty much convinced herself she would always be on her own. Now she was starting to remember what she had been missing.

CHAPTER 53

Gift of Concern

*M*att's time at the resort passed quickly. Unfortunately, not all of his short time could be spent behind Renee's closed bedroom door; some of it was spent cleaning, getting to know everyone ... and searching for answers behind what was going on at the resort.

He drove in and met with the sheriff. Renee had called ahead and explained who Matt was to Sheriff Thompson. She gave the sheriff permission to discuss all aspects of the case with Matt. Matt went alone; he wanted to be able to have an open, frank conversation but didn't want to scare Renee. His gut told him something serious was going on.

A young deputy took Matt back to the sheriff's office.

"Thanks for taking the time to meet with me, Sheriff Thompson," Matt said as he shook the older man's hand.

"Happy to meet with you," Thompson replied. "I understand you're a friend of Renee Clements? Shame that girl's havin' trouble out there already. I knew her aunt. Celia was a special lady. Hate to think someone might be hanging around, causing her niece trouble."

Matt nodded—he hated the thought, too. "That's why I stopped by. I was curious if you've come up with any suspects yet."

Thompson motioned to Matt to take a seat and slowly walked back behind his desk, dropping into a wooden desk chair; the chair groaned in protest, and Thompson groaned from the effort, limited though it was.

"Nah," he finally answered. "Nothing much to go on. Haven't had any reports of drifters through here lately. Renee and the rest of the folks out at the lodge didn't offer up any ideas to go on, either." His shrug seemed to imply *What more do you expect me to do?*, although he didn't say it out loud.

Matt sat forward in his chair, clasping his hands in front of him and leveling a no-nonsense look at Thompson. He really didn't like how nonchalant this guy seemed to be about the whole thing. "Have there been any other reports of vandalism in the area? Any kids causing problems? Sometimes kids get bored in the summer, start looking for trouble just to have something to do."

"Look, I appreciate your comin' down here to see if we have any updates. Celia was a friend of mine, and I'd like to help Renee with this, but like I said, we don't have much to go on. My crew here is pretty green, and there's never enough money to put on more staff or hire anyone with any goddamn experience."

Sounds familiar, Matt thought as he listened to the old man gripe.

Thompson rolled his shoulders and rubbed at his neck. "Sorry, don't mean to complain. I hate that shit, listening to people complain. Try not to do too much of it myself."

Matt knew he wasn't going to get any answers in this office today. He stood. "Tell you what. I'll talk to Renee some more. Maybe there's something or someone behind this she knows and she just hasn't put two and two together yet. I'll sit her kids down, too, have a heart-to-heart with them. If they share anything I think might be useful for you, I'll give you a call."

Sheriff Thompson rolled back in his chair, preparing to stand himself.

"No, don't get up," Matt said. The older man looked beat, and apparently that chair presented a real challenge to him. "I can see myself out." Matt pulled out his wallet and extracted a business card, handing it to Thompson. "If you do get any leads, give me a call. I'll be in the States for a few days yet. Appreciate your time."

"Sorry I couldn't be of more help," Thompson apologized, tucking Matt's card into the chest pocket of his uniform shirt.

***

When Matt got back to the resort, he asked Renee to walk him through the Gray Cabin. He agreed—it looked as if someone had stayed there in secret.

They walked back to the duplex. Together they sat at her kitchen table and carefully reviewed pictures of the vandalism in the other cabin, too. It was cleaned up now and she had a renter there, so he didn't go into the actual cabin.

"I'm sorry Thompson doesn't have any answers yet," Matt said, handing Renee's iPad back to her after studying the pictures of the damage. "I didn't get the impression any of this is high on his priority list."

Renee nodded. "He seemed surprised when I called and said you were coming down."

"Why don't we sit down with Julie and Robbie?" Matt suggested. "I think I need to talk to them. See if maybe there's something they haven't wanted to mention, or didn't think mattered. And, Renee, you *have* to tell Julie about the picture."

The kids were out back playing fetch with Molly. Matt had noticed they hadn't been around much while he was here. They were friendly enough, but mostly kept their distance. Still, he needed to talk to them about this vandalism.

Renee rose and walked over to the door, hollering through the screen to her kids to come inside.

She looked at him and sighed. "Shit. I know I need to tell her," Renee agreed, walking back to the table. "I've put it off long enough."

The back door opened on squeaky hinges and Molly bounded through, going straight to Matt. He petted the dog's head and she sat close to him, leaning into his leg and panting.

Well, he thought, *at least Renee's dog likes me.*

Julie held the door open. "Hurry up, Robbie, the mosquitoes are getting in!"

Robbie squeezed past his sister into the kitchen. "What's up, Mom?"

"Sit down, guys," Renee said, taking her seat again next to Matt. "We need to talk."

They sat, eyeing Matt. He petted the dog.

"You know we never like it when you start a conversation like that, Mom," Julie said.

"And you aren't going to like what I have to say," Renee replied, "but it's time."

Matt rose and scooped up Molly's water bowl from beside the fridge. He took it over to the kitchen sink to fill it, giving Renee space to talk to her daughter.

Renee took a deep breath. "Julie, remember when your grandfather and uncle discovered that mess in the bedroom in the Gray Cabin?"

"Yes ... but, Mom ... I told you, I didn't have anything to do with that," Julie said, immediately defensive.

Matt watched her closely as he rinsed out the water bowl.

Renee raised her hand. "I know, Julie, and I'm not saying you did. We probably should have told you this right away, and I'm sorry, but I didn't want to scare you."

"Wait ... what's going on, Mom?" Julie asked, confused when she realized she wasn't about to be blamed for something.

Robbie kept quiet, looking on.

Renee's purse was sitting in the middle of the table. She rummaged through it and pulled out a photograph, handing it to her daughter. "Grandpa George found this in a dresser drawer. Back in that bedroom."

Julie reached for the photo, looked at it, and dropped it onto the table, recoiling.

"Mom, why would you keep something like this from me? Are you crazy? I am *not* a child. I deserved to know." She swung her furious gaze to Matt. "Matt, what do you think it means?"

Matt set the bowl back down on the floor and Molly lapped greedily at the water. He pulled his chair around and positioned it in front of Julie. He sat down, facing the girl, and looked her in the eye.

"Well, to be honest, I'm not sure ... but I'm having a hard time coming up with any reason that doesn't worry me. Julie, can you think of anyone that might have an interest in you? Maybe someone you dated? Or turned down for a date?"

Julie eyed the photo lying face-up on the table, not immediately replying to Matt's question.

"What about that guy you were worried about at Christmas?" Renee asked. "Remember, you said he kept calling and you were worried he was acting obsessed?"

This snapped Julie's attention back and she swung to face her mother.

"You mean *Lincoln*? I haven't seen or talked to him since the holidays. When I got back to school in January, he wasn't there. I *told* you that. I ran into the guy he roomed with first semester, and he said Lincoln never came back when second term started. All of Lincoln's stuff had been cleared out of their room, and he never saw him after that. Lincoln sent him a text saying he wouldn't be back, was going to try something different. I was relieved he was gone—meant I didn't have to deal with it anymore."

Julie reached across the table and flipped the photo face-down, shuddering. Matt watched her walk to the fridge, pull out a Diet Coke and take a sip. She seemed nervous.

Matt pulled out his phone. "You might be right, Julie, the boy might not have anything to do with this. But why don't you give me his full name, number, and hometown. I'll do a little discreet checking."

Now it was Julie's turn to pull out her phone. "Well . . . OK . . . but just for the record, I think it's a waste of time." She pulled up his contact information and handed the phone to Matt.

Matt really did doubt the boy was involved. Kids dropped out after their first semester of college all the time. Julie hadn't heard from him in over six months. But Matt would do some checking to be sure.

Matt turned his attention back to Julie. "Anyone else you can think of?"

She took a sip of her Diet Coke, thinking for a long moment, then shook her head. "No . . . no idea."

"OK, well, keep thinking about it, and let me know if you think of anything else. Now, Robbie, what about you? Anyone been bothering you at school, or anyone you met around here this summer?"

Robbie had been messing around with his phone, content to let his sister answer the questions. Now he looked warily at Matt, fidgeting in his seat.

"Nah, it's been low-key here," he replied. "I haven't done much more this summer than work with Mom fixing this place up and mowing grass. The only two weird things I can even think of were what happened that night we dropped gifts off at Anna's and the guy at school who got mad at me when I didn't want to buy any of those pills from him."

"Wait, what? Back up a minute," Julie insisted. "Nothing happened when we dropped off Anna's gift. And what guy with pills?"

Now it was Robbie's turn to get up and grab something to drink out of the fridge. He popped the top on his Mountain Dew, leaning against the fridge door. "It probably doesn't matter now, but something *did* happen up at Anna's. I didn't tell you 'cause I knew you would tell Mom, and Mom already had way too much to worry about back then. Wasn't a big deal, really. Still bugs me a little, though ... it was so *weird*." He paused, sipping his Dew. "Remember, I put on that Santa suit and walked back through the alley to deliver Anna's gifts? After I gave her the box and she went inside, I was walking back through the alley and some guy came up behind me and knocked me down. I can't remember exactly what he said, but it was something like ... 'Stay away from her.' "

Renee inhaled sharply. "Jeez, Robbie, why wouldn't you tell us that? You could have been hurt!"

Matt glanced Renee's way, giving her a slight shake of his head when she met his eye. He needed her to let Robbie articulate what happened. He didn't want the boy to temper his recounting to spare his mother.

"I was ticked off and maybe a little scared," Robbie continued. "Took me by surprise, knocked the wind out of me for a minute. By the time I got my bearings, the guy was gone. I hurried back out to the street because I was a little worried he might have approached you, too, Julie. But you never mentioned anything and I figured you didn't see him. The guy was probably drunk or stoned or something, and seeing Santa walking down the alley maybe set him off for some bizarre reason. You know, Christmas is the most common time for suicide, biggest holiday for alcohol, crap like that."

"Did anything else unusual happen that night?" Matt asked.

"Not that I noticed," Robbie said with a shrug, pushing off from the fridge door and meandering back to his chair.

Matt could see Renee was biting her tongue.

"OK, let's assume for a minute that's all it was," Julie conceded, "but what about the other thing . . . a guy and pills?"

Robbie looked down sheepishly, fiddling with the tab on his soda can, sparing a quick glance at his mom. "That was me being stupid. I was working hard at basketball, trying to make varsity. There was this guy at school. I barely knew him, but he was trying to get kids to buy these pills he said he bought off the Internet. He said they'd help me be better out on the floor, quicker and stronger. He gave me a few to try. I took one and stuck the rest in my pocket. I got sicker than a dog from the one, had to go home from school. I forgot about the other two pills. Mom found them."

Julie stared around. "Oh my God, why do you people not tell me this stuff! I am *so* out of the loop."

Robbie shrugged again.

"Did the guy from school ever approach you again after you told him no?" Matt asked.

"Not really. He called me a pansy-ass one time when I walked by him in the hallway and he bumped into me hard one other time when he walked by, trying to act all tough. But he never gave me too much shit."

"Robbie, language!" Renee scolded.

"Oh, come on, Mom, give me a break. We're sitting here trying to figure out who is stalking us, and you're worried about a few swear words? *Damn.*"

"OK, first of all, we don't know that this is *stalking*, so watch what you say. And second of all, show some respect."

Matt got up and stood behind Renee. He laid a hand on her shoulder.

"It's all right, Renee. We're all a little nervous about what's been going on. Don't worry, we'll get to the bottom of this."

***

Nothing unusual happened while Matt was visiting, and then too soon, it was time for him to leave. The two of them managed to go out for a nice dinner the night before he left. Jess stayed at the resort with the kids. Of course, they were plenty old to stay alone, but given what had been going on, Renee wouldn't allow it.

Matt said goodbye to Renee's family, but not before making sure each of them had his number in their cell phones in case of any more emergencies. Renee walked him out to his car.

"Thanks for driving all the way out here to visit. I'm sorry you can't stay longer."

"I'm sorry, too . . ." He saw the look on her face and tried to cheer her up. "Come here, you. You gonna miss me?" Matt teased, pulling her close.

"Oh, you know . . . maybe a *little*."

"Any chance I can convince you to talk more than once a week? Maybe we can Skype, save on the phone bill. I want to know what's happening out here. And I know after spending time with you these last few days I'm going to miss you even more than I did before."

"Absolutely. Maybe we can talk every other day or so."

Matt kissed her and hugged her tight. He hated leaving. It had been fun to be around Renee and the kids. She was a great mom. She was doing an incredible job out here, too, getting the resort up and running. Part of him wished he could be part of it all—but he had other commitments, so best to ignore his second thoughts about leaving.

"Call me when you get back to your sister's, so I know you made it OK."

"Will do," he said. "Be safe."

And he was gone.

CHAPTER 54

Gift of New Ventures

*A*fter Matt left, Renee kept herself distracted fixing up the lodge and learning all she could about the retreat business. Susan was surprised but delighted to hear from her. They talked for over an hour the first time and multiple times after that, and Renee's initial ideas escalated into fully fledged plans. Before she knew it, Susan was booking a flight to meet with Renee and Jess.

Grant and Grace joined them for dinner at least two nights a week. Grace was benefiting from the fresh air and quiet. She was able to take longer walks as she regained her strength, and her most recent follow-up appointment went well. She wanted to start back at college in the fall, but Grant was trying to convince her to wait one more semester.

Grant was getting plenty of writing done, and seemed satisfied with his daughter's progress. Deciding to rent a cabin had worked out well for them both, along with Renee. She hated to admit it, but she slept better knowing another adult was close—and she could tell Matt was relieved to have someone there with her, too.

Either way, nothing more happened. Maybe that business was behind them.

***

Renee prepared a celebratory dinner for Susan's last evening at Whispering Pines. After three days of intense discussions, Renee felt better prepared to tackle her new business venture: Jess was committed to partnering with her on the retreats—*They have my back,* Renee assured herself—and Susan would continue to be a valuable resource in the future, but tonight was a time to relax.

Grant and Grace joined them for the evening. They all crowded around Renee's kitchen table. Grant, Jess, and Susan squeezed together on one side, with Robbie on one end of the table and Julie on the other. Renee placed a heavy bowl of corn-on-the-cob next to the potato salad, then sat in the empty chair between Grace and Lauren.

Grace was anxious to hear about their progress over the past few days (and Renee was tickled this young woman had taken such an interest in her resort's success). "Have you figured out what kind of retreats you plan to offer?" she asked.

"We don't have all the details mapped out yet," Renee said, "but in general, we want to offer women a place where they can learn how to take better care of themselves. Robbie, could you pass the burgers around, please?"

Grant accepted the tray from Robbie and asked, "Can you clarify what you mean by that, Renee?"

Renee smiled, excited to share more of their preliminary plans. "I know we want to offer healthy food and time to relax, of course, but I want it to be more than pampering. I would love to help women learn more about everything: finances, self-care, goal setting . . . what to do about relationships they feel trapped in . . . I'd love it if our retreats would include exercise, music, good food, learning, and camaraderie. Stuff like that. An *experience*, you know?"

They continued to pass dishes around the table until everyone's plates were full.

"That sounds really fun. Are you going to target a certain age demographic?" Grace asked.

"Why, Grace, you sound like a marketing major!" Renee kidded. "No, I don't think so—I want women of all ages, you know, so they can learn from each other and enjoy each other's company. Older women may have more experiences to draw upon, and wisdom to share, but younger women often have a fresh point of view. I like the balance."

Grant nodded his agreement, his mouth too full of burger to reply.

"Good point, Renee," Grace said. "You'll need to find instructors, unless you plan to lead sessions yourself."

Renee shook her head as she spread butter on her corn. "No, fortunately I'm not naïve enough to think I have the knowledge to do that. Susan shared some pointers on finding instructors."

"Once you have a better idea what kind of instructors we'll need, I can use local job boards to see what kind of talent is available," Julie offered.

"That would be great, Julie," Susan said. "You're going to want to use local people as much as possible to keep costs down."

Jess had been quietly listening to the exchange, having already discussed much of this with Renee and Susan, but the mention of instructors suddenly spurred an idea. "Renee, maybe you could offer long-term cabin rentals to people we hire. If their living expenses are lower, we might not have to pay them as much, and it would be super handy to have them right here."

"Hey—that's a *great* idea!" Renee said. "We'll have to take a hard look at whether or not we can winterize any of the cabins so they can be inhabitable in the winter."

"Speaking of winter," Grant said, "are you planning to live out here year-round then?"

Grant's question caught Robbie's attention. He still wasn't sure if his mom was going to make him switch schools, despite numerous heated conversations with her over the past two weeks.

"Well . . . yes, I plan to stay out here this winter. So does Jess. Julie will go back to college in the fall and Lauren is going back home to stay with her dad so she can finish out her senior year there." Renee paused, making eye contact with Robbie before she continued. "Initially, I assumed Robbie would switch schools and stay here with me this fall, but he has convinced me to reconsider. What if this doesn't work? I'm not sure it's fair to ask Robbie to give up his school until we know more. His best friend's mother called me earlier this week and offered to let Robbie live with them this fall. I'm seriously considering it."

"Yes!" Robbie exclaimed, pounding his fist on the table hard enough to make silverware jump. This latest update was news to him, and apparently he approved.

"But remember, kiddo," Renee spoke directly to Robbie now, "this is only temporary. We will reassess the whole school situation after we see how it goes the first few months."

Robbie gave Renee a thumbs-up and proceeded to fill his plate a second time, his appetite back now that he had his answer.

"Since that appears to be settled," Grant said with a chuckle, "when do you plan to offer your first retreat?"

"Ethan and Dad drove over and met with Susan yesterday. As long as I can get the financing figured out, Ethan plans to start construction on the lodge next week," Renee said, getting up to grab a pitcher of lemonade off the counter. She made her way around the table, refilling glasses.

"And I think," Susan offered, "if construction can be wrapped up in two or three months, they could shoot for early November as a tentative timeframe for their first retreat. They will want to start out with a few shorter retreats, no longer than, say ... a weekend. Once they get the wrinkles ironed out—and there *will* be wrinkles—they could offer some week-long retreats, too."

Renee sat back down. "I love the idea of a retreat in November focused on gratitude, what with Thanksgiving right around the corner."

"Oh, man, that would be a *great* way to start," Julie said. "Wish I didn't have to miss out on all the fun."

"Are you kidding, Julie?" Jess asked. "We're gonna have to work our butts off to make this happen. You may be glad you aren't in the thick of it!"

"I doubt that," Julie mumbled under her breath.

***

"Mom, I don't want to go back."

"What did you say?" Renee slowed mid-stride in her morning trek over to check progress on the lodge. "Go back where?"

"To school."

Renee pulled up short, stopping Julie with a hand on her shoulder. She was shocked at her daughter's pronouncement. Julie had never given her any reason to think she wouldn't go back to college in the fall.

"Why would you say that? I thought you liked school?"

"I've been thinking about it a lot lately," Julie tried to explain, kicking at a loose rock on the path. She knew what she was saying was a huge blow to her mother. "I still don't know what I want to declare as a major. It seems like a waste of money if I'm just there but not focusing on graduating. There's so much going on *here* . . . I'd rather stay and help get the retreats up and running."

Renee let out a sigh of frustration, pushing her sleeves up and then running her hands over her face. "Julie, quitting school is not an option. You worked way too hard to get to this point. Where is this *coming* from?"

Julie attempted to push her hair back from her face, but the steady, hot breeze off the lake whipped it around. She gave up the fight, gathered it into a ponytail at the nape of her neck, and secured it with a spare hair tie she always wore around her wrist. "Mom, I feel so lost . . . I don't want to quit—I *do* want to go back, just not right away. Besides, what good does college do these days unless you want to be a doctor or something? Look at what happened to you. You have your masters, and it probably helped you get your job, but then they fired you anyhow. Now you're doing something you wouldn't have needed college for in the first place."

This stung Renee, but she tried not to let it show in her face. "Stop right there, girl. Don't ever think college is a waste of time. A college degree is often a ticket to play, a way to open doors. Even if your future career ends up being in a totally different field from what you study, you'll miss out on opportunities without it. Employers often don't even *look* at you if you don't have a college degree."

"Mom, that's ridiculous. What if I wanted to work *here*, help you run the resort? You saying you won't even *look* at me?"

Renee narrowed her eyes at Julie. Now she was acting like a brat.

"Julie, I use skills here every day that I started to learn in college and continued to develop over the past twenty years. Same with your aunts and your uncle. Ethan has a successful construction company now, not only because he's excellent with his hands, but because he learned to run all the aspects of a business starting in college. I'm not saying college makes you completely prepared for the working world, but it does give you a stronger foundation. It shows you're willing to put in the time, resources, and hard work to develop professionally."

Renee could see this wasn't getting through to her daughter. She tried a different tack. "Here's the deal, Julie. If you don't go back now, it will be *way* too easy to never actually go back. And don't forget, Aunt Celia was very specific—if you don't finish college, you give up the fifty grand she left you. You'd have to be *crazy* to give that up."

Renee turned and recommenced her walk to the lodge, hoping this last reminder would knock some sense back into her daughter.

But Julie wasn't going to let that be the last word. She fell into step beside Renee. "Mom, you don't understand. Times are changing. A degree doesn't guarantee you a job like it used to."

Renee was so frustrated she wanted to scream. It was a given in her family that everyone went to college—it just was! She reached the lodge door. Placing her hand on the knob, she turned back to face Julie. "I understand there are success stories where people have made it big without going to college. But trust me, honey, they are the exception, not the rule."

"I still think it's a mistake, Mom."

"And I disagree, and in this case, you are going to have to trust me. You *are* going back. End of discussion."

CHAPTER 55

Gift of Neighbors

*R*enee hoped her talk with Julie had convinced her daughter she needed to continue with college. No more was said on the topic, although Julie was quieter than usual. Grace finally accepted her father's notion she needed more time to heal before she went back to school.

The late-afternoon sun beat down on Renee as she struggled to weed a large flower garden next to the lodge parking lot. The ground was rock hard following a week of blistering heat and no rain. The only thing thriving were the weeds. Grant approached Renee, cold drinks in hand.

"If one of those is for me, you are a lifesaver!" Renee said, groaning at the kink in her back as she straightened to greet Grant.

"It sure is," he confirmed, handing her a sweating bottle of water. "If you have a minute, I wanted to talk to you about something."

Renee nodded. "I always have time for you. But let's get out of this blazing sun. Come on."

She led him over to a bench in the shade.

"It's so peaceful here, Renee. Grace gets plenty of rest and isn't tempted to be out doing too much yet, and I'm getting lots of writing done. I was wondering what you would think if I asked to stay on at the resort for a few more months?"

Renee capped her water after taking a hefty gulp. "I think that would be fabulous. It's so great to have you here, honest. I truly feel like we're all getting to know each other so much better this way."

Grant settled back more comfortably, arms splayed across the back of the bench, relaxed now that he had his answer. "That's great—thanks, Renee. Maybe we can even help with your retreats. I've written ad copy in the past and could help with flyers and brochures. And Grace loves doing research. She could help you study hot buttons for women. Maybe she can come up with some ideas to help draw more people in."

"Grant, I want you to know you're welcome to stay as long as you want. I don't know how rough winter can get out here or if your cabin will stay warm enough when the bitter cold sets in, but as long as you understand that going in, it would be great to have you. As far as helping with the retreats, we can use all the help we can get—and God knows your Grace has a knack for marketing already—but I have to be honest: I couldn't afford to pay you."

Grant laughed kindly. "Don't be ridiculous. You've already done so much for us. You saved my daughter's life, Renee. We are so grateful to you. Helping with your retreats would be a small way for us to repay you."

Renee shifted on the bench to face Grant, giving his shoulder a friendly squeeze.

"Now *you* are being ridiculous, Grant. We're family, and family is always there for each other. We couldn't turn our backs on Grace."

There was a twinkle in Grant's eye at these words. "Really? So you mean to tell me you weren't a tiny bit tempted to ignore my letter to your in-laws? You had to know you were opening your family up to potential heartache, Renee, yet you had the guts to pick up the phone and call me. Everything could have turned out so different if you hadn't called."

Renee took another drink of her water, considering Grant's words.

"I suppose ... OK, you have a deal. I welcome any help you can provide, but on one condition: I don't *ever* want you to think you owe me or the kids. We didn't help out so you could be in our debt. We helped because it was the right thing to do. Deal?"

"Deal."

Grant and Renee shook on it, and then laughed and caught each other up in a hug.

***

By the end of August, the lodge was undergoing a major transformation. Ethan framed in rooms on the main floor. The "squirrel" bathroom was completely ripped out and a larger area, complete with showers, was roughed in. They decided to commandeer space for one additional sleeping room so they could host more guests. This meant a slightly smaller gathering area downstairs, but they still had a large area upstairs. A large hole was cut in the upstairs wall facing the lake and an impressive set of windows was installed, the resulting view breathtaking. The second floor remained a large, open space—except for the library. When the partitioning walls were up to create the special room, George built row upon row of shelves along three of the library walls; the fourth wall boasted the old fireplace. It was easy to envision how cozy the room would be on winter evenings with a roaring fire in the hearth. The floor would be covered with a thick rug, and comfortable sofas and chairs would complete the space. Lauren volunteered to round up books to start filling the shelves in the library. She recruited Julie to attend a bag sale at the county library with her and together they scoured thrift shops and rummage sales. It didn't take them long to gather an impressive variety of books to kick off a collection.

They experienced the typical roadblocks encountered in most construction projects, but for the most part, everything progressed on schedule. Cooler evenings and earlier sunsets signaled the arrival of fall. School would start the following week for both Robbie and Julie. Lauren was already home with her dad; Jess was in charge at the resort for the weekend. The cabins were full—all but the Gray Cabin, which was locked up tight. Renee ignored it, not wanting to spend any time or money to start fixing it up yet. Maybe in the spring. The place still gave her the creeps, from her nightmare or from the squatter, or perhaps from both.

"Robbie, do you have all of your bags loaded in the car?" Renee asked her son as he sat at the kitchen table, messing with his phone. "We leave in ten minutes."

He nodded absentmindedly and she finished packing some of his favorite snacks into a cardboard box.

"Julie, time to go!" Renee hollered up the stairs. "Tight schedule, let's go!" She needed to get Robbie dropped off and then head to their house to get all of Julie's college stuff rounded up. She would move Julie back to her dorm tomorrow.

Julie didn't answer or come down.

Frustrated, Renee headed up the stairs and poked her head in her daughter's room. "What are you doing, honey? We need to get a move on."

Julie sat unresponsive on her bed, head down, staring at her phone.

"Julie? Everything OK?"

Still saying nothing, Julie held her phone out to her mom.

Renee stepped inside and read the one-word text:

Packing?

Renee glanced at her daughter. "Who is this from? What does it mean?"

"I don't know, Mom. I don't know who sent it. I don't recognize the number."

"Maybe it was sent to you by mistake?"

As she said it, Julie's phone pinged again:

Are we leaving?

"Oh God," Julie shrieked, throwing her phone down onto her quilt. "What is *that* supposed to mean? Mom, is someone watching us? Watching *me*?"

"Now calm down, honey. Like you said, you don't recognize the number. Maybe these aren't even meant for you."

"I'm scared, Mom. Why is someone scaring me?"

"I don't know, sweetie. Give me your phone. I'll write down the phone number and call the sheriff, see if he can trace it. Then I'm going to turn your phone off. This afternoon, we'll go in and see if we can get you a new phone number. That way the texts will stop even if you're getting them by mistake. How does that sound?"

Julie nodded and pushed herself off her bed. Two large suitcases sat by her doorway, filled with her clothes. Renee grabbed the bigger one and lugged it down the stairs. Julie grabbed Teddy off her bed, tucked the old bear under her arm, and followed her mom downstairs with her second bag.

Renee finished packing the car and found Jess.

"Jess, Julie is getting weird texts. Feels like someone might be watching her. Be careful while I'm gone and be sure either Ethan or Mom and Dad stay overnight in the duplex with you. I don't want you to be alone."

Jess scoffed. "Things will be *fine*, Renee, don't worry. I won't be alone. You go get the kids settled. Maybe you'll feel better having them out of here until we can figure out what's been going on."

Renee's eyes filled, and Jess pulled her sister into her arms. Renee welcomed the hug, exhausted from worry and work. Jess could always sense what she needed. After taking a minute to compose herself, she headed back out to her SUV. She refused to let the kids see her upset—especially Julie.

Traffic heading back into the city was light. Most of the cars were leaving instead of going in for the long weekend. After dropping Robbie off with a tearful goodbye, Renee and Julie headed to the house. It had sat empty all summer and she'd only run home once in July. As Renee pulled into the driveway, she was pleasantly surprised when the yard didn't look too bad. The grass was dry but neat—it was early September and they hadn't had much rain—and only a few hardy perennials persisted. The lone tree in her front yard still held tight to its leaves, although gold started to tint the edges. Pulling into the garage, Renee relaxed back into her seat, her head falling back. It was a relief to be home. She loved living at the resort, but this was still home. Julie got out of the SUV and grabbed groceries out of the back. Renee was still getting organized, looking for her phone.

Julie pulled up short at the door to the kitchen. It was ajar.

"Mom . . . why is this door open?"

"What?" Renee was digging around in the trunk now.

"Mom, stop screwing around and get over here. Why wouldn't this door be locked?"

Finally hearing what Julie was saying, Renee dropped everything and rushed over. Sure enough, the door wasn't closed all the way.

"Maybe Tim didn't pull it shut hard enough the last time he checked the house," Renee said, referring to their next-door neighbor, who'd been checking the house weekly.

"Don't go in there, Mom," Julie warned in a harsh whisper.

Renee tried to shrug this off. She was tired. She didn't want to deal with this. "Don't be ridiculous. It's broad daylight. No one is in there. Stay out here if you want, but I'm going in."

Refusing to let an unlatched door unnerve her, Renee stepped into the gloom of her kitchen. It smelled closed-up, stale, and all was quiet. She pushed open the curtain and window over the sink, then made her way through the rooms, opening windows as she went to let in fresh air. She heard Julie come in and dump the bags on the counter. Renee headed upstairs. She poked her head in Robbie's room and felt a tug at her heart. She missed him already. Why had she let him go back to his old school? They had never been apart for long.

Everything looked normal as she made her way through the upstairs bedrooms and bathroom. She heard Julie come up the stairs, lugging her heavy suitcase. She opened both windows in her bedroom, fresh air flowing around her. All she wanted to do was lie down on the bed and go to sleep; she was bone tired.

A scream echoed through the house. Up in a flash, Renee bolted to Julie's room. Her daughter stood in the middle of her bedroom, hands covering her face, shoulders shaking.

"What's wrong?" Renee insisted.

Julie raised her head, tears streaming down her face. But she wasn't scared. She was laughing hysterically.

"Oh my God, Mom, I am so losing it," Julie said. "Just as I was trying to heave this ridiculously heavy suitcase onto my bed, I thought I saw someone standing in the corner."

She pointed behind Renee. Renee turned around and gave a little yelp of fright. Julie had left her black jacket on a hanger, hooked on the trim on the top of her closet door. She also left a pair of pants draped over the back of a chair. At first glance, the ensemble did have an uncanny resemblance to a man standing there.

"Oh, honey, we need to relax!" Renee started giggling, too. It didn't take long until they were both caught up in a fit of laughter. They collapsed on Julie's bed and laughed away the stress and exhaustion. Eventually, Renee rolled to the side of the bed and stood.

"I'll make you a deal, Julie. Get your stuff packed this afternoon, and we'll go out to P.F. Chang's for a girls' night out. Maybe we can get our nails done at that little place nearby, too, after we get your phone number changed. But only if you get everything pulled together. Then we can come home, get a good night's sleep in our own beds, and get you to school tomorrow morning. It's nice they give you a couple days to get settled in the dorms before classes actually start."

"OK, Mom," Julie agreed, grinning up at Renee from her bed. "That sounds fun. And you were right. It'll be nice to get back to school and a normal routine. No freaks hanging around, scaring the hell out of us."

"That's right, and by the time you come back out to the resort, I'm sure we'll have everything straightened out."

CHAPTER 56

Gift of Close Calls

*R*enee jolted from a sound sleep at the shrill ringing of her cell. She had been back at the resort for a week after getting both kids settled in for school; the ringing of the phone in the dead of night was enough to throw any parent into a panic.

"Hello?" Renee barked into the phone.

"Mrs. Clements?"

"Yes, this is Renee Clements. Who is this? What's wrong?"

"Mrs. Clements, this is Detective McGregory. I'm sorry to have to call you like this. I'm with the university's campus police. I'm afraid your daughter Julie was involved in an incident on campus tonight. We aren't sure what happened yet, but she's down at the local emergency room. They are checking her over as a precaution."

"Oh my God. Is she OK? What happened?"

"We're investigating now. We will know more after we get a chance to talk with Julie. We were alerted to a possible problem when someone hit one of the blue emergency signals near the library, shortly before midnight. An on-campus officer was able to get to her within a couple of minutes. When she arrived, Julie was curled up in a fetal position on the grass off the sidewalk, conscious but extremely distraught and non-communicative. Two kids were trying to calm her down when our officer arrived."

"Was she hurt?"

"We couldn't see any outward signs of trauma, but, as I mentioned, she was taken to the emergency room for an examination, since she wasn't able to tell us what happened."

"I'm leaving right now. It will take me three hours to get there. Is anyone with her, anyone she knows?"

"Yes, I believe her roommate is with her."

"Was Zoey with her when it happened?"

"No, we think she was probably alone when someone atta— . . . I mean, scared her."

Renee noticed the detective catch himself. *Attacked. He was going to say Attacked.*

"Do you think someone *attacked* her?"

"Please, take a deep breath and slow down, Mrs. Clements. As I said, we don't know much yet. We were able to locate her roommate by scanning her student ID, which we found inside her backpack. Zoey got there before Julie was placed in the ambulance."

"Oh my God, she went in an *ambulance?*" Renee's voice was rising in panic.

Jess must have heard her through the duplex wall. She had a key and Renee heard her sister come in downstairs. She heard Molly give Jess a rambunctious greeting, even though it was the middle of the night, then Jess sprinted up the staircase, a questioning look in her eyes.

"Something happened to Julie," Renee whispered to Jess.

McGregory continued to try to reassure her. "She appears to be fine physically, Mrs. Clements. Something has her upset. I'm sure you would feel better if you could see her, so why don't you drive over? But, for goodness sake, be careful—there's no need to speed. Julie will want you here in one piece."

"OK, tell me exactly where she is," Renee demanded, still scared to death but going into her tough functioning mode. She could break down later. The cop was right: now wasn't the time.

Hanging up after she had the address of the hospital, she threw on clothes and grabbed a duffel bag. Jess ran into the bathroom and scooped up toiletries for Renee, including her glasses and some disposable contacts. Dumping everything in a big baggy she found under the sink, she threw it all in Renee's duffel. Renee tried to fill Jess in, but she didn't know much yet.

"OK, Renee, breathe." Jess took hold of her sister's shoulders and forced her to look at her. "I'll stay here with Molly. You go, but be careful. I'm calling Mom and Dad, too. They may want to meet you at the hospital. I don't think you should call Robbie until you know more. No sense worrying him at this point."

"Right, right. But will you be OK here by yourself?"

"Yes. Tell you what. I'll give Grant a call so he knows what's going on. He's right here if I need anything. Now *go*."

Renee ran out to her Toyota, tossing her bag in the passenger side. She jumped in, slammed the door—then dropped her keys and couldn't find them on the floor. She could feel her panic rising. She was still so far away from Julie, and her daughter *needed* her. A tap came at her window and she screamed.

"Jesus, Grant, you scared the shit out of me!"

"Sorry, kiddo," Grant apologized, opening Renee's door. "It looks like you were having a little trouble getting going. Jess called. I'm so sorry something happened to Julie. Are you sure you're OK to drive? Maybe I should take you. Grace could go stay with Jess in the duplex."

Any other time, Renee would have refused. But she was pretty sure she wasn't going to be able to hold it together all the way to the hospital.

"Would you do that for me? I'm so scared," Renee admitted, a lone tear slipping down her cheek.

"Absolutely. Give me three minutes. I'll run back to the cabin and then we'll take off. I need my wallet."

"OK, please hurry. Julie needs me."

True to his word, Grant wasn't gone long. He threw the SUV into reverse and sped out of the lot, heading for Julie.

Renee knew Jess probably already talked to their folks, but she needed to talk to them, too. Sometimes you need your parents, no matter how old you are. Her mom picked up on the second ring.

"Honey, do you know any more yet? We talked to Jess. We're coming to the hospital, too. We don't want you to deal with this alone. Are you on the road?"

"Oh, Mom, I am so scared. Poor Julie. She's there all alone, and we don't even know what happened."

"Renee, remember, she has Zoey with her. She isn't alone. I'm worried about you driving when you're so upset."

"Actually, Grant offered to drive me. Grace will stay with Jess."

"Thank God."

"What time do you think you'll get there, Mom?"

"Your dad put the address in the GPS. We should get there at three-thirty-five."

"We should get there a little ahead of you. Call my cell when you get to the hospital, and we'll tell you where to come. I'm going to try to reach Zoey now. Maybe she can tell me how Julie is or what happened."

Renee fumbled with her phone, trying to find her daughter's friend in her phone contacts. Finally successful, she placed the call. The phone rang and rang. Zoey's voice came through, but it was voicemail. Renee asked Zoey to call her back right away.

"She's probably with Julie now. She might not even have her phone with her, running out when she found out about Julie," Grant attempted to calm Renee, reaching across the dark interior to give her knee a reassuring squeeze. "Do you want to talk, or would you rather not?"

Renee could feel more tears coming. "I should have listened to her, Grant. She didn't want to go back to school, and I made her go."

"Renee, this isn't your fault. You know that. Going back to school, even if she doesn't know exactly what she wants to do, was the right advice."

"But you wouldn't let Grace go back."

"That is different, and you know it. You're understandably upset right now, but you can't blame yourself for any of this."

"I know that in my head, but my heart is screaming something different at me right now."

"Believe me, I've been there, done that. But this wasn't your fault. We don't even know what happened yet. Let's not jump to any conclusions."

Renee didn't answer Grant, only gave a brief nod, turning her gaze out the passenger window.

It started raining, pavement a slick black stretching off into the darkness. Mile after mile, the swooshing of tires was the only sound. Finally, their surroundings became dotted with more and more lights until they reached the city. They pulled into the hospital parking ramp shortly before 3:00 a.m.

Grant barely had the car stopped before Renee shot out the door toward the bright red EMERGENCY sign. Wanting to be there for Renee, but not wanting to intrude, Grant hung back. He'd spent so much time in hospitals over the past two years, he wasn't anxious to enter another one.

Automatic doors were too slow for Renee; she repeatedly pushed the button displaying a wheelchair, as if that would slide the doors open quicker. Sprinting up to a reception desk, she impatiently waited for the man sitting there to get off the phone.

"I am Renee Clements. My daughter, Julie Clements, was brought in a few hours ago. Where is she?"

"Oh, yeah, the college kid," the man responded—slowly—searching a pile of paperwork on the desk in front of him—slower, still. He wasn't moving fast enough to suit Renee.

"Come on, buddy, where is my daughter?" Renee demanded.

The man raised his head and frowned at her. "I'll need you to fill out some paperwork," the man replied, not to be rushed.

"Oh, for God's sake, I am not dealing with that right now."

Renee gave up on him and approached a woman walking down the hallway in a white lab coat with a stethoscope hanging around her neck and a tablet in one hand.

"Excuse me, I am looking for my daughter, Julie Clements. Can you help me?" Renee asked the woman.

"And your name is?" the white-garbed woman replied.

"Renee Clements, Julie's mother. I came as soon as the detective called, but it was a three-hour drive."

"Yes, Mrs. Clements, I examined your daughter. Why don't we go have a seat in the family waiting room. I don't think anyone is in there."

Not waiting for an answer, she turned and headed down another hallway, Renee close on her heels.

The room was in shadows. The woman flipped a light switch, bathing the area in a warm glow. She took a seat at a round table to the right of the door and motioned for Renee to sit across from her.

"Mrs. Clements, my name is Dr. Roberts. I've been here since they brought your daughter in. After I finished examining her, I gave her a sedative to help her rest. The police are not happy with me because they want to talk to Julie, but since she wasn't talking anyhow, I thought it would be best for her."

"So what can you tell me?"

"I'm afraid I can't tell you much yet. But the good news is there is no evidence that your daughter was physically harmed. We did a thorough evaluation."

"So she wasn't raped?" Renee asked, her voice catching on the last word.

Dr. Roberts reached across the table to squeeze Renee's hand, tightly clenched on top of the laminate surface. "No, Mrs. Clements, we could find no evidence of any type of physical abuse."

"Oh, thank God," Renee whispered, slumping back in her chair. "You can't imagine all the scenarios that have been running through my mind. So she's OK?"

"Well, not exactly. Something has her extremely agitated. She hasn't said a word since she was brought in. There were no tears, but she was shaking violently. She didn't object to my physical examination, but she won't tell us anything."

"But . . . I don't understand."

"I ran a tox screen to see if there were any substances in her blood that could account for her behavior. I was checking the results when you arrived," said the doctor, tapping the screen of the tablet she carried. "I'm not seeing anything unusual here either. It's looking more like something or someone severely frightened your daughter, Mrs. Clements, but help may have arrived before she could be physically harmed. At this point, we may need to wait until she can tell us what happened before we get any answers."

"Can I see her?"

"Yes, of course. Please follow me."

Renee followed Dr. Roberts, spying Grant sitting in the outer lobby area as they passed by. She motioned to the room she was heading toward with the doctor, but he gave her a thumbs-up of encouragement and stayed where he was.

A uniformed police officer was leaning against the wall outside the room. He stepped toward Renee, but the doctor shooed him away. Renee nodded at him but kept going, wanting nothing more than to see Julie. Lights were dimmed inside the room. Julie was lying in the bed, looking still and fragile. Renee didn't see any equipment hooked up to her daughter other than a monitor softly beeping off to the left, showing her heartbeat on the black and green screen.

"Oh, honey, I'm here," Renee said soothingly, stepping to Julie's side and taking up her daughter's hand. She looked questioningly at Roberts when Julie didn't respond in any way.

"She'll sleep for at least another hour. She's sedated, so she won't know you're here yet," the doctor assured her.

A slight movement in the corner of the room caught Renee's eye. Zoey stood up from where she had been sitting, stepping to Renee.

"Oh, sweetie, are you OK?" Renee asked of her daughter's best friend. Zoey crumbled into her arms, tears flowing.

"Renee, I've been so scared. I don't know what happened."

Renee patted her back. "Start from the beginning."

"I was in our room, studying . . . Julie wasn't home, studying in the library, went to meet a new study group at nine, and I hadn't heard from her. My cell rang—campus police, telling me something had happened to Julie and asking if I could come over right away. When I got over near the library, I could see a group of people gathered under a street light by one of those blue alert buttons. The light was pulsing . . . it was so scary." Zoey took a steadying breath. "Julie was lying on her side, shaking but not crying or talking. Two medics were working to get her to stand up so they could help her onto a stretcher, but it was like she didn't know anyone was there. They got her on the stretcher, still all curled up in a ball. They let me ride in the ambulance with her when I told them I was her roommate. Oh, Renee . . . I'm so glad you're finally here."

"Oh, baby, thank you so much for being here for Julie. I would have gone crazy if I hadn't known you were with her, taking care of her until I could get here."

"I didn't do anything. I don't know how to help."

"Zoey, that isn't true. You have been a huge help. I'm sure Julie knew you were here, even if she didn't acknowledge you. That's what true friends do for each other."

"Maybe Zoey would like to go home now that you are here, Mrs. Clements," Dr. Roberts suggested. "She has to be exhausted."

"Oh, of course," Renee replied. "Zoey, do you remember meeting Grant, my brother-in-law?"

Zoey nodded, teary-eyed.

"He drove me here because I wasn't in any shape to drive myself. He's waiting out in the lobby. Would it be all right if he drove you back to the dorm? I'm sure he wouldn't mind."

"Oh, a ride would be great," Zoey said. "My eyes feel like sandpaper . . . I need to get these contacts out."

"Should I call your folks at all?" Renee asked.

"No, please don't call Mom and Dad. A phone call at three-thirty in the morning would freak them out. I'll be fine. I'll call them later. Will you let me know when you find out what happened?"

"Of course. Now come on, I'll take you out to Grant."

Grant stood as they approached. He gave Zoey a small smile and nod of recognition. Renee was grateful for his calming presence. She updated him on what she knew. She saw the flash of relief in his eyes when she reported Julie hadn't been physically attacked. Renee knew he harbored some of the same terrible fears. He was more than happy to give Zoey a ride back to the dorm.

Just as Grant and Zoey turned to leave, Julie's grandparents burst in. After accepting a teary hug from Lavonne and a hearty handshake from George, along with words of thanks for getting Renee to the hospital safely, Grant left with Zoey.

"How is Julie?" Lavonne inquired, hugging her daughter next.

Renee updated them with what she knew. George went in search of coffee for his girls while Lavonne and Renee sat by Julie's bedside waiting for her to wake up. Renee talked briefly with the police officer. He wanted to talk to Julie but was needed back at the precinct so asked Renee to give them a call immediately when Julie started to come around. Renee promised to do so.

Julie didn't wake up in an hour as the doctor had said; it took her almost three hours to come out of the sedation. The nurse kept assuring Renee not to worry—sometimes, she said, it took people longer to wake up.

***

The sun was up when Julie began to stir. Lavonne had just left to find a bathroom and both George and Grant were out in the waiting room. Renee hadn't let go of Julie's hand for the past two hours and she must have dozed off. She was awakened by a slight squeeze of her fingers. She opened her eyes to see Julie looking at her. It took Julie time to focus, to recognize her mom.

She must not have her contacts in was Renee's first thought.

"Hi honey, how are you feeling?" Renee softly asked her daughter.

A tiny shrug was all the response she got. No tears, no words.

"Zoey was here with you, but Grant took her home so she could rest. We can call her when you're feeling better."

Renee didn't know how to handle this. The shaking the doctor told her about was gone. Renee pushed the button to raise Julie's bed up so she was sitting more than reclining. She stood at her daughter's side, fingers softly brushing her hair back from her forehead.

A nurse came in. "Well, hello there, Julie. We were wondering when you were going to wake up," she said as she circled around the hospital bed, checking the single monitor and feeling Julie's pulse. "How are you feeling?"

Julie looked down at the blanket covering her. Renee met the nurse's gaze, silently asking what would happen now.

"I'll go let the doctor know you're awake, Julie. She will be in shortly to see you."

When they were alone again, Renee sat down on the edge of the hospital bed holding Julie's hand.

"Honey, do you want to talk about what happened?"

"Why . . . why am I here, Mom? Why are you here?"

"Do you remember anything that happened last night, Julie?"

Julie thought about it, a look of vague consternation on her face. "I remember eating supper and then meeting my study group in the library . . . we were studying for a math test. Oh my God, what time is it? I'll be late for my test!"

Renee jumped back up, placing her hands on Julie's shoulders and gently pushing her back against the bed. "Don't worry, honey, you can make up the test. Do you remember anything after you were finished with your group? Do you remember walking back to your dorm?"

"No."

"You don't remember anything at all?"

"No."

Renee wasn't sure whether that was entirely true. She thought she heard some hesitation in Julie's reply.

"Honey, I'm sorry, but the police wanted to talk to you as soon as you woke up."

Julie looked at her, scared now. "Why do the police want to talk to me? And why am I in a hospital bed? Mom, you aren't making any sense."

"Julie, something happened last night. Police were summoned to one of those on-campus alarm stations and found you there next to it, very upset. You were brought here so the doctors could check you over and you could rest. You were so upset, honey."

Julie looked at her mother as if she had grown two heads.

At that moment, Dr. Roberts came in.

"Hi, Julie. How are you feeling this morning?"

"Why does everyone keep asking me that? I feel fine, other than the fact that I'm freaking out a little because my first math test starts in an hour, and, oh yeah, I'm stuck in some stupid hospital room but I have no idea *why*."

"Julie, something happened that upset you a great deal last night. We couldn't get you calmed down, so we gave you something so you could sleep. Do you remember anything at all?"

"Did someone attack me? Oh my God . . . was I *raped?*" Julie's voice rose with the beginnings of hysteria.

"I examined you myself," the doctor assured her, "and I couldn't find any evidence that you suffered any kind of physical trauma at all."

Julie seemed to calm down a little at this. "I am so confused."

"Mrs. Clements, can I have a word with you please?" asked the doctor.

"Yes. Julie, your grandparents are here. I'll send them in so they can sit with you while I talk with the doctor, OK?"

"God, Grandma and Grandpa came, too? What is going on?"

"We'll get to the bottom of this, honey. Just relax, I'll be right back."

After sending her folks in to see Julie, Renee met with the doctor in the same family waiting room. She didn't bother asking the doctor anything, just sat with a questioning look, waiting for her to begin.

"Temporary loss of memory related to traumatic events is not unusual," Dr. Roberts began. "It could be that whatever scared her was so upsetting that her mind is holding those particular memories at bay. Sometimes the amnesia only lasts a few hours or a few days. Everyone is different. I will examine her again, but I would be surprised if I found anything we missed last night. She seems to be feeling all right, she's just confused due to her surroundings. That makes sense, too, because she isn't remembering whatever it was that scared her so badly. Why don't you go ask the nurse at the desk to call and let the officers know Julie's awake, and they can come talk with her. I will probably release her into your care after that."

Renee nodded. "What then?"

"I would like her to see her primary care doctor in a week. I am also going to refer her to someone that specializes in this type of situation. If her memories come back, she may need help dealing with them."

"I understand. Thank you for your help, Doctor."

But Renee still didn't understand what was going on, still felt that sense of helplessness. What happened to her daughter? What scared her so badly that she, or someone, summoned the police?

***

Grant drove back to the resort when Julie was released, not crazy about Grace and Jess being alone out there. Starving, George and Lavonne took Renee and Julie out for lunch. Her parents sat at a separate table, knowing Renee needed to talk with Julie in private.

Once they were seated and had ordered, it was time to talk.

"Julie, honey, I can't help but remember our earlier conversation, where you didn't want to come back to school this fall. I feel so guilty."

Julie shook her head adamantly. "Mom, you have absolutely nothing to feel guilty about. Whatever *did* happen to me, it had *nothing* to do with you."

"I don't know what happened last night," Renee said, "and I know you don't remember yet. You might remember at any time. Maybe I was wrong to push you to come back. I don't see how you can stay here, not knowing what made you so upset last night. Until we have some answers, I think maybe you should come back to the resort with me."

"But we're only one week into school. If I leave now, I'll get too far behind."

"Honey ... maybe we should see whether or not, under the circumstances, they would still let you withdraw without it impacting your college transcript or making us pay full tuition."

"You're right, Mom. I feel jumpy and scared. I don't know why, but I do. Since I don't remember anything, I won't feel safe here."

"Will you feel safe at the resort? It's been weird there, too."

"I know, but I'll feel safer if I'm with you instead of here on this huge campus with so many strangers. It doesn't mean I can't come back later, though. Hopefully we can find out what happened . . . I just don't want to always be looking over my shoulder."

Neither of them ate much of their lunch, but enough to sustain them for the time being.

***

The dean was agreeable to their request for Julie to withdraw for the semester. Of course, he wanted some answers, too. He needed to keep students safe. Rumors were already flying around, since others were there when the police and ambulance responded. The dean was trying to keep a lid on it, but that was hard in today's world of social media. There was plenty of speculation no matter what he did.

Renee worried about leaving Zoey without a roommate. Luckily, the other room in their suite had three girls versus the standard two, and housing agreed to let one of the three move in with Zoey. All five of the girls were friends; Zoey wasn't wild about the idea of a different roommate, but she understood why Julie didn't want to stay—she was scared, too. Her parents agreed to come visit her for the weekend. Zoey needed some family time, too.

Julie was subdued as they loaded her clothes and bedding into the back of George's extended cab pickup. Her girlfriends helped, all of them offering Julie reassurances. She could come see them any time. The poor girl had only been back for a week and was still settling in. But she was only pulling out for the semester; hopefully she could come back after the holidays.

Renee had called Matt earlier that morning, before Julie woke up. She stepped away to call him again and give him an update.

"Renee, do you know what happened?" he asked when he picked up after the first ring. "I have to admit, I've been going crazy with worry over here."

"Hey, Matt, sorry to call so early. I know it's almost morning for you. No . . . we still don't know what happened to her. She's awake, and feeling all right, but she doesn't remember anything that happened after their study group finished last night. She's still scared and jittery, but the doctor checked her again before releasing her and confirmed she couldn't find any signs Julie was physically attacked."

"What do the police say?"

"Not much at this point. Of course, they want me to get in touch with them right away if she does start to remember anything. There's some uneasiness around campus, not knowing what happened. Don't say I'm overreacting, but ... I pulled her out for the semester. I can't imagine leaving her here when we don't have answers yet."

Matt was quiet for a moment. "No, Renee, I don't think you are overreacting. I think that was probably a smart move. Something's happening around you, and that something, whatever it is, seems centered around Julie. Did you tell the police about what's been going on at the resort?"

"I did, but they didn't seem too interested. Didn't think there could be any possible connection. Actually, they're being pretty tight-lipped. I couldn't tell if they knew more than they were letting on or not."

"I already called Sheriff Thompson and let him know something had happened to Julie on campus," Matt told her. "I'll call him back, maybe he can get some information out of the campus police since he might be considered more local than I would be. I wish that damn sheriff would get off his ass and figure out what's going on."

"I do, too. Maybe it *was* just a drifter causing problems at the resort, and maybe whoever it was has moved on. Nothing else has happened since. Maybe the incident at school was unrelated. I might believe that ... if it weren't for that picture Dad found of Julie in the dresser drawer. I don't know how to explain that piece of this puzzle."

"I can't either, not yet. But I'll keep pushing for answers, too. How are you holding up? This is a lot for you to handle on your own. Did you get Robbie settled?"

"Robbie's settled. I guess I'm going to keep taking it a day at a time. Thank God for my family. They are my rock. Don't know what I would do without them. Grant has been helpful, too."

"I'm glad he drove you. Is he still with you now?"

"No, he was anxious to get back to his daughter. I hated to have him waste a whole day here with us. I wasn't sure yet what we were going to do. I suppose I'll have to call Robbie and let him know his sister is going back to the resort. I think I'll give him the abbreviated version. No sense worrying him."

"That would probably be all right for now, but I don't think you should keep this from him, particularly if you start to get some answers or anything else happens. He won't appreciate you keeping something like this from him."

"I suppose. Hey, how come you always give such good advice?"

"Because I care, Renee. Remember that. I wish I was closer so I could help more."

"I know you care, and I am so thankful you do. Sorry if we caused you a missed night of sleep. I miss you."

"I miss you, too. Believe me, I'm used to missing sleep once in a while. You better get back to Julie now. Thanks for the update. Keep me posted. Like I said, I'll call and pester the sheriff again, try to keep the investigation moving. Text me when you're back at the resort."

Once all of Julie's paperwork was complete, George took them all back to the resort. Despite their protests, he insisted on staying on at the resort for a bit. Even though Grant was at Whispering Pines, George didn't like the idea of his daughters and granddaughter out in the duplex alone.

Julie kept busy during the day helping plan retreats, but nights were a challenge. Soon after she got back to the resort, she started having terrible nightmares. They were vague—always a faceless stranger chasing her through the darkness, calling her name. She would jolt awake when hands reached out and grabbed her long ponytail, yanking her back off her feet. Maybe she was starting to remember what actually happened, but she never recognized the voice she heard in her dreams, and she never saw who was chasing her. As promised, Dr. Roberts arranged for Julie to meet weekly with a psychiatrist, but the sessions hadn't yielded any answers.

Renee called the campus police every week following Julie's sessions, but had nothing other than the nightmares to report. She always asked if there had been any further trouble on campus, but if there had been, they weren't telling her about it.

***

Matt tried to determine whether or not Julie's boyfriend from the first half of her freshman year had anything to do with their troubles. He couldn't find much on the kid. He was relatively certain Lincoln didn't go back to college anywhere after the holidays. The boy had a strained relationship with his parents, so they weren't able to tell Matt much; Julie's name hadn't come up, but that wasn't too surprising since they seldom talked. Lincoln called his mom a couple of times after the first of the year to tell her he was in Minneapolis, working odd jobs. He said he was thinking about going back to college to study computer science but wasn't sure when or where he might go. Now it had been months since they had heard from Lincoln, but Matt didn't get the sense they were particularly worried about their son. He tried to find out what caused the rift between the boy and his parents, but they refused to elaborate. His old college roommate hadn't known him before they roomed together and hadn't heard from him since he dropped out. His parents didn't know any friends he might have stayed in touch with, so that was a dead end. Any jobs he was working must have been under the radar, because there were no tax records of him working anywhere in the past year. If he had a car, it wasn't registered in his name, and Matt couldn't find any bank accounts in his name with activity since he had dropped out, either. If his parents hadn't heard from him at all since he dropped out, Matt might have been concerned something happened to the boy. He knew from experience people didn't fall off the grid unless it was intentional. His gut told him the boy might be involved.

He shared his musings with Sheriff Thompson, but since they were only speculation, he didn't say anything to Renee or Julie about his suspicions. It would probably scare them, and his hunch might be wrong. The sheriff always listened to what Matt had to say when he called, but Thompson never followed up on anything. He finally admitted to Matt he was having trouble keeping up with all of his department's cases. It wasn't only a staffing shortage. The sheriff was having a serious health issue and was considering turning in his resignation.

"Hard to leave, though. I got no one ready to step into my shoes around here. You met two of my deputies—still wet behind the ears, and the rest of them aren't any better. Say, you aren't looking for a new job, are you, son?" Sheriff Thompson asked Matt. "I know you run a decent-size crew out there on that island of yours, but you seem awfully interested in what's happening around here. It's got me wondering why you are so interested."

"Renee Clements is a special friend of mine, as you probably already concluded on your own. I actually *have* been giving some thought to moving back to the States . . . My dad passed away this summer, made me realize how much I was missing. But yours is an elected position. What happens if you aren't willing, or able, to complete your term?"

"Well, if I remember right, I think there is a provision that allows for the county commission to appoint an interim sheriff in the event I'm unable to work through the end of my term. Of course, I suspect anyone I would personally recommend would be given serious consideration. I've run this office for thirty years without too much trouble. That's one of the reasons I'm thinking I should get out before I end up botching things. I don't want to stay on too far past my prime."

Matt pondered how to respond.

"Tell you what," he finally suggested, "why don't we both sleep on it? I'll call you back in a couple days and let you know if I might consider such a big change. And you can maybe double-check the required procedures if you were to step down," Matt suggested.

"You got a deal."

"I do appreciate the offer and consideration, Sheriff," Matt said.

"Hey, you'd be doing me a favor. You might be my ticket to the beach and warmer weather, someplace where my old ticker could get some much-needed rest."

CHAPTER 57

Gift of Attention

*W*ithin two weeks, Matt had enough answers about the sheriff position to know he was interested in pursuing it. Thompson could arrange the necessary meetings with the decision-makers, but Matt would need to meet with them in person before they could commence with the process.

Matt knew he was intrigued about this particular position because it would put him near Renee, but in fairness to her, he didn't want to make that decision without talking to her first. It wasn't a conversation he wanted to have over the phone. Storm damage at his dad's old farm also meant his sister could use his help again. Despite the hit to his bank account for another expensive ticket, he arranged for time off from work to fly back. His superiors weren't too happy with him, given the time he took when his dad died, but Matt insisted. If they ended up firing him, it would make the decision to move back that much easier.

Renee was excited when Matt asked if he could come back for a visit.

"Oh, Matt, it would be great to see you again! But are you sure you can get away?"

"It isn't a problem. I have work to do with my sister yet on Dad's farm. Part of the roof ripped off our old barn during a thunderstorm last week . . . straight-line winds. And I want to see if there's any more I can learn about what happened at your resort and to Julie at school. But this time I didn't think it would be fair for me to drop in on you unannounced again."

"Well, the last time certainly was a fun way to reconnect," Renee teased, "but this way I can be sure I have time to spend with you, too. We have lots going on. We need to raise our profile at the resort . . . build interest for our retreats. Julie came up with the idea to hold a Halloween open house."

"That sounds cool," Matt said. "Something for kids?"

"Sure. We're going to advertise it as a family-friendly stop for parents when they take their kids trick-or-treating. We'll keep a bonfire going, weather permitting, and open up the lodge so people can see the new facility. We'll have a station to bob for apples, another for face painting, and, of course, candy and treats. Visitors can tour a cabin or two, as well. We'll have brochures available advertising upcoming retreats. Maybe try a suggestion box, too, asking people for input on topics that might entice them enough to sign up for a retreat."

"You *are* busy! Don't worry, I won't take you away from any of it. Let me help. I don't want Grant getting all the credit for helping you get up and running. I want to earn some points, too."

"Why, Matt Blatso, are you a tiny bit jealous?"

"Of course, I am! Why wouldn't I be? That lucky son of a bitch gets to see you almost every day while I'm thousands of miles away."

"Aww, that is so cute."

" 'Cute,' my ass. But seriously—I get in on October fifth. I'll stop and see my sister quick, take care of that business, then rent a car to drive out to see you. I should get there on the seventh. Will that work for you?"

"Absolutely—and if it doesn't, I'll *make* it work. Did you want to stay here at the duplex on the couch, or in Robbie's room?"

"Tell you what—while that's a great offer, why don't I rent a room in town? That way we might be able to have a little privacy if we can squeeze in a date night or two."

"Even better," Renee said, feeling herself blushing like a schoolgirl. What was it about this guy that made her feel flustered and on edge? She was going to have to watch herself.

Days leading up to Matt's visit passed quickly. Julie still hadn't remembered anything more than brief flashes of her attack, and it still wasn't clear if those were true memories or her subconscious plucking from her nightmares. Campus police stopped checking in, probably concluding Julie might never remember what happened. Renee did insist Julie keep going to her weekly sessions with her doctor, in case it would help.

Julie had a nice reprieve when Ben, one of the three young men that rented the vandalized cabin in late June, called and wanted to drive up to see her one weekend. They had kept in touch; he knew she was having a tough time since pulling out of school. He arrived on a Friday afternoon and planned to stay until Sunday. Renee was delighted when he agreed to stay with them. He would sleep on the couch—that way she could keep an eye on them; Julie wasn't in any shape to get serious about anyone right now, and it was nice to help them avoid any temptations.

George and Lavonne had headed home two weeks earlier. Ben and Julie stayed home with Renee and Jess Friday evening instead of going out. They enjoyed a simple dinner of homemade pizza and played a few competitive games of Whist.

On Saturday, Ben helped Ethan hang sheetrock in the lodge. Recognizing the kids deserved a little alone time, Renee kicked them out later in the day, insisting they grab dinner and a movie in town. Sunday morning all four of them got up and went to Mass. The weather was turning colder. They didn't have any renters for the weekend.

When they got back from church, they decided to have brunch before Ben headed back to college. Renee was out of coffee but remembered Val had left some in the lodge kitchen. She ran over there quick, promising to be right back.

She was startled when the front door of the lodge wasn't locked. Someone had been careless, surely, but still . . . it worried her. Making her way around piles of construction tools, she headed for the kitchen. She dug through the cupboard next to the sink, pulling out the can of coffee. As she turned to leave the kitchen, a sound stopped her.

What was that?

It sounded like dripping water. The sound was out of place in the empty lodge.

Following the sound, she headed back toward the bathroom. Sure enough, she definitely heard a steady *plop, plop, plop*. Renee opened the door to the bathroom, confused. Why would one of the shower heads be dripping so profusely? The plumbing in that room had been hooked up the week before; as far as Renee knew, there hadn't been any problems with it since. She reached over to the handle and tightened it, turning off the stream. Fortunately, it hadn't been a broken pipe. Knowing how devastating water damage could be, Renee had been holding her breath since first recognizing the sound.

Heading back to the duplex, Renee's mind jumped between everything she wanted to accomplish before Matt arrived. She forgot all about the dripping shower. Jess had a nice meal on the table when she got back, and Julie was more relaxed than she had been in weeks. Renee was glad Ben had come to visit.

She forgot to mention the dripping shower until mid-week when her brother came out. Ethan looked at her like she was nuts. He couldn't think of any possible reason a shower would be dripping. Sometimes, he suggested, the water pressure from the well was funky, but that was his best guess.

In the end, they chalked it up to a fluke.

***

The day Matt was due to arrive dawned cold and overcast. A stiff, damp wind blew. Fall was in the air, even if summer refused to completely yield to it yet.

With only three weeks until their open house, Renee wanted to get flyers up around the area. It would have been great to get a small ad in the newspaper and on the radio, but she needed to spend as little as possible on marketing the event—she needed funds for refreshments and decorations—so Julie was working on getting the word out via social media. Renee planned to distribute flyers and start looking for fall decorations early in the day, before Matt got in, but he pulled in earlier than expected.

"Hey there, welcome back," Renee greeted him as he hoisted himself out of a pickup. It was old and sported some rust. "Did you *rent* that beast?"

"Nah, it was my dad's. I was going to rent a car, but then I figured that was dumb. This old truck just sits there in the barn, needs to be driven once in a while. Now, come here. How 'bout a proper hello?"

Renee laughed as she settled into his arms to kiss him hello.

God, she had missed him since July.

A screen door slammed in one of the cabins. The old wooden lodge door groaned on its hinges as Ethan came outside, balancing a pile of lumber scraps in his arms.

"Hey there, buddy, get your hands off my little sister," Ethan hollered over at the two of them, a grin on his face. He dumped the lumber in the back of his trailer and headed their way. He extended his hand to Matt, welcoming him back.

"I heard you'd be coming back for a visit. Good to see you."

"Thanks, Ethan, good to be back. Sounds like you two have big plans for this place."

"Sure do. Renee can give you a tour. You won't recognize it. Lots of changes over the past couple months. Would give you a tour myself but I have to check on another job and get to a football game by 4:30. But maybe we can sit down for a beer before you have to head back."

"Sounds good, looking forward to it!"

Renee loved to see the easy banter between Matt and her brother. Even at her age, she still wanted her family's approval.

She walked Matt through the lodge, showing him the new configuration on the main level. Just as Ethan said, it was coming together. Matt led the way up the stairs but stopped at the top and Renee ran right into the back of him.

"Wow . . . check out that *view!* Opening up this wall was *brilliant*," he exclaimed as he made his way farther into the large open room, bringing Renee along by the hand. "Are you replacing these floors? 'Cause I wouldn't if I were you. I love the old, scarred look of 'em."

"Nope, I'm with you on that. We'll give them a good polish and make sure they're smooth and won't give anyone splinters. I want to use this area for exercise classes, maybe even yoga or dancing, in our retreats."

Matt again swung Renee into his arms, but this time he took her around the room in a quick little two-step, albeit without any music. Dancing led to a little more kissing and Renee finally had to pull back to catch her breath.

"I can see we might not get a heck of a lot of work done while you're here."

"Good point . . . I promise to behave—at least part of the time," Matt quipped.

Renee finished showing him the upstairs, especially excited to show him how the library was coming together. After the tour, they found Jess and Julie working back at the duplex. Following a warm round of greetings, Matt was curious what she had planned for the day.

"I have some errands to run and then I thought maybe we could go out for dinner. Jess is going to a class tonight at the tech school. It's on building entrepreneurial skills. I was going to go too, but since I would rather spend the evening with you, Julie is going in my place."

"In my experience, when a woman says she's 'running errands,' it usually means shopping," Matt said, grinning at Renee.

"I agree—those are often my code words for shopping, too—but not today. I want to hang flyers and start gathering some fall decorations for the open house."

"Oh, see, still a little shopping in there."

"Well, OK, a *little* . . . but totally business-related."

Renee and Matt continued with their bantering back and forth as they headed out of the kitchen. Jess rolled her eyes at their departing backs, and Julie made a gagging motion. They both dissolved into giggles.

"Those two act like a couple teenagers. I'm not used to seeing Mom flirt with a guy," Julie complained to her aunt.

"I know. This could get interesting. Have you noticed the way *Grant's* been hanging around more lately, too? I think he might have the hots for Renee. Having Matt around might not sit well with him."

"Wait, *what?*" Julie hadn't noticed Grant acting any differently. She never thought about her mom and men in the same sentence.

"Mark my words, there's going to be some male posturing going on here before too long. I don't think Renee's noticed Grant's interest, either. She thinks of him as a brother-in-law. But Grant never even *knew* Jim. He may not think of her like a sister-in-law, infringing on his dead brother."

"Oh God, Jess, I do *not* want to think about Mom that way!"

"Want to place a little wager?"

CHAPTER 58

Gift of a Pause

*M*att and Renee left in Matt's truck. After getting the flyers posted, they stopped at a farm stand along the highway. Renee introduced herself to the woman loading a roll of paper into a cash register.

"We're holding a Halloween open house at Whispering Pines, our resort out on the lake. Have you heard of us?"

"I know the place, but I thought it closed down a few years back," the woman—who'd introduced herself as Agatha—replied.

"It was closed for a while, but I inherited it from my aunt and have been able to get it opened this summer with lots of help from friends and family. I'm afraid most people around here either still think it's closed or don't know about it at all."

Matt began perusing wooden bins stacked high with produce, sensing this might not be a quick stop. Orange pumpkins ranging in size from baseballs to basketballs filled some of the bins, with still-larger versions laid out in neat rows on long wooden pallets. Other bins held gourds and squash, colors ranging from a deep green to gold, with some reds mixed in. He recognized some of the strangely shaped gourds—his own mom used to grow them in her huge garden when he was a kid. He only half-listened to Renee telling the woman about the resort, but eventually he sauntered back up to the two women, hands in his jean pockets. He was getting hungry.

Smiling at him and wrapping her arm through his, Renee made introductions.

"I was telling Agatha about our plans out at the resort."

"Did those plans include picking out some pumpkins before the sun sets?" Matt inquired with a wink.

"Why yes, sir, that *is* part of my plan. Guess we better get moving. How are your pumpkins priced?" Renee asked, turning back to Agatha.

"Tell you what, I want to help you make a go of this. I normally sell them by the pound, but for you, how does three dollars each sound?"

"Like a steal!" Renee replied, hardly believing Agatha's generosity.

"I also want to donate a bushel of apples for you to use. Why don't you give me one of your flyers, and I'll post it here on our bulletin board. We get lots of folks through here between now and Halloween. I'll be sure to promote it."

Together, the three of them spent the next half hour filling the back of the pickup with bags of apples, a pile of bright-orange pumpkins, a few white ones, and a variety of strange-looking gourds.

Hugging her new friend, Renee settled up with her and insisted she attend the open house.

"I wouldn't miss it! See you in a few weeks," Agatha said, waving them off.

As they drove away, Matt gave her a playful little fist bump on her shoulder. "Look at you, networking everywhere we go," he teased.

"But, of course, what kind of small business owner would I be if I wasn't putting myself out there, making contacts? Seriously though, I liked her. I felt like we connected. It would be nice to make some new girlfriends around here ... seems like all we've been doing is working since we moved."

"OK, are we done running errands? Because I'm starving," Matt complained. "How about if I stop by the hotel, get checked in, and we can go have dinner somewhere?"

"If we stop at the hotel first, are you sure we'll make it to dinner?" Renee asked, throwing him a sly smile.

"Why, Ms. Clements, what kind of man do you take me for? I wouldn't want you to think the only reason I came to see you is for a booty call. At least I have the decency to feed you first."

She snorted with laughter.

True to his word, he was the perfect gentleman. He checked in and they cleaned off the dirt streaking their hands and arms from loading pumpkins. They decided to try out the small Italian restaurant Agatha had suggested. Since it was a weekday, the restaurant wasn't busy. They were shown to a corner table. The atmosphere was pleasant: dimmed lighting, a candle on each table, rich linens. Both ordered a glass of wine.

"I feel a little under-dressed," Renee commented, fidgeting.

Raising his glass to her, Matt gave her an easy smile. "You look beautiful in the candlelight, Renee."

"Oh, now you're going to make me blush. Thank you. And thank you for taking the time to come visit, Matt."

He didn't have a chance to reply. The waiter picked that exact time to take the rest of their order. When they were alone again, Renee sensed a subtle shift in Matt's mood. The playfulness was gone, replaced by a more serious set to his shoulders.

"Renee, there's something I want to talk to you about. I didn't want to get into it over the phone, but it's one of the reasons I came to see you."

Narrowing her eyes, Renee gave him a skeptical look. "Should I be worried?"

Matt sensed her subtle withdrawal at his statement. "No, wait, that didn't sound right. Let me start over. I have a . . . unique opportunity I need to make a decision on, and I wanted your input. I didn't want to talk about it over the phone. I wanted to be able to get a good read on your reaction."

"Whew, you had me worried there for a minute. Now you have me curious. What is this opportunity that made you fly thousands of miles just to ask my opinion on?"

Matt took a sip of his wine, giving himself a second. He knew he had to be careful how he shared what he was contemplating with Renee. He didn't want to scare her off.

"You know I've been talking a bit with Sheriff Thompson? I've bugged him on a regular basis to try to figure out what's been going on around here. His lack of action, of *re*action, was surprising to me, not to mention frustrating," Matt said, pausing until Renee offered a brief nod. "He'd promise to look into something, and when I'd call him back, he hadn't done anything. He finally admitted he's been having some serious issues with his heart. He feels like it's time to resign and move somewhere warm, get away from the stress of the job and try to get his health back before it's too late. Problem is, he doesn't feel like anyone on his team is ready to step in to the role of sheriff. They're all either too inexperienced or too old to want to take on the extra responsibility. He asked me if I would ever consider taking over for him."

Renee didn't interrupt, but she was looking at him with an odd expression on her face.

"My first response was to remind him he is an elected official. He said he thought he remembered a clause in the rules that would allow a sitting sheriff to recommend a replacement in the event the elected sheriff resigned mid-term due to extenuating circumstances. Of course, the county commission would take a recommendation under advisement, and that group ultimately decides who they want to appoint to complete the remaining term. But Thompson has been around for thirty years and feels the commission would go with anyone he personally recommended for the job. He double-checked and let me know he did remember the rules correctly. I told him I might be interested, but I'd get back to him. Said I needed to think about it."

As Matt spoke, he rested both arms on the table, his hands laced together, his body leaning toward Renee. Renee sat back in her chair, arms crossed over her midsection. Her face did little to reflect what she was feeling. Matt hoped she wasn't thinking this was all a terrible idea.

"Renee, you know I've been thinking about moving back to the States. I feel like I'm missing out on too much, living so far away. So, what do you think?"

Renee took her time responding.

"Well, first of all, I have to admit I'm shocked," she finally shared. "I know you mentioned the possibility of moving, but Fiji is such an amazing place . . . I didn't know how serious you were about it. And I figured if you *did* move back, it would be closer to your sister and her kids, maybe even to your dad's farm. Not to . . . me."

"Fiji *is* a beautiful place, and I would probably miss it in the middle of winter. But living there is different from visiting. Because I'm still relatively new to the islands, I don't have family there and only a small handful of friends. All I do is work. If I do decide to move, I may keep my cottage there, rent it out. I remember you telling me how you wanted to build more than one income source after you lost your job and sole source of income. Got me thinking I need to do some of that, too."

"But what about your sister? And your extended family?"

"After living a long plane ride from home, a day drive in the car to get there would feel close. Besides, she has her own life and doesn't need me hanging around all the time. But it would be nice to be able to see all of them more often."

Renee let out a long sigh, shifting her posture to match Matt's.

"OK, that makes some sense. You've obviously thought this through, and I appreciate you sharing this with me, but I have to ask . . . why couldn't you talk to me about this over the phone? Why did you feel like you had to tell me face-to-face?"

"To be frank, you're one of the main reasons I'm considering this job, Renee. I haven't done any looking around for anything else, which would be a wise approach if I were doing this strictly in the interest of my own career. But to be fair to you, I didn't want to go any further with this until I had a chance to find out how you'd feel about having me living so much closer. I know our relationship is unique. Hell, some people *prefer* this kind of arrangement, where it isn't possible to get too serious given the logistics of a long-distance relationship. But if I were to take this job, we wouldn't be 'long-distance' anymore," Matt stated, emphasizing his final point with air quotes.

Renee folded back the napkin covering the bread bowl both had ignored up to this point. She pulled off a hunk of bread, handed it to Matt, and broke off another piece for herself which she buttered, her mind mulling over everything Matt had just shared.

"Wow . . . I never thought it would be possible to have a traditional relationship with you. Are you sure you want to live closer to me? I'm a package deal, you know: two teenage kids, a dog, a house with a mortgage, and now a barely solvent lake resort I'm still trying to figure out how to run."

Matt laughed. "Of course I know you're a 'package deal.' Your kids are great, and your dog loves me. Lots of people have mortgages. And having a lake resort to call your own is cool." Matt sat back. "What else you got for me?"

"Well . . . I guess that's about it." Renee gave a nervous laugh into her wine glass. "Like I said, I'm a little stunned right now. I don't know what else to say."

"I tell you what, here comes our meal. Don't say anything more about it right now. Take a little time to think about it. Hell, I've had *weeks* to think through all the implications of taking the job, but I'm just springing it on you now. Let's enjoy our dinner and talk about less heavy subjects. We can talk about this again later."

Matt gave Renee's hand a quick squeeze before she had to pull it back to make room for her entrée. They kept the conversation light for the rest of the meal, but Renee was more reserved than usual.

"What would you like to do now?" Matt asked as they walked back to the pickup, hands loosely linked.

"Would you mind terribly if we called it a night? I feel a headache coming on, and I want to get back. I know we only have a few more days of your visit, though, so I don't want you to be upset if we make an early night of it."

"Renee, don't be silly. I completely understand. I dropped a bomb on you in there. You want time to think, and you want to be sure everything is OK with Julie. I'm tired, too. I'll take you home so we can both get some rest."

She squeezed his hand. "Thanks, Matt. I appreciate how you always seem to get me."

As he walked her to her side of the pickup, he gave her a light kiss before he opened her door and said, "Hey, what's not to get?"

***

The resort was quiet when they got back. The duplex lights glowed through the trees.

"I'll walk you back to your place, all right?"

Renee tried to laugh. "I could pretend I'm a big girl and perfectly comfortable walking back there in the dark by myself, but I don't like to lie. Yes, I would love for you to walk me to my door."

As Renee hopped off her seat onto the gravel, Matt took something out of his glove compartment. It was dark as they walked around the far side of the lodge.

"You need to get a couple lights installed back here, Renee."

"Tell me about it . . . Was that a flashlight you grabbed? Can you shine it out in front of us so we don't trip?"

"Here, use my phone," he said, handing her his phone with the flashlight app turned on. The beam wasn't big enough to provide much light, but it helped. As they climbed the stairs to her front door, they could hear the television and voices inside. Matt pulled Renee up short before she could open the door. "Sounds like everything is fine in there, so I'll head on out. Can I at least have a goodnight kiss? I think I might have earned one after a full afternoon of running errands with you," he said with a chuckle. "Tomorrow, *I* get to pick what we do for at least part of the day, deal?"

Moving into his arms, Renee sighed. "God, you feel good," she said, raising her face for a kiss and wrapping her arms around his waist.

Her hands met cold metal. "What the *hell?*" She flinched hard and pulled away.

Shit, Matt thought, catching her by the wrists before she tripped on something and fell backward.

"Relax," he tried to assure her, "it isn't a big deal."

"What do you mean, 'it's not a big deal'? Have you been carrying that in your waistband all day?"

"No."

Renee paused. "Oh . . . that's what you grabbed out of the truck, isn't it? Not a flashlight like I thought. Why? Do you think that's necessary?"

He regretted tucking his gun into his waistband. Now he'd spooked her. "Mostly force of habit. But sometimes the boogey man does hide in the shadows." His joke fell flat. "Sorry, I shouldn't joke about that."

"Matt, do you think it's dangerous out here?"

Letting go of her wrists, he linked his fingers loosely with hers, swinging their hands softly side-to-side. "No, Renee, I don't think it is. Honestly, I grabbed it without thinking. I almost always carry a gun. When I'm not in the States, I'm usually on duty. I feel a little naked without it. Don't worry. I'm sorry if I freaked you out."

She wanted to believe him and slowly let herself relax against his chest. This time she kept her hands at his shoulders, not wanting to brush against that cold, hard metal again. At first he kissed her softly, but then he kissed her like he had been wanting to all day. She gave in to the sensations, and they made out on the porch like a couple of teenagers— until the porch light flicked on and off, and she could hear laughter inside.

Pulling back with a groan, Matt started to laugh, too.

"Oops . . . busted. Gotta go," Renee said, turning away with a little wave and opening the front door, letting out more sounds of laughter and pattering feet.

"Oh, man, OK, see you tomorrow. I'll come back mid-morning, if that works for you," Matt said as he took the steps down two at a time.

"It's a date!"

"Good night, Matt," Jess and Julie hollered after him through the open door, still laughing at their attempt to embarrass Renee.

CHAPTER 59

Gift of a Heart

*M*att stopped to visit the sheriff the next morning before heading back to Whispering Pines. Thompson waved him into his office.

"So does this mean you have an answer for me?" Thompson inquired after he shut his office door, giving Matt's hand a hearty shake. He motioned for Matt to take a seat.

"Leaning toward 'yes.' I'll decide after I have a chance to talk with your people tomorrow, but you can probably guess why I'm in town a bit ahead of schedule. Doing a little research on the area."

"Might be you came to see a certain resort owner, too," Thompson said with a grin, "while you're in town. If I were a betting man, I'd put money on it."

"Could be, could be. Gotta look at things from all angles, right?" Matt winked at the sheriff.

"See, now, that's why I think you're the man for the job. I can tell you're thorough and methodical as all hell. Not one to jump to conclusions without the proper legwork. I did some checking up on you, you know."

"I would have been disappointed if you hadn't. Find out anything interesting?"

Thompson took a seat across from him. "Maybe. You had an impressive career out East. But then you walked away. Want to tell me about the couple years you took off from law enforcement life? Anything I should know about?"

"Pretty standard stuff. The job was demanding, didn't leave time for anything else. My wife at the time didn't appreciate it, so she dumped me. I was sick of it all, thought I'd try something new."

"Simple as that?"

"Sums it up for the most part. I was involved in a tough case—missing kid—and the end result was . . . bad. Guess it was the final straw. Tried my hand at construction, refurbishing fancy old homes."

Thompson nodded. "How did you go from that to being a sheriff in Fiji? Didn't know that was possible for someone from the States."

"Life is like that sometimes, ain't it? My business partner was getting married on the island. One of those destination package deals. There was trouble even before the wedding, and suffice it to say I saw a side of him I didn't like. We parted ways. He went back home, still single, and I decided I liked the island life. I bummed around for a couple months, trying to figure out my next step."

Matt stood and opened the door, helping himself to a cup of coffee from the old pot just outside Thompson's office. He poured two, bringing one back in and handing it to Thompson before he shut the door again and continued with his explanation of his recent work experience.

"Fiji has a large national police force, responsible for providing law enforcement for all the inhabited islands. Pretty big task. With the growth of tourism and influx of more non-citizens moving to Fiji, they were stretched too thin. You have to be a citizen to be on the police force, but—this was five years or so ago, before I got there—the government was getting enough pressure from the tourism industry that they had to do more.

"They decided to set up supplemental offices in three of the more remote areas seeing lots of growth in tourism. These offices are staffed differently than the national police force, similar to how county sheriff departments are staffed in the States. You don't have to be a citizen of Fiji. Thought was, a more diverse law enforcement team might be better able to interact with the changing population and take some pressure off the national force. Anyhow, one of these supplemental offices had an opening. Without any better options, I was hired on as a deputy and eventually moved up the chain a bit."

The sheriff nodded at Matt's story. Matt suspected the old guy already knew most of this if he had actually done his homework. But Matt saw no point in glossing over any of the pain points; honesty was always the best policy, as his father used to say.

"So why are you so interested in what's been happening out at Whispering Pines?" Thompson asked. "You're like a dog with a bone, ya just can't let it go."

Matt considered Thompson's question before responding.

"I met Renee and her kids while they were vacationing in Fiji. Guess Renee and I clicked. We didn't spend much time together—I was working and she was only there a week—but we kept in touch after she left. We talked, emailed often. Still do. When my dad died this summer, I decided to drive up here for a visit after I got most of his affairs settled. I saw how hard Renee and her whole family were working to turn the resort around. It made me furious that someone was trying to throw cold water on their plans. I've learned on this job, both from cases out East and in Fiji, that there are some real nuts out there. I'm worried—particularly about Julie. She's a great kid. They're all great."

Thompson nodded. "Aunt was great, too."

"Celia, right," Matt said. "My gut tells me this situation still warrants our attention. I know there's only been a few instances, spread out over many months, but I can't ignore it."

Thompson eyed his coffee but pushed it away with a sigh. "Gotta stick to green tea these days, pisses me off. Anyhow, in this case, son, I hope you're wrong, because I would hate for those nice folks to have any more trouble. But I admire your tenacity. Back in the day, I probably could have been more help to you. But seems like I spend half my time at the damn doctor these days. Just can't keep up here."

"So why don't you tell me more about what goes on around here? I've been straight with you, and I'd appreciate the same candidness."

Sheriff Thompson complied with Matt's request. They spent the next hour talking through the types of cases his office commonly worked on, current trouble spots, and even some of the county politics Matt would get pulled into if he pursued the position. Nothing he shared gave Matt too much consternation.

"Thank you, Sheriff," Matt said, rising from his chair. "I've taken up enough of your time. I appreciate you sharing with me what I could expect. I also want to thank you for having enough faith in me, even though we hardly know each other, to suggest I consider this. Appreciate it. I'll see you tomorrow. If your people can get comfortable with me taking over for you, I'll commit to getting back to you within the week with a 'go' or 'no-go.' Work for you?"

"You bet. Sounds fair. You know what answer I'm hoping for. Sure would be nice to spend this winter somewhere away from the snow and ice!"

As he walked out to his truck, Matt wondered if he was ready to be back in the snow and ice himself. He did miss the changing of the seasons. As he drove back out to Renee's, he considered what Sheriff Thompson shared. The job did interest him. While they had serious issues here, like most everywhere, he wouldn't see the daily horrors that had so worn him down out East. Maybe he would even feel like he could make a positive impact here. Make a difference.

He found Renee painting in the lodge. He could hear her laughing as he walked in. It was hard to believe the transformation happening in the place. Grant was there, too, putting up trim around the windows after Renee got paint on the walls. He must have known Matt was in town, because he didn't seem surprised to see him—although Matt noticed his smile cooled a few degrees.

"Hey there, welcome back," Grant said, giving Matt a quick handshake.

"Grant," Matt acknowledged.

"Good morning!" Renee's dimples showed as she flashed him a big smile over her shoulder. "I need to get these last three sleeping rooms painted before I even think about doing anything else today."

"All right, then, got another roller? 'Many hands make light work,' as they say. I'm pretty handy with a roller, if I do say so myself."

"Actually, would you mind helping Grant with the trim? That's a bigger job and two of you could knock that out quicker together. I can handle the painting. It goes quick when I don't have to worry about keeping it off the trim. You guys can come up behind me after it dries a bit."

Matt and Grant eyed each other briefly.

"You bet," Matt said, "wherever you need me."

"Can you get those trim boards over in that pile cut down to size?" Grant asked, then added dubiously, "You do know how to use a table saw, right?"

"Yep," Matt replied. "Done a bit of construction in my day."

"Of course you have," was all Grant said, turning back to finish nailing a piece in place.

For the first time, Renee noticed a slight change in the atmosphere. She gave both Matt and Grant a thoughtful look and then got back to work. A boom box in the hallway was set to a local rock radio station, playing music from the '80s and '90s. The music filled the silence as the three of them got to work, the men talking only when they were giving each other work-related instructions. Renee had to pick up her pace to stay ahead of the two of them. She finished up one room and moved on to the next. She had to be careful of the ceilings, but since the trim was coming up behind her and the floor wasn't in yet, she didn't have to be as careful of the floor.

Lost in thought, Renee was about to start her fourth wall in the second bedroom. She stopped briefly to rub a sore shoulder. Matt quietly came up behind her to massage her shoulders. She didn't hear him coming and gave a tiny squeal of surprise, but leaned back into him when she saw who it was, closing her eyes to enjoy a minute of pampering. When Matt started nuzzling her neck, she shied away a little, turning to face him.

"Where's Grant?" she asked. "I don't want to embarrass him."

"He stepped out to take a call. No one's around but us."

"Well, in that case," Renee replied, grinning up at Matt, "I suppose I can take a little break."

He looked as good in the old jeans and flannel shirt as he had back on the island where he'd looked all official and sexy in his uniform. He wasn't built like a man who spent any time sitting at a desk. While she could see a bit of silver weaving its way through his hair, his body could pass for that of a thirty-year-old. She wished she was as fit as Matt, but she did notice her favorite jeans were almost too big on her these days. They had always been her favorites because they were soft and comfortable, but now they were baggy. All this physical labor seemed to have melted away her hated muffin-top.

Break ended too soon when Grant and Jess came back through the front door. Jess popped in to say hello and headed upstairs with a huge box of books. Grant lugged a second box up behind her before coming back down and getting back to work on the trim. After a few more hours of work, Renee called it a day—"We all call it a 'day,' dear," Matt teased—happy to have gotten so much accomplished. Grant headed back to his cabin a bit earlier, saying he was on deadline for an article. He had been quieter than usual, Renee noticed.

Julie made dinner for the four of them, testing out a recipe of Val's. Together, they all did some work on the design of brochures for their retreats planned for November and December. They wanted to have them available to hand out during the open house. Matt could see he wasn't going to get a chance to be alone with Renee, and he was tired. It had been a busy day. He said his goodbyes, but not before securing another dinner date for the following evening.

Renee knew she was going to have to talk to Matt about him possibly taking the new job. She wasn't sure why she had been putting it off, keeping them busy and not allowing much time for the two of them. A big part of her was excited by the possibility he might move closer . . . but she still couldn't understand why he would want to give up living in Fiji. Was it possible he felt strongly enough about her to give it up?

What worried her the most was the possibility he would see that her life wasn't that exciting and become bored with her if he spent more time here.

Matt didn't tell her where he was taking her for dinner, but he asked her to dress up. When he picked her up the following evening, he wore a dark-gray sports jacket over black dress slacks. She was relieved she had opted to wear her little black dress. She grabbed the silk shawl she bought for herself at the market in Fiji. The swirls of brilliant blues and turquoise reminded her of the ocean at sunset. Julie answered the door to Matt as Renee was coming down the stairs. Her heart tripped a little at the dazzling smile he shot her way.

"Mom," Julie said, a twinkle in her eye, "Jess bought that new movie everyone was talking about this summer, and I'm going over there for girls' night. So stay out as late as you want, and I'll crash over there with her. Don't worry. Grant said he and Grace were staying in tonight, too, so if I hear anything go bump in the night, I can call him. You two go out and have fun. All you've been doing is working since Matt got here."

Giving her daughter a quick peck on the cheek and grabbing her purse, she said goodbye and followed Matt out into the deepening dusk, not sure whether to thank Julie or scold her for being so obvious with her insinuations. She decided to let it go—Julie wasn't a little girl anymore, and besides, Renee didn't want to worry about anything back here while she was gone.

She was nervous enough as it was about the upcoming evening.

Matt was again the perfect gentlemen. His southern upbringing meant impeccable manners when he was on his best behavior, and apparently their date was one of those times. He opened every door for Renee and pulled her chair out for her at the fancy restaurant where he'd made reservations. Renee hadn't been there before and only knew of it because of research she'd done of the top-rated dining establishments in the area. The food was excellent, and the service wonderful. As the last of their plates were cleared away, Renee had a feeling of déjà vu as she held up her wine to clink glasses with Matt in a silent toast.

Matt finally started the conversation Renee knew was coming.

"Have you thought further on what I talked to you about a few days ago?"

"Of course I have," she replied as she gave Matt a shy smile. "I haven't been able to think about much else."

"So . . . what do you think? Would you be OK with me moving here to take the job?"

Renee could tell from Matt's tone he expected an honest answer. Knowing her response would impact both of their futures, she chose her words carefully.

"Matt . . . I appreciate the fact you care enough about what I think to come all the way back here to discuss this with me in person. The sheriff's department would be lucky to have you. You are an amazing person. But . . ."

She stared into Matt's eyes.

"Why me?"

Matt shook his head, looking bewildered.

"Renee, how can you even ask that? Why do you find it so hard to believe I want to have a shot at something real with you? You're smart, loyal, a wonderful mother . . . you've done an amazing job raising your kids, and when you face adversity, you don't run. You tackle problems head-on. How many people do you know that would have the guts to do what you are doing at the resort?"

"Matt, I wouldn't be at the resort in the first place if I hadn't gotten fired. I'm a middle-aged woman who hasn't done anything exciting with her life, not counting Whispering Pines—and even *that* was something that just fell into my lap. I color my hair to hide the gray, and parts are starting to droop on my body that I didn't even know could droop. How you could possibly be attracted to me is a complete mystery."

Matt sat back in his chair, aghast. "Jesus Christ, Renee, you're being ridiculous! I couldn't care less what color your hair is, and everything about your body is perfect to me. You know those stretch marks you tried to hide when we made love? Those remind me of the blessing you were given to be able to bear two wonderful children. I don't have any kids of my own. Any scars or sagging either of us has are well-earned and a testament to our years of living. Nothing less and nothing more."

Renee didn't respond immediately. She took a slow sip of her wine, set the glass back on the table and leaned back in her chair.

"How do you do that?"

"Do what?" Matt fired back; he was obviously still pissed at her for thinking so little of herself.

"How do you remind me that I'm more than I give myself credit for? It can be so easy for me to wallow in my own little pity party. To think because I have been single a long time and it has been a tough year, it will always be this way. Always me on my own, slowly ending up totally alone as my kids start to leave the nest. Right now, that feels less risky to me than letting you in, taking a chance with you. I might get hurt. And that scares the hell out of me."

"Do you think I would ever hurt you?" Matt asked, lowering his voice. He leaned forward and took up one of her hands in his own.

"Not intentionally . . . but life can get messy."

"Yep, it can, and it probably will, but the fact that neither of us are inexperienced twenty-year-olds means we're better-equipped to deal with the messiness," he replied.

Renee knew Matt was right. Each of them had lived through their fair share of heartache and loss, and they might have to live through more in the future—but Renee was tired of playing it safe. Her heart had shattered into a million pieces when Jim died. She hadn't been willing to put any effort into building a life with another man, was afraid to face that kind of pain again. Years later, here she was, having to decide whether or not to take a chance again, with a guy who put his own life on the line on a regular basis. Maybe that's what scared her the most.

"I *am* scared," she said again. "What if something happens to you? It isn't like you're in a safe line of work."

Matt nodded. "You're right, and I already lost one wife because she couldn't handle what I do for a living. I tried to do something different, but it didn't last long. Maybe I won't want to do this forever, but for now, it's what I do, and I'm good at it. If that's too much for you, tell me now and I guess we'll have our answer."

Renee considered his declaration carefully before answering.

"I didn't realize until tonight how terrified I am at the possibility of something happening to you on the job. I tried to block it out of my mind. But I'm not so terrified that I'm willing to walk away. I have lived through the death of a husband, and I survived. Maybe I am tougher than I give myself credit for," she acknowledged, smiling across the table at Matt.

Matt scoffed. "You think? And a hell of a lot sexier than you give yourself credit for, too, pretty lady. Now can we get the hell out of here? If you need any more convincing from me, I am done with words."

Renee laughed. "Lead the way, mister."

Matt tucked a wad of cash into the portfolio lying on the table, not willing to wait any longer. Still outwardly the gentleman, though, he stood and pulled Renee's chair back from the table, settling her shawl around her shoulders. He took her hand and ushered her out of the restaurant. To anyone watching, this couple would have appeared composed, but Renee's temperature was rising as she felt the tension radiating out of him. He helped her up into the pickup, her heels and short dress making the ascent more challenging. He gently tugged down her hem where it had ridden high on her thigh, letting his warm fingers trail down to her knee before slamming the door and hustling over to climb in on his side.

He pushed against the high end of the speed limit on the drive to the hotel, not saying a word but tapping out the beat of the Bob Seger song on the radio against the steering wheel. "Old Time Rock and Roll" was one of Renee's all-time favorites, and her foot kept time on the floorboards. The beat of the music kept their pulses from slowing.

This time Renee didn't wait for Matt to come around and help her out of the truck when they pulled in front of the hotel. She started to climb out but caught her high heel on the lip of a rubber floor mat, pitching herself off balance. She grabbed for the door jamb but wasn't quick enough. Bracing for a hard impact, sure she was about to break her neck falling out of the damn truck, she slammed her eyes shut—only to be caught up by a pair of strong arms.

"Whoa, there, pretty lady . . . what's your hurry?" Matt said, not completely able to mask a grunt as he broke her fall.

"Oh God, that was almost a disastrous end to the evening," Renee was able to gasp out, still shaken by her tumble out of the 4x4. "Thank you."

"My pleasure. Now come on, follow me."

Renee tugged her dress back into place with her free hand, stepping quickly after Matt as he hurried into the building, pulling her along behind him. The lobby remained empty as they waited impatiently for the elevator.

How can it be so slow when there's only four floors?! Renee's mind screamed.

A bunch of kids piled out, heading for the pool, and Matt and Renee stepped in.

"Ever fooled around in an elevator before?" Matt asked once the doors closed, standing behind Renee and holding her loosely against his chest with an arm looped around her neck.

"Nope, only fantasized about it after reading the steamy elevator scene in *Fifty Shades of Grey.*"

This had Matt groaning and pulling her in even tighter with his other arm now wrapped around her waist. "Remind me to book a room in a taller hotel next time to give us a longer ride," he replied as the door pinged open on his floor.

Renee led the way down the hushed corridor to the room she had briefly visited the day he arrived. He quickly unlocked the door, holding it open to let her enter the dark room ahead of him. He closed the door, throwing the deadbolt.

A slim column of light streamed through an open curtain, giving them enough light to see each other in silhouette. Matt crossed over to Renee and gently removed her inky blue shawl, tossing it onto the spare bed. Then he stepped behind her. The only sound in the room was the slow whisper of the zipper of her dress as he eased it down. When her dress hung loose at her shoulders, he gave it a light push and it fell in a puddle to the floor, leaving her in nothing but her undergarments and heels. Moonlight created a stark contrast between her alabaster skin and the black lace of her bra and panties. Matt reached out and caressed her breast through the tempting lace. She leaned into his hand, her breast heavy in his palm. When she reached to pull his shirt out of his waistband, he captured her fingers.

"Wait. Not yet. I want you to see how beautiful you are, why I am so attracted to you."

He again stood behind her, angling her slightly so she could see herself in the full-length mirror on the wall. There was something erotic about seeing herself standing in heels and black lace, a fully clothed male behind her, fondling her stomach and breasts. Her legs began to tremble as he continued his slow exploration of her body, and she felt like a voyeur watching it all unfold. He found the clasp between her breasts and gave it an expert twist. Tension released, the thin lace cups popped back, and her breasts fell loose. The chain of her long silver necklace was cold against her skin, and as it caught on an already sensitive nipple, it sent a shudder through her body.

"Are you cold?" Matt murmured, feeling the tremor.

With a nervous laugh, Renee assured him she was far from cold.

Ending the exquisite torture, he scooped her up and laid her down on the bed. He made quick work of stripping down and joining her. Together they explored each other the way they hadn't taken the time to do before. There was no fear of someone walking in and discovering them this time. They made love slowly, enjoying each other and their private time.

***

Later, as they lay in each other's arms, Renee thanked Matt.

"I don't believe anyone has actually thanked me at a time like this before," Matt laughed.

"That isn't what I meant!" Renee said, embarrassed. "I meant . . . thank you for helping me realize how much I do want us to work out. It would be amazing to have you close. Now I hope you actually get the job, if you decide to throw your name in for it. I'm going to let myself get my hopes up, fear be damned. Have you decided what you want to do?"

"Sure have. I think this is the right next step. I'll call Thompson tomorrow and let him know I want it, find out if I passed muster today with his cronies ... though that interview felt like a formality. I'd be surprised if they didn't offer it to me. Thompson's recommendation carries a lot of weight."

"Where will you live?"

Renee felt him shrug his shoulders beside her. "I'll look for an apartment or small house I can rent. I don't want to buy right away. I do think I will try to keep my place in Fiji as a rental, and I'll have to keep my dad's place up, too. Would you like to maybe help me look around a little tomorrow, get a sense for what's available?"

"Maybe we could fix up the Gray Cabin," Renee suggested, only half kidding, "and you could stay there for a while."

"While the idea of living that close to you is tempting, I think there might end up being a bit too much testosterone out there right now."

"What do you mean? The only other guy out there these days is Grant."

"That is exactly what I mean."

"Grant's a nice guy!"

Matt laughed. "I'm sure he is. He also has a thing for you, and I'm not real crazy about it."

"Oh, you are *nuts*. He does not have a thing for me! You don't have any idea what you're talking about. He was my *husband's brother*, Matt. Even if they never knew each other, that would be weird. I think of him as family, not like that—not like I think of you," she assured Matt, snuggling in closer.

"While I'm glad to hear that, I can tell he isn't any crazier about the idea of having me around than I am about him."

Renee propped her head up on her fist. "I can't kick them out, Matt."

Matt leaned up and kissed the tip of her nose. "No, no, I would never ask you to do that. I honestly feel better having a man out there. Hope that doesn't sound sexist because I don't mean it to. But I don't like it that he doesn't think of you as a sister-in-law."

Renee laid her head back down on Matt's shoulder. "But how do you know that? Has he ever said anything to you about me?"

"Nope, didn't have to. Trust me, I'm right about this," Matt replied, stroking her hair. "But enough about Grant. Do you want to help me look at places tomorrow?"

"Yeah, that would be fun. But I suppose I better get home now . . . it's getting late."

Renee sat up, holding the sheet over her breasts as she flipped on the bedside lamp.

"You know . . . you could stay here. Julie made it pretty clear you had the green light to spend the night with me."

"I know, but I don't like the message that sends. You understand, don't you?"

"I do." Matt rolled to the edge of his side of the bed and stood, grabbing his pants off the chair and pulling them on. "Come on, I'll take you home. Why don't I sleep on your couch? Then I don't have to drive all the way back here. Would that feel too awkward for you?"

Renee smiled at Matt, giving herself permission to enjoy the view of his naked chest as he stood facing her, hands resting on his hips.

"No, that would be fine. Julie and Jess aren't dumb. They probably know right where we are about now, so if you spend the night on our couch, that isn't going to make it any more or less awkward. Now, if *Robbie* were home, that might be a different story."

CHAPTER 60

Gift of a Sixth Sense

The open house was tomorrow, but they weren't ready and Renee was nervous as hell.

Matt would try to be back in time for it, but flight times would make it tight. She would like his moral support, but he had lots going on now, too. It had been a whirlwind few weeks since he told Thompson he was interested in the job. A few days after Matt flew back to Fiji, Sheriff Thompson suffered a minor heart attack and an emergency county commission meeting was held; all were impressed with Matt's credentials, and they asked him to start as soon as possible. The office in Fiji was larger and there were deputies ready to step into Matt's old role, so his superiors allowed him to give a two-week notice. The council had agreed to a six-month trial period, after which, if it went well, Matt would be installed as Thompson's replacement for his remaining two-year term. After that, Matt would have to be elected to hold his position. All the stipulations made Renee nervous, but Matt already made up his mind he was moving. He was confident this job would work out, but if it didn't, he assured her he could find something else. He didn't see it as a big risk, and besides, one of the apartments Matt liked was still available. The pieces, he told her, were falling into place.

Renee considered calling him, but since her "to do" list was long and she knew he was probably busy moving out of his cottage, she decided against it. Half of the day had already slipped away.

***

Renee ran back to the duplex to check on the beef roast. She planned to make an easy dinner and use any leftovers to make sandwiches for her help—which would be most of her family—on Halloween.

"Honey, what are you doing?" Renee asked Julie as she entered the kitchen.

"*Shit*, Mom. You scared the crap out of me! Don't sneak up on me like that!"

Her daughter stood at the window over the sink, staring into the gloomy woods beyond. Shadows were lengthening, and Renee doubted Julie could see much.

"I didn't sneak up on you. The door was locked and I had to use my key to get in. Molly was barking at me. Didn't you hear any of that?"

"Um . . . no, I guess I didn't. Sorry to snap at you."

"Julie, is everything OK? I haven't seen much of you today."

"Oh, sure, everything's fine. I've been working on games for tomorrow."

Renee wasn't entirely sure she believed her, but didn't push it. She knew her daughter missed being away at college. After tomorrow, they needed to visit about Julie's plans for the upcoming semester. They still didn't know what happened on campus that night, but nothing unusual had happened at the resort since Julie had been back. It was time to get back into the routine of things.

Renee put potatoes in to bake and headed back to the lodge until dinner. Julie came along to wash apples. As they were leaving the kitchen, Julie's phone vibrated but she said to leave it, she would check it later.

They went on with their night, and Julie forgot about her phone.

***

The main level of the lodge was set up to serve multiple purposes for the open house. Val would serve healthy snacks and meal samples while Jess hosted an information table about their retreats, answered questions, and explained their concept to those interested. Getting word out about their retreats was one of the main reasons for the Halloween open house. Two new sleeping rooms would also be open for display. Right now they were bare, with no linens on the beds or pictures on the walls—all details Jess planned to have done before the open house.

It was cold for October and the only cabin rented was to Grant and Grace. Grant and Luke would keep a bonfire burning and one of the kids would help keep s'more supplies stacked. Cabin #1 would be open for viewing.

In the lodge's upstairs, the library looked amazing. It was, by far, Renee's favorite room at the resort. They would open it for the public during the open house. Overstuffed loveseats and club chairs sat on a dense shag rug of deep burgundy. End tables were placed strategically to hold cups of tea or glasses of wine while guests immersed themselves in books of their choosing. The rest of the upper floor turned out better than Renee hoped as well. The view through the new windows, looking out over the lake, was magnificent.

Julie and Grace would be in charge of the apple-bobbing station. Renee vetoed the idea of letting people bob for apples with their mouths; she was afraid the health department would shut them down for sponsoring a germ fest. Instead, the girls came up with a fun game using a special scoop they designed to catch an apple.

***

By five o'clock the next evening, all was ready.

Since it was Halloween, most in Renee's family opted to wear fun costumes—nothing too scary for kids. Julie and Grace looked amazing in their Hansel and Gretel get-ups. Since Grace was a little taller, she wanted to play Hansel; her white-blond hair was tucked inside a bowler hat, and she wore knickers and suspenders. Julie's hair, nearly the same shade as Grace's, hung in two long braids and she wore a blue-and-white gingham dress with a white pinafore and clogs. Renee was struck again by how much they looked alike. They could easily pass as siblings (in this case as brother and sister).

It would be Robbie's job to keep moving amongst the kids, handing out snack-size packs of baked goldfish and glow sticks. He was dressed like a clown, but Renee didn't let him use any face paint. Fully made-up clowns gave lots of people the creeps, including her.

Luke wasn't crazy about wearing a costume. Val convinced him to go the cowboy route. He always wore boots, anyhow—all he had to do was throw on his Stetson and one of his flannel shirts and he would look like someone out of the Wild West as he helped man the bonfire. Val looked good on his arm in one of Lavonne's square-dancing dresses and boots of her own.

Even though they planned for people to start arriving at 6:00, visitors started showing up earlier. Apparently there was still plenty of interest in the old resort. George added Halloween tunes to the old jukebox, laughing when Lavonne suggested he dress up like Frankenstein's monster and dance around to "The Monster Mash." He opted to pass on that idea. Flashing lights and festive music helped set the tone. Outside a nice fire burned and there was no wind, so people congregated out there, too. Little costumed creatures were everywhere. Adults appreciated the impressive array of food samples and treats, and since they kept candy to a minimum, kids weren't getting crazy on sugar highs. Agatha, Renee's new friend from the farm stand, came early dressed as a scarecrow and was proving to be a big help in the kitchen. She appreciated the small tent cards Renee placed strategically around the lodge thanking Agatha for contributing to the decorations and produce. Jess tried to keep track of the number of people coming through the lodge: she estimated a hundred came through during the first two hours. There were hourly giveaways. Lavonne prepared three gift baskets for prizes; visitors tossed their names and contact information in a box for the drawings. It was a great way to start a mailing list, and they would count the number of slips to estimate how many adults visited.

Renee shouldn't have worried about the open house being a flop. Now she worried about running out of food.

***

By 8:00, the girls were running low on apples. One last bag was out in the shed, and Julie offered to run and grab it. Grace waved a quick hand at Julie in acknowledgment but was busy helping a three-year-old who was struggling to catch an apple; the cute little witch was having trouble with the scoop.

Other kids kept coming through the line. Before long, only four apples floated in the big, galvanized tub. Grace looked down at the apples and then at the fresh batch of kids headed her way. What was keeping Julie?

"Hey, Robbie!" Grace motioned him over. "Have you seen your sister? She went to grab apples out of the shed but hasn't come back."

"Nope. Want me to go ask Mom if she knows where she is?"

"Yeah, you better. I'm almost out of apples."

***

Robbie headed off in search of either Renee or Julie, his big clown shoes flopping and threatening to trip him up. He ran upstairs, but Grandma Lavonne was up there talking to two women. Thinking he might find them by the bonfire, he headed out there. Grant was talking to some guys—probably dads whose kids were having too much fun inside to leave.

"Grant, you seen either Mom or Julie?"

"No. Aren't they in the lodge? I thought Julie was working at the apple station with Grace."

"She was, but she went to get more apples. That was a while ago, and she hasn't come back yet."

"That's strange. Maybe she's having trouble finding the extra bag. Why don't you stay here and watch the fire? I'll go see if I can find her."

Robbie frowned. "I'm supposed to be inside handing out these stupid cracker bags."

"You can go back in when I get back. Stay here for a few minutes, all right?"

"If you say so," Robbie replied reluctantly. He didn't want his Mom ticked off at him.

***

Grant made his way back toward the shed with a bad feeling in the pit of his stomach. He didn't want to overreact, but he didn't like hearing Julie hadn't come back. And he didn't want Renee to hear Julie was missing— she had enough on her mind. It was dark between the lodge and shed. Too bad the wand he carried as part of his Harry Potter getup couldn't light the way. He pulled his phone out and used the flashlight app instead.

The shed door was partially open. A large bag of apples leaned against the shed wall. Grant heaved the heavy bag over his shoulder. He wasn't sure Julie could have carried it inside herself. Maybe she tried but gave up, going instead to get help.

Grant made his way back through the still-crowded lodge to Grace. Her tub held only water.

"Oh, hey, Dad. Thanks for bringing more apples. Julie said she was going to get more, but she totally ditched me."

Grant dropped the bag by the tub and straightened up. "You mean she still hasn't come back?"

Grace shrugged. "I haven't seen her. Robbie ditched me, too."

Grant shook his head. "He's out by the fire, and neither of us can find Julie. I don't want to scare Renee . . . maybe Julie is talking to someone. Why don't you run some of these apples into the kitchen, get them washed up, and let more kids play? We have less than an hour left."

Grace's eyebrows shot up and she slapped her forehead. "Wait! I should have thought to try her cell right away!" She pulled her phone out of her pocket and dialed Julie.

Within seconds, they heard Julie's ringtone coming from a jacket thrown over the back of a nearby chair. Grant pulled a phone out of the pocket.

"Darn," Grace said, disappointed, "I suppose she didn't have any pockets in that dress."

Grant spied George coming down the stairs and went to talk to him. George hadn't seen Julie, but he was immediately concerned when he heard she was missing.

"Is there any chance she might have run back to the duplex to grab something?" Grant asked.

George looked grim. "I doubt it. I'll go check with Jess, you talk to Val. Ethan had to leave about an hour ago. If Val and Jess don't know where Julie is, either, we need to tell Renee and all look harder."

*****

Val hadn't seen Julie. Jess hadn't either.

Hating to do it, George headed upstairs to talk to his daughter.

"Renee, sorry to interrupt, but I need to talk to you for a minute."

"I'm sorry, ladies . . . if you could excuse me for a minute, I will be right back," Renee said politely to the two women, leaving them again in Lavonne's hands. She followed her father over to the top of the stairs, confusion and frustration clear on her face. "What's up, Dad? I was close to talking those two into signing up for our November retreat."

"Honey, I don't want to scare you, but have you seen Julie?"

"What do you mean? She's downstairs helping with the apple bobbing."

George shook his head patiently and explained the situation, careful to keep his voice calm.

Renee was down the stairs in a flash, her cape billowing behind and one hand securing her witch hat on top of her head, George barely keeping up with her. She ran over to Grace, almost mowing down a little toy soldier and a princess in her haste. "Pardon me—excuse me—" Renee said as she rushed by the kids and their mother. "Grace, where's Julie?"

"I don't know, Renee. I'm starting to get scared."

George came up behind Renee, placing a firm hand on her shoulder. He sensed she was within a whisper of falling into a full-blown panic.

"Now, don't assume the worst, honey. Maybe she ran to the bathroom and then started talking to someone. Or maybe she had to go back to the house for something. There could be a reasonable explanation, and she isn't going to appreciate it if you raise the alarm. Try to stay calm."

George glanced at his watch. It was getting late.

Renee hustled over to Jess, who was standing near her retreat table anxiously scanning the room, whispered something to her, and then came back to her dad.

"Jess is going to keep watch out here," she told him. "The crowd is thinning. It's getting late for the little ones, and the open house is almost over. I want everyone else in the kitchen."

Renee bit her lip to keep it from trembling.

"Dad, we *need* to find Julie."

***

He hid it well, but George was worried sick. His mind flashed back to the bedroom of the crappy old cabin where he had found Julie's picture. Slipping quietly out of the lodge, he carefully made his way back to the cabin now. He used the mini-flashlight on his key chain to light his way. He had to make sure Julie wasn't back there.

All was quiet. The cabin door was locked, as were all the windows.

George picked his way through the dark back to the bonfire. Luke was sitting next to Robbie.

"Robbie, come inside with me. Luke's gotta stay out here with the fire. We still have guests."

Robbie stood, grim-faced.

George turned to his son-in-law before walking back to the lodge. "Luke, do me a favor. Give Ethan a call, OK?"

Luke nodded, and without another word, George and Robbie headed to the kitchen.

***

Inside, most everyone was gathered in the kitchen with Renee. She, Grant, and Val were debating whether or not they should call the police.

Renee's phone rang. *Matt.*

"Matt, thank God. Where are you?" she said, hurrying off into a corner to talk.

"What's wrong, Renee?"

"We can't find Julie." She was almost in tears now, she was so scared. She briefed Matt on what little she knew.

"Renee, listen to me. Hold it together, OK? Stay calm. I want you to hang up and call Sheriff Thompson right now. He isn't on duty tonight—still recuperating—but he'll know who is and what to do. I'm only ten minutes out. Be sure everyone else is accounted for and don't let anyone go wandering off in the dark looking for her. I'll be there as quick as I can."

Renee hung up and made the call.

Sheriff Thompson answered quickly, but those three rings beforehand felt agonizingly slow to Renee. "Hey, Renee, did Matt get in?"

"Sheriff, we have a problem out at the resort. My daughter went outside, and now we can't find her. We're having an open house and there are lots of people around—lots of people we don't know." A new thought struck Renee and she gasped. "Oh my God, what if someone took her?"

"Slow down. Back up. Is Matt there?"

"No, but he will be in a few minutes. He told me to call you right away."

"All right, now stay calm," he said, echoing her father's and her boyfriend's words. "She's probably fine, but I understand your concern. I'll send a car out there right away. Sit tight. Call me back if she shows up."

When he hung up, Renee groaned.

How in the hell *do they all expect me to stay calm?*

***

Sheriff Thompson knew this was potentially serious if Matt had told Renee to call him right away. This shot his plan to spend a quiet night at home and let his deputies handle any Halloween nonsense. He hadn't been off duty on Halloween for thirty years, but he hadn't been feeling well enough to work tonight. It looked like he wasn't going to spend a quiet night at home in front of the fire after all. He called Dispatch to send a car over, grabbed his badge and gun, and headed out.

His doctor was going to give him hell for this.

***

Matt got to the resort first.

He scanned the parking lot when he pulled in. There were a number of cars he didn't recognize—people there for the open house. He parked next to Renee's SUV and headed for the lodge, watching closely for anything suspicious. Once he was inside, Jess pointed him toward the kitchen. She was thanking people for coming out, obviously trying to keep a normal atmosphere for the visitors. He recognized the woman from the farm stand, handing out food samples, but he didn't recognize anyone else.

Matt saw most of Renee's family in the kitchen when he entered. He wasn't sure what condition Renee would be in, but when she turned toward him, he could see she was dry-eyed. A little pale, but in control of her emotions, which he was instantly grateful for.

She rushed to his side. "Matt, what should we do? Where could she be?"

"Did you call the sheriff?"

"Yes—he said he'd send a car right over, but they aren't here yet."

"OK. They should be here soon. Come on, I need to talk to Grace."

Together they made their way over to the scared-looking young woman standing in the corner next to her dad. Matt asked her to tell him everything Julie had said before she left, how long it had been since she headed outside, and anything else she could think of that seemed strange or out of place tonight. Matt questioned Grant, too, since he had already done some searching for Julie.

"Thanks for helping keep Renee calm," Matt said to him in a low voice. "Can you break this group into two search parties? I want the younger kids to stay inside with an adult. I'll be back in a few minutes, and we'll get a search organized."

Grant nodded to Matt and started organizing the family.

George approached Matt.

"Hey George, sorry y'all have to deal with this now," Matt said, shaking the older man's hand. He could see the ache of worry in George's eyes.

"Listen, Matt," George said, "I couldn't help but wonder if somehow this might all be related to that damn Gray Cabin."

Matt nodded. "That cabin was gonna be the first place I was going to look."

"I already did. Checked it out a few minutes ago."

"Alone?" Matt asked, arching a disapproving eyebrow.

"For God's sake, *yes*, alone. She's my *granddaughter*, dammit," George replied, as if that fact justified his going off into the dark by himself. Matt didn't press the matter. "Never mind about that. The place was locked up tight as a drum. No one was back there. The important thing is to find Julie."

"All right, thanks for letting me know. That'll save me some time. From now on, though, no one is to be outside searching alone. Got that?"

George nodded. "Agreed."

Matt walked over to Renee where she stood with her arm around her son. Robbie was visibly shaken.

"Why don't you come outside with me, Renee? We can see if anyone from the sheriff's office has shown up. We don't need uniformed officers traipsing through the lodge while you still have visitors here."

Renee turned to Robbie. "I'll be right back, OK, honey?"

Robbie nodded, but Matt could tell he wasn't doing OK. "Hey, Robbie," Matt said before he and Renee walked away, "nice clown outfit."

***

Renee followed Matt out, thankful he was taking charge of the situation. She was trying hard to remain calm—but where the hell was Julie?

Fewer cars remained in the parking lot now. A woman was loading a sleepy toddler into a car seat and another car was driving away as a sedan pulled in. The open house was winding down. Sheriff Thompson got out, dressed in street clothes. Renee groaned at the sight of him. Had something else gone wrong?

"What the hell are you doing here?" Matt asked. "You just had a damn heart attack! You should be home."

"It was a *mild* heart attack, son, but don't worry—I won't do much. A deputy is on his way. Any updates since I talked to Renee?"

***

All the visitors were gone now, so with the coast clear they went back inside the lodge and made their way to the kitchen. Renee was getting agitated. This was taking too long. She needed to get out there and find her baby. Matt gave her hand a quick squeeze.

The group was divided as Matt requested. It was quickly decided Matt would lead one group in the direction of the shed and then check the duplex and surrounding areas. Grant would lead the other group in the direction of the lake.

Renee hadn't even considered that big black lake out there, and swayed a little at the thought.

Robbie and Renee would be part of Matt's search group. Younger cousins were to stay at the lodge with Val. Both Sheriff Thompson and Grace were to stay at the lodge, too, neither well enough to go roaming around in the dark. Both Matt and Grant were to check in with the sheriff every ten minutes via cell phones. Before the search parties could set out, two deputies arrived in a squad car, and they had a supply of flashlights in their trunk. Each of them joined one of the two groups.

They made for two odd-looking search teams, a wide range of ages and at least half of them still in costume.

***

Sheriff Thompson listened with approval as Matt took control.

He'll make a good sheriff, he thought.

"If you see anything unusual, be sure to tell me or one of the deputies," Matt instructed. "Stick with your assigned group, and be quiet so we can hear anything out of place. Grant and I will call for Julie as we go. Remember, she may be close by. Maybe she got turned around in the dark, or took a tumble and is sitting out there with a bum ankle. Don't assume the worst. If we don't have any luck in the next hour, we'll bring in more help."

Both groups headed out and Thompson got comfortable for the wait.

Ten minutes later, his cell rang. Like clockwork. Matt reported they didn't find anything in or near the shed and were heading to the duplex. Grant's call came shortly after to report that his team was checking the shoreline and trees rimming the water.

Ten minutes passed, and subsequent check-ins brought no answers.

Thompson felt restless. He hated being stuck in the lodge. An idea occurred to him, and he handed Grace his cell. "You need a code to unlock it when it rings—extra security app the guys in tech added, since I tend to leave the damn thing behind sometimes. It's eight-seven-one-seven. Can you remember that?"

"Eight-seven-one-seven."

"Good. Make sure both groups call in. Tell 'em I'm in the bathroom. I should be back before they give their second report, anyhow, but I just wanna check something quick."

He ignored Grace when she warned him not to go outside. He had remembered the photo Julie's grandfather showed him, the one he'd found in the little cabin on the back of the property. Thompson knew it was a long shot, but he wanted to see if anyone was back there now.

It was a dark night. He should have brought his damn flashlight. He picked his way carefully across the black lawn. He could see the cabin in the moonlight, silhouetted against the woods. All was quiet. He approached the cabin from the side, not wanting to give up his element of surprise if anyone was in there. Wooden steps creaked under his weight, causing the sheriff to swear under his breath. He stilled, but couldn't hear any movement inside. He advanced again, reaching for the door knob. Off to his left, an owl hooted, damn near giving him another heart attack. He turned the knob, and the door swung inward on creaking hinges.

Fumbling for a light switch, the sheriff gave up trying to be quiet. If anyone *was* inside, they would have heard him by now. A single, naked bulb over the kitchen sink blinked on, offering a small amount of light. The kitchen was empty, and at first glance the small living area—what he could see of it at least—looked empty, too. He took a few cautious steps farther into the kitchen. A large ring of keys lay on the table. The light wasn't bright enough to chase away all the shadows, but Thompson had developed a kind of sixth sense over the years, and he knew he wasn't alone in here. As his eyes adjusted, he could see someone standing in the far corner by the fireplace. The figure was wearing a large red cape with a hood pulled down low, obscuring all facial features.

"I can see you standing there, so you might as well tell me who you are," ordered the sheriff. He could tell it wasn't Julie—this person was taller. He positioned himself near the door so they would have to go through him first if they bolted. But he hoped to God they didn't. Not in his condition.

But the figure didn't move, nor did they answer.

"Who are you and what are you doing here?" he asked again.

"She shouldn't have ignored me," the figure said.

"Who shouldn't have ignored you? Julie?"

"I thought she loved me. But then she left and wouldn't take my calls. Just like the other one. They use me, and then they ignore me. I'll show them both."

"Are you talking about Julie, young man?" He still couldn't see the figure's face, but he was positive he was right about it being a young man. "Do you know where she is? There are lots of folks worried about her right now. In fact, I'm expecting half a dozen of them to show up here any minute. You want to tell me what's going on?"

The masked figure continued to mumble about "showing them," but the words were hard to understand. Then Thompson thought he heard a moan from the back bedroom—just once, but he was relatively certain someone was back there. The figure in the corner was getting more agitated, shifting from foot to foot, his mumbles completely incoherent now. Thompson knew it could all deteriorate quickly, and he wasn't confident he could physically handle this guy if it came right down to it. He had his firearm in its holster, but he didn't want to have to use it. This was just a kid.

The door into the kitchen swung inward.

"Sheriff, are you in here?"

Thompson recognized the voice immediately and groaned inwardly. *Grace.*

***

Matt called Thompson's phone to check in for the third time, halfway through their one-hour search.

The phone rang half a dozen times and went to voicemail.

"What the hell?" Matt muttered.

"What's wrong?" Renee asked, her anxiety ratcheting up as their search continued to turn up nothing.

"Thompson isn't picking up. Call Val."

Renee pulled out her phone and started to call her sister but stopped with a groan. "I forgot. She left her purse and phone back at the duplex."

"What? Why?"

"No pockets in her costume. *Crap!*"

"I think we ought to go check on things back at the lodge."

***

As soon as Val told Matt that Sheriff Thompson had went to check on something and Grace had followed him out of the lodge a short time later, he feared their problems had just magnified. It took all his restraint not to yell at Renee's sister for letting an old man and a teenager—both of them ill—go wander into the dark alone, but he knew that would only make things worse. He called Grant and the other search team back to the lodge. Upon their return, Matt updated Grant and watched as the man immediately started calling his daughter's cell, but based on Grant's stony expression, she wasn't picking up.

Matt let out a whistle to quiet Renee's family.

"All right, everybody needs to stay calm," Matt ordered. "I would prefer it if all of you stayed here while we go find these three, but I'm afraid we need your help. We haven't checked all the cabins yet. Grant, take your group and start checking at the first cabin on the east side of the pit. My group will start at the other end. Renee, do you have the keys?"

"Just a sec," she said as she hurried over to the drawer in the lodge kitchen where she kept her spare set, then: *"Shit!"*

"What's wrong?" someone asked.

"The keys," Renee replied, "they're gone."

Matt hurried over to her side. "What do you mean, 'they're gone'?"

"My extra set of cabin keys! They aren't here!"

"That is *not* good news," Matt said. He faced the groups and rolled his shoulders in an effort to dispel the tension gathering there. "Let's move, guys. Stay with your groups, and for God's sake, be careful."

***

"Oh good, there you are," Grace said as she walked into the cabin, phone in hand, oblivious to the potentially dangerous situation she was putting herself in.

"I told you to stay put," the sheriff reprimanded her sharply, grabbing her arm to prevent her from going any farther into the room.

"Jeez, *sorry*. I forgot the security code to unlock your phone. Matt and Dad tried to call but I couldn't answer, so I had to come find you," Grace babbled. She gasped when she saw the figure standing in the corner.

"Oh God, *who's that?*" she asked Thompson, as if whoever it was couldn't hear her.

"And there's the first one," the figure said, his voice rising from incoherence, "finally she comes to see me. I'll show her. I thought she cared. But she's just like all the girls. Uses you and forgets you. *Tsk tsk*, now she's going to pay." His voice droned on in a sick sing-song.

This had Grace stepping backward until the door halted her movement, clearly terrified by what she was hearing. Thompson kept a firm grip on her arm.

Voices reached Thompson's ears from outside—not yet close but coming closer. "Sheriff, Grace, where are you two?"

The figure stilled his fidgeting, clearly realizing his window of escape was about to slam shut, and then sprang into motion. He made a break for the door—Grace jumped out of the sheriff's grasp with a shriek—and he bulldozed right into Thompson, knocking them both to the ground. In the struggle, the hood fell away and Grace gasped in shock.

Everything happened at once. The fleeing figure extricated himself from the sheriff and Thompson tried to grab his foot, but he wasn't quick enough. He could see it was indeed a young man, one sporting a scraggily beard, but nobody he knew. The guy kicked hard at the sheriff as he struggled to get away, and grabbed for Grace as he ran for the door, but he missed her when she recoiled.

He ran out the door and was gone.

***

Grace stared around in shock, first at the open door, then down at the sheriff. The kick had caught him on the side of the head, and he lay there for a moment, clearly dazed. Grace knelt at his side to check on him.

A whimpering sound came from the back bedroom. Grace turned toward the sound, listening.

"Sheriff," Grace whispered, "someone's back there. It . . . it sounds like Julie."

Grace started to stand, but the sheriff grabbed her wrist.

"Wait," he grunted. "Don't go back there. Let one of my men check it out. I can hear them outside."

"But it sounded like Julie," Grace repeated in a high-pitched voice. "I need to make sure she's OK!"

The sheriff labored up into a sitting position. "I know, but we have no way of knowing if she's alone. There might have been more than one punk."

***

Matt led his team toward the Gray Cabin and instantly saw that the front door was wide open. Then a skinny figure appeared in the doorway and he heard Grace's voice yelling for them to hurry. Matt held up an arm at the bottom of the stairs, signaling everyone to stay put. He entered the cabin, looking from Thompson, struggling to rise, to Grace, and around the rest of the front part of the cabin.

"Someone's back there," said Grace, motioning toward the bedroom. Matt saw the fear in her eyes. "It sounds like Julie."

Matt moved forward cautiously, drawing a gun out of his waistband and holding it poised in the air. He held a flashlight in his other hand, aiming the beam into the dark room ahead. It was a small room, and unless there was someone hiding under the bed, he was sure the only person in the room was lying on the bed. He instantly recognized Julie, crying softly and holding her head.

Matt did a quick sweep of the room and under the bed with his light and then put his gun away, flipping on a lamp.

Julie started to cry harder when she saw Matt.

Sitting down gingerly on the bed next to Julie, Matt quickly looked her over. She was wearing some kind of dress—some kind of costume, probably—and didn't appear to be harmed other than where she was holding her head.

"Your mom is right outside, Julie. You stay here for a minute. I will go get her and be right back, OK?"

Matt left the room, asking Grace to sit with Julie for a minute. He needed to talk to Thompson before calling Renee in. He knew she was sick with worry over her daughter—was surprised she hadn't charged in here herself—so he had to make it quick.

He knelt down by the older sheriff and asked, "What the hell happened?"

"When you guys weren't finding anything, I was getting antsy sitting there waiting for news. I remembered the weird deal earlier this summer when someone appeared to have been holed up back here and how Julie's picture had been tucked into a drawer. Thought it was worth checking out. Probably would have been a better idea to bring one of my deputies along."

"Ya think?" Matt asked. He was disgusted with Thompson for taking such a risk. "Julie's grandfather already checked this cabin once tonight. Was Julie here alone?"

"Shit, no, didn't you guys grab the guy that ran out of here?"

"What guy that ran out of here? We didn't see anyone."

"Oh, God," Thompson said, shaking his head. "We need to find him, Matt. There was a guy in here, and he was rambling on like some lunatic. He stood over by the fireplace when I came in, trying to hide in the shadows. When he heard you guys outside, he freaked and ran, knocking me down in the process. He looked about Grace or Julie's age, but pretty tough. Dirty and unshaven. He's still out there. What if he went to the lodge where the kids are?"

"Oh, Christ . . . Val's with them, but still—stay here with the girls. I'm sending Renee in, too. Try to keep everyone in here so they aren't out wandering around with a nutcase on the loose. I'll take the deputies with me."

Running back down the stairs, he told Renee that Julie was back in the bedroom and she needed her. Everyone needed to stay together; he would be back in a minute. One of the deputies was close by and understood Matt's body language to follow him. The other deputy was walking up with Grant's group.

"What's going on?" Grant demanded, stepping in front of Matt. "Did you find Grace? What about Julie?"

"Yes, they're both back in that cabin. I sent Renee in there. Go in there with them. Keep your eyes open for trouble. We have a guy on the run, and we need to find him. And Grant, keep them safe."

Grant didn't need any further direction. He headed for the girls, leaving Matt to try to wrap up this messy business.

Their first stop was the lodge. Thankfully, Val and the kids were fine. They were told to lock the doors and stay inside.

A noise in the parking lot caught Matt's attention. He ran out of the lodge in time to hear a spray of gravel and a crunch of metal. Tail lights raced out of the lot. It was the small blue Honda that had been sitting off on the edge. Matt noticed it earlier because it had out-of-state plates, but there were so many strange cars in the lot at the time, he hadn't given it much thought.

"Goddammit!" he yelled.

***

Matt and the deputy jumped in the patrol car—now sporting a long dent down the passenger's side where the Honda caught it with a bumper—and they gave chase to the fleeing car.

They were gaining on it when the car reached the main road, taking a hard left. There was a squeal of tires and the car almost turned into an oncoming pickup. Both drivers swerved sharply to avoid a collision, but the Honda driver overcorrected and lost control. It veered off the road, into the ditch, and there was another sound of crunching metal, but this time the impact was with a tree. The Honda was going no farther, crumpled against a massive pine.

The deputy pulled quickly to the side of the road. He grabbed a fire extinguisher while Matt called in for an ambulance. If whoever was driving that car survived the impact, he'd need medical assistance. The second deputy arrived behind them, jumping out of Thompson's car. The three of them approached the crumpled car, guns drawn. Steam spewed from the decimated hood. A figure draped over the steering wheel. Matt cautiously reached through the shattered windshield. There was a pulse, but it wasn't going to be easy to get the driver out of the car.

The pickup the Honda almost hit was pulled over on the far shoulder. Matt signaled to the deputies to stay with the wreck, and he walked back up to the road, wanting to keep any witnesses out of harm's way. He was surprised to see Ethan climb out of the pickup.

"Matt? What the hell is going on?"

Matt couldn't believe it. He actually laughed. "Was that *you* that jackass almost hit, flying out onto the road like that?"

"Luke gave me a call, said Julie might be missing. I was partway home but turned around. Oh God . . . tell me I don't know anyone in that car down there," he said, motioning toward the wreck.

"Ambulance is on the way. I don't know who he is, and I only see one guy in the vehicle. He's in tough shape. Might be someone Julie knows."

Ethan's eyebrows shot up. "And Julie–?"

"We found her," Matt assured him, "and I think she's OK, although she might have a nasty bump on her head."

Ethan's expression hardened. "Did that guy hurt her?"

Matt held his hands up. "Hold on, Ethan. You know I can't let you go down there. We'll figure out what's going on, I promise. I think this is probably the guy Sheriff Thompson found in that little cabin Renee hasn't gotten around to fixing up yet."

Ethan looked at him sharply. "The cabin where–"

"Where you guys found her photo, yeah. Julie was back there, too. We'll get answers. Why don't you let us deal with this and head on back to the lodge? Check on everyone."

"Yeah, OK. Should I let them know you caught the guy?"

"Well, I can't be a hundred percent sure, but it's looking that way."

Sirens were approaching.

"On second thought," Matt said, "why don't you sit tight for a minute? These guys will need to follow the ambulance, but I want to get back to the resort, too, and they were my ride. Can I catch a ride with you?"

***

The rescue squad cut the driver out of the wrecked car and loaded him in the ambulance. He was unconscious and losing blood fast. A tow truck arrived to take the vehicle in. It would be searched for evidence, but that could wait until daylight.

Ethan and Matt found everyone in the lodge. One of the deputies had phoned ahead to let Sheriff Thompson know about the accident, and since the guy driving was wearing a red cape, it looked like they had their man.

The sheriff had allowed everyone to go back to the lodge instead of waiting in the dingy old cabin. Julie, Renee, and Grace were waiting in one of the sleeping rooms. The sheriff didn't want the girls talking to anyone until Matt got back. Since Matt would be taking over for him within days, Thompson wanted Matt in on all parts of the investigation.

There was some debate whether or not Julie should be taken to the ER, but she was still traumatized from the incident at college and was adamant she didn't need to be checked. As a compromise, Thompson called a doctor buddy to come examine her. If the doctor thought she should go in, there would be no further debate. Thompson needed to be checked, too, anyhow.

There was no way Renee was leaving Julie's side, so she was allowed to wait with the girls. Grant was concerned, as Grace was visibly upset about something, too, but she hadn't said anything yet. He waited with everyone else. With Matt's permission, Ethan convinced the rest of his family to call it a night. Val's family would spend the night in Cabin #1 as planned and Lavonne and George in #2. Instead of getting a third cabin dirty, Ethan would stay with his sisters in the duplex. Matt convinced Grant to go back to their cabin as well—Grace needed to be questioned about her part in tonight's debacle, and Matt promised to personally walk Grace over soon. They would probably know more tomorrow about what had happened, but for now, everyone in the family was safe.

After the lodge cleared out, Matt suggested they head up to the library where it was more comfortable while they discussed the events of the evening. Renee smiled her appreciation at him, and he gave her hand a quick squeeze as she followed Grace and Julie out of the smaller sleeping quarters.

Hoping to ease the tension, Matt whispered in Renee's ear as she climbed the stairs in front of him, "By the way, you're the *cutest* damn witch I've seen in a long time."

The fire smoldered low in the fireplace behind glass doors. Matt threw another log on to chase away the chill. Grace and Julie took a seat on the long, comfy couch, and Renee sat down right next to Julie, needing to stay physically close to her. Matt pulled two club chairs in to face them and the men took their seats, too. Thompson nodded to Matt, signaling he should lead the conversation.

"Julie, can you tell us what happened tonight?"

"I . . . I can't remember everything."

"That's OK. Tell us what you *can* remember," Matt encouraged her.

"Well . . . we were almost out of apples, and I knew we still had one big bag out in the shed. There were so many people around, it wasn't like I was afraid of getting snatched up or something, you know? I forgot how dark it can be back there. I got back to the shed, and it took me a minute to get the door rolled back. I went into the shed but it was pitch-black, so I had to feel around. I couldn't find the apples. My hand brushed against something. It felt like someone's leg, and I heard this creepy breathing sound, too, all heavy. It scared me so bad, I freaked. I tried to run, but . . ." Julie shook her head, tears standing in her eyes. "That's the last I remember until I saw you, Matt, in the little cabin."

"Did you hear or see anything else?" Matt prodded.

"Maybe someone saying something? I kind of remember a guy's voice, but not what he said."

"Do you remember seeing anyone?"

She thought for a while before replying, "I'm sorry, I don't."

Matt turned to Sheriff Thompson to give Julie some time to think.

"Tell me exactly what you saw and heard in the cabin, Sheriff."

So the sheriff told him, step by step, what happened between the time he left the lodge up until Grace came barging into the cabin.

"All right. So you thought you heard someone in the back of the cabin, and the guy was muttering about being ignored, when Grace came in." Matt didn't want anything the sheriff reported seeing or hearing once Grace got there to influence what Grace remembered, so he said, "Let's stop there and let Grace tell us what she remembers." He turned to her, and was glad to see that she seemed to be doing slightly better since he'd found her in the Gray Cabin. "Grace, tell us everything you remember."

Nodding, Grace gave a little shiver of apprehension and began. She told Matt how the sheriff had given her his cell and left, and how she'd forgotten the code.

"And where was Val when this happened?" Matt cut in. "Why couldn't you have gone to her about it?"

"I . . ." Grace frowned. "I don't know. I guess the whole night had me shaken up. She was up here in the library with the kids, I think, and I honestly didn't even think about it. I knew you or Dad might freak out when no one answered his phone," Grace said, nodding her head in Thompson's direction. "Plus, I'd heard something about his having a heart attack recently, so I was getting a little worried about him."

Matt nodded. "It's hard to think clearly under pressure like that, Grace. I understand, trust me. Go on."

Grace smiled appreciatively, then continued. "I never imagined he found anything. When I came out of the lodge, I noticed a light on in the littlest cabin. No one ever goes back there so I thought it was odd—"

"Nobody had told you about everything that had been happening there," Matt interrupted again, "over the summer?"

"I . . ." Grace stammered, her apprehension back. "My dad mentioned it, I think, but it'd slipped my mind. I just wanted to find Sheriff Thompson. I know how stupid that sounds, but it seemed like the right thing to do at the time."

Grace shifted uncomfortably on the sofa. She was exhausted.

"I had a flashlight. I could see where someone had walked through the grass, back in that direction, so I followed the path. The door wasn't locked, and I thought I heard a voice inside. Again, stupid, I know, but I went in. Sheriff Thompson was standing with his back to the door. It took me a minute to realize he was talking to someone I couldn't see at first. He grabbed my arm so I wouldn't walk past him, wouldn't go any farther into the cabin. That's when I saw *him* standing back by the fireplace. He was wearing a long red cape with the hood up so I couldn't see his face, but I could hear him talking."

Grace visibly shivered. "I have to admit, what the guy was saying gave me chills. It was like he was talking about *me* when he saw me standing next to the sheriff. Then there were voices hollering outside and the guy spooked. He ran at us, and when Sheriff Thompson tried to block him, he ran right into him, and they both fell down. The guy was crazy, kicking and yelling. He wasn't going to let anyone stop him. He was able to get back up first, and when he ran to the door, he grabbed for me but missed. He kept going, thank God . . . you got there pretty much right after that."

Matt nodded. "Did you ever see his face?"

Here Grace paused for a minute, looking down into her lap and wringing her hands.

"Yes. I saw his face. When he was fighting with the sheriff, his hood fell off," Grace said, pausing again before continuing in a rush. "Before, when he was saying stuff, I thought his voice sounded kind of familiar, but I wasn't sure. At first, when his hood came off, all I could see was a scruffy guy, and I didn't recognize him."

Now Grace was fiddling with her phone. Matt didn't know if she was stalling. He gave her time.

"I got a good look at him when he tried to grab me. I'm pretty sure it was him," she said, handing her phone to Matt. On it was displayed a picture of a clean-cut young man, smiling at the camera.

After studying the picture, he handed the phone to the sheriff and asked Grace, "What's his name?"

"Lincoln Sorenson. He lived next door to us."

"Wait . . . *what* did you say?" asked Julie. "Let me see that picture."

She got up off the couch and took Grace's phone from Thompson.

"Oh my *God*. Are you sure? Are you sure it was Lincoln?"

"How do you know Lincoln?" Grace asked Julie, confused now.

"OK, girls, let's slow down here," Matt said. "Grace, let's start with you. Tell me what you know about this kid." He gestured at the phone still in Julie's hands, its screen displaying the college kid Matt himself had tried to check out.

Grace shrugged. "His family moved next door to us a few years ago. Lincoln was a little younger than me. He used to come over to our house, and we got to be friends. When I was a senior in high school, and he was a junior, he asked me to go to prom with him. But I always thought of him like a younger brother, not like someone I'd date. I tried to explain, but he got mad. We didn't see much of him for a while. I graduated and then started college in the fall. He was a senior in high school."

Grace looked down at her hands, back to their wringing. "But then I got sick, and he started to visit again. He never mentioned the prom incident, and things seemed to go back to how they had been between us before. He and Dad got kind of close, too. Lincoln is good with computers and finding stuff on the Internet. He helped us research my disease and look for possible cures. When Grandma died and Dad found clues in her paperwork about his twin, Lincoln helped research that, too. Together they did a bunch of digging and found Jim's parents. Once Dad had their names, he wanted to take it from there. Dad wanted to be careful with how he approached his brother's parents, you know? Lincoln, on the other hand, wanted to contact them right away and find out if Jim's kids might be a match for me. It was like he was obsessed with the notion. Again, I had to tell Lincoln to back off, and so did Dad. Reluctantly Lincoln agreed, but he stopped coming around again. I was too sick to do much and Lincoln left for college. We didn't hear from him again, and his parents moved." She shrugged again. "I never heard where they went."

"OK, thanks, Grace, that's helpful." Matt turned to Julie, who was sitting on the couch again. "And you know this boy Lincoln, too, right?"

***

Renee eyed her daughter carefully, still scared for her welfare despite the fact she was sitting right next to her now. Julie nodded her head, her skin pale. She'd listened quietly to everything Grace had to say, and now that it was her turn to talk, she seemed reluctant to start.

"Come on, honey, it's all right, tell us what you know," Renee encouraged her daughter. She was thinking back to the time in Fiji, when her daughter confided in her about the boy she dated at college, but he had become too serious too fast and Julie hadn't been interested. She also remembered the stream of texts on Julie's phone from a Lincoln.

"I met Lincoln at a football game on campus, and he invited a bunch of us to a party afterward. He was nice, and cute," she said, holding up Grace's phone as if to say that was obvious from the picture. "I wasn't the only one that thought so, but he seemed to like me, too. He called me the next day, after the party, and we studied together in the library. Over the next few weeks, we saw more and more of each other, and all of a sudden it was kind of like we were a couple."

"Why didn't you tell me about him right away, Julie?" Renee asked, a little hurt that Julie would have kept something like that from her.

"Mom," Julie said with an eye roll, "it was fun to be off on my own. I was making lots of new friends. I thought if I told you about Lincoln, you'd lecture me to be careful, not let a guy put a damper on meeting more new people as a freshman, all that kind of stuff."

She turned back to Matt, color coming back to her face. "Anyway, I was already starting to feel overwhelmed by all the attention Lincoln was giving me. He got upset when I told him I wouldn't go home with him for Thanksgiving, that I was going to a friend's house with a group of girls. I ignored his calls and texts while I was gone that weekend. When I got back, he said he was sorry, said he was embarrassed he had gotten so mad and it wouldn't happen again. He seemed so sincere . . . I kinda believed him. We started studying together again, and we did some Christmas shopping for our families. He even helped me work on that photo album I made for Robbie. But it didn't take long until he wanted to be with me all the time again. I started to feel claustrophobic, just like the last time. I tried to tell him I wanted to cool it before leaving for Christmas. He said he understood, but I think he was just saying that. When I got home for break, he kept texting and calling. I only answered him a few times. When we went to Fiji, I left my phone home, and it felt so good to be unplugged from everything."

I should have taken Julie's comments about the boy more seriously, Renee thought. *I was too wrapped up in my own drama.* She forced her attention back to Julie.

"By the time we got home, he'd stopped. No contact. I figured he finally took the hint. I was nervous to see him when we got back to school. I felt kind of bad, totally ignoring him like that, but nothing else seemed to work. I didn't hear from him when we got back, and about a week into classes I ran into his roommate Tyler. He told me Lincoln didn't come back after break. All his stuff was gone from their room and he'd left a note saying he switched schools. Tyler sent Lincoln a couple texts, tried to call him, but never heard from him again. It was weird, but I was also relieved . . . I figured we were done with any of that business."

"Matt, what do you think it all means?" Renee finally asked, once Julie seemed to be done sharing.

Matt shook his head, frowning. "I don't know yet. It seems like an awfully big coincidence that Lincoln ended up at the same school as Julie after helping Grace and Grant try to find out more about Jim's family. And I learned a long time ago that true coincidences are pretty rare. But I don't want to speculate too much. Obviously we need to talk to Lincoln and dig into his background. Grace, how sure are you the guy you saw tonight was Lincoln Sorenson?"

"I'm sure," Grace responded. She shivered a bit, but this time there was no hesitation in her answer. She was sure.

A knock at the lodge door echoed up from below and everyone but Matt and the sheriff jumped where they sat.

"That would be the doctor," Sheriff Thompson said, hoisting himself out of his chair.

CHAPTER 61

Gift of Answers

The man injured in the car accident was indeed identified as Lincoln Sorenson.

He suffered a broken arm, broken collar bone, and a deep cut on his head, along with a concussion. Lincoln's parents were called, and they drove over the following day. According to his folks, Lincoln was supposed to be on meds to help control severe mood swings and other challenges he'd battled since childhood. When he came home for the holidays last December, he was severely depressed; he stopped taking his medication and started using street drugs, and his parents kicked him out of the house as a result. He checked himself into rehab, but that only lasted a few days, and then he left the facility and disappeared. His parents had given up, not knowing where he was or how they could help him anymore.

Lincoln's father insisted he not talk to anyone until they arrived. While it frustrated Matt, he knew that was the right call for a parent to make. Besides, Lincoln was incoherent; little of what he said made sense.

Law enforcement combed through the Honda. Lincoln had been living out of the vehicle—when he stopped squatting in the Gray Cabin, of course. A pillow and blanket were in the backseat along with plenty of trash. In the trunk was a small suitcase full of things sure to keep Matt up at night: numerous pictures of both Grace and Julie—some were old, and it was a mystery how he got his hands on those; others were newer, taken at the resort—and small mementos Lincoln stole from the girls, including hairbrushes, trinkets, and even undergarments.

Matt knew this whole situation could have ended horribly if they hadn't found Julie so quickly. Lincoln was a sick young man.

Once Lincoln's parents arrived, they hired a lawyer to determine next steps. Their son faced possible assault, stalking, and kidnapping charges. A doctor examined his mental state and worked to get his medications back in balance. The local hospital wasn't equipped to keep him for an extended period of time, so he was admitted to a high-security facility for violent individuals with mental illnesses. It would be some time before they could even determine if Lincoln was fit to stand trial for his crimes.

Julie suffered no physical injuries requiring treatment. She confessed she'd received disturbing texts over the past couple days leading up to the attack at the resort but hadn't wanted to upset Renee. She didn't recognize the phone number and it turned out to be one of those burner phones.

Among the pictures, two were taken on campus, date-stamped the same day as Julie's first attack. There were also a few from the backyard of Renee's duplex. Based on the angle, Matt guessed they came from the camera he'd pulled out of the tree in July. He remembered that when he'd taken it down, the SD card was missing. There were other pictures with backgrounds Matt didn't recognize. He showed them to Ethan (consciously deciding against showing them to Renee). Ethan confirmed some were outside Renee's home in the city, and others were outside George and Lavonne's home.

Christ, Matt thought. *This kid was following Julie around more than any of us imagined.*

In piecing together the puzzle, Matt doubted it was a coincidence Lincoln and Julie ended up at the same state university. Lincoln may have first been obsessed with Grace but when he wasn't able to get anywhere with her—and after she became so sick—he transferred his obsession to Julie. And why not? As far as Lincoln was concerned, they looked alike and were first cousins, something Lincoln could have known based on his research with Grant. While Grace wasn't interested in a relationship with Lincoln, Julie was attracted to him—up until his possessiveness turned her off.

It took a few days for nerves to settle down at the resort, but there was an immediate sense of relief. While Matt and the rest of the sheriff's office dealt with Lincoln—Matt's first official case in his new position, some would say—Renee tried to move on and made the final push toward their first retreat. The open house helped generate interest and eight registered for the weekend before Thanksgiving. Another half a dozen registered for a December weekend retreat. They planned to hold a combination of both week-long and weekend retreats throughout the winter months.

Matt just hoped—and he was sure Renee felt the same—this retreat would help everyone at Whispering Pines move on and enjoy a safer resort.

CHAPTER 62

Gift of a Tribe

*S*oft morning light bathed upturned faces. All paused to reflect and breathe following an early yoga session. The earthy scent of fresh coffee floated up the stairs. A fire crackled in the hearth, chasing away the morning chill. Music played softly.

Women sat on the wooden floor in two semi-circles on green yoga mats with fluffy white towels around their necks. Guests ranged in age from mid-twenties to late-sixties. Each shared a bit about themselves the previous evening during their initial group discussion. Most were mothers; two were not. Half were single; half were not. Some worked outside of the home; some did not. All were battling issues. Some were tight-lipped about their troubles while others were more open, and this was OK.

Since it was nearly Thanksgiving, *gratitude* was the theme of their first weekend retreat. Guests enjoyed healthy food, group discussion time, exercise and fresh air, and plenty of rest and reflection. Each received a beautiful journal upon arrival to capture thoughts, contact information, "ah-ha" moments, and anything else they wished to record.

Unfortunately, Susan wasn't able to join them for their first retreat, but she continued to provide Renee with helpful advice leading up to the big weekend.

Renee and Jess were open with this initial set of retreat guests. While Susan provided a basic framework and helpful tips for running a retreat, this was going to be a "learn as you go" process, and they had lots to learn. They encouraged each woman to share what she liked about the retreats but also wanted to hear any and all suggestions for improvements.

Renee understood a few days or a week wasn't going to be enough time to resolve the complex issues these women were dealing with in their own lives; her goal was to provide them with an experience where they could reconnect with themselves, remember their own self-worth, and hopefully make fulfilling connections with other women. Renee suspected many felt as she did: life could be busy with jobs, raising and running kids, caring for loved ones, but that "busyness" (or, in Renee's case at her old corporate job, "business") often left women feeling lonely and isolated, lacking in simple joy. It was important to take a step back from it all to give yourself space to recognize and appreciate life's blessings, big or small. She hoped this weekend would help these eight women do exactly that.

"Val has a wonderful breakfast prepared for us downstairs. Please place your mats and towels in those tubs and go get something to eat. After you finish, feel free to freshen up, and we will reconvene at nine o'clock."

After all the guests made their way downstairs, Renee and Jess thanked their newly hired yoga instructor—in fact, their very first official Whispering Pines hire.

"I should be thanking *you*," Peggy replied, giving Renee and Jess each a quick hug. "This is a beautiful space, and it's so nice of you to let me stay in one of your cabins for the weekend. This is a fun group. Maybe some of them will turn into clients for me at my studio, too."

"It's our pleasure," Renee said. "You're a perfect fit here."

Renee had reservations when she first met Peggy for coffee. The woman had short, spiky gray hair, and cheaters hanging from a silver chain around her neck. Renee was ashamed to admit that in a terrible case of stereotyping she'd expected a young, perky blonde before actually meeting Peggy. Luckily Peggy quickly won her over. Observing today from her own yoga matt in the back of the room, Renee could see Peggy was the perfect choice. Her maturity was an asset. Older guests couldn't use their age as an excuse not to try the various poses—Peggy wasn't much younger than they were—and the younger women couldn't let a gray-haired lady show them up, either. All in all, Peggy did a fantastic job leading the group.

Saturday morning and afternoon were filled with fun activities interspersed with quiet times for napping or reading. Most of the women interacted well with the others; only one, Desiree, remained aloof. Susan had warned Renee this might happen. "Some women," she'd said, "are either more private or are reluctant to open up to strangers. This doesn't necessarily mean they aren't enjoying themselves or benefiting from the retreat. You just have to let them be themselves. Remember why they are here, and take heart in knowing that you are giving them the retreat they need."

***

After a light dinner of grilled chicken breasts, steamed vegetables, and an orange gelato for dessert, they reconvened upstairs. It was Renee's turn to share her own story with their guests. She took a seat facing them and inhaled deeply to calm her nerves.

"One year ago," she began, "I was sitting in an office at the same job I'd been at for twenty years. A bit boring, but it paid the bills. Then came the fated conference call, two weeks before Christmas. Major cuts, effective immediately."

"Right before Christmas?" someone asked in surprise.

"Exactly my initial thought!" Renee confirmed, pausing for a sip of water. "I was done immediately. Tough discussion, telling my kids. But we decided to make the best of it. We visited family for Christmas, something we hadn't made time for in recent years.

"I should probably back up a minute," Renee said, realizing she needed to include Jim in her story. She hadn't rehearsed this and feared she was jumping around too much. "Eleven years ago, I lost my husband to aplastic anemia. I became a widow at thirty-five, a single mother to my two young kids. Grief can do funny things to people. His parents, my in-laws, blamed me for their son's failure to get medical help sooner. Thought that might have made a difference. After Jim's death, we lost touch. I regret that now.

"So last Christmas we were visiting my side of the family, and my kids wanted to reach out to their paternal grandparents, too. Thank God we did. During our dinner with Marilyn, Jim's mom, she finally shared with us, after all these years, that my husband had been adopted. His twin had recently reached out to her, seeking information. I took a chance . . . contacted the man . . . and I am so thankful I did. If you see a man here at the resort this weekend, it's probably Grant, my 'new' brother-in-law."

Am I boring people? Renee wondered, seeking out Jess in the crowd. Jess met her eye with a wink and nod of encouragement. Glancing around, Renee could see she had their guest's attention.

"One of the crazier things we did during the holidays was take a trip to Fiji," Renee said, her comment met with more than one groan of envy. "Yep, I know—how crazy, how *irresponsible*, right? I'd just lost my job! But if this last year has taught me anything, it's that life shouldn't be all about the rational."

"Amen, sister!" one of their older guests agreed, garnering laughs around the room.

"I had been a single mom for a decade, focused on providing for my kids, keeping a roof over our heads. I never made time for romance. But . . . what better place for romance than a beach at midnight on a tropical island?" Renee laughed with the crowd. "I had a couple 'run-ins' with the local sheriff where we were staying. All innocent enough. I found him more than a little irritating at first, but handsome as hell."

"I like where this is going," another guest chimed in.

"Yep, me too," Renee confirmed, a broad smile lighting up her face. "I got myself a sexy new boyfriend out of the deal. God, that sounds so *weird* to say out loud! But it's true. If we wouldn't have made that crazy trip, I would've been slogging my way through this past year without the support of an awesome guy."

"So, Renee, how did you end up here?" Desiree prodded, surprising Renee with her contribution to the discussion.

"Well, Desiree, I was sick to death of the type of environment I used to work in. I was tempted to go back to it, because that's all I knew. But, as fate can often do, I was presented with a very . . . *unique* opportunity. For reasons that are still revealing themselves to me now, my dear Aunt Celia chose to leave this beautiful resort to me when she passed away. Celia was an amazing, strong woman. Looking back, I think she could see my disenchantment with my work, and my failure to cultivate relationships beyond my immediate family, well before I could. It's funny how that can happen."

"We never seem to do a very good job seeing our own shortcomings," Beth, another guest, shared. Renee nodded her agreement.

"I didn't know how I could make it work, running a resort two hours from home, and having zero experience, but it was like this place embedded itself in my soul, and I couldn't ignore it. I came here as a kid, felt the same pull back then. So, with the encouragement of my amazing family"—Renee motioned to her sister with a thumbs-up and a smile, and Jess returned the gesture—"I took a chance and committed to bringing the resort back to life."

"Did you always know you wanted to incorporate these retreats into the resort?" Desiree asked, again surprising Renee. The woman hadn't said more than two words up until tonight.

"No—but again, life can be full of serendipity. You just have to watch for it. I met an amazing woman on our flight to Fiji. We struck up a conversation and she told me all about a retreat business her sister had started after suffering a number of traumatic events in her own life. We exchanged contact information and I ran into her again on the island. We clicked, you know?"

Renee made eye contact with a few guests to gauge whether or not they were following her haphazard account of her past year. Nods of confirmation encouraged her to continue.

"I only have five cabins out here, four I can rent out right now, and summers in Minnesota are short. We needed to do more than just rent cabins to make this place economically viable. I remembered my conversation with Susan on the plane and knew this might be the answer I was seeking. The bumps on my own road, mild compared to many, taught me enough hard-earned lessons for me to know I wanted to find a way to help other women navigate their own paths when the going sometimes gets tough. Us girls, we need to stick together!"

Renee laughed. She could feel the pieces of her jumbled life fall into place as she openly shared her journey with this room of near strangers.

Silence followed her words . . . and then applause broke out. She was shocked by their reaction. She was starting to realize how powerful sharing the truth was in spreading her message.

***

After hugs were shared and a few tears were spilled, Jess started a playlist and Peggy got everyone up dancing on the scarred wooden floors. Val set up a table of crystal glasses, bottles of wine, sparkling drinks, and a large glass decanter filled with iced water and cut lemons. They spent the next hour dancing with new friends. It felt good to stretch and move to the music. Most of the women hadn't danced in years. No one judged and everyone participated.

Guests were free to relax or retire after the dancing. Many got comfortable around the fire in the library, joining in quiet conversations or reading. Once Renee and Jess were sure their guests were settled, they headed home to an excited Julie and Grace, who wanted to know everything about the day.

***

Loud knocking on her front door yanked Renee out of a deep sleep. She fumbled for her glasses and hurried down the stairs.

"Who's there?"

"Renee, it's Peggy. Open up."

She flung open the door to find the yoga instructor in a less-than-Zen state.

"Something's wrong over at the lodge. We better get over there. And," she paused, her face serious, "you might want to call the police."

"Mom?" a voice came down the stairs, "what's wrong?"

"Julie," Renee yelled back, "can you call Matt and ask him to come right away? I have no idea what's going on, but it can't be good. I'll grab Jess and head over there. You stay here until I call you, understand? Don't leave this house!"

Renee used her key to enter Jess's side and hollered up the stairs. The three of them sprinted over. Peggy pulled them up short behind the lodge.

"I'm not sure what's going on, but there's a bunch of yelling and screaming. I woke up to a car honking its horn. Didn't you hear it?"

Renee shared a panicked look with Jess. "No, I guess we were tired," she said. "And maybe the furnace was running?"

"Well, someone is pissed. I hear male and female voices yelling. I don't think we should go up front. If you have your key, let's go in through the back door and see what's going on."

Renee hoped Julie was able to reach Matt. She wasn't sure she should handle this without the police.

Good thing you're dating the sheriff, she thought to herself.

Five of their eight guests huddled in the kitchen. One woman rushed over to them, eyes wide with fear and hands trembling.

"Oh, Renee, Jess, something terrible is happening. There's a crazy man outside, screaming for Desiree to come out."

"Did she go outside?"

"Yes, she's out there, and so are Beth and Liz. Oh, I hope they're all right! What do we do?"

There was the sound of breaking glass, and Renee was afraid they lost one of the front windows on the lodge.

"Oh my God! What is going on out there?" Renee hurried out of the kitchen toward the front door, followed closely by Jess and Peggy.

"Renee, wait," Jess said, "I don't think we should go out there. Wait until Matt gets here."

"Nope, not a chance. We can't just wait in here! If some idiot is out there breaking windows and threatening our guests, we have to see what's going on."

With that, Renee rushed out the front door.

The front of the lodge was illuminated by the bright headlights of a jacked-up pickup. Next to the running vehicle stood an irate man in a torn black parka, hands on his hips, glaring at the three women before him. Desiree stood slightly behind the other two. Renee pulled up short at the scene. Tiny little Liz, one of the older retreat guests, was giving the man a piece of her mind. She jabbed a finger at the guy to emphasize her words, stepping closer to him with each jab. Her hair would have stood on end if it wasn't wrapped so tight around big pink curlers. She was livid.

"*Who* do you think you are, coming around here, *drunk* as a skunk and *yelling* at our Desiree? This is a *women-only* retreat, and *no men* are allowed, especially *scumbags* like you. I was married to a guy like you once, and I let him *push* me around for *years* before I got up the nerve to chase him off. Last time I saw him he was nursing a sore ass full of *buckshot*, and he never came around again. *Maybe* I should do the same to *you!*"

Now Liz was close enough to jab the guy in the chest with her finger. Grant ran up behind her, easily lifting her off her feet and pulling her back a safe distance. "Why don't we all take a minute and calm down before someone gets hurt?" Grant tried to reason.

"Who the hell is that guy if this stupid sleepover is just for women?" the drunk shot back.

"It's a retreat, not a sleepover, and he's a long-term renter at the resort," Renee answered heatedly.

Renee hurried over to Grant. "Where did you come from?" she asked, surprised by his sudden appearance.

"Jess came over and banged on my door. I was writing and had my headphones on. Sorry, I didn't hear any of this. Why didn't you come get me right away?!" Grant asked, pinning Renee with a glare.

"Probably should have." Renee conceded. *I didn't want to bother him again,* she thought.

Pushing past her three guests, Renee stood directly in front of the obnoxious man hassling Desiree. She looked between him, Desiree, and the other two women. "Do you mind telling me what is going on here?"

"I'm so sorry about this, Renee," Desiree said. "This is Chuck, my husband. I told him I was going to stay at my mom's for the weekend. I knew he wouldn't want me to spend the money to come to your retreat. But then my stupid sister blabbed her big mouth and he found out."

Wow, Renee thought, *that's the most words I've heard Desiree say all day!*

"*You're* the stupid bitch, not your sister," the man spat. "Spending my hard-earned money on some fufu weekend instead of staying home with the kids where you belong."

Renee saw red. She couldn't believe what she was hearing. Who talked to their wife that way? He was drunk, but that was no excuse.

Beth had been quiet up to this point, but she tried reasoning with the man.

"Why don't you go on home, now, Chuck? The retreat will be done tomorrow, and Desiree will be home."

The man turned to Beth, taking a step toward her and Desiree. "Oh, shut up, you stupid bitch!"

Renee shoved hard at the man, trying to push him back from Beth. It was like pushing on a brick wall. He didn't look big, but must have been solid muscle. He glared down at Renee and then pulled his fist back. Renee saw the swing coming and heard Grant shout a warning at her, and ducked out of the way. Chuck missed the first time, but she saw him come at her again.

Suddenly, Chuck was yanked backward, staggering and clawing at his throat.

In all the commotion, no one had noticed Matt drive up.

***

The noisy diesel engine drowned out the sound of Matt's car. Seeing the situation quickly spiraling out of control, Matt snuck up behind the distracted man. While they were of similar height, the man was easily fifty pounds heavier, but Matt had the element of surprise on his side. He locked his arm around the guy's throat and twisted Chuck's other arm up hard behind his back.

"Let me go, you son of a bitch!" Chuck screamed in outrage.

Wanting to help, Liz tried to go after Chuck again, but this time Grant saw what she was up to before she could get far. He held her back, and Beth tried to calm her. Desiree stood there, shivering but quiet, and Jess carefully walked up beside her and put an arm around her waist in a show of support.

"Renee," Matt said as he struggled with the large man, "run to my car and grab the handcuffs out of the glove box. Grant, help me hold this idiot down until I can get him cuffed."

Together, they got Chuck under control. Matt cuffed him to the roll bars fixed to the back of the truck box until a deputy arrived to take him in. He was going to sleep off his drunk in a jail cell; then he would face a litany of charges, including destruction of property for the broken window, attempted assault, and disturbing the peace.

***

As the cruiser pulled away from the resort with Chuck in the backseat, everyone except Matt and Renee went inside. Renee needed to compose herself before facing her guests. Their first retreat had been going so well, and now this. The weekend was ruined. She didn't know how she was going to make it up to everyone.

"You know, honey, hanging out with you is certainly proving to be action-packed," Matt joked to lighten the mood. He wrapped his arms around her and pulled her close, rocking gently back and forth, his lips resting on the top of her head.

Tears of frustration soaked his shirt. *We all worked so hard,* Renee thought, *and now this.*

He gave her a minute and then pulled back a little so he could see her face.

"This isn't your fault. Some guys are assholes. If you're going to work with the public, this can and will happen. Comes with the territory."

"He was disgusting. How can anyone treat people that way, especially his own wife? Belittling her like that in front of other people, telling her she belongs at home. What a pig. How can she live with that?"

Matt smoothed the hair back from her forehead, doing his best to calm her.

"Some women find themselves in difficult, controlling relationships. If you've never personally lived through something like that, it's hard to understand how hopeless it can make people feel, to be controlled by someone bigger and meaner than they are and not know how to get out of it. Maybe Desiree came to your retreat for that reason. To try to find the strength to leave that son of a bitch and make a better life for herself and her kids."

Maybe Matt was right. She remembered the stories Susan shared with her about her sister and the abuse she suffered. If Renee truly wanted to help people, sometimes it might get messy. Like tonight.

Taking a deep breath, Renee felt calmer. She needed to check on her guests. Giving Matt a quick kiss, she thanked him again for stopping the guy before he slugged her—or worse. He kissed her back and followed her into the lodge.

Now all eight guests were gathered in the kitchen. Someone thought to put on a pot of tea, and Desiree was holding a warm mug.

Renee faced the group and said, "Jess and I would like to apologize to all of you for the disruption tonight."

Desiree held up her hand to silence Renee. "You have nothing to apologize for, Renee. This was all my fault. I'll gather up my stuff now and head home."

This was met with protests all around.

"You will absolutely do no such thing, missy," Liz said. "You are staying right here with all of us. Tonight was an unfortunate mishap. I would venture to guess how that husband of yours treated you tonight is nothing new." Liz's tone softened. "You can't change the past. All of us have made mistakes in our lives. He happens to be one of yours. Doesn't mean you can't change your future."

Renee remembered what the older woman said out in the parking lot about an ex-husband. She could probably relate to how Desiree was feeling.

A tear slid down Desiree's face, and Liz reached out her arms to the woman. The single tear turned into a flood and Desiree collapsed into Liz's embrace. Others insisted Desiree stay too and offered their encouragement.

In the end, Desiree agreed.

***

Matt found a piece of plywood in the shed and Grant helped him nail it up to cover the window Chuck threw a rock through. One by one, everyone headed back to bed. Grant went back to his cabin and Matt walked Jess and Renee back to the duplex. Julie was furious no one called her to let her know what was going on, so she stomped off to bed after she heard the story. Jess headed to bed as well, leaving Renee and Matt alone in her kitchen.

"So other than what just happened, how did today go?" He had been curious how the first retreat was going but hadn't expected an update until Sunday evening, once everyone went home.

"You know . . . I think it went great."

She told Matt about the different parts of their day. When she told him how their guests reacted when she shared her own story, her eyes welled up. She still hardly believed anyone found her story inspiring.

"Renee, you never give yourself enough credit. You have done amazing things. Thank God one of those things was a crazy trip to Fiji with your kids." Matt chuckled. "Who does that right after they lose their job?"

"I'll assume that's a rhetorical question and not one you expect me to answer?" Renee laughed as she sat down on Matt's lap at the kitchen table. She cozied in, getting comfortable. "I am glad I was so scatterbrained that first day."

Matt caught her up in a kiss.

"Woman, you drive me crazy. It's hard to get you truly alone. I have an idea. Any interest in making that trip to Fiji over the holidays an annual event? You know I still have my house on the island."

Renee stared at him. "Are you *serious?* You want all three of us to go back there with you for Christmas this year? We could go to the New Year's party—together this time—and I might even let you kiss me on the beach again at midnight."

"Well . . ." Matt gave it some thought while he kissed her. "What if this year we make it just the two of us? We could spend Christmas here with our families, and then you and I could celebrate the anniversary of you locking your keys in the car back in Fiji. As I recall, our last trip to the beach was interrupted by my work. This year, I couldn't respond to an emergency if I wanted to . . . we'd be thousands of miles away."

EPILOGUE

A mist rose from the lavender surface of the sea and early-morning sunshine kissed the beach pink. Renee soaked in the view, a steaming mug of coffee in her hand, and her bare toes curled in the cool sand. A screen door swung open and shut. Matt sauntered out in running shorts and his favorite gray sweatshirt.

"Care to join me on a run this morning?" he asked, stealing a sip of her coffee and a quick peck on the lips.

"Hmm ... no, why don't you go ahead? I'm going to sit here, relax, and enjoy my coffee."

"Save me a cup, I'll be back in an hour."

Renee watched Matt jog off down the beach until the mist swallowed him up. She didn't plan to sit and do nothing—that wasn't her style. She reached into her beach bag and pulled out two items. One was a creamy linen envelope, and the other was her journal.

She pulled the letter out of the envelope and her eyes fell lovingly on her aunt's handwriting. She read again Celia's final words meant for her alone. Two paragraphs in particular spoke to her this time.

You will never have the regret of missing out on raising your own children. You were blessed with a husband you loved, but you lost him too soon. Don't give all of your time and energy to your work and your children. Save enough of yourself so you have the strength and desire to forge strong relationships with people who will light your days and carry you through to your own sunset. Don't depend on your children to do that for you. They need to build lives of their own.

My only other significant regret is something I never shared with anyone. Most people think because of my success that I must have loved my work. I enjoyed the work and the people; however, it always felt like something was missing. I longed for a deeper connection or sense of peace and fulfillment from my work. I never found it. Some lucky people do. I suspect you have not yet found this type of connection either, my dear Renee, but my hope is that you will.

How could she have known, when she first read those words one year ago, how much her life would change? Matt came into her life, and she hoped he would be with her for years to come.

If only Renee could have one last conversation with Celia, she would thank her for the path her aunt provided her. Folding up the letter, Renee carefully tucked the envelope back in her bag. She opened her journal, took another sip of coffee, and started making plans for their upcoming retreats. Matt would be back from his run soon.

Did You Enjoy
Whispering Pines?

Thank you for reading *Whispering Pines*. I am so grateful you selected it and I hope you enjoyed the first book in my Celia's Gifts series.

If you liked *Whispering Pines*, I invite you to check out *Tangled Beginnings*, the second book in my series. What is next for Renee? Will Jess get the fresh start she's looking for?

Celia's Gifts follows a tight-knit family as they navigate the challenges and celebrations of modern life.

There are many adventures yet to come for this family. If you enjoyed *Whispering Pines* and would like to read about other ways Celia managed to leave a legacy for her family, please join my Reader's Club for updates on future books in this series and my other writing projects.

Did you notice the chapter headings in *Whispering Pines?* I believe life offers so many gifts. These chapter names also provide a writing prompt for my blog.

You can join my Reader's Club, find my blog, access book club questions, and other projects on my website:

www.kimberlydiedeauthor.com

Or email me at kim@kimberlydiedeauthor.com

Finally, if you enjoyed this book, I'd like to ask you for a big favor: Please post a review for *Whispering Pines* on Amazon and Goodreads. As an indie author, this is the best way readers can help me!

Your feedback and support are invaluable in helping me not only improve this book, but my future writings as well.

All the best,
Kimberly Diede

ACKNOWLEDGMENTS

First and foremost, thank you to my husband, Rick Diede, and our kids, Amber, Alecia, and Joshua. I so appreciate your patience with me throughout this process. Writing my book took a long time, tucked into the nooks and crannies of our already-full lives. While I know you didn't always understand my near-obsession to write, you never stopped encouraging me. I hope this book can serve as an example to you how dedicated, consistent work on your own goals can take you where you want to go in life.

Thank you also to my parents, Linda and Larry Hansted. You were my earliest readers and your interest in my book kept me going when I was ready to give up on it.

I am so grateful to other family and friends as well for helping me on this journey. Thank you for not laughing out loud when I told you what I was up to. To my brother Jon Hansted—I was so nervous to hand my early draft over to you, perhaps because your opinion means so much. Maybe together we can convince Tom to read the finished product!

Thank you to my life-long friend, Deneen Axtman, for continuously holding me accountable to see this through and for reading my near-complete manuscript during your family camping trip. So many more of you also encouraged me along the way. You know who you are and I truly hope you know how much your support means to me!

While encouragement from friends and family was invaluable in my pursuit of becoming a published author, writing was only half the battle. I will be forever grateful to the Self-Publishing School community for teaching me how to go from a rough draft to a published book. Thank you Chandler Bolt and Sean Sumner for the Mastermind Community and the wonderful resources you make available. To my coach RE Vance—

thank you for opening my eyes to what it takes to be a fiction author in today's world. Without all of you, my book would likely still be residing quietly in a binder in my desk drawer.

Despite reading more books than I can count over the past few decades, lots of reading doesn't automatically translate to the ability to actually *write* a story that will pull readers through from beginning to end. I needed lots of professional help and was so lucky to have the assistance of two gifted people. Thank you Yvonne Fugelstad for your generosity in helping me with my early draft. You set me on the right path. Then my amazing editor came along—Spencer Hamilton of Nerdy Wordsmith Ink— and he worked tirelessly with me to bring my story to a level I never could have reached on my own. You made me laugh, and at times nearly cry, when you pushed me for more and never let me settle. Thank you, Spencer—here's to more books with you in the years to come!

They teach us in SPS the importance of having an accountability buddy. Thank you Lisha Lender for giving of your time and encouragement over these many months. I have gained a friend in you and together we are both finding our way to "published"!

To the many other wonderful people in our SPS community—I have never before been exposed to such an amazing group, willing to share trials and tribulations, all with the ultimate goal of helping each other achieve our dreams.

A huge thank-you to all of the amazing, selfless people on my *Whispering Pines* book launch team. Thank you Sarah Magarey for your careful review and suggested corrections. Writing a book begins as a solo project but getting it out to the world can't be done alone.

I also want to thank Amanda Wolf with Lemon Drops Photography (www.lemondropsphotos.com). You are talented and a blast to work with, but even more than that, I admire you for pursuing your own dreams. You go, girl!

And finally, as with any "gift," the beautiful wrapping is important, and I want to thank my cover designer, Cakamura DSGN Studio, for sharing your talent with me.

About the Author

Kimberly Diede's first novel, *Whispering Pines*, was inspired by her real-life "Aunt Celia," Mary K. Nierling. Aunt Mary was a generous, extraordinary, slightly formidable woman who excelled in a "man's world" in the mid-1900s. The Celia's Gifts series is Kimberly's way of honoring her great-aunt and the legacy she left behind.

An avid life-long reader, Kimberly would occasionally read until the sun rose, before adult responsibilities made the habit unsustainable. Her love of reading has evolved into a love of writing as a creative outlet from the demands of thirty years in corporate America. She is currently at work on future novels in her Celia's Gifts series.

Kimberly lives in North Dakota with her family and spends as much time as possible at the lake in the summertime.

You can visit her website at www.kimberlydiedeauthor.com.

Made in the USA
Middletown, DE
04 September 2020